THE ETHEREAL SQUADRON

SHAMI STOVALL

THE ETHEREAL SQUADRON

BY SHAMI STOVALL

Published by
CS BOOKS, LLC

Cover Design: Darko Paganus

Editors:

IF YOU WANT TO BE NOTIFIED WHEN SHAMI STOVALL'S NEXT BOOK RELEASES, PLEASE VISIT HER WEBSITE OR CONTACT HER DIRECTLY AT

s.adelle.s@gmail.com

ISBN: 978-1-7347587-7-1

To John, for being the first to see.
To Beka, for all her support.
To Gail, for her unending enthusiasm.
To Big John, for his fatherly advice.
To Tiffany, who helped shape Vergess.
And to history, for being so interesting.

Author's Note

This novel takes place in an alternate history of World War I. While many of the events are similar to reality, fictional characters and magic have been woven into the timeline, which changes a few things. If you read this series thinking you know every battle or how the Great War ultimately concludes, you may find yourself surprised.

Without further ado, please enjoy the novel.

ONE

Verdun
____

The machine gun fire wouldn't last forever.

Florence Cavell held her Springfield rifle close as the bullets whistled overhead. Soon they would engage the enemy. Would there be landmines between her and the Germans? Zeppelins? Sorcerers? Florence didn't know, but as her boots sunk farther into the trench mud, she pushed the thoughts from her mind.

"Here comes our opening," Cutter said, his voice sharp enough to pierce through the din of war. "You ready, Geist?"

Geist. Her codename. Her true identity among allies.

She gave a curt nod.

"Good. You're with me. We'll rush the bunker and get the POWs. Little Wick and Buttons will take the gunners."

"Understood," she said.

Geist and Cutter shared a quick smile and salute. Ice still gripped her heart, but Cutter's presence thawed her anxiety. *I'm a fool for worrying,* she thought.

The light of the full moon lit the battlefield despite the midnight hour. The enlisted men squeezed together in fraternal huddles throughout the trenches, keeping their heads low and their eyes to the ground. While Cutter tensed in preparation to leap, Little Wick held a hand to his heart and spoke aloud, defiance in his words.

"Almighty and Everlasting God, by Whose grace Thy servants are enabled to fight the good fight and prove victorious, we humbly beseech Thee to inspire us! Save us and our foes, as they know not what they do. Lord our God, accept this prayer on behalf of all the wretched men of war. *Amen.*"

And as though God himself had touched the enemy guns, the stream of bullets ceased.

Cutter jumped up first, eagerness evident in his movements. Geist followed after, her fingers gripping the muddy edge of the trench without slipping. Little Wick, without a rifle, climbed the ladder out of the pit of French soldiers, a bag of shirt buttons hanging from his belt.

The moments between the reloading of the machine guns were short. Geist had a narrow timeframe to cross the distance between trenches—No Man's Land—a kingdom of death between men standing in shallow graves. The eerie gray landscape revealed only the red of French trousers and the horizon-blue of infantry coats.

The unblinking eyes of corpses unnerved Geist as she wove through the dangers of the desolate terrain. She controlled her breathing and focused on the drum of her heartbeat.

Where barbed wire would stop normal men, it ripped at the edges of Geist's uniform but passed through her flesh without harm. Even the bullets from German rifles tore her clothes but left her skin untouched.

Geist had heard the rumors, but even the stories of 'guardian angels on the battlefield' didn't come close to the truth. What ordinary soldier would believe that real, live sorcerers were fighting alongside mortal men in the trenches at Verdun?

But they were real, real as the magic that flowed in her veins. A covert UK-US joint task force made up entirely of magic-users known as the Ethereal Squadron.

Sorcerers going to war.

Cutter ran the length of No Man's Land with a sprinter's enthusiasm and stamina. He leapt the barbed wire like hurdles, and when the hail of 7.92mm Mauser rifle bullets came to slow his progress, he met them head on. His laughter, loud enough to hear over the gunfire, echoed into the night. Soaked crimson and high on adrenaline, Cutter waded into the fray with a berserker's smile on his pale American face.

The German front had two parallel trenches that ran to each horizon. A multitude of smaller ditches connected everything like a maze with no beginning or end. In between muddy furrows sat giant machine gun turrets and mountains of sandbags stacked chest-high. The sentry posts, stationed every hundred yards, lit up with the burst of rifle fire from the men on duty.

Geist stepped up to the edge of the first German trench and pointed her rifle down. Surprised soldiers could only half-lift their weapons as she fired. One soldier, tucked away in the shadows, his face muddy and his hands unsteady, managed to fire on Geist before she could ready her rifle for another round.

His shot pierced the collar of her uniform but flew off into the night, her power momentarily causing her skin to shimmer and fade.

"*Geist,*" the soldier mouthed. German for *ghost*. She had earned the codename from a hundred men murmuring the same thing just before they had died.

Geist stabbed down with her bayonet, plunging it deep into the soldier's neck and lifting up. The short knife snapped off her rifle as the German stumbled backward, his back hitting the dirt wall of the trench as he choked on blood and panic.

Cutter, his rifle too slow for his bloodlust, jumped into the German frontline trench with nothing but a Bowie knife. He bled from scores of bullet holes, yet his body refused to succumb to his wounds. Each injury stitched itself back together with superhuman speed, never allowing Cutter to fall.

As he advanced, sharp claws sprouted at the end of his fingertips. He slashed with a knife in one hand and boney talons on the other, tearing through enemy soldiers and staining their dark green uniforms with hot blood.

Geist took advantage of the Germans' stunned disbelief. Like her namesake, she slid through the moonlight shadows, leaping over the trench and firing from behind, catching them at their most vulnerable. The enemy watched Cutter with terror in their eyes. They never saw Geist coming.

Little Wick, slow to cross the horror of No Man's Land, arrived with a grim expression etched into his face.

"Fear not," he said, "for our Lord is a consuming fire."

With a wave of his hand, flames erupted. They scorched the mud and chalk and panels of the trenches, lighting everything in deep, hellish reds. The fire answered Little Wick's every thought and gesture, dancing at his command and tearing through the enemy lines unimpeded. Ash swept over the battle as he set the sentry posts ablaze, creating a pyre for the soldiers trapped within.

Little Wick grimaced each time a German fell. "Forgive me, please. Forgive me."

The reloaded machine guns swiveled into place. Everyone but Cutter—even the Germans—raced for cover as the orange-yellow burst of fire erupted from the barrel of the nearest turret.

Little Wick tossed a shirt button over the machine gunner's bunker and ducked away. The button, nearly invisible in the darkness, landed behind the German soldiers. A man slipped into reality right where the piece of apparel had landed—Buttons, the last of the Ethereal Squadron's trench cleaners, had arrived. Geist smiled. His khaki British uniform marked him as an ally.

Buttons stood and seemed to get his bearings, then pulled a Webley revolver from his holster and shot the machine gunner in the chest. Moving to wield the machine gun himself, Buttons swiveled the heavy weapon to the edge of its arc, firing into the western German trenches, pulping the sandbags and ripping the supports for the enemy ditches apart.

The Germans scrambled through their narrow labyrinth, falling back to defensible positions. The hundreds of dead at their feet slowed their progress as they stumbled and slipped through the mud at the bottom of the trench.

Geist pursued, her intangibility allowing her to navigate through the sea of corpses with ease. Even amidst the chaos of battle, she kept her wits about her. Rigorous training had killed idle fear years ago.

Four sorcerers versus a platoon of normal men? Geist wasn't surprised it had ended in a massacre. She ran through wave after wave of bullets, her confidence building.

The enemy soldiers might see her magic in action, but they wouldn't live to tell the tale. And those lucky few who survived would be accused of hallucinating—nightmares brought on by the horror of war.

Geist turned her gaze to the enemy command bunker. The closer she got, the colder the air seemed to become. Magic could always feel the presence of magic. Ethereal Squadron sorcerers had gone missing, and intelligence said they were trapped in the front-line bunkers.

Why keep prisoners so close to the front? Geist asked herself as she sprinted toward the building. *A trap?* She shook the thought from her mind. Even if there were a possibility the information was false, she wouldn't risk leaving a teammate behind.

Cutter waded through the quagmire of combat, far behind but awash in enemy blood. Geist thought she could hear him laughing.

I shouldn't wait. I'll have to go in alone.

Geist kicked through the door and dove into the room with her rifle at the ready. German soldiers fired Luger pistols, tearing more tiny holes in her uniform. Geist moved between them, using their panic to her advantage as they shot each other through her shimmering form. The last soldier standing emptied his gun but kept firing, the empty gun clicking limply. Geist leveled her rifle and fired, and the Luger fell to the floor just before he did.

She turned and ran down the bunker hall and stopped at the first door she came upon. A pile of corpses sat shoved into the corner of the room. Each body—once a man—had been stripped down to his drawers and discarded. Their skin had a waxy sheen under the dim lighting of an oil lantern, as though they were made of candle wax and partially melted.

What... happened?

A twist of pain knotted her gut. Geist recognized two of the distorted faces as sorcerers of the Ethereal Squadron, codenames Lock and Chorus. The sight of their deformed corpses sent shivers down her spine.

I'm too late. They've been mutilated.

She stepped back when she realized she wasn't alone. One man lay atop a gurney in a shadowy corner of the room. His chest heaved, and she could hear unsteady breaths rattling his lungs. Geist slung her rifle over her shoulder and rushed to his side, thankful that at least one soldier would make it out.

The sorcerer on the gurney had a cold aura. He writhed as though caught in a night terror, his eyes squeezed closed. Unlike the corpses, he wore a pair of trousers and boots, his circular ID tags flat on his bare chest. His skin wasn't distorted, and Geist couldn't find any injuries, but icy sweat gushed from his every pore.

"Wake up," Geist said, giving him a shake.

The man took in gulps of air and opened his eyes, his gaze locked on the ceiling.

"I'm Geist—with the Ethereal Squadron in Verdun. What's your name?" she asked.

For a moment, the man struggled to lift himself onto his elbows. *"Wilhelm Richter,"* he muttered, his pronunciation German in every regard.

Geist glanced at his ID tag. Nationality: American. Name: William Black.

Before she could question him further, an enemy soldier entered the bunker room, his Luger pistol in his hands.

Geist turned as the soldier lifted his weapon. In the fraction of a second she had to think, she realized becoming intangible would result in the bullet passing through her and striking Wilhelm. Instead, she drew her Colt .45 and remained corporeal, hoping to beat the soldier on the draw.

They both fired.

Geist's bullet pierced the soldier's skull, but her enemy managed to strike her right side just below the ribs. He hit the floor and Geist staggered back into the gurney, pain surging through her body.

She glanced back at Wilhelm, relieved to find him unharmed,

but it didn't ease the hot agony pounding her ribs. He stared at her, his eyebrows knit together as he took another deep breath.

"You…"

"I'm going to get you out of here," Geist said through her teeth.

She stepped away from the gurney. Warm blood soaked into the bottom of her khaki tunic and the top of her trousers. Geist's hands shook as she opened her medical pouch and withdrew a small handful of cellucotton and gauze. She knew she had to stop her bleeding, but removing her tunic would reveal her identity as a woman…

Geist pressed a hand over the injury and gave Wilhelm a sidelong glance. With each beat of her heart, her pain intensified.

Wilhelm grabbed his forehead and returned her stare with one eye tightly shut.

Geist took a deep breath. Duty came first. Duty always came first. Her orders were to rescue the POWs, and Geist *would* save them—even if it meant dragging them from hell itself.

I can't hesitate, she thought. *And searching for a private room would take too long… If we're both to survive, I've got to act right now!*

TWO

Grave-Maker Gas

G eist ripped off her tunic, exposing the taut binding over her chest, and applied the cellucotton to both the entry and exit injury. The enemy's bullet had passed straight through—the Luger pistol's 9mm rounds were smaller than her Colt .45, which meant less potential damage—but this gave Geist little comfort.

Muscle memory took over as she wrapped the gauze around her waist. Geist had done it so many times to her chest that the entire process took less than thirty seconds to complete, despite the dim lighting and slick blood.

Wilhelm groaned and shook his head. "You're a…" He spoke in English, staring with narrowed eyes.

Geist snatched up her tunic and pulled it over her head, her right side ablaze with every move. Her chest tightened at the thought of dealing with just *what* the soldier had seen. But perhaps Wilhelm could be convinced he was hallucinating.

"Come," she said, breathless. "We need to go."

Wilhelm slid off the gurney and stood on unsteady feet. Geist held her side and motioned for him to follow. Together, they strode down the bunker hall, stepped around the German corpses, and made it back to the trenches.

"Abscheuliche Soldaten," Wilhelm whispered, drawing Geist's attention.

A group of men ran into the battlefield from the German side. They were soldiers unlike the disbelieving men in the trenches: They were *Abscheuliche Soldaten,* Abomination Soldiers. German sorcerers meant to deal with the likes of her.

Geist slung her rifle off her shoulder and unloaded.

The group of enemy sorcerers broke apart and returned fire— two running to deal with Cutter in the trenches, one to deal with Little Wick by the sentry posts, one for Buttons at the mounted machine gun—but the commander turned for Geist.

"Kill these Huns quick," Cutter shouted from down below, his voice ringing with excitement. "Tonight, we break their lines!"

Buttons belted out a laugh. "Hear, hear!"

He fired another hurricane of ammunition, but Geist didn't have time to watch. The commander of the Verdun Abomination Soldiers met her on the field in a matter of seconds. She pushed the unarmed Wilhelm away and clenched her jaw.

The commander, unlike the others dressed in a uniform of dark green, wore an officer's outfit of black and blue. A stitched line marking his status as a commander—colored red, white, and black —gleamed in the rays of the moon as it hung over the collar of his tunic.

She met the first lieutenant across the gap of the second trench, her aim off thanks to her injury. Geist took a full breath to steady her rifle despite her shaking hands. The commander's name, stitched in bright ivory above the breast pocket, caught Geist's eye.

First Lieutenant Agustin Fechner.

But before she could pull the trigger, her mind flooded with grating noise. Her eyes were bombarded with flashes of light that lingered as bright stains on her vision.

Fuck—this is his doing, she reasoned. *What sorcery is this?*

In her confusion, Geist missed the moment the commander leapt across the gap dividing them. He pulled out a combat knife from a sheath on his belt and slashed wide, clipping her forearm and drawing blood in one brutal swing.

Geist stumbled back. She needed to focus in order to become intangible. But the terrible noise in her head broke her concentration again and again. When the commander slashed again, he laughed, slicing through part of her ear and sending a long shiver of agony throughout Geist's body. These cuts wouldn't kill her quickly, but blood loss would finish her if she wasn't careful.

"Are all American men so small?" Fechner asked in German. "I'm disappointed."

She met his excited gaze with her own steely stare. Adrenaline masked the pain from her injuries, like they had all bled away, leaving her whole.

The commander thrust his blade forward, but it flew through her cheek without making contact, her skin shimmering in defiance. He stepped back, a smile creeping across his face.

"Fascinating. Maybe you'll make a good trophy after all."

Bring your tricks, Geist thought. *I'm ready.*

The machine gun fire stopped, and the irregular crack of rifles sounded from the German defense lines. Geist heard the enemy rally. They had returned to help their fellows, and when she chanced a glance, she spotted them hiding among supply boxes and ducking between trenches under cover of darkness.

Accosted with another round of lights and a deafening bust of raucous sound, Geist stifled a shout and slid back over a pile of sandbags. Her back hit the dirt as her mind searched for focus. She needed something to hone her thoughts, and a memory wormed its way into her mind.

Prove me wrong! her father shouted. *If you're not worthless, prove me wrong!*

She chewed her tongue and tasted copper.

First Lieutenant Fechner leapt over the sandbags, his uniform straining over his bulk. Geist scrambled to her feet and reloaded. The first lieutenant swung and she buried the end of her rifle barrel into his shoulder before firing. He grunted and fell back on his heels, his shoulder mangled and streaming blood.

Geist turned to run, but the first lieutenant lunged forward clumsily, slamming into her and sending them both to the ground.

Her rifle slipped from her grasp. Geist couldn't become incorporeal or fade fully into the dirt with Fechner on top of her. By grappling with her in the mud, the first lieutenant had limited the usefulness of her magic.

Fechner struck downward, opening a gash across her face with jagged knuckles.

As Fechner readied a second swing, Geist jammed her thumb into the gaping hole of his wounded shoulder. He cried out as she torqued him to the side and mounted, reversing their positions. She bashed her elbow down across his nose, and blood exploded onto his chin and uniform, breaking his concentration and causing his magic to fail.

A bullet clipped Geist's sleeve. She jumped off the first lieutenant and took cover, her chest heaving.

"*Auslöser das Grab-Hersteller Gas,*" the Germans shouted from the far lines. "*Auslöser das Grab-Hersteller Gas!*"

It took Geist only moments to translate the words literally: *Trigger the grave-maker gas!*

"No…" the first lieutenant gurgled through a mouthful of blood. "*No!* Not now!"

Geist took in controlled breaths. Gas? She had heard of deadly gases used in the trenches, but not yet in Verdun. What were the Germans planning?

She turned and spotted Wilhelm pressed against the side of the bunker, keeping out of enemy fire. His body glistened with sweat in the moonlight, his chest rising and falling with ragged breaths. Geist didn't know what ailed him, but she knew they needed to retreat before the gas hit.

She limped to his side and motioned toward No Man's Land. "We've got… got to hurry."

Wilhelm replied with a curt nod and a groan.

A loud explosion shook the ground, sending shivers down Geist's spine. A shell landed in between the German trenches—between her and the other members of the Ethereal Squadron. Through the debris, she could see the German sorcerers fleeing, leaving Little Wick, Cutter, and Buttons in control of the line.

Fog poured from the shell. The gas, a cloud of sickly yellow and green, crept across the battlefield with an almost slither, seemingly attracted to life. It slipped into the trenches, washing over the German soldiers as well as Little Wick and Cutter. Buttons sat in the machine gun turret and covered his mouth with a handkerchief—one printed with the stripes of the United Kingdom's noble flag.

First Lieutenant Fechner forced himself to stand. He waved his one good arm. "Fall back! Run! It never should've been released this close!"

The screams that followed came straight from Geist's nightmares.

She watched from around the corner of the bunker, her body tense. The German men clambered over each other in their haste to flee, but the gas seemed to chew through their flesh and turned their eyes to jelly. Skin sloughed off in hideous clumps, the soldiers' uniforms turning into bags of blood and organs. Soon they couldn't even scream.

"Wick!" Geist shouted, her voice high and strained. "Cutter!"

Cutter stared from within the cloud. Geist knew his sorcery had long since killed his fear of death, but she could only watch as his confidence shattered in an instant. The gas melted his flesh, first to a waxy sheen and then liquefying his whole body. By the time he actually realized what was happening to him, he fell apart in chunks of red, pink, and putrid yellow, his uniform sinking into his body as though disappearing into a pool of bloody quicksand.

No. Not Cutter. He can heal. He'll get up, and...

Even in the most desperate of straits, Cutter had returned to the squadron commander without fail. He had lived through every injury imaginable, including near decapitation. Nothing slowed him. But the gas...

Cutter didn't get up from the gas.

Little Wick attempted to burn the fog away, but to no avail. His fate came just as swiftly as Cutter's, and as he cried out, his voice faded into strangled sobs.

"Dear Lord, not now... not before I've told Ellen... *Please*... I'm not ready..."

Geist turned her attention to the first lieutenant, but his shock and horror matched her own. Had he not known?

No. He had to have known. It was his weapon.

The *Grab-Hersteller Gas* shifted without the wind, snaking up out of the trench and toward Geist and Wilhelm with supernatural precision. She saw it swell and waft forward in a thick, semi-opaque cloud. She pulled on Wilhelm's arm, prepared to run, but First Lieutenant Fechner lunged toward her. He punched her in the side, right on the bullet wound, sending Geist to her knees.

Wilhelm shoved off the bunker and cocked his fist, but First Lieutenant Fechner struck first, knocking Wilhelm back into the wall.

"Traitor," Fechner hissed. "You'll die here."

Geist's vision darkened for one terrible second, a small portion of her mind on the gas at all times, panic blocking out all other information. She inhaled, jumped to her feet, and slammed her shoulder into Fechner. The German officer toppled into the nearest trench as the gas came on, hungry for flesh.

Geist grabbed Wilhelm the moment the yellow-greenish *Grab-Hersteller Gas* grazed the skin of her arm. The odd pinprick sensation —a prickling that went deep and flared into a heated pain— returned her to her senses.

She ran, Wilhelm in tow, leaving the first lieutenant to his fate.

Her feet struck the packed earth in rhythm, matching the pounding tempo of her heart. Bullets followed her, but she didn't fear them like she feared the gas. She felt pity for the soldiers close enough to fire. Soon they would know why she ran…

No Man's Land greeted her with a fog of death all its own. Amid the corpses, barbed wire, and posts, Geist saw nothing but phantom visions of her comrades melting away. She slowed and came to a stop halfway back, turning to get one final look. Her fingernails dug furrows in her scalp as she ran a hand through her crew-cut hair. The sensations made the situation real.

The machine gun turret stood empty, Buttons's fate left unknown. Had he used his magic in time to escape? Only if he was lucky.

All rifle fire ceased.

The *Grab-Hersteller Gas* remained suspended in the moonlight, looming like a reaper. She had never seen such a weapon before. A mix of technology and magic? *Impossible.* Such a thing couldn't exist.

And yet, the shell… The German men—non-sorcerers and mundane in every regard—had been the ones to unleash the weapon. It had to be a product of science if they could wield it.

She had to report to Major Reese. It was imperative.

He has to know.

Wilhelm placed a hand on her shoulder, snapping her out of the mounting dread. "We must continue," he said, his voice a dry rasp.

Geist gave herself the once-over before continuing through the impromptu graveyard. As long as most of her uniform remained intact, she wouldn't need to steal pieces from the dead men all around her.

Buttons. Cutter. Little Wick.

She had thought they would see the Great War through till the end.

The *Grab-Hersteller Gas*—the wretched grave-maker gas—she had never seen a tool of war so horrifying or so efficient at killing sorcerers.

Never.

THREE

Fort Belleville

After a short wait, a Fort Belleville nurse joined Geist in the examining room. "Remove your clothes, sir," she said as the nurse shut the door behind her.

Geist gripped her coat sleeve and turned away. "My physician is Matron-in-Chief Johnson. I'll wait for her."

The nurse, a lanky woman in a long gray medic coat, tightened her lips and raised an eyebrow. Her cheeks shifted to a rosy hue for a brief second. "All nurses write the same reports. You are not entitled to a specific one."

"I'm a member of the 2nd E Squadron," Geist forced herself to say.

The Ethereal Squadron was a classified organization that kept to itself but, during times of war, it often shared facilities with other soldiers. French, British and even a handful of American men filled the halls of Fort Belleville. In times of overcrowding the sorcerers referred to their group via a code to avoid revealing information about their true nature.

"Chief Johnson is very busy," the nurse stated. "I'm more than capable of prepping you for her. Strip off your uniform and I will take all the preliminary notes."

Geist exhaled and stared down at her tattered clothing. She couldn't take it off. Not in front of the nurse—not when her medical file read *male* under all the reports. "I'm not... comfortable," Geist said, her lie ringing hollow, even to her.

"Come now. This isn't the place for such frivolity. It's a nurse's office. You stripped for your first medical evaluation."

"I'll wait for Chief Johnson."

"Young man, you have no need for modesty. Other soldiers require my attention. Now *strip*."

Her voice, so commanding and authoritative, echoed throughout the tiny examination room. Geist found herself chuckling. The nurses of Fort Belleville were as formidable as any soldier.

Stalling for time, Geist undid the fastenings of her uniform, starting with her trousers. The nurse tapped her foot and kept the sharp point of her pencil poised over her clipboard. She had to be younger than thirty-five, but the stress and lack of sleep added ten years to her face. She held herself with a matronly confidence, a stern but gentle expression etched into her haggard features.

The door to the room opened, and Geist flinched on instinct. She held her uniform tight, her pants half-off.

Matron-in-Chief Mattie Johnson stepped through the door, her bright blue eyes snapping to Geist in a heartbeat.

"I have everything under control now," Chief Johnson said. "Thank you, Nurse Rodgers."

The other nurse frowned but gave no resistance. She nodded, placed the clipboard on the center table, and strode from the room. Chief Johnson followed behind and locked the door, leaving Geist as the only other occupant in the small space.

Chief Johnson turned to Geist and shook her head. "You had me worried."

"I got in at an odd time," Geist replied. "And my report took precedence. I'm sorry. I should have come here first."

"I can't be awake at all hours of the day."

"I understand."

"You don't want to be discovered, do you?"

"No. You're right. I understand."

Geist had nothing else to say. She knew the risks of walking into the medical wards without planning her visit ahead of time, but she had done so without thinking. Images of the battle had played in her mind, distracting her. Geist could barely focus and her body refused to stop shaking.

Chief Johnson picked up the form report and lifted an eyebrow. "What happened out in the field, Mr. Charles Weston?"

"Don't call me that," Geist snapped. She threw off her pants and undid her coat and shirt.

Geist undid the first of her chest bindings, allowing herself to breathe easy. "We should go by codenames when we're alone. It's better that way. I like calling you 'Cross.'"

"I like hearing it," she said with a genuine smile.

"What happened out there, Geist?" Cross asked, her smile never fading.

"It was gas. I wrote about it in my report to the commander."

"What kind of gas?"

"Something new. Something I've never seen before."

"Did Little Wick report on it as well? His writeups are always so detailed. The commander will want to see them."

Geist's throat seized. Did Cross not know? Of course not. It had all happened last night. How could she know when the Ethereal Squadron kept their activities classified?

"Little Wick…" Geist fished for words. She ripped off the last of her bindings and took a seat on the cold counter that lined the wall of the room, biting back the stabbing pain of her gunshot injury. With a long sigh, she shook her head and stared at the floor. "Little Wick and the others didn't make it."

Cross's smile disappeared in an instant, replaced with a tight frown. "All of them?"

"I don't know about Buttons."

"Cutter? Surely, he didn't go like the rest."

Geist nodded once.

"But, Cutter, he——" Cross cut herself short. Geist met her gaze and found nothing to read. No fear. No pain. Cross dealt with more loss and death than anyone—it came with her job. Geist admired the emotional fortitude, but Cross hadn't seen the *Grab-Hersteller Gas* with her own eyes. Would she be so stoic then?

"Have you seen Buttons since last night?" Geist asked.

"No. I haven't heard from anyone in your team until now."

With no more words to pass between them, Cross turned her attention to her work. She jotted down a few simple notes and went to examine Geist.

Cross grazed her fingers over Geist's narrow frame and then through Geist's blackish-brown hair, easily mistaken for tar, it was cut so short. Such a trim figure made masquerading as a man a simple task, but in moments of vulnerability, naked in front of another, Geist couldn't help but wonder how life would have been different if she had possessed a different sort of body, something closer to Cross's hourglass curves and golden-wheat hair.

"Cross," Geist said, her voice hushed. "Have you treated the man I brought back to the fort? His dog tag said his name was William." *Even though he said his name was Wilhelm.*

"Of course."

"Did he… mention me? Or anything strange about the rescue?"

"No. Why? Is something wrong?"

"No. It's nothing."

Perhaps he doubted his eyes.

But Geist knew she couldn't take that chance.

With the care befitting a master physician, Cross ran her fingers over Geist's body. Such contact from anyone else would have left her feeling vulnerable, but Cross's touch came with a warmth and soothing comfort unlike any other. Her magic was so potent—Geist's hardly compared. No other sorcerer as young as Cross could hope to be as proficient.

Every wound, big or small, relaxed and mended itself. The knife slash down Geist's forearm closed, leaving no scar in its wake. The bullet wound in her side ceased its throbbing pain. Her sore feet, aching from miles of marching in worn boots, rested easy. Even internal bruises faded, leaving Geist awash in relief.

Except her left wrist.

Cross touched Geist's wrist, and a terrible pain flared throughout Geist's body. Geist jerked back, holding her arm close to her chest.

"Cross," she breathed. "What was that?"

Cross met her question with a furrowed brow. "I… didn't do anything. I was healing you."

Geist glared down and held back a gasp. Her left wrist, though fine the day before, had a waxy sheen to it and a piece of fabric—khaki like her uniform—embedded in the flesh. Geist clawed at the inch-long, half-an-inch-wide distortion, hoping to rip it from her body. Blood welled at her fingertips and ran in rivulets down her arm, falling onto her bare lap.

"Stop," Cross said. "You're hurting yourself. Let me try again."

She ran her hand over Geist's and caressed the wrist. Pain flared once more. Geist fought the urge to pull away. The flesh healed, but the fabric remained. And the longer Cross attempted to fix it, the more agony built up in Geist's arm. The sensation of burning became too much.

"*I can't,*" Geist snapped, ripping her limb away from Cross. "This isn't working. It's the gas. It did this." She held her arm close to her chest and scrunched her eyes shut. The gas had touched her for but a second.

"Gas doesn't make injuries like this."

"It was magic. It was… sinister." Geist's voice trailed off. Cross stood a breath closer.

"If it was magic, I should be able to heal it. It must be something else or—"

Geist shook her head. "No. You weren't there. There's no doubt in my mind. It's *tainted* me."

When Cross reached to examine the arm a second time, Geist shot her a grim glower. What use was it for Cross to look at the mark? The tiny injury didn't require her attention. It would be hidden by the long sleeve of Geist's uniform. She didn't want to dwell on it any further.

"Scars don't taint you," Cross intoned.

"This is different. Something worse than a scar. It killed my whole team."

It killed my whole team. Geist hadn't meant to blurt out something so macabre. But what else could she say? Cross didn't understand.

Silence settled between them. Cross brought a hand to her cheek and frowned.

"The weight of suffering may never go away," she said, "but it's the strength you derive from carrying it that matters."

Geist sighed and turned her gaze to the window. "I don't need this right now."

She can keep her nonsense poetry for the shell-shocked soldiers.

Cross placed a hand on Geist's shoulder and drew her in for a gentle embrace. Geist, confused and stiff, bunched her shoulders up around her neck.

"You're so strong already," Cross whispered into the nape of Geist's neck. "I can only imagine what you've gone through in your life. Forgive me."

"Cross… This is inappropriate." Geist awkwardly patted Cross on the back with her one free arm. "You have nothing to apologize for. Just finish the examination. C'mon now, get up."

"You're my responsibility. You wouldn't even be here if it weren't for my intervention. I should've thought this all through."

"Stop this. If you hadn't, I would've just found another way to—"

The door's lock clicked without a key, causing both Cross and Geist to tense. The door flew open half a second later and a man burst in without knocking. In the remaining half a second that Geist had to comprehend the situation, she held Cross close, keeping the nurse between her and the soldier, hiding her curves against the other woman.

"Hey, Cross," the man said. "I need something for—*whoa!*" He tucked his hands into his khaki trouser pockets and cocked a smirk. "What've we got here? *Geist?* Is that you?"

Icy dread and red-hot embarrassment sluiced through Geist's body. What could she do? She couldn't release Cross without revealing who and *what* she was to this man—but she couldn't stay frozen like this forever, either.

The man waited, as though for an explanation.

Then Cross sobbed, her voice shrill and loud. She shook against Geist and clung ever tighter, her face tucked away into Geist's collarbone, stifling her sniffles. The man raised both eyebrows, his bravado waning.

"Oh, shit," he muttered. "I'm sorry. I didn't know—"

Geist forced herself to glare through her flushed red face. "*Tinker!* Get the hell outta here!"

"R-right."

Tinker fled the room, shutting the door and locking it with his magic as he went. After a long moment, Cross's faux-sobbing transformed into genuine laughter. She snorted and stepped away, her own face rosy.

"I can't believe he just walked *in* here," she said between chuckles.

"Cross, what were you thinking? What if the commander gets word of this? He might have us both discharged—for indecent conduct."

"It already looked bad. I didn't make it much worse."

"A woman crying in the arms of a naked soldier? Damn it all, I can already hear the rumors…"

"I'm a member of the Ethereal Squadron," Cross stated matter-of-factly. "They won't lose me because of some idle tittle-tattle. We won't make a fuss about it, and no one will reprimand us. Trust me. I've seen other nurses in more compromising positions. *Much* more compromising."

Geist allowed herself a single chuckle. "All right. Thank goodness for your quick thinking, then. Hand me a uniform before we have to do it all over again."

"But I haven't finished the exam."

"Make something up," Geist said as she slid off the counter and crossed her arms over her chest. "I'm done here."

I'm just shaken, she thought. *Once I get assigned to a new team and get back to my routine I'll be fine. No more close calls. Well, as long as Wilhelm didn't see anything.*

Cross withdrew a smaller-than-average uniform from the tallest cabinet. The khaki outfit, folded neatly, had a fresh scent. Nothing like Geist's old clothes—weeks of trenches and warfare had left them a tattered mess.

Geist held up the garments and examined them with a sigh. Tailored for a man and ill-fitting. She slipped into the trousers. She gestured to Cross for medical bandages, and the other woman brought over two rolls. Geist proceeded to bind her chest all over again, quick and practiced in her motions.

"If you need any more cellucotton, you should tell me," Cross said. "We run out of supplies constantly. One nurse used her petticoat as bandages the other day, God bless her heart, but I've stored some things away in case you start bleeding."

"Thank you, Cross. I'll let you know."

"Don't dwell on your past battles, Florence. I tell the other soldiers the same things. Only fools trip on things already behind them."

"Where is the POW?" Geist asked as she pulled her coat tight and hooked each button with hasty motions. She finished her dressing by securing her belt and fitting her cap atop her head.

Cross sighed. "In recovery room three. Why?"

"I need to see him."

Cross stared, her face emotionless, and Geist gave her a curt nod before walking up to the door and fumbling with the locked handle. Cross walked over and unlocked the heavy door with her key.

"The commander called a debriefing," she said. "Don't take too long."

"I know. That's where I'll head afterward." Geist stepped out of the room. "I'll visit later."

Cross said nothing.

Fort Belleville, like most forts Geist had been in, stood sturdy and proud, crafted with fine masonry. The narrow halls and small rooms weren't designed for comfort or large crowds. Rooms had been converted depending on the need of the situation. Somehow, despite the chaos, the noncombatant personnel made everything work.

She rounded a corner and jumped back. Tinker swung a heel off his foot and pushed away from the wall to stand straight in her path. A swagger to his stance, Tinker folded his arms over his chest and tilted his head.

"Geist. You dog."

Caveat, another sorcerer stationed at Verdun, hovered behind Tinker without speaking. He shifted his weight from foot to foot, his rotund frame a contrast to Tinker's lithe and lanky stature. Geist shot Caveat a glare before returning her flustered gaze to Tinker. Did Caveat know? Had Tinker already told everyone? What would their commander say?

Tinker snorted and shrugged. "Don't worry. Your secret is safe with us. I didn't know Cross was your sweetheart. I won't be gettin' in the way."

"I wish I had a gal as swell as Cross," Caveat muttered.

"Hah! *I* have a girl waiting for me back home." Tinker motioned to his full head of blond hair—a perfect slicked-back hairdo complete with stylish waves on one side of the part. Geist wondered where he had found pomade out on the frontlines.

Caveat pursed his lips and grumbled, patting his own bald head. "Women always fall for the quiet ones," he said, his voice growing bolder. "You should read the letters my sister wrote about the boys of her neighboring academy. Her fawning borders on obsession."

Tinker threw a long arm around Geist and pulled her down the hallway. "Isn't that always the way? Women love the brooders. I guess it makes up for how short you are—eh, Geist?" Tinker tousled the top of Geist's head, ruffling her cap.

Geist gritted her teeth and kept her gaze straight ahead. At least *they* didn't know.

But there was still Wilhelm to deal with.

"What're you, five-six?" Tinker asked. "Five-seven? They have shoes to make you look taller, ya know. Fancy things. I've seen 'em for sale in the New York shops. All you need is a few inches and you'd be knockin' the ladies dead."

"Don't go givin' him any more of your boneheaded advice," Caveat said. "He already has Cross."

Tinker snapped his fingers. "Oh, it all makes sense now! You always visiting Cross? You've been sweethearts since you enlisted, haven't you? You sly dog. I should've put it all together sooner."

"Huh. I thought Victory was sweet on Cross. Maybe he's pining in secret."

"Victory's a prick." Tinker snorted. "That guy can stand to lose every now and then."

"Might want to keep that to yourself. He's bound to be here for the debriefing."

"Ah, it doesn't matter. What's Victory going to do about it? Beat me at a game of cards?" Tinker stopped at an intersection in the hallway and pushed Geist forward. "Get on over to the commander's office. We'll meet you there."

Caveat nodded and followed Tinker down the northern hallway, his fidgeting creating as much noise as their boot steps.

Nice talk, boys.

With a sigh, she turned for the western hall and headed straight for recovery room three. All the recovery rooms had once been storage closets, but they had since been converted. Seeing as Wilhelm was a member of the Ethereal Squadron, though different than the sorcerers of Verdun, it didn't surprise Geist that he would have his own special room.

Once Geist found herself outside the door, she took in a deep breath. *There's no need to fear. He likely saw nothing.*

She turned the handle and entered.

The tiny space, more cramped than the exam room, had no windows, a single cot, and a stand for linens. Wilhelm sat up on his cot, a thin blanket draped over his legs. He wore no tunic or shirt, his dog tags dangling from his neck and resting flat on the center of his chest.

He glanced up when Geist stepped forward, his eyes narrowed and discerning.

Geist cleared her throat and attempted to keep her voice deeper than usual. "I don't know if you remember me, but—"

"I remember," Wilhelm interjected gruffly. "You're the soldier who rescued me."

Soldier. Not *woman*.

But not *man*, either.

"I came to ask you a few questions, Wilhelm," she said.

The mere mention of his name caused Wilhelm to tense. "William. My name is William."

Geist shook her head. "You're German, aren't you? I heard you speak on the frontlines."

He threw back his blanket and stood from the cot, confident and uninjured in every regard. Geist crossed her arms over her chest as he stepped close. He was a good foot taller and she craned her head back to match his serious gaze.

"I'm American," he said.

"Perhaps you're American *now*," Geist replied. "But I know a German when I see one." *I've met and lived with many back in Austria-Hungary. There's no doubt in my mind. His accent is native. I'd bet my life on it.*

But then it struck her. If he had once been German, it meant he was a defector. Even the enemy lieutenant had recognized Wilhelm during their escape. He had called Wilhelm a traitor. If that were the case, he wouldn't want his nationality known. Many hated the Germans and Austro-Hungarians for declaring war on Serbia, and animosity ran deeper than the trenches that separated the soldiers. The other men might not trust a German defector. They might even still consider him an enemy.

"What's your code name?" Geist asked, her mind stewing in the revelation.

"Vergessenheit," he replied.

Vergessenheit—*oblivion* in German.

Having a German code name didn't mark him as German—Geist's name was German in origin—but the name's significance wasn't lost on her.

Geist exhaled. "Your identity is safe with me, Vergess. It doesn't matter where you come from, so long as you're with us now. You are with us… aren't you?"

"Yes."

She found it ironic she would need to hide a secret for the man, especially when she had entered the room fearing he knew hers. She held back a chuckle.

"And what about you?" he asked in a rough whisper. "Do you always conduct yourself as a man?"

Geist lost her breath.

He knew.

"I thought the British held themselves as gentlemen, but here they have women fighting their war for them." Vergess glowered down at her. "Or do they not even know?"

"Not everyone," Geist managed, her lies stitching themselves together as her mind raced. "I—well, there are reasons—spies need to be versatile. So many have been caught already."

That wasn't untrue. Female sorcerers, from dancers to singers, traveled between the warring countries, performing for all manner of soldiers and officers. They reported back their findings, but two had already been caught and executed for their treachery.

"So the others here are aware?" Vergess asked, his tone implying he would check if she gave an affirmative answer.

"No," she said. "No one knows outside of General Pétain and Fort Belleville's Matron-in-Chief. It has to be kept a secret—do you understand? You must never mention it to anyone or you'll compromise my usefulness."

Geist knew Cross would play along if Vergess approached her, and it was unlikely that General Pétain, the head of the Verdun front operations, would have an audience with Vergess simply to confirm his stories.

Vergess took a breath and tensed. "A spy-agent. In the Ethereal Squadron. I see."

A moment passed between them, and Vergess gave her the once-over, as if seeing her truly for the first time.

The other soldiers never looked at her like they looked at wartime dame entertainers or the fair ladies they marched by during their trek to the trenches. It was easy to push aside carnal feelings when she considered her fellow Ethereal Squadron members all the same—soldiers carrying out a mission, no difference between them, everyone a cog in the bloody machine of war.

But Vergess had changed that. He *knew*, and for the first time, Geist saw him not as a fellow soldier, but as a man. His shirtlessness showcased a lean, muscled physique and broad shoulders. He held himself with a stiff posture and a cold presence, his body coiled, as though he could lash out with lethal force even from his compromised position. He was an impressive specimen, even among soldiers.

Geist gritted her teeth, the heat in her veins angering her. She had kept her desires locked away for so long… To have them resurface now, in the middle of her frontline assignment… it felt like weakness.

"I don't like the idea of women getting hurt in the war," Vergess said, drawing Geist from her thoughts. "But you've done me more than one favor. I'll keep your secret, as you've agreed to keep mine."

"You swear it?" Geist asked.

Vergess huffed. "A soldier keeps his word."

"You'll have to forgive me for not immediately trusting the word of a defector."

He caught his breath and clenched his fists. Geist could sense his rage, but it waned with each breath that followed.

"I'm sorry," she said. "It must've been hard to leave your motherland." Geist switched to German and continued, "I understand. I truly do."

She knew her accent had the tint of the south, specifically an Austro-Hungarian dialect. Although she didn't care to share her history with others, she felt assuaging Vergess's fear was worth this small omission.

"I—" Vergess began. Then he, too, switched to German and said, "You have my thanks."

Geist gave him a single nod. Unsure of what else could be said, she fumbled over her words. "Yes, well, th-thank you."

After another quiet moment of staring, Vergess turned away, his face a slight shade of red. He grabbed his tunic off the edge of the cot and threw it on, keeping his back to her at all times. He wore the

American khaki uniform with a small 48-star American flag tied across the left sleeve.

"I need to go," he said, curt and in English. "Pardon me."

Vergess stepped around her, giving her a wide berth as though afraid to get too close, and opened the door. He cursed under his breath in German and then disappeared into the hall.

FOUR

Team Assignments

The commander's office served as the field command for the Ethereal Squadron in Verdun, and Geist knew it well enough to find her way there without difficulty. She stopped at the door and narrowed her eyes.

Blood stained the stones of the hall and the wood of the door, fresh enough to be noticeable, but old enough to have faded to near-black.

Geist turned the handle and stepped in. To her surprise, the room already had several occupants. She glanced between them, half to see who they were and half to see if anyone was bleeding. Thirteen of the twenty Verdun Ethereal Squadron sorcerers returned her gaze. None of them had injuries to speak of, and Geist glanced back down at the floor to find that the trail of crimson stains continued all the way to their commander's desk.

Major Archibald Reese stood behind a solid piece of oak desk. His broad shoulders, half-moon gut, and well-kept beard set him apart from the rest—not to mention the crown-shaped insignias lining his uniform. Sorcerers in the squadron referred to him simply as "Commander," but face-to-face, Geist fell back on formality.

"Afternoon, sir," she said with a salute.

He returned her greeting—a casual gesture, more of a half-salute—and motioned for Geist to take her place among the ranks. The men of the room stood still and waiting. Smoke lingered in the air as a thick haze with each new cigarette. The windows remained shut for security purposes, cutting off all possibility for airflow. The room stunk of men's sweat.

Geist disliked the silence.

She had been in many debriefings. The ones with bad news always started quiet.

Her gaze shifted to Vergess, who lingered in the far corner. He stared at her but looked away when she met his eyes. He stood separate from the others, and Geist recognized the way he kept to himself to avoid attention—she had become the master of this technique herself.

The door to the office opened and closed, revealing Tinker and Caveat. Before they could mutter greetings or apologizes for their tardiness, Major Reese pulled down a scroll map mounted on the wall behind his desk. A web of hand-drawn red, black, and blue lines covered the topographical map of France and the surrounding countries.

"Gentlemen, we have a sorcerer from Marne here with us," Major Reese said in a baritone voice that shook the room. "Vergess has served with the Ethereal Squadron for some time now and will be stationed with us in Verdun until called to another special assignment."

The men of the room gave Vergess a quick glance before returning their gaze to the map. Geist took note of their narrowed stares and dismissive waves of their hands. People seemed to know of Vergess—either through reputation or personally, though Geist wasn't sure which.

"But now we need to focus." Major Reese struck the map with a finger along the red line. "We failed to move the frontlines north."

Geist winced. That had been her assignment—hers and the rest of her team's—to save the POWs *and* to move the Triple Entente farther north.

"What?" a soldier leaning on the far wall asked. "Then why is

Geist back? His team was assigned that battle. They should still be there. The Germans are already too close to Paris. If they take France, they'll be free to focus on the Russians."

"Yes," another soldier said, chiming in. "We should send them back until we've broken the lines."

Major Reese held his hands behind his back, silencing the crowd as though with sheer will. He glanced between the men before speaking. "Geist has made his reports. Sorcerers attacked in the trenches. Cutter, Little Wick, and Buttons are dead."

Shock rippled through the room.

One sorcerer shook his head. "Not Cutter. He didn't die. He *can't*."

Everyone turned their gaze to Geist. She hesitated for a moment before holding her head high and nodding. "I saw it with my own eyes. Cutter died fighting."

"And Buttons?" Tinker asked, his voice distant. "The same happened to him?"

"I don't know what happened to Buttons."

"You didn't stay?" one man blurted out.

Geist turned her attention to the speaker, the highest-ranking member of the Ethereal Squadron outside of Major Reese himself —Victor Hamilton, codenamed "Victory."

"You left them to die?" Victory asked.

The accusation in his voice cut deep. The eyes of the others tracked Geist's every move and motion, judging her. She stepped forward and, through restrained rage, chose her words carefully.

"I would never leave them behind. I stayed until the last moment. They were in the trenches—I tried to warn them, but it was too late. We didn't understand the threat. I watched Cutter and Little Wick *melt* in front of me before I turned to flee."

The others glanced amongst themselves and shared silent conversations. They lit a whole new round of cigarettes. Vergess returned his gaze to her, unflinching and intense.

"Then what happened to Buttons?" Victory asked.

"Buttons used his magic to return," Major Reese interjected.

"He made it to my office before dying. His wounds were consistent with Geist's report."

Geist went to speak, but the words never came. Her eyes dropped to the floor and to the commander's desk. Bloodstains. Bloodstains everywhere.

He came here, Geist thought, her mind's eye picturing Buttons in a state of horrific agony, similar to Little Wick and Cutter. *He came here to make his report. To warn the commander. God, what could he have been thinking? Why didn't he go straight for Cross?*

Words filled the room, but Geist couldn't hear them.

She was the sole survivor.

"Geist."

She heard her name, but it didn't register.

"Geist."

Their faces flashed through her mind—Cutter, Little Wick, and Buttons. Had she failed them somehow? Victory seemed to think so —and Victory was never wrong. Could she have done something else to help them?

"Charles!"

The sound of her assumed name broke her trance. Geist snapped her eyes up to meet Major Reese's steely gaze. "Yes, commander?"

"Did you get a good look at any of the Abomination Soldiers? Do we know who is responsible for creating the gas?"

"I identified First Lieutenant Agustin Fechner, but otherwise, I didn't get a good look at any of the others."

Geist stepped forward before any follow-up questions could be asked.

"A sorcerer didn't create the gas," she said. "It came from a shell. None of the sorcerers activated it, either. The soldiers on the battlefield did."

Again, the eyes of the room honed in on her.

Major Reese shook his head. "Impossible. That's not how sorcery works. It cannot be stored and activated by someone else."

"But—"

"Enough, soldier. It's a fact of magic. You create it and control it. No one else. You can't simply dole it out like rations."

Geist took a deep breath and stopped herself from speaking further. It was inappropriate to argue with a commanding officer, especially in the middle of a debriefing. But she knew what she had seen.

Then again, she knew the limitations of her magic. Her father had made sure of it. Magic, fueled by the sorcerer, could only be wielded through will and focus. Those without the gift could never wield it for themselves.

So how had the soldiers unleashed the weapon?

I have to say something. He has to know.

"Sir," Geist said, her voice steady. "The German soldiers fled once the weapon was deployed. And, I know I didn't write this in my report, but the enemy first lieutenant died in the fighting, consumed by the monstrous gas." She hadn't seen his death, but there could only be one outcome.

The members of the Ethereal Squadron murmured things amongst themselves, their faces set in glowers. Major Reese exhaled.

"Older sorcerers are capable of a great many things," he said. "Perhaps an unknown sorcerer could have been on the battlefield in an unfamiliar form."

The others nodded in agreement, but Geist's frown deepened.

Victory stepped forward, his posture straight and his uniform well-pressed. "We need to identify this sorcerer posthaste. Assign me to the task. I'll handle it."

Standing near the front of the room, his chest out and his chin forward, Victory looked every inch like a wartime propaganda poster boy. His dark hair shone, parted neatly to one side, and his muscled frame rippled even under layers of clothes. They said he had a perfect record, that he'd earned his codename in a hundred splendid conquests, maybe more.

Another sorcerer stepped forward. "I'll go with him."

It was Bernard Hamilton, codenamed *Blick*, Victory's first brother, a bulky mountain of muscle with stubble shading his square chin. He placed a hand on Victory's shoulder and smiled wide.

"Very well," Major Reese stated. "You and Blick will act together on this. You're to identify the enemy sorcerer and neutralize him. Your top priority is this task and this task alone. Everything else is on hold."

Victory nodded; Blick answered in kind. Although Geist disagreed with Major Reese's assessment, she breathed a sigh of relief. *Victory will handle everything. Whatever the source of this evil might be, he'll find it.*

The door opened, setting everyone on edge. Geist glanced over her shoulder and spotted Cross. The Matron-in-Chief stepped into the commander's office and saluted. Major Reese rolled up the map of France and covered the paperwork of the latest assignments before answering Cross's gesture with a salute of his own.

"To what do we owe the pleasure?" he asked.

"Word has come from Fort St. Michel," Cross replied. "They have injured there who need emergency care. St. Michel is only a short distance east. I want permission to go before disease sets in."

"Sounds dangerous."

Major Reese's words were punctuated by a low rumble that shook the office. Aerial bombardments and German artillery could be felt from more than a hundred miles away. The relentless enemy assault had wiped entire nearby towns off the map and permanently rearranged the landscape. Everyone knew getting caught out in a bombing raid was a death sentence—sorcerer or no.

"They need my care," Cross said. "I can travel with the medics."

"I already have to write the parents of three fallen soldiers today. I won't write your mother, too, to say her daughter died fighting a man's war."

Cross's shoulders stiffened, but she held her head high. "I knew the risks when I joined the Ethereal Squadron, and I understand that—"

"We allowed you to join the Ethereal Squadron because of your extraordinary abilities. You aren't military, so I'll overlook this outburst, but as your commanding officer, I am the one who decides what risks you take. Do I make myself clear?"

A host of expressions lit across her face. A child would continue to protest. A civilian would be indignant. But Cross, a soldier in her heart despite Major Reese's remark, seemed to realize the conversation was over and slumped her shoulders.

"I understand, sir. If you'll excuse me, I'll return to my duties."

She turned and left without another word, leaving the room to its silence. Tinker—who had slithered along the wall until stopping at Geist's side—elbowed her in the shoulder.

"Cross is a real live wire," he whispered. "You better look after her."

Geist ignored him. She watched Major Reese unfurl the map and uncover the assignments, seeing the pain that lingered in his stern eyes. She trusted the commander. He'd never send his men into danger unless it was absolutely necessary.

But then again, he wouldn't trust her, not if he ever learned her secret. She would become something else to him—not a soldier, but something fragile and demure. Something that needed protecting.

Geist felt her gaze drawn inexplicably to Vergess. He had accepted her, hadn't he? He knew her secret and hadn't immediately dismissed her. Perhaps it was because he had seen her fight, or perhaps it was because he owed her his life, but it didn't matter to Geist. His respect, whatever its source, eased the loneliness of her long masquerade.

But would the others be so understanding?

She shook her head and dispelled the thoughts. What would her father say if he knew her doubts? No—no need to ask that. She already knew.

You're going to fail. You can't pretend to be something you're not.

Geist glared at the floor.

Major Reese tapped his fingers on his desk. "Gentlemen, until this threat is taken care of, all engagement with enemy sorcerers should be avoided. This *Grab-Hersteller Gas* will henceforth be referred to as GH Gas in all reports—and, obviously, it should be strictly avoided until we can find a way to counteract it."

"Commander?" Caveat asked, his voice a mere whisper among rowdy men. "Won't the Germans break the French lines with the GH Gas? If we avoid fighting, they'll head straight for Paris."

"Your assignments for the time being will be to target enemy sorcerers and neutralize them as always." Major Reese picked up a stack of papers and waved them for the group to see. The information on each page detailed a member of the Abomination Soldiers —information that Geist suspected had come at a high price.

Major Reese motioned to three men. "Tinker, Trilogy, Big Wick —you're to accompany the ground troops at Fort Souville. All details of your target can be found here." He folded up the paperwork and slid it into a stiff envelope before handing it over.

Tinker, Trilogy, and Big Wick, the tallest men in the room, regarded each other over the heads of everyone else with nods and slight smirks.

"Geist," Major Reese said, his gaze shifting over with a discerning quality. "Are you capable of handling another mission so soon after the last? You haven't been yourself today, son. Be honest with me. I need you at your fullest, or I need you recovering."

Geist straightened herself. "You have me at my fullest."

"Good man. Then I want you with Percival."

Chuckles escaped the mouths of the other soldiers. Percival Hamilton, a small man who blended with the shadows of his corner, stepped forward. He was only a few months out of school and barely eighteen—the youngest member of the Ethereal Squadron by far, and the only member who had yet to experience combat and thus hadn't earned a codename. He was also the younger brother of Victory and Blick—but compared to his brothers, Percival looked almost childlike.

Then again, the Hamilton family always produced exceptional sorcerers. Surely, this Hamilton wouldn't be any different.

"Are you grouping us based on height?" Tinker quipped, ruffling Geist's hair through her cap and nudging Percival with a narrow elbow. "Look! It's Team *Teensy-Weensy!*"

Chuckles turned to laughs as Percival stepped up next to Geist, proving Tinker's point. They stood at nearly the exact same height —both a few inches shorter than Caveat, the next shortest soldier in the room. Percival kept his gaze low. His cheeks flushed bright red and his body stiffened with embarrassment.

Geist didn't mind the japes. The men just needed to blow off steam. Geist understood. After everything she had been through, she needed a good laugh, too.

"Is this a training mission?" Geist asked, eyeing Percival.

He had the wiry body of a student athlete, not the bulk of a soldier. Had they even sent him through basic training? Geist knew times were desperate. The French were trained by fifty-year-old men brought out of retirement—everyone had to do their part, even if that meant sending a sorcerer out onto the field before he was ready.

Percival glowered at her, his eyes a mix of unreadable emotions. "I don't need any further training. I'm quite capable."

"This is an evaluation mission," Major Reese stated. "Geist, you'll give me a detailed report on Percival's sorcery and how he uses it in battle. You'll both be stationed at Fort Souville. We have reason to believe that zeppelins will join the fray and bombard the countryside."

The mere mention of the zeppelins got certain men uneasy; half the room squirmed, each puff of smoke shorter and shakier than the last. Even the most powerful sorcerer had reason to fear a zeppelin: They were huge flying machines, heavily armed and heavily protected, and could wipe a town clean off a map with one of their bombardments.

Major Reese pointed to another man in the room. "Albatross has already been briefed on your target, Geist. He'll take point."

Hubert Haas, codenamed "Albatross," stepped forward, a half-smoked cigarette hanging on his lips. Although Percival was younger, his age differed only by a few years for most in the room. Albatross, on the other hand, took the award for oldest in the squadron—beating out Major Reese and even the sixty-year-old General Pétain. Although he had graying hair and a face marked with heavy lines, the standard uniform fit him fine. No extra flab in the gut, no shrinking from age—at least, not yet.

"Major," Vergess said, silencing the room with his gruff voice. "May I have a word?"

Major Reese nodded. "Of course, son."

Vergess walked up to the commander's desk and leaned against the edge. He whispered something to Major Reese, his words washed away by the conversations growing within the room. Geist strained her ears, but nothing came of it.

She couldn't help but hold her breath. What if he was exposing her right now? *He might be telling Major Reese I can't handle the mission. Or that I shouldn't be in the army at all. Or maybe he's—*

"All right," the commander said, once again silencing the other soldiers. "Vergess will also be assigned to the zeppelin raid. He knows the airships, and it's imperative we knock these floating metal monsters out of the sky."

The men in the room cheered.

Geist felt the same tightness in her chest and gut. He had requested to join her team? Why? The rest of the room buzzed with excitement as the last of the assignments were doled out, but Geist couldn't conjure the will to pay attention.

At least Vergess hadn't outed her. He had kept his word, like a good soldier.

Tinker jabbed her with his boney elbow. "Hey, you ever worked with Vergess before?" he whispered.

"No," she said. *I always had my old team.*

"Well, even if Percival is a greenhand, Vergess will cover you. That guy's a killer."

"A killer?" Geist repeated. *With a German codename like "Oblivion," I can see why.*

"Yeah. He's ruthless. He fought and killed ten Abomination Soldiers singlehandedly. That's what my mates at Marne say at least."

Geist nodded along with the words, taking them in one at a time. There had been no need to know the capabilities of the other teams when she'd had a permanent one of her own. Geist regretted not knowing more about the others, but there was nothing to do about it.

I wish I knew how someone like Vergess got captured, Geist thought as she stole another glance. *But at least I won't have to worry about him pulling his weight.*

Major Reese motioned Geist close and handed her a packet of paperwork. "While Tinker, Trilogy, and Big Wick secure the ground, you four will take to the skies."

Geist simply nodded and took her paperwork to the back of the room. Percival followed, his eyes glued to the envelope. The hazy lighting made for poor reading, but Geist opened up the packet regardless.

Before Geist could read up on their target, Percival positioned himself behind her and stood on his tiptoes to read along. Geist sighed, turned around, and pushed the paperwork into his arms.

"Tell me when you're done," she said.

Percival held the paperwork out. "We can read together."

"I don't like people standing so close."

Percival stepped back and continued to read.

Blick, on his way out the door, turned and gave Geist the once-over. She lifted an eyebrow.

"You better bring my brother back," Blick said. "Albatross might be team leader, but the commander paired Percival with you personally."

Geist nodded. "I'll bring him back."

For a moment, they stared at each other, and Geist couldn't help but feeling that unspoken accusation again. *She hadn't returned with her old team.* Did Blick still doubt that she'd stayed until the end? His gaze betrayed him, and his skepticism stung sharper than barbed wire.

Percival kept his eyes on the paperwork. "I can look after myself."

"There are no certainties in war," Victory stated as he walked over. "Watch yourself. Blick and I look forward to hearing about your first combat, but that won't happen if you're careless."

His demands made, Victory exited the room. Blick, hesitating for a long second, opted not to speak at all. Geist knew the three to be full-blooded brothers, and perhaps they were just concerned, but family politics were never simple. *Especially sorcerer families.* She didn't want to fail House Hamilton and become a target for their ire.

Thinking of families got her thinking of her own. Geist leaned against the far wall and stared at her boots, wondering whether her family had given up looking for her yet.

Of course, she thought. *It's been so long. Why would they continue?* The thought of her mother gave her pause. *I should've left her a note. I shouldn't have put her through that grief, not a second time.*

Vergess stepped into view, ending her parade of black thoughts. She stared up through the haze of smoke, one eyebrow raised.

"I look forward to working with you," he said.

Geist nodded.

After a silent second, Vergess sighed and continued to the door.

Tinker snorted. "What a kook. All that posturing. What's he got to be nervous about?"

"I don't know," Geist muttered.

It occurred to her that most of the Ethereal Squadron in Verdun likely hadn't worked with Vergess before. He had been a POW from another division stationed at Fort Douaumont before it had been captured by the enemy. And all those sorcerers were dead or had been reported missing. Vergess had no one among the soldiers here to call a confidante.

"Hey. No need to brood," Tinker said, grinning. "You're makin' the shadows look bright."

Geist couldn't help but laugh. She shrugged. "Practice makes perfect."

"Don't get funny on me. That's my job."

The talking in the room ceased. On instinct, Geist and the others turned their attention to their commander. Major Reese stroked his peppered beard and took them in as a whole. Fear darkened the lines of his face, but determination shone in his eyes.

"You'll all take transports tomorrow morning to your designated destinations," he said. "Reports are to be written and addressed to me until your objective is met. The rest of you are dismissed."

DEAR MISS ELLEN LUXTON,

I do not know how to start this letter. I write to you, regretfully, to inform you of Douglas Croft's death. We knew him as "Little Wick." I was not his commanding officer, but I was with him in the end. He spoke of you with his final breath, and I am certain he loved you with all his being. In confidence, he told me that, despite his family's wishes, he would return home and marry you—eloping if need be.

I know this letter will likely bring you distress, but I thought you would want to know regardless. Douglas was a close friend. We were together most days of the year. I could trust him with my life and, when the odds were low, he would—

The transport shuddered, and Geist's pencil point snapped. She exhaled, staring down at her incomplete letter. With a huff, she crumpled it and threw it out the back of the truck, watching the horse's hooves crush it into the mud.

How could she write Ellen? How could she tell her anything? Nothing she could say would bring her anything but heartache.

Geist ripped off her cap and ran a hand through her hair. Little Wick's family would never want Geist to send such a letter. Wick, a sorcerer, had been forbidden from marrying Ellen Luxton, a normal human woman, one who didn't even know about his power. Writing to tell her that Little Wick would have eloped with her regardless? It was too cruel.

The world shuddered with each distant bombardment. The horses whinnied in protest, but they were drafted soldiers, like the men around them, unable to shirk their duties. Geist pitied them, for they couldn't even take solace in what few victories they helped win.

The truck jerked to a halt and then lurched forward as the driver wrestled with the reins. Geist gripped the tarp hanging over the truck bed to prevent herself from spilling onto the feet of the other soldiers.

Percival hadn't been as agile. He tumbled about, apologizing to the others each time he collided with them. His gracelessness bordered on slapstick. Vergess grabbed him by the collar and forced him upright.

"Sorry," Percival said.

Vergess snorted but otherwise gave no response.

When the motor transport got close to their destination, the soldiers crowded the back, ready to jump. Geist found herself moving away from the others as they bumped up close, the closeness of their bodies more anxiety than it was worth. To her surprise, Vergess put himself between her and the others, shielding her with his own body. She glanced back at him through her eyelashes, but he kept his gaze locked on the war-torn countryside.

"I never properly thanked you," he said, keeping his voice low. "And after hearing what happened to the rest of your team, I realize the mission must've been difficult."

Geist almost choked, but she managed to nod regardless. It *had* been a trying mission.

"I—" Vergess took a moment, his voice unsteady, "—once knew a spy. Someone like you."

A woman, by the sound of his shaky voice, Geist was sure of it. But had she been a spy for the Germans or someone else?

"What happened to her?" Geist asked.

Vergess exhaled. When he spoke, he did so slowly and with strain in each syllable. "Isidora was a member of the Black Hand, a Serb fighting for her country. She... didn't make it."

The raw emotion in his speech resonated with her. "I'm sorry to hear that," she whispered.

War took everything if you let it. Geist knew this, and Vergess's words only made it ring truer. So many dead. It was her duty, as one of the few left with magic in her blood, to make things right. She wondered if Vergess felt the same way.

"Let me help you maintain your disguise," he said.

Geist rubbed her neck. "No. We should pretend we barely know each other—for both our sakes." She'd seen it before. Getting involved with another soldier, even to keep secrets, could lead to something... distracting. She had a mission to do, and compromising it was out of the question.

Geist jumped out the back of the vehicle the moment they arrived. Albatross and Vergess were close on her heels. With her pack slung over one shoulder, she made her way out of the supply train and into the ranks of soldiers near the frontlines.

The dazzling beauty of France's countryside captivated her as she walked. Thick, golden dust hung on the orange rays of the sunrise. It gave the sky a delicate sparkle the likes of which she had never seen in America. Was it pollen? Dirt from the boots of the soldiers? Geist didn't know. All she knew was the halo it gave the horizon—mesmerizing and utterly glorious.

Stopping under the morning shade of a sessile oak tree, Geist threw down her pack and rubbed her chest. The bindings made it difficult to breathe. *I secured them too tight this time.*

Albatross, Vergess, and Percival walked over to meet her. They, too, threw their packs down and surveyed the area. Albatross's silvering hair hit the gold of the sunrise at the perfect angle, giving a hint of color to his otherwise wan complexion.

"I thought Fort Souville was on the frontlines," Percival commented, his hands on his hips and his eyebrows knit together in confusion.

"It is," Albatross said as he withdrew a pack of cigarettes from his trouser pockets.

"I figured there would be combat. Where are the Germans? Why aren't we fighting?"

"Kid, nine time out of ten, you just have to pass the time. *Hurry up and wait*—that's the military's motto."

"What happens the tenth time?"

"You try not to die."

Percival fell silent.

Albatross clamped his lips on another cigarette and searched his back pockets, his hands patting around his body. Geist pulled a pack of matches from her pouch and tossed them over. Albatross offered a one-sided smile in thanks.

"So," he said, striking a match against his teeth. "We have to evaluate your sorcery, kid. What school do you practice?"

"Potentia," Percival replied, obvious pride in his voice.

Geist and Albatross exchanged questioning glances. *Potentia?* Geist thought. *What the fuck is that?* She knew, at one point in history, there had been hundreds of schools of sorcery, each guarded by a family hellbent on keeping their magic a secret from all others. Over time, families had combined and married while others had died off —or they had simply bred amongst themselves, keeping the secret intact no matter the terrible price.

Geist couldn't be expected to know them all.

"I should've known you would have something bizarre," Albatross said, exhaling a line of smoke. "You Hamiltons collect all sorts of weird magics into your bloodline."

"*Useful* magics," Percival corrected.

"All right. Impress me. What's so useful about this potentia?"

"I heighten the magics of other sorcerers."

Percival made his statement with his head high and his thumbs hooked in his belt loops—the dictionary picture of smug. Again, Geist and Albatross exchanged dubious glances.

"So," Percival continued, "I was thinking… my codename could be 'Enhance,' or 'Surge,' or—"

"That's not how it works," Albatross interjected. He took a long drag on his cigarette. "You *earn* your codename through combat. It's a rite of passage."

Geist crossed her arms over her chest and examined the tiny man in front of her. "You said you heighten the magic of others, but what can *you* do?"

"So…" Percival stopped himself short and took a quick breath. "Not much. Potentia is a difficult magic to learn. It's the only sorcery I know, but it's very useful."

"You always need another sorcerer to use your magic? There's nothing you can use on your own?"

"I—well, er… No."

Albatross laughed. "I hope you like *Deadweight* as a codename."

Geist and Vergess chortled.

"Don't laugh," Percival said in a heated tone. "We can't *all* be Victory. Some of us have to develop other kinds of magic. I'm still a valuable asset to the Ethereal Squadron."

"Keep your britches on, kid. If your magic is useful, we'll see it when the fighting starts."

"You already think I'm worthless."

"Geist, Vergess, and I can handle this mission with our magic *as is*. Whatever you bring to the table is extra. No need to get worked up about it right now. This is the time for breathin' easy."

Major Reese always gave the men one battle to get comfortable with their abilities. Geist knew it was why Percival had been assigned to her: This was his first time seeing actual combat. She needed to keep him safe so they could assess his abilities for use in later missions.

Their intimate and quiet setting was assaulted by the exuberant energy of Tinker's arrival. The taller sorcerer jumped into the group, a bandolier of ten grenades hanging loosely from his gaunt shoulders. With a wicked grin, he pulled a fatter grenade from his trouser pocket and tossed it end-over-end in the air.

"If it isn't Team Teensy-Weensy, led by Captain Old Man," Tinker said. "Who here wants to see a Mills bomb go off?" And he tossed the grenade straight into the hands of Percival.

FIVE

Fort Souville

Flailing, Percival threw the bomb onto the road. He dove for cover behind the oak tree, hitting the dirt on his knees and covering his ears. Geist, Vergess, and Albatross remained standing, the two men watching Percival roll in the dust with obvious amusement.

When no explosion came, Percival stood and glanced around the trunk of the tree. Tinker roared with laughter. Geist sighed. The stunt had been fun the first time, but Tinker's antics grew stale after the fifth go-around.

"You can get up," Geist said at last. "It won't explode."

Slowly, Percival stood, recognition, then anger rising on his face. "You… you…" he spluttered. Tinker only laughed harder.

Vergess, unamused, walked over and snatched up the fat grenade from the ground. In the next second, the device rotted away in his hand, disintegrating into fine dust. Geist stared. Her briefing notes told her he had destructive powers, hence his code-name, but she had never seen sorcery do that before.

"Okay, okay," Geist said, noting Percival's growing resentment. "Tinker, why aren't you with Trilogy and Big Wick?"

Tinker wiped tears from his eyes as he walked over to Geist and pulled a heavy satchel off his shoulder. "The commander ordered me to make these special for you."

He handed the satchel over and Geist threw back the flap to inspect the contents, half-expecting to see another gag. To her surprise, the satchel contained two thermite charge incendiary grenades. They were dangerous devices all their own, but if Tinker had meddled with them, they weren't to be trifled with.

"You read your packet?" Tinker asked. "You gotta get these suckers up near the hydrogen in the zeppelin. Pull the pin and they'll bake for two whole minutes before they're ready. Pretty good, right? Longer than any other. You don't want to be on the ship when it goes down. You should have plenty of time."

Geist ran her fingers over one of the incendiary grenades. The device had no magic, but she couldn't help but wonder, *What if?* The Germans had somehow constructed a device that had married sorcery and technology—why couldn't Tinker?

What did the Germans have that they didn't?

"You like them?" Tinker asked.

"Yeah."

"Good, because I named them *Cross and Geist's Little Babies.* Look there, I even gave them faces."

Geist turned one over and rolled her eyes. The device had a crudely drawn happy face on the side of the metal casing. Drool dribbled from one corner of the lip and a pacifier hung from the other. *Where does he get the time to do all this? I swear he never sleeps.*

Tinker fell into another fit of laughter.

"I even made this one stumpy," he said in between chuckles. "So there's a family resemblance!"

Sure enough, when Geist examined the grenades, one *was* shorter than the other. She smiled in spite of herself. How long had it taken him to craft one grenade smaller? Had he been giggling the entire time? Geist didn't doubt it.

Albatross finished his cigarette and tossed it to the ground. "You and Cross, huh? I thought that was a rumor. Did you speak to her family already? Do they know you practice specter magic?"

Geist tied the satchel to her belt and held back an exaggerated sigh. *Goddammit, Tinker.* There were no secrets in the Ethereal Squadron. If one person on the team knew something, it was a mystery. If two people knew, it might still stay secret. But if *three* knew, *everyone* knew.

"Back in my day, they didn't let young sorcerers mingle until it was time to seal the deal," Albatross said. "You were lucky if they let you see the girl once or twice at fancy family functions. There wasn't much romance to it, ya see. Marriages were bargaining chips—for alliances and such."

Vergess gave Geist a quick glance before crossing his arms.

Tinker's continued laughter turned into a coughing fit. Once he straightened himself, Geist asked, "Is there anything else?"

"No," he replied, one last chuckle escaping him. "That's it."

"Then we'll see you once our missions are complete."

"Yeah. See you on the other side."

He slapped Geist on the shoulder and took off toward the fort. The fortification, though intact, had shattered trees and roads riddled with craters all around it. Bombs left scars on the land, but the squadron's engineers kept the fort alive.

Percival watched Tinker until he disappeared out of sight. He turned to Geist with a frown. "Is that really how sorcerers treat each other in the Ethereal Squadron?"

"Yeah," Geist said. "What of it?"

"It doesn't bother you? I don't know if I can handle being around someone like him for very long."

"If that's how you feel, you should resign now."

Percival snapped his gaze up. "How could you say that?"

"If you can't handle that, you're not suited for war. It gets a lot worse out there."

The look he gave in response took Geist by surprise. Indignation? Worry? Shame? Percival turned away before Geist could identify his expression. She wanted to say something more, something poignant like Cross would say, but the words never came. Instead, they stood in silence. Albatross, a few yards away, kept to himself, and Vergess seemed lost in deep thought.

Nothing like my old team.

Morning turned to day, day to late afternoon, and soon dusk settled onto the horizon. Geist would have been content to have a day free of worry, but no one rested well during wartime.

THE TREMBLE in the earth heralded the attack. Warning bells followed soon after.

Geist, Albatross, Vergess, and Percival got to their feet and scanned the skies. Pillars of fire from aerial bombardments lit the battlefield at sporadic intervals. Enemy biplanes roared overhead, their wings marked with Germany's black cross. The pulse of warfare thundered on, spurring each member of the Squadron to hoist their weapons. It was time to fight for their country.

Bullets whistled through the air by the hundreds, and the sound flipped a switch in Geist. Moments before, she had been lost in her own musings, but now she reverted fully to a soldier: emotions deadened, her training and instincts driving her forward.

Fort Souville's strength rested in its single armored turret. The path up to the fort, stationed on the stump of a hill, offered but one narrow avenue of attack. Enemies caught in the strait of fire could not hope to survive long, but the Germans were no fools. A second attack came from the left wing—three army corps hoping to circle around and overwhelm them.

Albatross pulled Geist and Percival to the second line of trenches, far from the front. Vergess followed with ease, the only one who didn't seem on edge in the midst of gunfire. They took up positions near the sharpshooter posts, their backs against the wood beams.

German, British, and French soldiers alike shot back and forth across the barren lands of war, attempting to snipe the opposing commander. The German officers, wise by now to the tactic, wore ordinary uniforms while the English officers still gave themselves away with their high leather boots and sword belts. Geist saw the cap of one Englishman fly off the head of its owner—a hole the size of a quarter torn through the front and back.

I guess that's the price of etiquette.

Percival huddled close and squinted through the debris caught on the wind. "Why aren't we fighting? Shouldn't we run to the front?"

"Remember the mission," Geist replied. "We're here for the zeppelin, nothing else."

And then, as if summoned by her voice, the infernal airships came into view. They were behemoths in the sky, black and ominous, each stretching over five hundred feet in length. Soldiers would whisper superstitions—getting caught in the long shadow of a zeppelin meant you were sure to die. And many of them weren't wrong.

Albatross grabbed Vergess's arm and gave him a nod. The two men left the safety of the post and charged toward an outcropping of trees and bushes—a straight line toward the zeppelin they had been ordered to bring down. German soldiers hid among the trees, but they kept their route.

Geist held her satchel of explosives close. One wrong move could get her killed. If the grenades were shot, she wouldn't get a second chance. She grabbed Percival by the collar of his khaki uniform. "Keep this safe." She ripped the satchel off her belt and shoved it into his hands.

"What're you doing?" he asked.

"Clearing a path."

"Wait, let me help you!"

Geist hefted her Springfield rifle. "Just protect the explosives until I get back." She stepped around the sharpshooter post, but Percival jogged after, tying the satchel to his own belt in the process.

"I meant with my magic," he said. "I can—"

"I don't need any of your magic right now. Wait here. That's an order."

"But—"

A bombshell cut Percival off with a deafening explosion and ear-shattering after-burst. Her ears ringing, Geist took off to join Albatross and Vergess. Germans hiding behind trees didn't frighten her, but the possibility of Abomination Soldiers was a real threat.

Percival hung back as instructed. Geist appreciated his eagerness, but she didn't want his help—not yet at least. Grenades went flying into the tree line from nearby French soldiers. Albatross hung back until the branches stopped raining down around him, but Vergess continued regardless, heedless to the dangers, as though they couldn't affect him. When he got near enemy soldiers, he fired with incredible precision. When a tree collapsed in his path, he grabbed the branches and the vegetation rotted in mere seconds, crumbling into a pile of withered ashen flakes.

Albatross charged ahead the moment he could, moving with all the speed and agility of a much younger man. Geist took his flank as they made their way through the decimated grove. When a German rounded a trunk, Geist fired. A second enemy soldier caught her by surprise, but his first three bullets whizzed through her sleeve and arm without making contact.

Geist cried out as the fourth bullet grazed her left wrist. She ducked back behind a tree, shock blanking her mind and thoughts.

How is that possible?

She stared at the injury—a cut above the waxy sheen of her misshapen wrist—but the implications staggered her. *I was ghosting,* she thought, trying to reason with herself. *That bullet never should have touched me. Never.*

But the GH Gas had changed her. Even thinking about it left Geist gritting her teeth.

The crunch of boots on disheveled earth brought Geist back to the battlefield. She jumped back as the German soldier rounded the tree with his bayonet raised. Her back struck the tree trunk as the enemy screamed with bloodlust and plunged the blade through her left upper arm.

Geist couldn't remain intangible forever.

Her incorporeal state lasted for fractions of a second—her clothes stayed on her body, after all—her magic maintained long enough for bullets and weapons to pass harmlessly through her, but then she became solid once again.

The bayonet, still in her body when her sorcery had failed, was pinned in the tree behind her, spearing through the flesh of her bicep. Geist reared back and kicked the German, sending him stumbling away.

Before he could pull his pistol, Geist shot him in the chest and sent him flying to the ground, one last groan escaping his lips before he died. She grunted and removed the bayonet from her arm. Holding back frustrated tears, Geist administered the bare minimum field medicine necessary to prevent blood loss—slapping cellucotton over the injury and holding it in place with rough linen gauze.

Bullets pelted the trunk of the tree. She didn't have time to mend her wounds further, not here. Geist gritted her teeth and pulled her rifle close to her chest. Her left arm worked. Hurt like a bastard, but it could move. That was all she could ask of it.

Running out from her safe position, Geist shielded her wounded wrist with the butt of her weapon. The Germans who had fired upon her stepped back in surprise as she ran forward, brazen and heedless to the danger. Vergess had taken down the main group and those who remained were torn between two targets. Their indecision cost them their lives.

Geist fired with her rifle and, rather than reloading, she pulled out her handgun from her side holster and continued firing. She focused on maintaining her magic, but the pain of her injuries intensified the longer she fought.

"Get the kid," Albatross called out once the trees were clear of hostiles. "The zeppelins are starting their run!"

Sure enough, the black behemoths had formed a line in the sky, their bay doors open and their payloads ready to be dropped onto the ground below. The zeppelins could kill all the French soldiers in one go if left to float through the sky unopposed. They didn't drop bombs one at a time, but by the hundreds, blanketing the landscape with destruction.

French anti-air guns chattered, attempting to knock the monsters from the sky, but their shots were weak at best and embarrassingly off-target at worst. The head zeppelin, Geist's target, actually seemed to deflect incoming fire. She saw bullets and bombs alike blown away from the engines by powerful winds.

Magic! A sorcerer is protecting that zeppelin.

Before the ships could begin their pass, Geist pushed off the shattered trunk of a tree and ran for the sharpshooter posts. Panicked looks were all around her. The men, their faces caked in mud, cowered like prey animals. Those in the backlines shivered in clumps. Those on the front fought through disorientating explosions to fire at the enemy, most barely bothering to aim.

War took its toll on everyone. Even Geist felt her focus divided.

She rounded the sharpshooter post and grabbed Percival by the shoulder. He took one look at her and paled. "Geist," he said. "What's going on?"

"We're heading up," she replied.

"Now? In the middle of the fighting?"

"Before they pass. On your feet. Let's go."

He pushed away from the post and followed her toward the trees, his attention on everything other than the path in front of him. Geist made it to the broken forest and spotted German soldiers moving into the area she had cleared. They would fill the gap in their lines and Geist cursed under her breath. There was nowhere to go but forward, which meant the Germans would cut off her escape route to the French.

Could she keep fighting if her magic failed her?

Geist made it to the other side of the grove and stopped. A wide dirt road separated her from Albatross and Vergess. They stood in the shadow of a half-shattered building, motioning for her to cross and join them. The corpse of a dead horse and a splintered cart stood in her way. Geist took a moment to lean against a still-whole tree and catch her breath. Dust caught in her lungs and she coughed.

Percival kept his hip to hers as he glanced around. The roar of the zeppelins' engines rolled in like a bank of fog.

"Are you okay?" Percival asked, motioning to her arm. "I thought you never got hurt."

"I'll live."

"I can help."

I don't need it, was what Geist wanted to say, but she held back her words. She needed to assess his sorcery at some point. And would she have denied Cutter, Buttons, or Little Wick? No. She would have taken their aid without hesitation. She held out her right hand, palm up.

"Let's see what you've got," she said.

Percival gingerly placed his hand onto hers. The feeling—it was like Cross's healing—was intense and comforting all at the same time. Geist closed her eyes. She had been close to exhausted before Percival had touched her, but afterward she felt as if a whole new pool of energy had been dumped into her.

Standing straight, Geist took a deep breath and relished the new strength. Percival pulled his hand away. The vast well of energy disappeared, but the added power lingered. She wanted to place her hand on his again, to feel the full potent force that he could add to her magic, but she restrained herself.

"I can only maintain this for so long," he said, almost apologetically.

Geist nodded. With his extra energy, like coffee fresh in the morning, she shook off her fatigue. She sprinted across the road and dove into the shadow of the broken building. Percival chased after and slammed his back against the wall as the zeppelins drifted overhead, their engines a constant hammering of sound.

Vergess glanced down at her bloodied arm. "What happened?" he shouted.

Geist shook her head. "I'll be fine."

"Stick close to me."

"I can handle myself."

"I owe you a few hits."

Vergess motioned to his side and Geist smirked. He must've seen when she had taken the bullet for him. *I guess he does owe me,* she thought, her smile widening.

"This is how we're gettin' up," Albatross yelled.

He pointed to the half of the roof still intact. Geist eyed the distance and frowned. Even with her newfound strength and energy, she wouldn't be able to scale the wall in time to board the zeppelin. Hell—the longer she stared, the more she realized the roof wasn't high enough to reach their target, not by a long shot. She knew Albatross would need to get them there, but she had never personally witnessed his tempest magic in action.

Albatross kept his eyes up on the black blimps. The shadow of the beasts swept over them as all four zeppelins flew overhead. They were colossal—the largest Geist had ever seen, each over a hundred feet across, longwise.

Geist gritted her teeth and placed her hand on her weapon. What could her rifle do against the giant machines above her? She had to get up and kill the crew if she was to have a chance at defeating such a monstrosity.

"Get ready," Albatross said.

Percival glanced around. "Get ready for what?"

"Kid, listen up. I'm gonna get us up there. Stick close to me, and you'll make it back in one piece. If we get separated, well… things aren't gonna go well for you."

"Oh, I get it," Percival said with a forced laugh. "Like an albatross. But how, exactly, are we…"

Albatross chuckled, Percival frowned, but before further words could be exchanged, Albatross threw his hand up into the air. Dirt swirled around his feet. Then…

Geist lost her breath as gusts of wind dragged her into the air, lifting her far from the ground in a swift ascent. Albatross, Vergess, and Percival followed soon after, the wind tunnel sending them straight for the zeppelin above. Albatross kicked off the dilapidated roof on his way up, increasing the strength of the wind so quickly, it took Geist's breath away.

"You're gonna have to grab on," Albatross shouted. "I'm not so good at landings!"

SIX

Zeppelin

G eist didn't breathe the whole time it took to clear the distance between the ground and the zeppelin. Her cap flew off as she drew near, spinning down toward the ever-shrinking scenery below her.

Geist attempted to grab the duralumin girder of the rigid airship, but with only one arm, she flailed and missed her chance. Vergess latched on to the zeppelin and caught her by the collar of her uniform. He pulled her down onto the underside platform with little effort, then wrapped his arm around her while the wind continued to whip by, her eyes thick with water.

Percival's magic maintained throughout the flight, and she vowed to compliment him on his concentration once the mission ended. Focusing to maintain sorcery was sometimes a lifelong journey. Most sorcerers had to train their entire lives to maintain that kind of concentration, and she knew the youth had to be scared.

Albatross slid onto the platform, his gray hair disheveled but a wide smile across his face. "I don't get to fly often," he said through strained breaths, his voice barely audible over the engines. "Too flashy. It's a kick, though. When we get back, I'm gonna ask the commander to put me in charge of an aircraft of my own."

Percival steadied himself against the metal railing, landing hard on his shins but otherwise managing to stay upright. Albatross allowed his magic to fade, but steady winds washed over them regardless.

Vergess kept his protective hold, but Geist jerked away and took a few ragged breaths. "I'm fine."

He said nothing.

The underside platform, a mere five feet wide, no more than a loading area when the airship was on the ground, sat between two gondolas filled with German soldiers. The blimp above contained eighteen gas ballonets carrying over nine hundred and fifty thousand cubic feet of hydrogen—Geist's target. She motioned for Percival to pass her the satchel of incendiary bombs. He handed the satchel over as fast as he could untie it from his belt.

The rumble of bombs and the chattering of machine guns filled Geist's ears. She winced at the cacophony and pointed to the ladder and catwalks between the gondolas.

Albatross gestured to the bow. "Vergess and I will head for the pilots and the captain." He pointed to the rear gondola. "You two clear the back. We meet in the middle." With a jerk of his head, he motioned to the blimp above.

Geist nodded.

Ernest Meier captained the ship, an Abomination Soldier who had studied the same school of sorcery as Albatross: The school of tempest magic, the ability to control winds, lightning, and the occasional blast of hoarfrost. Albatross had made it clear that he and he alone would be the one to confront Captain Meier.

But Geist worried. Yes, Albatross had been practicing his magic for decades. He could keep up with the best sorcerers in combat, but Geist wondered if it would be enough.

Before Vergess turned to follow, he gave Percival a stern glower. "Don't get in Geist's way, Deadweight."

"That's…" Percival clung to the railing, his breath short. "That's *not* going to be my codename!"

Vergess snorted and headed for the front gondola. His confidence was infectious, and Geist admired it from afar. *We can handle this. We can.*

The wind rushed past and Geist gripped the railings to stay aboard. She realized then that the bullets and bombs must have been missing the engines of the zeppelin because of Captain Meier's magic. The wind acted as a shield—perhaps it knew she had come to harm the ship, as with each powerful gust, she felt her grip slip a little farther toward oblivion. *We need to get inside.*

Geist steadied herself and traversed the narrow catwalk toward the rear gondola. The farther she went, the harder the gale attempted to wrench her from the underside of the airship. The short path between gondolas became a deadfall unlike any Geist had ever experienced.

Once at the end, she grabbed the handle of the gondola door and yanked hard. The door didn't budge. Locked. The wind intensified. Percival strangled the railings, half-doubled over one, but still, his focus and magic held strong.

What am I going to do? Geist thought, her eyes scanning the ground. Trees exploded into deadly splinters with each bomb that fell. Giant fireballs lit the sunset battlefield—no doubt Big Wick's contribution—and German soldiers stormed toward the fort with gusto.

And below her, the drop…

Thoughts of falling the three thousand feet to her death nearly overwhelmed her as Geist yanked on the stubborn door handle a second time. She hefted her rifle, intent to shoot her way through, but she stopped the moment Percival placed a hand on her shoulder. He motioned to the door with a grunt, unable to hold on to her long before returning his hand to the railing.

Does he want me to use my magic? It'll never work. I can't pass through a solid metal door. She couldn't fade longer than a flicker, which meant she would get caught in the metal of the door once her magic failed to maintain. *Or is Percival saying I should try it now with his help?* she thought. *Will I be able to maintain my intangibility longer?*

Geist held her breath and focused on using her newfound strength. She suppressed a gasp when the magic came effortlessly.

Within an instant, she shifted and shimmered, her whole body becoming incorporeal—even her clothes were caught up in this new power.

Fearing the wind might succeed in throwing her off the zeppelin, Geist plunged her right arm through the metal of the door. It went straight through and continued to remain intangible. By sheer instinct, she reached around to unlatch the lock.

Then she had a second revelation.

I'm invisible. Geist stared down at where her body should have been. *Fully invisible. I've never managed this before.*

The feeling of the door passing through her arm sent a shiver through her body.

Unbelievable. God, I feel invincible.

Geist threw open the unlocked door and charged forward, her rifle at the ready. She was a true specter in her new state—incorporeal and unseen by naked human eyes. Percival's magic had pushed her to heights she hadn't imagined possible.

Per the mission packet, the zeppelin crew was twenty-eight men strong, and more than a third of its fighting force stood before her. One by one, she shot at the soldiers manning the machine guns and ammo lines, her bolt-action rifle gunning down man after man. Their eyes were wide, but there was nothing for them to see. Only the cracks of gunfire gave away her location.

The gondola erupted into a firefight. The Germans swiveled their machine guns around and fired wildly in her direction. Bullets passed through her body and clothing, burying themselves in the duralumin shell of the airship. Geist's bullets left her sphere of magical influence and became visible only just before they pierced the bodies of the lightly armored German soldiers. Their caps and windbreakers, suited for the blustery cockpit of an airship gondola, provided little protection against a pointblank rifle shot.

It didn't take long for the narrow space to fill with corpses. Ten of the twenty-eight crew members would never man the machine guns of a zeppelin again.

Percival clawed his way inside once the last shot was fired. The wind slammed the door shut behind him, but he didn't flinch. Geist exhaled and allowed her magic to drop, rendering her visible once more.

Such power, she thought, nearly overwhelmed by adrenaline.

She glanced back at the panting and bedraggled Percival. Maybe she had underestimated him.

"We're going up," Geist shouted, motioning to the hatch above them.

Percival nodded as he shambled forward, the slick mess of blood on the steel floor making his boots slip and slide. Before he made it to the hatch, he grabbed the body of a downed German and ripped off the parachute, but bullet holes from the firefight had rendered the chute useless. Percival manhandled a second corpse as he searched for a parachute that wasn't ripped to shreds.

Geist pushed open the hatch to the inside of the blimp. "We don't have time for that! Albatross will get us to safety! Get up here!"

With a furrowed brow, Percival ignored her. He scrambled through the carnage until he found what he had been looking for—a parachute in working condition. Percival threw it over his back as he jogged to the ladder. Geist shook her head. If things went south, falling would be far from their biggest problem.

The inside of the blimp was massive. The metal ribcage of a frame held the blimp canvas taut, keeping the wind and noise at bay. Separate steamer-sized gasbags, eighteen in total, were held in place with nets. A central walkway, stretching the full five hundred feet of the blimp, connected all gondolas through hatches and ladders. Despite the dim lighting, Geist rushed forward, her gaze up and locked on the white ballonets of hydrogen gas.

I've only got two grenades. I've got to make them count.

"Wait," Percival called out. "Geist, you can't get too far."

Sure enough, as Geist made it halfway down the walkway, Percival's magic waned, as if there were an invisible tether between them. She stopped and allowed him to catch up. *I need to keep in mind he's my battery.*

"Look out!" he gasped, pulling up his rifle.

Percival fired the half-second after. Geist whipped around and spotted a German soldier diving onto the floor of the metal walkway. The bullet ricocheted off the blimp frame and through the black outer canvas, tearing a tiny hole.

"Careful," Geist said, glancing up to the bundles of gas. She had no idea what would happen if they were shot, and she didn't want to find out.

Percival fired again, hitting his target, who went flying to the floor. He ran up to Geist, but an unexpected jolt of the zeppelin sent him tumbling to his knees. Geist grabbed hold of the railing and steadied herself as a far hatch blew off its hinges from a powerful gust of wind.

Albatross and Captain Meier exploded into the blimp compartment, both men locked in combat and barely turning their attention to their surroundings. Captain Meier, twenty years Albatross's junior, moved with the grace of a summer breeze. The gale force surrounding him prevented Albatross's bullets from finding their mark and allowed Meier to fly into the open areas of the blimp, unhindered by gravity.

Despite the sheer spectacle of the fight, Geist forced herself to return to her task. She pulled out the incendiary grenades and ran to the gasbags. Shock overcame her when she glanced up to the metal beams between the giant white ballonets. There was magic embedded in the very steel around her. She could sense it—a cold pulse of power no metal should have had.

Geist lifted an unsteady head and grazed her fingers over the blimp's foundation. *How is this possible? Is this Captain Meier's work? Or is it like the GH Gas—magic fused into technology?*

Albatross and Captain Meier landed hard on the walkway. Percival ducked back behind the first ballonet, staggering into a defensive position. Geist, shimmering into her invisible state, tied her grenades to the metal support beams between gasbags.

Wind kicked up throughout the blimp.

Albatross attempted to calm the squall, but his magic couldn't overpower Meier's. Instead, Albatross held out his hand. Blue-white electricity arched from his palm with a powerful crack that popped Geist's ears. The jagged strike of raw lightning flew past Meier and struck the canvas on the far side of the blimp, ripping yet another hole. Meier, his face set in a stony neutral expression, swept his hand out in front of him.

The wind spiraled at deafening speeds, ripping the breath from Geist's lungs and shattering her focus. Her magic dropped.

Sorcerers were all different, even if they studied the same school of magic. While Albatross let loose lightning strike after lightning strike, his ability to control the wind paled in comparison to Captain Meier's. Likewise, Meier didn't seem to have the ability to control lightning like Albatross could. He stood back, biding his time, using defensive maneuvers and guile while he waited for the best opportunity to strike. Nothing Albatross threw at him seemed to hit, and soon the ferocity of the wind would leave everyone unable to breathe.

The ballonets shuddered and quaked thanks to the sheer intensity of the magical hurricane. The strain on the zeppelin sent the groans of creaking metal echoing throughout the blimp. Geist waited to pull the pin of her grenades until after the confrontation —they would only have two minutes afterward to make their escape.

Struggling for air, Albatross turned around and shot a bolt of lightning directly at the ballonets.

"What are you doing?!" Captain Meier yelled, his German one angry unpunctuated shout.

The white-blue bolt *had* been aimed for a gasbag, but the strike of energy curved around and instead hit the metal between the hydrogen containers. The support beams glowed with the intake and, like lightning rods, diverted the energy and absorbed it all, leaving the ballonets unharmed.

Captain Meier let out a heavy breath, his body relaxing as he watched the magic disperse harmlessly. Albatross craned his neck back to stare in disbelief.

Oh, God, Geist thought as she stepped away from the super-charged metal. *This isn't powered by Captain Meier's magic at all. It's just like the GH Gas… some sort of magic-technology hybrid.*

Albatross lifted his rifle and fired upward. The wind ripped his bullet from its path, protecting the shaking ballonet. He pulled a knife and Captain Meier did the same. Albatross charged, but all Captain Meier did was release the hold on his weapon.

In one sick instant, the fight ended. Meier's trench knife, propelled forwards by the wind, sliced through Albatross's throat in one precise plunge. Albatross flew backward, head first, and hit the walkway limp. Without his magic fighting against Meier's, the storm intensified, throwing Albatross's twitching body into the ribcage of metal at the back of the airship.

Geist couldn't breathe. She gritted her teeth and blinked her watery eyes.

Percival stepped back and fell from the force of the wind. He tumbled off the walkway and landed on the taut black canvas of the underside blimp, half-bouncing as if hitting a trampoline. Captain Meier snapped his attention over to the younger man, and Geist took the opportunity to shift back into her invisible state.

But with each passing second, it became harder to concentrate. The roar of the deafening wind, the thinning air, the unsteady feeling when caught in the current… Geist squinted. Captain Meier strode straight toward Percival, and Percival didn't have the magic to fight back. He flailed about the canvas with a frantic energy— even his empowering magic felt as though it could slip from Geist's grasp at any moment.

Pull it together, Geist! He needs you.

Through sheer willpower, she ghosted more and more of her body—allowing the wind to pass through her without resistance— while simultaneously staying aboard the aircraft. The possibility of slipping straight through the floor and falling to her death kept her focus sharp.

Percival pulled a Lancaster pistol from his belt and fired four rounds at the captain as the man drew near. They never made contact, but Geist understood what he was doing. While Meier focused on diverting the bullets, Geist lunged forward. Without the storm holding her back, she unsheathed her Bowie knife and stabbed, fueling the strike with all the rage and anguish brought on by Albatross's death. To her surprise and momentary disbelief, her incorporeal state allowed her hand and knife to slip through Captain Meier's torso without harm.

He gasped upon "impact" and turned on his heel, his eyes frantically searching the chaos of the wind spiraling all around him.

Geist slashed again, this time allowing her magic to drop midswing. The blade, along with a portion of her hand, became solid inside the body of the captain, just beneath his ribs. When she pulled out, her knife and knuckles took a satisfying chunk of raw flesh with them.

Captain Meier screamed, the fillings in his back molars gleaming. The hurricane petered out, and Geist took in a deep breath of much-needed air. She kicked Captain Meier and sent him stumbling back.

While the captain cradled his mangled torso, Geist took the moment to lean over the railing and outstretched her hand. Percival clambered to her and managed to pull himself back onto the walkway with her assistance. His shaky hands betrayed lingering terror.

"I won't let you have the ship," Captain Meier said in haggard German as he bled out over the walkway. "I won't."

"I don't *want* your damn ship," she growled.

Geist turned to run back to the grenades but slowed herself halfway to her destination. *Did* she want the ship? *The commander needs to see this,* Geist thought, her gaze trailing up to the magically enforced steel framework rising all around her. *This ship would prove my theories. He would have to listen then.*

The entire zeppelin jerked to the side. Geist flew off her feet and slammed onto the unforgiving walkway floor. Percival followed suit, but upon impact, his magic finally failed. Geist felt his strength dissipate, leaving her weaker than she had ever felt before.

Metal creaked and groaned. The ballonets jostled in their nets. Geist heard the sound of canvas ripping. She looked up—Captain Meier had managed to stand, and his magic had returned in full force. He wasn't using the wind inside the blimp, however. He was controlling the plummet of the zeppelin, ensuring the airship would crash to the ground below.

Geist fired her last two handgun rounds, but the German officer deflected them with ease. Before Geist could formulate a new plan, Vergess opened the cockpit door, his uniform stained crimson with the blood of the pilots.

Captain Meier turned to face him, but it was too late. Vergess sprinted forward, his celerity in a league of its own, and grabbed the man by the neck before the wind could push him away. The moment Vergess's skin made contact, a blackness spread across the captain's skin, rotting away the man's throat and spreading to his clothes. He choked and spasmed as Vergess lifted and tossed him aside.

Captain Meier crumpled into a pool of rotted flesh and blood.

But that didn't stop the zeppelin's fall.

Barely able to get to her feet, Geist hobbled for the far exit hatch. "Vergess! The cockpit!"

Percival jumped to his feet and ran over. "We have to get off this thing! It's going to crash!"

"It's heading for the fort," she said between the crushing groans of metal that echoed all around them. "Someone has to turn it."

Vergess nodded and headed back inside, stepping over the pile of bodies.

While he adjusted the course, Percival slid off his parachute and handed it over. "You put this on. I'm going to search for another one."

Geist took it with a grimace. She glanced up at him, frowning.

"I'm sure there are more," Percival said over the sounds of the airship ripping apart. "Go! I'll meet you on the ground!"

Before she could comment further, Percival turned toward the stern of the airship and ran off down the narrow walkway. Geist slung the parachute over her shoulders and fastened the straps as tight as they would go.

She had never used a parachute before.

Geist hobbled for the nearest hatch as the zeppelin tilted downward. Walking on a slanted surface didn't help her speed. She half-slid to her destination and threw open the hatch as fast as her hands would allow.

Breathe, she told herself. *You're almost out. Just stay calm.*

Glancing over her shoulder, Geist kept her eyes fixated on the cockpit hatch. Seconds passed as hours, every breath a lifetime. She didn't want to leave without knowing Vergess would escape, but staying much longer could prove fatal.

Slowly, but obviously, the zeppelin changed course. Vergess had succeeded. She forced herself to take even inhales and exhales. *Did he find his own parachute? Has he already jumped?*

As if to answer her unspoken questions, Vergess reemerged inside the blimp, a parachute on his back. He ran over and examined the exit hatch.

"Jump!" Geist commanded.

He regarded her with a hard look, his eyes narrowed. "What about you?"

"I'll be fine. I need to watch over Percival."

Vergess nodded and leapt out of the zeppelin. Not a trace of hesitation.

Hurry, Percival.

Geist knew she couldn't go without him. She wouldn't lose another teammate.

Then she saw him. Percival climbed up from the gondola and into the blimp. Then he jogged to her side. His pale expression was clear as day—nerves slowing his movements. He relaxed the moment he reached Geist.

"You waited?" he shouted, his voice taken with the rush of the wind.

"Hurry!" she yelled. Percival stumbled as the metal ribcage frame tore asunder. "Did you find a parachute?"

"There were none."

Fuck.

"Go," he said, his voice weak. "I'll try to find another."

"There's no time! Tie yourself to me."

His face drained of color. "Will it hold?"

Geist removed her belt and slipped it through the parachute straps. She secured it around Percival, creating a makeshift tandem attachment and securing them close. *We're Team Teensy-*

Weensy, for fuck's sake, she thought with a dark smile. *If anyone can do it, we can.*

The zeppelin turned, slowly spiraling, and Geist pulled Percival to the open hatch. They jumped together, sailing straight out of the vehicle and entering a freefall. The weightless sensation and vertigo caused Geist's muscles to seize up.

The few seconds it took to hit terminal velocity were among the worst in her life.

The black of night surrounded them. She couldn't tell how close to the ground they were, or how fast they were falling. The lights that dotted the landscape whizzed by in a blur as Geist tumbled through the air.

After a terrifying moment of fumbling, her fingers found the string of the parachute and pulled. The sudden painful jerk of the chute catching left her winded. Percival hit the end of his makeshift attachment, and the belt and straps held strong. He threw his arms around Geist's body and dug his nails into her skin through her uniform. She didn't protest—she *couldn't* protest, couldn't *breathe*— and instead tightened her grip as well.

The evening wind caught in the chute and dragged it away from the falling zeppelin, throwing it back away from Fort Souville and straight beyond enemy lines. Geist didn't know where it would take her. She didn't even know if she could control her descent. Twisting and turning, the parachute bobbed through the air, dragging her with it. They only thing she could feel beside the cold sting of the wind on her face was the mad beating of Percival's heart.

A horrifying crunch preceded the massive explosion. The zeppelin hit the ground, only to rupture moments after. The incendiary grenades, still mounted to the inside frame, went off at the impact point, causing a chain reaction that turned the whole airship into a gargantuan ball of flame. The fire that ensued lit up the surrounding area like an erupting volcano. Geist could only make out part of it as she sailed away, farther and farther from the sounds of battle.

An updraft rocked the chute and spun Geist around. Percival's panicked breaths were stifled by her uniform collar.

Geist had no sense of time. Everything had happened so quickly that even gliding on the wind felt rushed and frenzied. She wondered when the ground would meet them. Despite having a parachute, they fell so fast, she was sure they would suffer severe injury—assuming they didn't die on impact.

The trees were upon them before Geist could draw a breath. Branch after branch snapped as they hurtled through the canopy, shredding the chute above them. Percival grunted but otherwise kept silent. His grip grew weak. The chute caught on the trees and ripped, swinging them in frenzied circles.

The straps tore. Percival fell.

"No!" Geist shouted, her voice hoarse. The parachute ripped again and Geist plummeted after him.

She hit the ground sooner than she had expected, leaving her dazed. Geist couldn't move. All she could do was stare up at the canopy of leaves above her. Everything hurt, but every agonizing breath told her she was still alive. The shredded cloth of the parachute hung from the branches above and swayed with the breeze.

Her father's voice echoed in her ears. *The worthless stay down.*

Geist scrunched her eyes closed as she forced herself to roll over and stand, no matter the pain that flared throughout her body. *I'm getting up,* she thought, half reassuring herself and half in defiance. *I won't stay down.*

Standing on unsteady feet, Geist braced herself against a nearby tree. A throbbing agony filled her head. She pressed the palm of her hand over her forehead and tried to focus.

Percival.

The light of the crescent moon couldn't pierce the canopy of leaves. Geist couldn't see more than a few feet ahead of her. She stumbled forward, determined to find Percival before anything else could happen. Within a few seconds, she found him under a tree, sprawled out on his back.

Despite his ragged uniform and scuffed knees, Percival appeared unharmed. Geist breathed a sigh of relief.

He gazed up at her, his expression one of disbelief and worry.

"I can't believe we did that," Percival murmured.

"Man was never meant to fly," Geist replied, her tone dry. She looked him over. "Are you okay?"

"I thought we were going to die."

"Well, we didn't. But we're not safe yet."

"I didn't think fighting in the war would be like this."

"Like what?"

Percival pushed himself up onto his elbows. He frowned. "Like… this." His melancholy tone reminded Geist of a hundred other soldiers who shared the same sentiment.

"Get up," she commanded. "We need to go back."

Percival sat silent and unmoving.

Geist held out a hand. "C'mon. I can't do this without you, Battery."

He turned to her with a furrowed brow. "What did you call me?"

"You heard me. *Get up*. I'm not going to repeat myself again."

SEVEN

Fort Douaumont

Battery patted at his belt. When he came up emptyhanded, he glanced around. Geist watched him search the surroundings with his eyes, but she had no idea what he was looking for. Before she could ask, Battery jogged over to the nearest tree and scooped up a Lancaster pistol nestled between two exposed roots.

"Good thinking," Geist said. "I lost my weapons during the fighting. We'll need something to protect us." She felt around her waist. Even her knife had disappeared during the confusion of the airship battle. Fortunately, she still had a trench dagger—a little dull and used more for cutting cloth or leather—but it could still kill.

"It's out of bullets," Battery said with a half-chuckle. "But this pistol was my grandfather's. I don't want to lose it."

He tilted the gun, allowing the moonlight to spotlight the custom grip and ornate finish. It was a handmade weapon. Each Lancaster pistol was one-of-a-kind, and Battery's had four barrels.

"Your grandfather gave it to you?"

Battery let out a long sigh as he tucked the weapon back into its holster. "No. He gave it to Victory." He returned to Geist's side and kept his gaze down. "Even though *I'm* the one named after him."

"So you stole it."

Battery glared. "I didn't steal it." After a few moments of silence, he relaxed and continued. "Victory gave it to me before he left for the Ethereal Squadron. He said it should've been mine from the beginning… that he felt guilty having it."

"That was noble of him."

"Yeah," Battery said with a scoff. "I'm sure that's what he'd want you to think. But forget I said anything. Let's get going."

Geist hiked up her pants, suddenly lost in thought. She couldn't relate. Her younger brother had given her all sorts of gifts when they had been younger, especially after she had been scolded by their father.

I wonder how he's doing now.

She shook her head. Without the stars or lights on the horizon, Geist knew they had bigger problems. "I got turned around when we fell. Do you know the direction back to the French lines?"

"I have a compass."

"Those aren't standard issue."

"I've always carried one, even before the war."

Battery withdrew a brass Cruchon & Emons compass from his breast pocket. The device fit in the palm of his hand, and as he flipped open the lid, he brought it close to his face.

"If we're behind enemy lines," Geist said, "we need to head southwest." Her body felt heavy, as though soaked in water and dragging her down. *Push through it. Just push through it.*

Battery pointed. "That way."

The trees blocked their path, but together, they marched around.

The longer they walked, the slower Geist became. She fell behind, her body drained and weak. At times her knees would give out, causing her to half-stumble, but she managed to catch herself before falling. When Geist rested against the trunk of a tree, Battery stopped and turned.

Neither spoke. Battery walked back and offered his shoulder. Geist hesitated—she didn't like getting too close, but the parachute ride down had thrown that excuse out the window. They had practically become one with the force of their freefall embrace.

After a long, silent moment, Geist leaned her weight against Battery's shoulder. He tucked his arm around her back and brought his hand up the side of her ribs. Too close. On instinct, she shoved him away and recoiled, her arms folded tightly across her chest.

"What's wrong?" Battery asked.

Her injured arm stung with the sudden movement. Geist half-doubled over and gritted her teeth. *What am I going to tell him?*

"I need to rest," she said, curt.

"Right now?"

"Yes."

"But the sooner we get you to Cross, the sooner—"

"*I can't,*" she interjected.

Again, silence settled between them. Battery took in a deep breath and then exhaled. "Okay. You're in charge. What should we do?"

"We should move away from the front. Find a place to hide."

"You want us to go in the opposite direction?"

Geist forced herself to nod. The farther they were from active troops, the less likely they would get caught. Despite the darkness, Geist knew a soldier or two would have spotted the parachute. Even a small team of scouts could kill them, given the state they were in.

If only Battery had studied any school of magic other than potentia.

"Can you walk by yourself?" he asked.

"I'll get far enough... Just lead the way."

Battery held his compass close. "All right."

REST CAME IN FLEETING MOMENTS. The snap of twigs could be an approaching soldier. The chirp of birds could be snipers' signals. The howl of the wind could be another Abomination Soldier using tempest magic. The potential threats made Geist's heart seize up with dread.

Their hideaway—a clump of mutilated trees far from the front-lines—provided enough cover to make a small shelter. Geist curled up onto her side and rested her head on the soft grass. Her thoughts lingered on Albatross. He had died so suddenly; she hadn't been prepared.

Slowly, she slipped into a kind of waking dream. One moment, she would be back on the zeppelin, fighting for her life. In the next, she danced with Vergess in the ballroom of the Schönbrunn Palace, dressed in the spring dress her mother had commissioned for her engagement. Her fears, desires, and memories all rolled together into a roiling mass, and sweat coated every inch of skin on her body.

She jolted upright at the crunch of leaves. Battery lifted his head, his eyes wide.

Vergess slipped into the leafy shelter. Both Geist and Battery let out quick exhales of strained relief. Geist's heart relaxed back into an even beat knowing that at least he hadn't been discovered by the enemy.

"How did you find us?" Battery asked after a round of shallow breaths.

"Scent," Vergess replied. He sat down on the grass and allowed the foliage to fall back into place. "I found traces of you both walking deeper into enemy territory, so I followed your trail."

"That's… incredible."

"Hardly."

Scent? Geist thought, her memories still swirling in the forefront of her thoughts. *He can pick up human scent? My notes said he practiced destructive sorcery. Does he know another?*

"How long have you been searching for us?" Battery asked.

"I've scoured this part of the woods for twelve hours now."

Twelve hours? Geist shook her head and then glanced up. An orange-tinted sky greeted her. Sunset? Sunrise? She had lost all track of time.

"I spotted a fort not too far from here," Vergess said. "Fort Douaumont."

Battery sat up straight. "Truly? I didn't know we were *that* far behind enemy lines."

Her stomach growled. She clutched her side. "If I knew we were going to be stranded like this, I would have brought rations."

"I never leave without emergency supplies," Battery said. "We can split what I have."

He opened a pouch on his belt and removed a single iron ration. The small tin container held three cakes made of beef bouillon powder and cooked wheat, along with three tiny bars of chocolate. He broke apart the rations and handed Geist half.

She took the offering and inhaled it without tasting. The nourishment eased the aching of her stomach but didn't cure her overall fatigue.

"Good thing you came prepared," Geist muttered upon finishing.

"I always plan ahead. My brothers say I'm a doolally, but I doubt they'd be mocking me now."

Geist nodded, her eyelids heavy.

"Feeling better?"

No.

Vergess shook his head. "There are soldiers all around us. Once it gets dark, we should head out. It'll be our last chance to make it back to Fort Souville."

Geist watched the waning light and shivered. They couldn't stay behind enemy lines forever. She inhaled and exhaled, trying to gather her strength.

"We'll wait here until then," she said.

The other two nodded.

Silence stretched between them until Geist turned her attention to Vergess. "I need to know. What other kinds of sorcery do you practice?"

"Besides ruina, I practice apex sorcery."

Apex sorcery? Geist remembered—her mother and father had practiced the same sorcery in lessor degrees. Those with apex magic often developed peak physical abilities. Night vision. Enhanced strength. Supernatural fortitude. *Heightened senses.* How could she have forgotten?

"Ruina sorcery," Battery interjected. "Of course. Everyone's seen you destroy things just by touching them. Living and dead."

Vergess glowered.

"Two?" Geist asked. "You've really mastered *two* schools of sorcery?"

"Yes," Vergess replied.

"You're so young."

"I've practiced since I was a child."

Geist held her breath, torn between admiration and curiosity. Studying two schools of sorcery was *possible*, just as a man could be both a professional baseball player *and* a boxer, but the likelihood of mastering them at the same time was a feat of unrivaled skill.

Then again, many sorcerers developed small amounts from other schools of sorcery, taking abilities that complemented their main areas of expertise. Perhaps Vergess knew only a little of either.

Though from the skill he'd demonstrated thus far, this didn't seem likely.

Battery lifted an eyebrow, his gaze serious. "Did you know the Kaiser trains special sorcerers to keep him and his family safe? He forces the sorcerers to develop two schools of sorcery. He beats and twists them until they comply. I've heard horror stories about his methods."

Vergess went still, not bothering to reply.

Geist had heard about the Kaiser's guard. They were often described as emotionless vessels of destruction, ruthless in every regard. It made sense that someone like Vergess would result from intense physical and emotional training. The man didn't look like he had enjoyed a pleasant childhood.

"We better hope we don't run into any of them," Geist said. "They would be formidable foes."

"I think we *have* run into one," Battery whispered, his attention still locked on Vergess.

Geist, thinking fast, offered a weak chuckle. "Who? Vergess? The Kaiser wouldn't let one of his pets escape him." She had said she would help Vergess maintain his secret, and if he didn't want to confirm or deny his past in the Kaiser Guard, she wanted him to have an out.

"Everyone's heard the rumors," Battery said. "He speaks fluent German. And look at his face. That's what all Huns look like."

Battery's timid tone gradually shifted to one of confidence. "What if he's here to infiltrate the Ethereal Squadron? With his abilities, he could cripple us if he struck at the right moment."

"*I* can speak fluent German. You're jumping at shadows."

"I want to hear him say it," Battery said. "Are you a sorcerer from the Kaiser's Guard?"

Vergess sat back and glared. "I'm an American soldier."

The silence grew between them.

"We're behind enemy lines," Geist said at last. "We don't have time to cast doubt. Vergess is an ally, and I won't have any more talk of it."

Even if Vergess was a German ex-patriate and a member of the Kaiser's Guard, he had still helped them in their mission. He had earned the right to call himself American.

The two men regarded each other with a long stare before nodding. Geist breathed easy. *As long as we can get through this, everything will be fine.*

The dying sun cast the wooded terrain in dark shadow. Although she hadn't fully recovered, Geist knew she didn't have the luxury of resting.

"I gotta take a piss," she said. "And then we leave."

"Let me help you up," Battery said. "I'll lend you what strength I have."

Geist took his hand and stood, the power of his sorcery invigorating her all at the same time. Pain faded and exhaustion slipped away. She kept her hand on his for a second longer, enjoying the intense yet soothing presence of his magic.

Battery stared down at their grip. "Your hands are really small."

Geist jerked away, breaking contact. A fraction of Battery's power lingered, but it was enough for her to function.

"I'm sorry," he muttered. "I didn't, er… I didn't mean it like that. There's nothing wrong with being smaller than, well, you know, *average.*"

"Let's not talk about it."

"Yeah. Sorry. Right."

Ignoring Battery's floundering, Geist pushed passed the foliage and trekked through the trees. Once in a secluded spot, she undid her pants, her mind on distant thoughts. *Battery's sorcery is useful. If it can give me invisibility* and *the ability to go incorporeal, I wonder what it could do for the others.*

Once finished, Geist secured her belt and rounded the tree. There stood Vergess. He had his back to her as he leaned against a tree, his glare set on their surroundings.

"What're you doing?" Geist asked.

"Keeping an eye out," he replied.

"For what?"

"For you. To make sure you're not discovered."

Geist chuckled. "That's how you're going to help me?"

"Yes."

"I went an entire year without getting caught. You don't need to worry."

Vergess glanced over his shoulder and stared down at her. "I would've figured it out the moment we were put into a team together. You're not as covert as you think you are."

She let out a single, huffed laugh. "Is that right?"

"You smell like a woman."

Geist's face flushed. "Really?"

"I'm an apex sorcerer. How do you think I found you and Percival? You stand out."

"I—" Geist floundered for the right words, struggling to articulate her position. "I can maintain this ruse without any assistance, thank you. It would only compromise my operations if you're always skulking about."

Vergess laughed. "Skulking about? That's not what I intended to do, I assure you. I'm here to watch your back."

"Now isn't the time. I'm capable for the moment."

"Because of Percival."

"His name is Battery," Geist said shortly. "And there's nothing wrong with drawing strength from your team."

"What's going on?" Battery called out from behind a thicket. "Are you two bickering?"

"N-no," Geist stammered. "Of course not."

Vergess snorted. "We're fine. We're perfectly fine."

"Uh-huh," Battery said. "Well, we should be going."

Together, the three of them moved through the trees, Geist's mind on Vergess's statements. *Could he really have figured me out? No. I've been so careful before. He's just worried—but why? It's not his neck if I get caught.*

They had to stay stealthy, even at night. Soldiers marched from location to location heedless of the weather or time of day. Although Geist felt proud wearing her uniform—the proudest moment in her life was the first time she had donned it—the American-khaki under moonlight would identify her as an enemy even at a distance.

And German snipers were deadly, even at night.

Battery kept pace. His gaze darted to every movement and dark shadow, but he didn't flinch. Geist admired his vigilance, though she knew stress could wear down anyone's mind. *How long has he been on the alert? He'll need to rest soon.*

"What is that?" Battery asked as he pointed.

The evening blanket of black shrouded the surroundings, but Geist could still make out the outline of a large form lying on the ground. She stopped and reached for her weapon, but she came up empty.

Vergess held out a hand. "It's a deer."

A deer? Here?

The sounds of the wood were dead. Animals didn't dwell long near battlefields.

Geist approached the beast, curiosity fueling her steps. *Is it injured? Maybe a stray bullet brought it down?*

"Wait," Vergess muttered as he glanced around. "What's going on?"

Battery shivered. "I can't see a thing."

The closer she got, the more confused Geist became. The "deer" was much larger than any she had seen before. It twitched and writhed and took in raspy breaths at odd times, like it had two pairs of mismatched lungs. When she drew near, the beast jerked and kicked, tossing up leaves and dirt, but it settled down soon after with a long groan.

Geist caught her breath.

It wasn't *a* deer. It was *two*—a doe and an antlered buck—melted together to form a horrendous amalgam. Both heads twisted about, and all eight legs twitched and spasmed, their bodies jammed into one deformed lump. And the waxy sheen of the hide… Geist grabbed at her wrist, feeling the fabric that had fused to her flesh.

The Grab-Hersteller Gas.

With her eyes fully adjusted to the night, Geist panned her gaze to her surroundings. The road ahead was crimson with pools of gore. Everything stood still but the wind. Magic lingered on the air, as did the aroma of death.

It was all around her.

Battery walked up to get a look at the creature. He recoiled. "What a horrible monster. How is it still alive?"

Geist grabbed his arm and jerked him back. "We have to run."

"What? Why?"

"It'll come for us. It might already be too late."

"What will?"

"*Run.*"

Ice sluiced through Geist's veins, washing away all feeling. She dragged Battery away from the monstrosity and sprinted in the opposite direction, hoping Vergess would keep pace. As she wove through the trees, a yellow-greenish mist wafted between the trunks—slithering close, reaching out—but Geist leapt away, heedless to her new direction.

A yearling buck, crazed and wild, bounded through the haze of the gas. It crashed into Battery and collapsed to the mud and detritus, its legs folding in on themselves and sinking into its very body. The animal screamed and flailed as Battery staggered to his feet.

"What is this?" he asked, his voice breathless and shaken.

Vergess leapt to the beast and briefly grazed its neck with his fingers. The rotting power of his ruina magic killed the animal before it suffered any longer.

The gas hungered for more. It came closer and closer, relentless in its thirst. Geist took Battery by the arm, and on the heels of panic, ran faster than she ever had before. Together, they burst from the tree line and out onto the empty military roads of France. Wagon lines of muddy water glistened in the crescent moonlight. Vergess sprinted out after them, coming to a halt by Geist's side.

With the option to go north or south, Geist hesitated. South would lead them toward the Triple Entente, their allies, and north would take them to the German-controlled Fort Douaumont, the enemy.

A small piece of Geist had hoped that the GH Gas used to destroy her team had been a fluke. Seeing it a second time stirred a deep hatred within her. She hated running. She hated feeling helpless. She hated that the gas had such power over her.

But I'm not going to let it control me. I'm not going to sit by and do nothing. I won't. I can't. I can do this. I have to.

Geist's resolve burned hot in her chest and quickened her heartrate. But how could she combat the GH Gas when her commander wouldn't believe her about the source of its power? No sorcerer was in the woods controlling the gas… It was simply *there*, lingering, looming just out of sight among the trees.

The gas had likely been deployed from Fort Douaumont.

Geist turned northward.

Battery shook his head. "That's the wrong way."

"We need to bring back evidence," Geist stated simply. "The commander needs to know that GH Gas was here."

"*That* was the GH Gas? Why didn't you say so?" He ran both hands through his dark brown hair. "It all makes sense. You should have said something." Battery furrowed his brow and frowned. "You want to infiltrate the fort? Us? There're Abomination Soldiers in the fort. Everyone knows. If we're caught—"

"We're wasting time," Vergess said. "We need to make a decision."

Battery shook his head. "This isn't our mission. Our mission was—"

"We're members of the Ethereal Squadron," Geist interjected. "Our objectives are greater than a single mission. Information about the GH Gas could be a turning point for the whole war."

Battery fell silent. He ran sweaty palms over his tunic and stared at the dirt road under his feet. Geist took the moment to relax her muscles and stare back at the tree line. The gas had yet to follow, but she didn't doubt that it would pursue them if they stayed. Somehow, it always knew where they were.

"We can't stay here forever," she whispered. "I need to know. Are you two with me?"

Battery took in a ragged breath. "We already lost Albatross."

"We'll lose a lot more if the enemy continues to use and develop GH Gas. Can you imagine men twisting together like those deer? We need to know how it works."

"Fine," Battery said. "I'm with you."

Vergess nodded. "You don't need to convince me. I'm in too."

FORT DOUAUMONT SAT on the highest ground in the area with a pentagon-shaped wall and a moat surrounding the base of the hill. Stillness settled over the German-manned 75mm guns and 155mm turrets on the parapet. Anti-personnel cannons swiveled on the corner wall towers. Off in the distance, still visible from the edge of the fort, stood the village of Douaumont, half-destroyed.

Vergess knew the inside, he'd told them. He had been stationed at the fort before he had been taken as a POW. The plan, as Geist laid out, was to sneak in, disable the guards, search for any information, either in the form of paperwork or smaller bombs, and escape the fort without raising an alarm. With Battery, Geist could become invisible. With Vergess, they could destroy any walls or doors that would prevent them from taking their evidence.

It all seemed plausible to Geist, so when the enemy guards on the walls shuffled from one post to another, she knew she had to act.

Geist ran to the wall. Her invisibility protected her better than any armor—she relished the feeling of power and ease of movement and silently thanked Battery for his empowering sorcery. The masonry of the wall, once an obstacle she wouldn't be able to scale, no longer prevented her passage. She slipped through it, slow and careful, concentrating the entire time.

I wonder what would happen if my power dropped halfway through. Would I be harmed? Would it kill me? The thoughts haunted her every inch of stone she passed through.

I really am a ghost, she thought, releasing her held breath once on the other side. *I never knew specter sorcery could be so powerful.*

Geist ran to the corner tower, but the strength of Battery's sorcery gave out halfway to her destination. The tether between them was too short. She slammed her back against the wall and edged her way to the ladder. Exhaustion took hold, but she pushed it from her mind. As soon as Battery got close again, she would be fine. She just needed to last a little longer.

Climbing the ladder took time. Geist's arms shook as she reached the last ten rungs—especially her wounded arm, as the injury reopened and began to weep. If she made a noise, the gunner in the tower wouldn't hesitate to fire down on her. She gritted her teeth and pressed upward.

Geist pulled herself up onto the tower platform. The gunner at the cannon heard nothing. She held her breath, inched forward, and withdrew her trench dagger from her pocket. The German soldier hummed a gentle folksong.

Gunshots would only attract attention. Geist punched her short weapon into the side of the soldier's neck. Unfortunately, it didn't kill the man instantly. He whipped around, blood gushing from his neck, his hand shaky on the butt of his handgun. Geist stabbed his neck again as the man yanked his weapon up, his eyes wide and already unfocused.

Geist then grabbed for the firearm. The man grunted and tried to shout, his voice drowned in hot blood. The noises reminded Geist of the melting men in the GH Gas. It took all her willpower not to imagine Cutter liquefying before her eyes.

She jerked the weapon from the soldier's grasp and stabbed him a third time, this time right between the ribs. The man fell forward in a slump, soaked in crimson. Geist exhaled, thankful to have taken the man without the other towers noticing.

With the corner tower unmanned, Geist signaled from the gunner window. Battery and Vergess crept out of their hiding spot near the shrubbery of the moat and ran to the wall in a half-crouch. Geist let down a rope and allowed them up, unnoticed by the enemy. Together, they slid down the ladder and stood in the moonlight shadow of the wall until the patrolling soldiers of the fort courtyard made their rounds. They spoke no words, and, once assembled, Battery empowered Geist once more.

Of the nineteen forts that surrounded Verdun, Fort Douaumont had been one of the first to fall. It stood as an outlier, not as strategically important as the other forts, but the loss had still struck a blow to the morale of the French soldiers. Its insignificance meant it wasn't as manned, not even by the enemy: perfect for prowling about.

They darted across the courtyard and ran straight for the side door into the main building. Locks no longer held the challenge they once did. Geist pushed her good arm through the metal and unlatched the door into the fort. Battery and Vergess slipped in after and together they stood in the dim hallway with a sense of unease.

"Where to now?" Battery whispered.

"Wait," Geist said. "Do you speak German?"

"Of course. Two of my uncles are from House Vogt of Trier."

Geist snorted. *I should've guessed that the Hamilton family would have connections with every major house this side of the Black Sea.* "Good."

Vergess gave the other man a sidelong glance. "And you gave *me* trouble for knowing German?"

"You're different. You know… Secretive. And the way everyone talks about you is—"

"Enough," Geist said. "We don't have time for this. We need weapons and uniforms."

Vergess nodded. "I know where the armory will be."

"Of course you do," Battery muttered under his breath.

"I'll get the guns," Vergess said, ignoring Battery's remark even though Geist was certain he had heard.

"Very well," she muttered. "If you get us some rifles, Battery and I will head for the barracks for uniforms. We can meet at the entrance to the barracks afterward." She nodded to Vergess and then grabbed Battery by the sleeve. "C'mon. Follow me."

Battery replied with a nod.

Vergess jogged off in the opposite direction and disappeared around a corner. Battery glowered in his direction, and Geist sighed. The two men were just determined to dislike each other.

Geist had been stationed in enough French forts to know they shared a similar layout and construction. It didn't take long to navigate the narrow hallways. Geist scouted ahead, invisible, but the soldiers were few and far between. Despite that, Battery dawdled behind, almost cowering in Geist's shadow.

The barracks were occupied. Hundreds of soldiers slept in cots, unaware of the enemy lurking not twenty feet away. Geist, alone, ghosted into the main room and rummaged through the trunks and containers for the dark green uniforms of the German army. The darkness hindered her sight, but not her movements.

I should develop a magic that would allow me to see in the dark, she thought as she snatched a belt off the post of a nearby cot. *I know my father and mother can, so it has to be in my bloodline. If I had known apex magic was so useful, I would've learned it sooner.* She chuckled to herself. *Maybe I could ask Vergess to teach me.*

Geist hadn't seen the soldier wandering from his cot. The man tripped on her invisible form and caught himself before he went face-first into the concrete flooring. Geist held her breath and slid under the nearest cot, panic overtaking her thoughts.

"What's that?" the soldier asked in groggy German. "Who's there?"

He got on his hands and knees, his eyes wide despite the sleep in his voice. Geist remained still—a surreal feeling of disbelief washing over her as the man turned his gaze upon her several times without seeing.

"Koch," another soldier whispered in a heated tone. "Get some sleep."

"I thought I tripped on someone."

"You're dreaming of phantoms."

"Will you both *be quiet?*" a third soldier chimed in. "Koch, you shell-shocked lunatic, *get back to your cot!* We wake at dawn."

The worried soldier—Koch—got up off the floor and brushed himself off. "I could have sworn…"

"If you don't get back to your cot, so help me, I'll—"

"I have to piss."

"You *always* have to piss. Hurry up."

Under the cover of Koch's heavy steps, Geist rolled out from the cot and stood. She didn't have complete uniforms, but it would have to do. The soldiers were antsy and sure to stay awake for several minutes longer. She didn't have time to wait.

Geist slid through the wall between the barracks and the hallway to find Battery muttering to himself. He had his head down and his shoulders bunched up around his neck.

"If we make it through this, I swear I'll—"

"Battery," Geist whispered. "Get ahold of yourself and change."

He snapped his gaze up to the sound of her voice, but his eyes remained unfocused. "You have the uniforms?"

She handed one over. Once out of her grasp, the fabric shimmered into view.

Battery looked over the garments and frowned. "Where's the rest?"

"That's all I could get. I doubt anyone will notice. Just put it on."

Battery awkwardly unhooked his belt and peeled off his British-khaki tunic. Geist would have ignored him, but something on the youth's back caught her attention.

Geist suppressed a gasp. All across Battery's spine, from between his shoulder blades down to the small of his back, were long medical scars, each more jagged than the last. Not a handful, or a dozen, but *hundreds*. And some were fresh—less than a year old. Tiny fragments of opals were inlayed in the wounds, adding a twisted sparkle to the scars.

Battery caught her staring.

"It's no big deal," he said, his tone terse.

Geist turned away.

She had seen such injuries before. They were archaic attempts to help sorcerer children. Opals had a latent magic that had attracted sorcerers since the dawn of time. Some jackass had had the great idea to alter sorcerers who couldn't focus properly with the stones, and because of its success, the practice had gained popularity.

But the surgery, when done young, stunted your growth and shortened your lifespan. Sure, the fledgling sorcerer focused—sometimes too much, almost to the point of mania—but the procedure still worked, no matter how barbaric it all was.

"Did Victory and Blick have the same surgery?" Geist asked.

"No," Battery said as he rammed a foot through the uniform pant leg. "They didn't have problems focusing. Just me."

Trouble focusing. That was why some sorcerer parents mutilated their children.

Geist returned to changing. She had never done so in front of a man—she had avoided it at all costs, for obvious reasons—and the faux-exhibition caused her to flush. Geist couldn't see the bright red of her skin, but she could feel it. She also couldn't see the clothing she was stepping into, making dressing an arduous ordeal. With all the grace of a blind child, she groped around her uniform and fumbled through the motions of dressing, hoping everything went together.

Battery, finished long before Geist, straightened his collar and folded the bottom of his pant legs to compensate for his height. "Potentia is difficult to learn," he said, his voice still shaking. "It's far more demanding than other schools of magic. Most sorcerers would struggle with it, I think."

"Probably. I've never seen it before."

"You study specter magic, right? Was it… difficult for you?"

Geist slid the German belt through the loops and cursed at the odd latch and fastening system. *Why aren't belts universal? Why are they all so different?*

"It wasn't difficult," she said absentmindedly. "It came natural."

"I just figured that since you're also, you know, *smaller*, that you had maybe—"

"No. I've never been operated on."

Battery fell silent. Geist finished dressing and dropped her invisibility. Her uniform, ill-fitting, needed adjustment. She tucked and straightened what she could, but her attention fell back to Battery on several occasions. He stared at the floor, unseeing.

I can't let him dwell like this.

"That doesn't mean I didn't have a hard time studying magic," Geist said, keeping her voice low and hoping to cheer him up. "My parents disapproved of me developing specter magic. They wanted me to study corpus magic instead."

"Like Cross?"

"Something like that. They wanted me to *alter* flesh instead of mend it. Needless to say, that didn't work out. My father isn't a patient man. When I didn't meet his expectations, he… let's just say he wrote me off as a failure. He was too busy with my brothers to notice anything else I might be doing."

"I know a thing or two about that," Battery said with a sardonic smile.

Geist chuckled. Free of his melancholy, Battery gathered up their old uniforms and crammed them into a cootie bag. The lice-ridden clothing inside the bag would hide any trace of their presence until it was too late.

Vergess rounded the corner of the hall, his back to the wall at all points. He carried three Mauser rifles close to his chest but relaxed the moment he spotted Geist and Battery. When he jogged over, Geist tossed him a uniform.

"Hurry and change," Battery muttered. "We've been in the hallway too long."

Vergess glanced down at the garment and then up to Geist. For a long moment, he did nothing, a slight redness to his face and ears. Battery flailed his arms around, gesturing to the uniform with exaggerated movements.

"What's wrong? Get out of your old uniform already!"

Again, Vergess hesitated.

Geist grabbed Battery by the arm and forced him to turn around with her, both their backs to Vergess. "He's shy," she said, forcing a playful tone. "Maybe he's a member of Team Teensy-Weensy after all."

"Th-that doesn't matter. We're all men here! We don't have time for modesty!"

"Keep it down."

Vergess undressed hastily. Geist could almost swear she heard him muttering, *I can't believe she'd say that.* It made her laugh, but Battery didn't join in.

"We could be killed," Battery said. "We don't have time for games."

"Tinker is rubbing off on me," Geist quipped.

"God help us."

"I'm done," Vergess stated.

Both Geist and Battery turned back around, and Geist caught her breath.

He looked born to wear a German uniform. Sleek. Handsome. Fit and warlike. And he knew how to properly buckle the belt and fold the sleeves, a very German habit.

He's practically giving himself away.

Vergess handed over the rifles.

"C'mon," Geist said, rubbing at her arm and turning her gaze away. "We need to get moving."

Battery and Vergess nodded. They followed behind Geist as she led the way through the fort. There were armories and equipment rooms meant to house all sorts of high-powered explosives, from hand grenades to daisy cutters, and Geist banked on finding what she needed in one such room.

She rounded the corner and slammed her feet together in a full stop. There were two German field officers and their personal retinue blocking the hallway—standing right in front of them.

EIGHT

Testing Grounds

"Kommandant," Geist said, forcing her German out as masculine as she could muster. She saluted with her right fingertips against her eyebrow, attempting to mimic everything she had ever seen enemy soldiers do before.

The field officers wore their tassels and insignias in plain view—not the practice of officers ordered to the frontlines. Geist recognized the rank on both men and tensed. One, the older with a thin mustache, wore the rank of *feldwebel-leutnant*, a warrant officer, while the other, a thicker, younger man with broad shoulders, wore the pomp and frills of a colonel.

The harsh green against the bright colors of the officers clashed strikingly, further indication neither was meant for the heat of battle. *Administrative types,* Geist surmised as both men looked her over with hard gazes of scrutiny and suspicion.

To Geist's surprise, Vergess saluted and then kept his gaze to the floor and his body turned away from the men. Did he fear recognition? If he had been with the Kaiser on more than one occasion, a colonel might have remembered his face. *Fuck. I guess it's up to me to get us out of this.*

Although she couldn't sense magic within the two men, killing them in the middle of the fort would be the same as putting a bullet in her head. No doubt there were Abomination Soldiers close by, and news of officers being assassinated would draw out all kinds of sorcerers Geist wasn't prepared to handle. And while she and Vergess might be able to flee, Battery wouldn't have such luck.

"Where's your Stahlhelm, boy?" the colonel asked.

Stahlhelm? Ah, he means those coal scuttle helmets. Geist ran a slow hand over her curly brown hair. "I'm not on duty."

"Do you think the enemy knows that?" the officer bellowed. "This is *war*. You're *always* on duty."

His reprimanding tone cut deep, despite her actual position. A small piece of her wanted to go back and get the helmet—but she pushed the foolish urge aside.

"I woke up not feeling well," Geist said, struggling to find the correct German words for the conversation. She spoke Austrian-German and knew it to be a dialect distinct from others. The last thing she wanted was more questions. *Best to keep sentences short and sweet.*

The warrant officer, calmer and more reserved than the colonel, narrowed his eyes. "Woke up not feeling well?"

"I keep needing to… relieve myself, sir."

The man stroked his mustache. "Ah. That damned infection keeps spreading."

"Get to the medics quick before you give it to the rest of the 24th," the colonel said, waving her to continue. "We can't have our men pissin' themselves to death before the enemies arrive."

Geist saluted a second time. "Yes, sir."

She stepped around the two officers and through the other soldiers, feeling the weight of their gazes upon her. Battery and Vergess shadowed her steps.

"Wait there, boy," the warrant officer said, holding out a hand to stop Battery. "What's that around your waist?"

Geist glanced back. Battery's belt—it was the British uniform standard—nothing like the odd German belt she had fastened around her waist. She clenched her hands into fists, ready to ghost and fight the soldiers if needed. *Damn. I should've paid more attention in the barracks!*

Battery turned and motioned, not only to his belt, but to his British-standard boots as well. "Souvenirs," he said. "It's not like that island monkey was using them anymore."

The Germans laughed.

Geist forced herself to smile, but she couldn't believe Battery spoke such fluent—and *crass*—German. Even Vergess gave Battery a sideway glance, a slight smile on his face.

The colonel patted Battery on the shoulder. "If you're all visiting the medics, bring this report. It's for the doctor there, you understand? Now hurry up, soldier. You should be back in bed before the sun rises."

One soldier among the retinue handed Battery a thick file of paperwork.

"Of course, sir." Battery took the file and turned away without further incident.

The moment they rounded a corner, Geist shot Battery a half-smile. "I'm impressed."

Battery scoffed and held his head a little higher. "I said I'd be useful, didn't I?"

"Maybe. But I bet if *Victory* were here, he would've somehow convinced the Germans to surrender the fort back to the French."

With a look of indignation, Battery glowered. Geist responded with a chuckle. For a moment his anger persisted, but eventually, he relaxed.

"Very funny," he murmured. "At least I can properly conjugate German verbs. You sounded like a yokel back there."

Geist and Battery shared another laugh. It reminded Geist of her old team.

Vergess stepped between them. "Is it wise to go around speaking English in a German-occupied fort?" he asked, his German so authentic that Geist understood why he tried hiding it around other squadron members.

"You're right," Geist replied.

Battery straightened himself. "Any idea where we should be going, Mr. American?"

The sarcasm caused Geist to chuckle again, but she knew Vergess wasn't pleased. *I'll need to talk to Battery. This isn't helping anything.*

They stopped talking once a pair of soldiers passed them in the hall. Vergess motioned them to follow without a single word. Geist and Battery complied. The remainder of the walk occurred in silence.

The gray walls and gray flooring blended together to create a bleak, drab atmosphere. The walls seemed to suck the heat out of the air, leaving only the chill of early spring. At the end of the main hall, Battery turned in the opposite direction. Geist stopped and lifted an eyebrow. He motioned to an open door—the medic's ward —and then waved his file of paperwork. Geist cursed under her breath. Did they really need to follow the enemy colonel's orders so exactly?

She shrugged, and the three walked to the infirmary.

No one was around. The room stood empty.

Although Geist's intent had been to drop off the file and leave, she stopped and lost her train of thought the moment she spotted a caged deer in the corner of the large rectangular room. All at once, the reality of the GH Gas in the woods hit her hard.

"A deer," Battery whispered. He walked over to the tiny cage— not big enough for the animal to stand—and stared at its ears. "It's tagged, just like the others."

"Tagged?" Geist asked, nervous jitters coursing through her. "What do you mean?"

"Didn't you notice how the other deer had tags on their ears? The ones out in the woods? Just like this one."

Geist hadn't seen—she had been too focused on fleeing the area.

Vergess nodded. "I saw the same. You've got keen eyes."

Geist returned her attention to the room. The ward had boxes of supplies piled on beds and countertops, and paperwork littered every surface. Several empty cages were piled in the corner next to a solid metal door.

And no injured soldiers.

Glancing at the paperwork, Geist gritted her teeth. In German, it read:

VERDUN TESTING GROUNDS

DAY: *18*

Test Site: *Gamma*

Description:

Two does, three yearling bucks and forty French POWs released into test site. Three shells detonated. All POWs with gasmasks. Ten-hour timeframe starting at 1700 hours.

Sweep Results:

GEIST TOUCHED THE PAGE. The results were left blank, but she already knew the outcome. The pools of blood on the road? French soldiers. Even with their gasmasks. The doe and bucks? Fast enough to escape dying in the gas, but perhaps their fate had been worse than death.

It can't be… They're testing the GH Gas here, of all places. They might've even been testing it when they used it against us on the battlefield…

She remembered the POWs, and how they were kept so close to the German frontlines. *So close to the GH Gas shell.* The purpose struck her, and Geist closed her eyes. *They were using the POWs as test subjects, just like the deer. The same thing would've happened to Vergess if I hadn't arrived on time.*

Geist opened her eyes and flew through the paperwork, throwing files out of the way in a haphazard manner and tearing through drawers to find more. Most medical records were on German head injuries and how the latest helmets alleviated the workload for most medics—nothing about the GH Gas. Frustration welled within her as she tore through the tenth drawer and came up emptyhanded again.

"Geist."

She glanced up and saw Vergess standing by a far door. It was unlabeled, but Vergess inhaled deeply.

"They kept deer just beyond here," he said.

What were they hiding? Geist jogged over, intent to find out. Using her magic, she ghosted through the metal and unlatched the lock. Vergess watched, silent, and waited for Geist to go in first.

With bated breath, Geist crossed the threshold into, anticlimactically, another hallway. She froze, confused by the four additional doors. She went to the first and found it unlocked. Vergess walked to the second and discovered the same. Battery joined them in the hall, his gaze flitting to each shadow.

Geist held up a hand. They all held still and waited. Nothing. No movement. They were alone in the small hall and adjourning rooms.

"Stay close," Geist whispered, eyeing the terrible lights and thick shadows that crowded the corners. "But search quickly. We should get out of here as soon as we can."

"Agreed," Battery and Vergess replied in unison.

Battery disappeared into a room to search and Vergess slid farther down the hall. Geist focused—harder than she had needed to before—and became invisible. *I wonder how long Battery can keep this up. We need to hurry. If his power gives out, we'll be in a world of trouble.*

She entered an odd medical room and froze. In the center, on a surgery table, sat a man covered in thin blankets. Geist held her breath and shut the door behind her, confident in her cloak of invisibility. The harsh click of the door betrayed her.

"Nurse?" the man rasped, his voice both grating and familiar.

Geist swallowed her breath as her mind raged with indecision. Would she have to kill a bedridden soldier? *Could* she?

When the man turned, she widened her eyes. His face was wrapped in crimson bandages, his eyes completely covered.

"Please," the man continued. "I need water."

A pitcher of water and a clean glass sat on the countertop nearby. Geist stared for a moment longer before walking over and pouring a glass. She stole glances back at the injured soldier. His blankets, pink with blood, were numerous. The only visible parts of his body were his neck, chin, and mouth.

With the glass of water in hand, Geist drew close and narrowed her eyes. His face and neck had a waxy sheen. His lips had melted into the skin of his face, becoming smoothed and wide. His bleeding gums gave his teeth a sick blackish-red tint.

Geist brought the glass to his mouth and tilted it up. The soldier drank and coughed, spilling half the water onto his blankets. She waited and helped him again, patient despite the odd circumstance of their situation. Once finished, the man turned away. Geist placed the glass on the stand next to the medical table, her attention drawn to his personnel file.

The soldier sighed. "Thank you."

Geist leafed through the paperwork, her horror growing with each new sentence she read.

First Lieutenant Agustin Fechner. The same Abomination Soldier she had met on the GH Gas-ridden battlefield the night Cutter, Little Wick, and Buttons had died.

Her hands shook as she read the accounts of the overseeing doctors.

First Lieutenant Fechner has stabilized. His body, while malformed, is still intact. It appears that brief exposures to the Grab-Hersteller Gas can result in permanent alteration. No theories yet on whether or not this can be reversed.

Geist leafed through further reports, struggling to keep her breathing even.

First Lieutenant Fechner is in a great deal of pain. Surgeries have been done to deaden the nerves. This seems to have helped. He can sleep now.

First Lieutenant Fechner's sorcery is unstable. It no longer functions like it should. Attempts have been made to help him focus. The abilities he displays are unlike the ones he wielded previously.

First Lieutenant Fechner complains of blurry vision, but his eyes were liquefied during his exposure to the Grab-Hersteller Gas. Will need to conduct further tests to ascertain what he is complaining about. The current recommendation is to open the eye socket and check the status of the retina. Further testing at the frontline command facility Oberste Heeresleitung would be preferred.

"How is it?" Fechner asked in a quiet voice.

Geist fumbled with the paperwork, startled by the soft question.

"Are the treatments working?"

She took a breath and relaxed her throat. "The treatments… yes. They appear to be helping." It felt strange using her normal voice after purposefully deepening it for so long. Geist's natural speech, gruffer than most women's, still held a feminine twang that sounded foreign to her ears.

"I'm in pain."

Geist said nothing. Fechner had been the Abomination Soldier responsible for her old team's deaths. Then again, he was a shadow of his former self now. Weak and mewling—she could kill him with little effort. But did he deserve to suffer? Did he deserve to become a twisted monster like the deer in the woods? He was a soldier, just like her, following orders and fighting the enemy. He hadn't even been the one to order the GH Gas.

Geist lifted the thin blankets and regretted her action the moment she caught sight of his disfigured form. His left arm, tucked close to his side and resting on his stomach, had fused with the flesh of his torso, creating a deformed mass. Shattered opals had been stitched into his waxy skin and muscles. Open sores, weeping blood, littered his discolored body. She threw down the blanket, unwilling to stare any longer.

There would be no fixing what had been done. Perhaps the Germans could find a way to save him—perhaps they could alter him to become useful once more—but he would never again be a man.

Geist's gaze fell on a scalpel sitting on the side medical table.

"You don't have to suffer," she whispered. "I could end this for you, if you wanted."

Fechner grunted as she shifted around the table. "End this…?"

"I'll make it quick."

"Is that what you would do, if you were me?"

There had been a single instant in which Geist had contemplated such an act herself. A moment so powerful she could never forget—the night she had escaped her home and made her plans to join the Ethereal Squadron. Death would have been an easier escape from her suffering, but giving up, especially when others would have taken delight from seeing her fail, had lit inside her passion hotter than any other emotion she had experienced in her life.

Living was the greatest defiance of all.

"What happened to the other sorcerers under your command?" Geist asked, ignoring Fechner's question. "The ones on the battlefield with you when the gas was released?"

He took in a ragged breath. "They didn't make it."

Geist touched her disfigured wrist. She refused to pity him—he had still taken the lives of her teammates—but what anger she had melted away.

Geist turned her attention to the bottles scattered around the countertops. She picked up a half-empty container of barbitone and returned to Fechner's side. "Here," she said. "This will help you sleep."

He took the medication without fuss. Geist gave him another sip of water before gathering up the paperwork in the room. Records of the GH Gas, mention of the effects on sorcerers, even the history of the test sites, were all within her grasp. She took everything and turned to leave.

"You're beautiful," Fechner murmured. "I hope… you get assigned to this ward again."

"I *sound* beautiful," Geist corrected, her hand frozen on the doorknob. Could he see? She chuckled under her breath. *No. Obviously not—or else he wouldn't be saying I'm beautiful. I'm disguised as a man, for fuck's sake.*

Fechner groaned and shifted. "Your colors are so… vibrant."

"You're delirious. Get some rest."

He fell quiet. Geist fled the room before he could speak again.

Vergess stood waiting in the hall, his gaze vigilant and scanning the surroundings. "What happened?" he asked, keeping his voice low. "I heard you speaking."

"It's nothing," she said.

"Are you unharmed?"

"Yes."

"Your heartrate is up."

Geist placed a hand on her chest. "I'll be fine," she stated. "What about the other rooms?"

"Battery and I have searched them all."

"I have paperwork here. Information on the GH Gas."

"So do I. You need to read this."

Vergess handed her a single sheet of paper. It read:

FORT DOUAUMONT – Medical Staff – March 1916

In accordance with the Kaiser's New Schieffen Plan, testing results must be concluded by June. Special attention is to be paid to gas concentrations and the viability of standard countermeasures.

Unless otherwise instructed by the Kaiser himself, no other commands are to take precedence.

Oberste Heeresleitung Command

"THE NEW SCHIEFFEN PLAN?" Geist asked, rereading the note a second time.

"They plan to bomb Paris with GH Gas shells."

"*What?*"

Geist momentarily lost her voice. The shock—the outrage—it coursed through her so thoroughly she felt gut-shot. They were planning on using the GH Gas *en masse?* After seeing what it could do?

Of course they would target Paris. The sooner France surrendered, the sooner Germany could turn their full attention to the Russian Empire. One devastating blow to the heartland would cripple the French morale. Without an effective means of combating the gas, the French wouldn't stand a chance.

"We have what we came for," Geist whispered. "We need to leave."

Vergess nodded. "I couldn't agree more."

She couldn't mention Fechner, nor could she bring herself to go question the man. Seeing him had left her uneasy—and what more could he tell her that the reports didn't?

I've left him to his fate. There's no need to get involved with him any further.

The trek out of the fort occurred in silence. Geist tucked the papers into her oversized uniform; Battery and Vergess did the same. They exited out the back, in front of the patrolling soldiers, and kept their gaze straight ahead. With confidence as her disguise, Geist walked out the back gate and nodded to the Germans manning the heavy artillery. So long as they were walking away from the front, the other soldiers paid them little heed.

The moment they rounded the far bend, Geist, Vergess, and Battery made a wide loop around the forest doubling back to head for the western front.

NINE

Fraternizing

The strain was getting worse.

The bleeding, the injuries, the stress, the fatigue, relying on Battery just to move—Geist could feel her resolve slipping. For two days, they had traveled the back roads and military supply trains in an attempt to get closer to the French frontlines. Casually approaching was out of question while they wore German uniforms.

Vergess's insistence on safety over speed meant longer routes than Geist would have ever taken, but fatigue took away her greater judgment. All they needed to do was get back to Fort Belleville. Could she make it? She was less and less sure every step she took.

Geist stopped walking and leaned against the post of a broken country fence. Once, before the trenches and aerial bombardments, farmlands had dotted the hills. *War changes everything.*

Battery took the opportunity to catch his breath. Although they had gone through the same ordeal, he hadn't been bleeding from a bayonet wound—he still had energy to spare.

Vergess, on the other hand, didn't appear strained in the least. Geist knew apex sorcery could keep a sorcerer going far longer than normal human endurance allowed. She gritted her teeth and swore to her herself: *I'll have him teach me. Apex sorcery is in my bloodline as well. I need to be able to pull my weight.*

But developing the sorcery would take time. It wouldn't help to start out on the road between frontlines.

"Fort Belleville is on the horizon," Vergess said.

Battery breathed a sigh of relief. "If we surrender ourselves, we'll be taken as POWs. With our identification tags, they'll notify Major Reese, and he'll straighten everything out. But there's a chance the snipers might see us before we reach the soldiers. We can remove our tunics and cover the green of our uniform with mud and—"

Geist slipped and hit her knees on the packed earth, her body trembling.

Both Vergess and Battery flinched. They stared for a moment, their brows furrowed.

"Are you all right?" Battery asked, hovering close.

Geist cringed away, her hand tightly wound into her tunic.

Vergess glared at the smaller man. "Give him some space. He needs to breathe."

"A-all right."

Battery took a few steps back and tucked his hands into his armpits, his frown deepening. "I can't," Geist forced herself to say. "Leave me and—"

"We're not leaving you," Battery said, cutting her off. "We can make it together. We're so close."

Vergess knelt by her side and reached for her, but Geist shoved him away as hard as her arms would allow. Her heart beat a mile a minute, sweat drenching her clothing. Vergess slid one arm behind her trembling shoulders, but Geist shook her head.

"Don't," she hissed.

He got close, his breath on her ear. "Relax. I already know."

"I…" Even in her exhausted state her heart reacted to his closeness. Knowing he could sense it brought a flush to her face.

"I'll keep you safe. I swear it."

"I can't go back like this," she rasped, straining to speak through the weariness. The siren song of sleep haunted her thoughts. "What if… what if someone…"

I can't go back. The first field medic who examines me won't hesitate to inform command of my disguise. I have no choice.

"I won't let anyone discover you."

Vergess's voice came as sweet relief. Geist hadn't realized how afraid she had been of discovery. Having one other person—just one—who was looking out for her made a world of difference.

"Wilhelm," she whispered. "Please. I need Cross. *Only Cross.* Promise me."

"I promise."

"I… well…"

She couldn't articulate the urgency well enough. The helplessness that came from being unconscious frightened her. Unable to control her fate—the frustration ate at her willpower. Hot tears burned the corners of her dry eyes.

Vergess effortlessly lifted her into his arms. His body—so solid, so warm, so comforting—helped Geist relax. He held her close to his chest, allowing Battery to take the lead and guide them through the war-torn French countryside.

"I'll keep you safe."

Thank you was what she wanted to tell him, but the words never came.

Geist took in a handful of deep breaths and closed her eyes.

THE BUSTLE of a full medical ward woke Geist long before she wanted to wake. Nurses, medics, wounded soldiers, and delivery servicemen crowded the cramped Fort Belleville hall just beyond her private recovery room. Simple cots were assigned to men with minor injuries, but the sick and diseased were kept separate to prevent outbreak.

Geist fumbled with her heavy blankets, confused and covered in sweat. Taking in even shallow breaths proved difficult. The bandages over her chest were numerous and unforgivingly tight—

thick enough to obscure curves. Her arm had had the same treatment.

The door opened and closed, revealing a bag-eyed Cross. Even in her worn state, she held herself with ladylike grace, as always.

"Geist," Cross said, her eyes widening. "You're awake."

Geist's dry throat made it impossible to speak. Her chapped lips clung together; the pounding headache that followed didn't help, either.

Cross brought over a short glass of water. Geist threw back the beverage and motioned for more. Cross gave it to her slow, one cup at a time, and observed with a critical eye.

Cross's magic mended wounds, but it couldn't refuel a tired body like Battery could. Hunger still clawed at her belly.

"Cross," Geist muttered, her throat wet at last. "Why are these so tight?" She rubbed at her chest and grimaced.

"I'm sorry. Percival refused to be kept out of the room. I figured with enough gauze, no one would be able to tell. He was by your bedside until thirty minutes ago."

"No one found me out?"

Her heart raced the moment she had asked. Vergess had promised, but perhaps he had been negligent in his duties. And what if Battery had figured everything out simply from close proximity?

"Percival said nothing to me," Cross replied. "But he's been quite chatty since he's returned. Way different than when I first met him."

Geist smiled and pulled at her medical dressings. "And what about Vergess?"

"He refused to stay in the room while I treated you. He's been standing out in the hall."

"Hm."

When the bandages didn't loosen, she stared up at Cross. "Can I get rid of these now?"

"I told Percival you let your injuries go untreated too long—that my sorcery could only help a small amount—which is why I kept the bandages on you."

"Is that true?"

"Of course not. I also told him you had a chest wound, which is how I bound you without further question. Keep that in mind if someone else asks."

Geist breathed a sigh of relief.

Cross took a seat on the edge of the bed and sighed. "Percival insisted that he use his sorcery to empower me. His magic is incredible—I felt as though I could heal anything, even your wrist. But it wasn't enough. I'm sorry."

Geist ran a hand over the distorted skin. "It's fine."

"You'll be back to combat shape in no time."

"Thank you, Cross. For everything."

"No need to thank me," she said. "I'm just glad you're not dead."

"You can thank Battery for that."

"Battery?" Cross asked.

"Percival."

"Ah. It all makes sense now. I wondered whom the others were talking about."

Geist rotated her arm and smirked. *Cross is amazing. That bayonet wound would have sent a normal soldier home.* She settled down and stared at her blankets. Most men would give anything to go home—even an arm. *And here I am, celebrating staying on.*

Cross touched her shoulder. "How did this happen? I thought your specter sorcery kept you from harm?"

"I couldn't use my magic. I lost my focus."

"Lost your focus?"

"It happens." *My wrist will never be the same.*

Thoughts of cutting her flesh away and removing the tainted fabric-skin hybrid crossed Geist's mind. Another part of her wanted to keep it forever—to remind her of everything that had happened.

Cross turned away. "I see." She stood and smoothed out her frazzled blonde hair. "I need to go. You should rest for the remainder of the day. If anyone asks, you're still injured. I'll be back to check in on you." She turned to the door, and without another word, she exited.

Geist knew something was wrong. Cross was always so positive, despite the often grisly nature of her work. She'd seen the worst war had to offer, and nothing had cracked her resolve yet. At least, nothing Geist had seen.

So why is she so sullen now?

Shaking her head, Geist allowed the questions to fade from her mind. She had a million other things to worry about—from the New Schieffen Plan to Vergess to Battery—and sitting around in a bed wasn't going to get her any answers. She threw off her blankets and slid off the mattress onto firm legs. *Cross works miracles.*

Geist found her uniform in the standard hiding place, folded neatly and ready to go. Another one of Cross's many favors. Geist dressed with mechanical efficiency and headed for the mailroom. The grime of three days' worth of field travel clung to her skin beneath the clean fabric of her uniform, and Geist craved a shower.

The lull between major battles allowed soldiers from the front to return and change places with a fresh batch of men. The crowding in the fort got to the point of claustrophobia, but there was nothing to be done. Geist waded through the soldiers with her gaze down and her mind elsewhere.

The mailroom swarmed with activity. All soldiers loved delivery day, each praying for a letter from a loved one or a parcel from home, and the static trenches at the frontlines meant that soldiers were easy to track down and deliver to.

Geist approached the counter and veered off to the side. There was no point in asking if she had any mail. *Charles Weston* didn't have family—and nobody would be writing *Florence Cavell* out on the German front.

The back room, a narrow storage space behind the mailroom, was reserved for the members of the Ethereal Squadron. The sorcerers of Verdun had their own lockers and couriers, their parcels handled a little more delicately than the rest. This impromptu space was all Fort Belleville could spare on short notice, though the room served its purpose, given how few sorcerers Verdun actually had scurrying about.

Geist walked into the back, surprised to see three others rummaging through their lockers.

"So it's true," Tinker said, slamming the door of his locker and fiddling with a small brown-paper-wrapped package. "You're already up and moving."

That's already common knowledge? Geist thought with a side-smile. *Of course it is.*

Tinker rubbed a thumb over his nose. "I knew you'd live. You're like a weasel, ya know that? We had a weasel problem back home. Damn things never go away."

Yeah. Thanks.

He continued, unabated: "I'm surprised you even got *hurt!* Cross said you got stabbed in the arm *and* the chest. Shows what a bruiser you are, though. Most men choke to death on blood when they get a bayonet that close to the heart." Tinker punctuated his statement with a quick smack across Geist's chest.

She recoiled, bright red in the face, and pulled her uniform collar close to her neck. *Goddammit, Tinker!*

"Oh, fuck," Tinker said, holding up a hand in apology. "I'm sorry. Cross said you were still injured, but I just, well, didn't *believe* her. You know how some nurses get. It won't happen again, I swear."

Geist glared, still flushed with embarrassment.

He held out his package and shook it about, the sound of a hundred small objects tumbling inside. "You wanna share my cookies? My gal back home made them special."

"I don't want your cookies," she stated, her mouth salivating at the mere mention of homemade treats. *I'll eat later, once everything gets sorted out.*

"Suit yourself." Tinker pulled the box back. "My gal is as cute as a button. These are gonna taste like heaven. Plus—and this is the best part—she said she sent me photographs."

"Wow. Fantastic."

"Heh. Don't get too jealous. You can still change your mind."

"I'm not changing my mind."

With a crooked smile, Tinker pushed away from the lockers.

"Okay, well, I've got important cookie business to attend to." He strolled out of the backroom, his brown paper-wrapped parcel tucked under his left arm.

As Geist turned to glance back at her locker, she noticed Caveat staring. His round face, set in a frown, drooped more than usual. Geist couldn't help but sigh and engage the man.

"Is Tinker's gal even real?" she asked with a forced chuckle. "I wouldn't put it past him to bake his own damn cookies."

"Oh, she's real," Caveat replied. "They've been betrothed since they were children. You know how it goes."

Geist snorted. She knew all too well about arranged marriages. Anything to guarantee the babies would have the right mix of sorceries. She had avoided hers without a second's regret.

Caveat continued, his voice quiet, "He only just met her before he was deployed. He says she's beautiful—from House Rosenthal, you know how striking they can be." With a mumble and a sigh, Caveat shut his locker and ambled over to stand near Geist. "I hope I live long enough to find someone."

"Why do you say that?"

"Commander ordered all Verdun sorcerers back to the fort after he thought you, Vergess, and Battery had died."

"Everyone's here?"

"Oh, yeah." Caveat's face lit up, dispelling all traces of his sullen state. "And you should've seen Blick after he heard Battery hadn't returned! He was so livid when he thought his little brother had died. He practically demanded to get assigned the next zeppelin raid—like destroying all the zeppelins would bring his brother back. I've never seen him lose it like that."

"How did Victory take the news?" Geist asked.

"I'm not sure. He disappeared for a while. No one saw him till earlier this morning. Maybe he knew Battery was still alive. Who knows with his magic."

Before she could ask any more questions, Caveat stepped closer and leaned in close. She leaned away, narrowing her eyes in suspicion, but the man either didn't notice or didn't care. He glanced over his shoulder before asking, "So what's going on?"

She stared at him in silence. Although Geist felt the information paramount, she trusted the commander to dole out intelligence as need.

"Something big is happening," Caveat continued, his hushed tone laced with excitement. "The commander called in a special sorcerer from the Sinai and Palestine Campaign—all the way from the Middle Eastern Theater. He's some sort of infiltration specialist."

Caveat scooted in closer. Geist stepped back.

"C'mon," he said. "At least tell me if something's going on."

"Something's going on."

Caveat snapped his fingers. "I knew it. Tinker is gonna want to hear this. He's been talking about striking back for some time now. Those damn Huns have been asking for it. First Lock and Chorus, then Buttons, Little Wick, and Cutter—and now Albatross and Forest... Everyone wants to get serious and end this."

Albatross. The name gave her pause. Of all seven sorcerers who had died at Verdun, Geist had been present for more than half of them. She didn't believe in omens, but even Belshazzar had been able to see the writing on the wall.

"What happened on Tinker's assignment?" Geist asked, attempting to escape her thoughts. "He was ordered to kill the Abomination Soldier on the ground while we took the zeppelin."

"The yellowbelly never showed. Big Wick and Tinker covered the whole battlefield in fire. The Huns won't forget that fight, that's for sure."

Geist remembered the magic built into the zeppelin and wondered if it, too, had been scheduled for testing. *Perhaps the enemy sorcerers didn't show because they were afraid of the zeppelin's capabilities.*

Murmuring the entire time, Caveat secured the buttons of his uniform, fastening everything into place while he spoke. Geist didn't bother to tune in. With a nod and an "uh-huh," she opened her own locker and took stock of her meager supplies. Underneath an extra box of cellucotton and behind her one spare uniform and trench knife sat a black-and-brick-red ribbon. She fiddled with the smooth, delicate cloth before pulling it out and wrapping it around her deformed wrist, covering the fabric fused to her skin.

"That from Cross?" Caveat asked, pointing to her wrist.

She secured the ribbon and refused to answer. It was a gift from her younger brother, one of the few people in her early life she remembered fondly. She needed anything to liven her spirits, lest she fall into despair.

"I hate to be the one to tell you this," Caveat said, once again leaning in close. "But Victory is trying to steal your girl."

Geist held back a laugh. "What do you mean?"

"I mean, he sent Cross's family a marriage proposal. Her family denied him—surprisingly—but now everyone's been talking about how he's trying to steal her from you. I'd suggest you write to her family, but if they're denying men from House Hamilton, you *know* they're going to deny a family as obscure as House Weston. No offense, of course."

"Did anything else happen?" Geist asked, shutting her locker door.

"Tinker said you should pop Victory right good in the jaw. That's a little barbaric, if you want my tuppence-worth. They might discharge you for it, too."

Geist opened her mouth to speak but stopped the moment she spotted Big Wick lumber through the door. The gaunt Englishman trudged in with a knapsack and ammunition belt hung around his neck like a pair of deadweights. He let out a strained sigh as he threw his burden to the floor.

"Geist," Big Wick said, his voice the harsh rasp of a lifelong smoker. "Vergess has been asking about you."

"All right," Geist said. "Thank you."

Before Caveat could continue, Geist slipped from the room. She had heard enough. Rumors usually didn't hold her attention for too long, but Caveat's ramblings did indicate why Cross might be upset. Geist scoffed as she rounded the sharp corners of Fort Belleville and headed for the wall. Nothing wound her up quite like family politics.

I need to nip this in the bud before it gets out of control. I'll speak to Cross and straighten things out. But first, I need to shower. And then maybe I'll see Vergess. And I need to speak to Major Reese.

She cursed under her breath. *I'll drown in my own to-do list.*

Geist shook her head. Everything had to be put on hold.

Fort Belleville had a limited selection of showers that the enlisted men cycled through. Although she had used fort showers once or twice in the past, the overcrowding made it impossible without getting caught. Instead, Geist headed for the medical showers. Cross had given her a key to the facility, which was reserved exclusively for the nurses and Red Cross volunteers.

Geist jumped in the first one available, gritted her teeth through the icy water, and washed without a second's delay. Then she jumped out of the water, half-slipping on the concrete floor, and stumbled into the towel cabinet. She dried herself and pulled back on her clothes.

But she wasn't done.

Maintaining her disguise included a certain amount of façade. Geist exited the medical shower and headed for the washroom. Everyone had to shave—it was required for all enlisted men—and Geist couldn't avoid showing up for the routine, even if she could avoid being seen in the showers.

The washroom had rows of mirrors and sinks mounted to the wall, each smaller than anything found in a comfortable home. Straight razors and face soap sat in the dozens, provided free to the soldiers, waiting for soldiers who needed to trim their whiskers.

Geist took her position at the farthest station. *Act natural,* she told herself.

She had faked her way through shaving before, but not without cutting herself. The straight razors were kept sharp by the maintenance staff. *Too* sharp, in Geist's opinion.

She covered a brush in soap and painted it onto her cheeks, chin, and neck. It was all for show, but Geist enjoyed the way the soap felt on her face. It didn't last long, not with the mud of trenches, but the brief moments of cleanliness were worth the awkward dance of shaving hairs that weren't there.

Once her face was covered, Geist brought the straight razor up to her cheek and slid the blade around, cleaning off the soap in whatever zigzag of a line she could muster.

"Pathetic."

Geist locked up and turned her head. Vergess stood next to her, leaning against the wall with a sardonic expression, one eyebrow up, and crossed his arms over his muscular chest.

She looked around. The other men were too absorbed in their own shaving.

"What're you doing?" she asked under her breath.

"Watching you smear soap across your face."

Geist grew hot in the cheeks despite the cool presence of the soap. "No one's ever commented."

"They're being polite."

Stifling a laugh, Geist returned her attention to the mirror. "I haven't cut myself." She sheepishly added, "Today."

"You haven't learned yet?"

"My father didn't think it necessary to teach me," she quipped.

"I'll show you."

His declaration sent shiver's up Geist's spine. She refused to meet Vergess's eye on the off chance he could read her emotions. *He can probably smell it,* she sarcastically mused, but she still didn't want to risk it.

Vergess stepped up close and held out his hand. Geist placed the straight razor in his palm. To her surprise, he took her chin in the other hand and tilted her face up, forcing their gazes to meet. She was half-tempted to push him away—that was her tactic whenever the other soldiers got close—but Vergess already knew her secret.

Blood rushed to her cheeks as she stared into his hard, blue eyes. He had an intensity about him, even when doing something as mundane as shaving.

He placed the razor on the side of her face, the blade against her burning skin.

"You start below the ears and stoke down, slow and consistent."

Geist wanted to nod, but she couldn't. Instead, she focused on his set expression, on the angled lines of his masculine face.

"Hold the skin taut with your other hand. That's the key to a close shave. Let the blade do all the work."

His calm and instructional voice was pleasant. He sounded stern yet regal, like he was teaching a prince.

"Then you lather up a second time," he said as he grabbed a brush covered in soap. "And this time, you go against the grain."

Vergess reapplied the soap to her face, rinsed off the blade, and went to work yet again, shaving her already smooth skin as though there were whiskers to remove. Geist swallowed hard, enjoying the feeling of his rough hands against her chin. Although callous, he was never forceful with his touch.

"Lastly, you wash your face with cold water and aftershave, if you have it." He set the blade down and cocked an eyebrow. "Did you get all that?"

Geist felt over her smooth cheeks and nodded.

"Good." Vergess handed her the straight razor. "Then show me."

"Show you?"

"That's right. To see if you were paying attention."

She half-smiled. *I didn't know there would be a test.* With hesitant movements, Geist grabbed the brush and brought it close to her face. Vergess grabbed her wrist and shook his head.

"On me."

Geist blinked, expecting him to reveal his jest at any moment. He didn't. Instead, he grabbed a chair near the back wall and dragged it over to the sink. He sat down and tilted his chin up to expose his neck, a smirk clear on his face.

It wasn't uncommon for older soldiers to help the newer soldiers shave. And sometimes, with men who were missing fingers, or their injuries caused their hands to shake, the camaraderie was necessary. But Geist had never done anything similar, and the idea of touching Vergess's face made her palms sweaty.

My father would be furious, she thought with a smile.

She applied the soap, rinsed the straight razor, and placed the blade near his sideburns. With slow strokes, she removed the fine amount of stubble that lined his cheek and jaw. Geist's hand shook as she worked, her mind blank except for the occasional doubt.

She cleaned away the soap and then reapplied a second layer. He stared at her the entire process, his gaze locked on her expression—on the slight smile she couldn't stifle. The combination of nerves, excitement, and guilt affected her like heavy alcohol. She felt flushed and almost silly but happy to be experiencing the moment with Vergess.

She shaved against the grain, removing the last pepper flakes of a beard. When her task was complete, Geist ran her knuckles over the smooth jaw, enjoying the warmth of his skin.

"What's going on here?"

Geist whipped around at the sound of Tinker's voice. His face was set in equal parts bemusement and delight.

"Uh," Geist began, her mind grinding to a halt and speeding up again within seconds. "I was showing Vergess how to shave."

Tinker snapped his attention to Vergess. "You don't know how to shave? What kind of man are you?"

Vergess squared his shoulders but said nothing.

Tinker smacked him in the gut and chuckled. "You really didn't know how? *You?* Oh, I can't wait to tell the others." His chortling soon devolved into full-on laughter that echoed throughout the washroom. Others joined in, if only because of Tinker's manic declarations.

After sneaking a glance and catching Vergess's stern expression, Geist mouthed a quiet, "Sorry."

He gritted his teeth and narrowed his eyes, but otherwise kept silent.

She knew it would be frontline news for all the members of the Ethereal Squadron within a few short hours. Anything that wasn't war-related—and was even slightly happy—traveled faster than a flu in a schoolhouse.

"I have to go," Geist said. "Major Reese needs to see me."

She dashed for the door, still flushed from the encounter.

TEN

Operation Prometheus

Fort Belleville had open courtyards that separated the main facility from the walls by a good two hundred feet. The flat land beyond the walls, barren and stripped of trees, made for easy observation once up in one of the six watchtowers. The snipers at their posts regarded Geist with curt nods.

The northeastern watchtower greeted her with the cold chill of a building seldom ventured. Geist walked up the spiral staircase to the top landing, pushing through the burn of her muscles by the time she finished the last few steps.

Major Reese stood at the sniper window, staring down the scope of a rifle while the gunnery waited nearby. Geist saluted.

"Reporting, sir," she said.

"You never salute without your cap, son," Major Reese drawled. "Standing at attention is fine." He aimed with the rifle and fired. The crack of the weapon echoed outside of the tower, the kick barely affecting the major. With a frown, he handed the weapon back to the gunnery. "Your sight is faulty. Get down to the arms room and change out your rifle for something reliable."

The gunnery nodded. "Yes, sir." He stepped past Geist and made his way down the long, spiraling staircase.

Alone with the major, Geist kept her back straight. "You sent for me."

Major Reese stepped away from the window and paced the small, circular room, his gaze on the floor and his hands clasped together behind his back. His gut protruded more than normal, but he moved with a warrior's gait.

"Battery and Vergess informed me of your *frolic* into the enemy base."

Geist held her breath and waited.

"They said you came face-to-face with the GH Gas," he continued. "That you went looking for proof of your theory. They say you insisted on going behind enemy lines and broke into a German-occupied fort." He paused. "They also mentioned Albatross's death and the… what I'm going to call the *magi-tech* zeppelin that crashed behind enemy lines."

His tone barely concealed his anger, and Geist could understand. His orders had been to avoid the GH Gas at all costs. Entering an enemy fort was also a huge risk; getting caught could have been disastrous, especially considering the experimentations the Germans conducted on the French POWs. She braced herself for reprimand.

"I apologize for disobeying direct orders."

"Don't bother," Major Reese stated. He halted his pacing and turned to face her. "We both know I'm the one who needs to do the apologizing."

"Sir?"

"You were right about what you suspected. I should've listened to you. You were the only one to see the GH Gas in action. I had no basis to doubt you."

Geist narrowed her eyes and met Major Reese's gaze straight on, relieved he saw things how they were. "What're we going to do about this, sir? It's like nothing I've ever seen before."

"It's like nothing *I've* ever seen, either," he replied with a long sigh. "The fact of the matter is that the Central Powers have the upper hand. The potential of this new *magi-tech* puts them leagues above our own might. Add to that the fact that the Russian Empire is slowly collapsing from within means that Eastern Front may vanish, and *soon*, leaving the Germans and the Austrians to turn their full might on the Triple Entente. France is only hanging on by a thread."

"Then I'm willing to do whatever it takes to stop them."

"I'm glad to hear that, son. That's why I'm ordering the formation of a special team to infiltrate the German frontline command and bring back the blueprints for magi-tech inventions. This operation—*Operation Prometheus*—is our play to even the odds. If we have magi-tech of our own, we can fight fire with fire and hopefully defeat Germany and Austria-Hungary once and for all."

Geist nodded. "I heard you sent for a sorcerer from the Middle Eastern Theater."

"Dreamer's unparalleled in their schools of magic. We need the best of the best."

She took in a deep breath, honored that the major would consider her good enough to be one of the best. "I'll join the team proudly, sir."

"Oh, Geist," Major Reese said with a chortle, stroking his short, peppered beard. "You're not going to serve on the team. You're going to *lead* it."

"Me?" she asked, letting her voice slip into something more feminine than she would have liked. She cleared her throat and continued, "Sir, I—"

"Your initiative got us this information," he stated. "And you've proven resourceful in every mission you've ever been on. Your record speaks for itself."

My success record? The one written in the blood of my teammates?

Geist gritted her teeth. "Sir, with all due respect, I think you might be making a mistake. I've never led an operation before."

"You've never submitted yourself for a leadership role."

"I'm not looking for prestige."

"The best leaders never are."

"I've only been in the military for a *year*," she retorted, doubt welling within her. "I didn't even know that I shouldn't salute without my cap. I'm not experienced enough."

"This isn't a test of what you know," the Major replied. "When you become a leader, you give up thinking of yourself. If you don't know something, you ask the man who *does*. The *team* succeeds or fails—no one individual or another."

"I wasn't strong enough to protect the other members of my team. You should have Victory lead the operation. He never fails. He can see the future, for fuck's—" Geist stopped herself cold, "—er, pardon my language. Sir."

Major Reese folded his arms across his chest and exhaled. For a moment he said nothing, allowing his gaze to settle on the floor. A cool breeze swept between them.

"Victory will be the man I turn to if you're adamant in your refusal," he said. "But I wanted you in charge for the very reason that you *have* lost teammates."

"What do you mean?"

"This operation is a thousand times more dangerous than anything I've ever assigned before. Victory's future sight isn't flawless, and sometimes I fear it may lead to disaster. He's never lost before. What if someone dies on his watch and he can't handle it?"

"You think *I'm* handling it well?" *I sure as fuck don't.*

"You know the weight of failure. He doesn't. And you've already proven you're still willing to take risks for the greater good. *Think,* Charles. You could've ordered your men to retreat to safety the moment the zeppelin crashed, but you pressed forward regardless. You got us vital information, while keeping two other men alive."

Geist remained quiet. Major Reese took advantage of her silence.

"Charles," he said. "Take the rest of the day. Tomorrow I'm breaking the men into two teams—one to attack Fort Douaumont, the enemy base of experiments, and the other to infiltrate the German frontline command and steal the magi-tech information for ourselves. I need to know your answer before then so that I can plan accordingly."

Geist replied with a single nod.

"You're dismissed, soldier."

ELEVEN

Team Assignment

"Victory wants to marry me," Cross said.

Geist listened without speaking as she downed a swig of pale-red brandy from a dented tin can. The evening winds were quiet.

"He sent word to my family, but my parents wouldn't allow it," Cross continued. "They want me to stay with House Moreau."

Tiny points of light sprinkled the tall grass surrounding Fort Belleville like flickering stars dotting the night sky. Geist had never seen so many glow worms in one location, nor had she seen them so close. Back home, she had chased fireflies as a girl, and the field of glittering lights brought back pleasant memories. She stroked the ribbon on her wrist, and for the first time since she had left, a twinge of homesickness struck her.

"Do you want to marry Victory?" Geist asked, pushing the urges from her mind and steering the conversation away from the depressing.

Cross leaned back against the shattered trunk of an oak tree and sighed a wistful sigh. "Have you ever felt your heart flutter, Florence? Felt your pulse quicken when you get close to somebody else?"

Maybe. Hard to tell sometimes.

"Of course not," she forced herself to say. "I'm a soldier. I can't entertain such thoughts."

Cross smiled. "It's intoxicating. Nothing like it in the world, nothing at all." She closed her eyes and spoke as though lost in thought. "When we're together, time passes too quickly. When he meets my gaze, I feel dizzy. When he grazes my cheek…" Cross chuckled. "I lose my train of thought."

"Sounds like an illness," Geist quipped.

Cross laughed. "Maybe it is."

"I should probably avoid it."

"Love transforms even the wisest of men into fools."

"You're not convincing me it's a good thing."

Cross opened her eyes, her smile widening. "Explaining the joy of love to someone who has never experienced it is like explaining faith to the faithless. You'll always sound crazy."

"Heh," Geist said with a smirk. "What's so great about Victory, anyway?"

"He's a gentleman through and through," Cross replied, blushing. "I've never met a man who understands me so well or who takes my words to heart so closely. I would be honored to have him as a husband and to be called his wife."

Geist finished her drink and snorted. "Then why listen to your family? Just do it. I mean, *look at me*. I defied my family. They wanted me to get married—but here I am."

"I won't abandon my family. Besides, I've got work that needs doing here. The war comes before my own personal pleasures."

Geist nodded along with the words. "If Victory is so in love with you, why not ask *him* to elope?" she asked.

"Victory has responsibilities beyond his position," Cross stated, turning away. "You know that. We all know that. He's heir apparent to House Hamilton, he's an older brother to seven siblings, and he's second-in-command here in Verdun. Just as I can't leave my post for love, neither can he. And I would never ask him to."

Geist tied the tin cup to her belt. *What's Cross saying? That running from your family is selfish? That the responsible-minded would never do that? Is duty really more important than freedom?*

Cross turned and gave the Geist the once-over. "What's wrong?"

"I… I'm just lost in thought."

"Are you going to accept the commander's assignment?"

"I can't. It wouldn't be right."

"Why not?"

"I'm lying to them," Geist stated, her tone heated. "All of them. They don't even know me. They don't even know what I am." She ran her hands through her hair, dragging her nails across her scalp. "I'm supposed to lead them? They're supposed to trust me when I can't trust them?" Geist closed her eyes.

Cross's words echoed in her mind. *I ran from my family. I ran from responsibility. Is that really what a leader is? A liar? A deserter? If the commander knew… if he had any idea…*

"Don't you fight alongside them?" Cross asked.

"Of course."

"And you'd give your life for the fight if absolutely necessary?"

"I get it," Geist snapped. "This is different."

"Is it? You're made by your actions, not circumstances beyond your control. The others know that. They trust you, or else they wouldn't stand beside you."

"That doesn't change the fact that I'm lying."

Cross folded her arms tightly across her body and shuddered as the wind howled past.

"Then deny the commander's request."

"I will."

"Perhaps it's for the best." Cross fell silent.

Geist gritted her teeth and glared at the moonlit dirt road. She could hear all of Cross's unspoken words. *Then perhaps you're not suited to lead,* Cross was saying. *You're more concerned about what people think of you than you are the team. You're selfish.*

Geist hung her head and fought back tears. *Why am I crying?* she thought with a forced laugh. *Why am I so afraid?*

But the images of fire and gas and corpses swirled in her mind. Watching her new teammates die—knowing it could be her fault—it burned and frightened her. More than running from her home. More than her father. More than her own inevitable death…

"What if…" Geist began, her voice quavering. "What if I fail them?"

"Now you're thinking like a leader," Cross said. She walked over and placed a tender hand on Geist's tense shoulder.

"What if it's my fault the others die? This isn't just another mission. It's *the* mission. It's more important than any other—the commander said so himself. What if—"

"What if they need you?"

"They *don't* need me," Geist said, jerking out of Cross's grasp. "They have Victory."

Cross lowered her voice to a whisper and said, "He told me once that… he sees his own death in his visions."

"W-what?" Geist asked, turning her gaze to meet Cross's.

"Victory. When he uses his magic, he sees the future. He told me he sees branching paths and, in some, he sees his own death." Cross chuckled, her eyes becoming vacant as her thoughts drifted inward. "He told me it weighs on him. That sometimes he thinks… he might be forced to pick the path that results in his own death, all for the greater good… or worse yet, that he may have to choose the deaths of his brothers. It's a heavy burden."

"I didn't know," Geist murmured. "He's never explained his magic to me before."

"Everyone has their demons, Florence. Do you really think yours are so unique that you cannot shoulder the mantle of responsibility?"

Geist caught her breath and stepped back. Cross's words hurt—but they were true. She ran a hand over her face and steeled herself. Joining the Ethereal Squadron had been difficult, and Geist had never thought it would go so far, but she was already in so deep. There was no turning back.

Geist exhaled. "Cross… Thank you."

Brushing her blonde hair aside, Cross smiled. "We've been out too late. The others are sure to question our absence. We should return to the barracks."

THE ETHEREAL SQUADRON at Verdun had shrunk in the past few weeks. They had once been a force of twenty, but Geist only counted thirteen, including herself, as she walked into the commander's office. The tiny tactical room of Fort Belleville made it easy to identify everyone but difficult to breathe. The stifling atmosphere got everyone agitated.

Battery stood among his brothers, Victory and Blick, but his attention had been fixated on the door. The moment he spotted Geist, he broke away and crossed the room, ignoring all others. Geist turned away and veered off to the corner. Tinker and Caveat had claimed the space, but they stepped aside to allow her room.

"Geist," Battery said as he approached. "I've been searching since yesterday for you."

She crossed her arms. "What is it?"

"I need to speak with you."

"We're speaking now."

Battery darted his gaze to Tinker and back. "In private."

"Sure," she said, forcing a casual tone.

When Battery didn't leave, Geist lifted an eyebrow. He gestured to the door. *I guess he means now.* Reluctantly, Geist followed Battery out of the room and stopped just outside the door.

Battery, confused, turned around a few feet away and then walked back. When he realized she wasn't going any farther, he lowered and his voice and asked, "Geist, what happened yesterday?"

Geist wanted to ask what he meant, but the look on Battery's face stopped her cold. His expression told her now wasn't the time to joke—he was worried about her stay in the infirmary. On the other hand, she knew she could never tell him the truth, trapping her in a silent conundrum.

"You don't have to keep anything from me," he said. "I mean, you already know about *my* alteration."

"Alteration?" Geist repeated.

"The opals in my back. To help me focus. I don't like calling it an operation. What I'm trying to say is, why can't you trust me to know you've been altered as well?"

Geist held her breath. *The scars on his back. He thinks I have the same thing.* Her silence only served to anger him.

Battery glared. "I know Cross is lying to me. I know you're not suffering any *lasting damage.* I empowered her healing sorcery. Why bother with this charade? I'm not like Tinker. I'm not going to spread rumors."

"But—"

"Here's what I know," he interjected. "You keep to yourself. You only let Cross see you undressed. You didn't want anyone touching you. And, just like me, you're on the, well, smaller side." He huffed and turned away. "But not too small. Just… smaller."

Damn. Vergess was right. I do need to be more careful with my disguise.

"I get it." Geist sighed. "And you're right. You figured me out."

"*Really?*" Battery half-gasped as he whipped his attention back to her. "I knew it! Why didn't you just tell me back when we were in the enemy fort?"

"I'm embarrassed about it," she said, hating herself for every second of her alternate lie. *God, nothing I say to them is ever the truth. I hope I'm not making a mistake.*

Battery exhaled and then laughed, a visible relief washing over him. "I'm so glad you told me. I thought I was the only one in the entire squadron. I know this'll sound crazy, but… I dreaded being the only one. Like it would somehow prove I was lesser than everyone else. That I needed help—that I'd never be as competent or as accepted by the others."

Like being the only woman among men?

"But everyone here likes you," Battery continued. "Which proves the alteration isn't a handicap—if anything, it's more of an enhancement. I can be a sorcerer of the Ethereal Squadron just like any other man here. You agree, don't you?"

"Of course."

"And," he said, holding his head high and buffing his fingernails over the chest of his tunic, "not that I want to toot my own horn, but I did figure everything out through deductive reasoning."

"You're a regular Sherlock Homes," Geist drawled, restraining the urge to roll her eyes.

Like an untied balloon, Battery deflated. With a deep frown, he said, "Ha-ha. I get it. You want me to stop."

She slapped him playfully on the shoulder. "Where's the fun in that?"

In the quiet moment that followed, Geist felt a sudden camaraderie with Battery. Even if he wasn't in the same situation as she was, it was close enough. Her worries and concerns didn't feel so alienating, not when someone else was going through something similar.

And it struck her then—Vergess was in almost the same position. The only German defector. Different from the rest and hiding it. They were a trio of secret misfits. And Geist was the thread that bound them together.

Funny how people are more similar than they realize.

Geist glanced over Battery's shoulder and jumped to attention as Major Reese turned into the hallway. She saluted and Battery turned on his heel to do the same.

"Sir," she said.

A strange man followed Major Reese, but Geist didn't give them much of her attention. The commander motioned to the meeting room door. Geist and Battery went in first and reassumed their positions in separate corners.

The newcomer followed Major Reese into the room and stood at attention in front of his desk. Everyone fell silent. Geist couldn't help but stare. *Is he the specialist?*

"Gentlemen," Major Reese said, waving smoke from his face. "We haven't the time for pleasantries. I'm going to cut straight to the chase."

The murmur of conversation swirled around the room for a moment before each sorcerer gave Major Reese their full attention.

He held his hands behind his back. "This man here will help us with our current operations, all the way from the Middle Eastern Theater. Welcome Agent Oliver Evans, codename Dreamer."

Geist kept staring. He stood almost impossibly tall, his shoulders and back straight, his British uniform crisp and neat.

"It is a pleasure to work with the men of Verdun," Dreamer said, speaking the Queen's English so precisely, one could mistake him for royalty. "I look forward to the assignment."

"I heard this guy was Arab," someone whispered behind Geist.

"Doesn't look Arab to me," answered somebody else.

Dreamer's hair, sandy-blond and thin, was leagues from the black and dark brown most Arabic men possessed. And he had the pale skin of an Irishman or North Englishman. Even Vergess's skin was darker, a color he had earned from hours out under cloudless skies.

But although Dreamer's articulation and word choice reflected English high society, the dialect of his speech indicated English was not his first language. The Arabic tint to his pronunciation still shone through.

"These are dire times," Major Reese said, shaking his head. "The GH Gas is something far more sinister than I thought we would ever encounter. We have no counter for it—not gasmasks, not suits, not anti-agents—and its lethal touch spreads like wildfire.

"But the gas is just a symptom of something much more pressing. The enemy has magical technology and we don't. They have a terrible advantage. And now we have two important objectives. Everyone is to aid in these operations—you're to give everything you can to their success. I can't stress enough how the fate of France, perhaps even the Triple Entente, rests in your hands."

His grave tone and unsteady voice got everyone in the room shifting their weight. Even Geist turned and watched the commander choose his words wisely, knowing full well his mood would spread to every man in the room.

Major Reese continued. "First, the majority of you will be attacking Fort Douaumont, the enemy base of experimentation and research. Your goal is to stop them at whatever costs necessary. We cannot have the enemy using their magi-tech on the frontlines any longer."

He took a moment before resuming his speech, his gaze downcast and set on the desk in front of him. "Second, a small handful of you will be infiltrating the *Oberste Heeresleitung*—the German frontline command known as the OHL—in the center of Spa, Belgium. You will retrieve the secret of magi-tech and deliver it to our headquarters here."

"Bruno," Major Reese said, turning to face the sorcerer leaning against the far wall. "You will lead the attack of Fort Douaumont. Tinker will act as your advisor."

"Yes, sir," both Bruno and Tinker replied in unison. Tinker's exuberance and excitement laced his words. Geist hoped he knew what he was getting into.

Turning to each man he mentioned, Major Reese said, "Caveat, Trilogy, Big Wick, Gunner, Foolhardy, Quake, Vergess, Dirk—you all will make up the attack team. I'm counting on you to bring Fort Douaumont back under French control."

All eight men answered the statement with confidence, but Geist still couldn't shake her doubts. The GH Gas could made quick work of talented men. The thought of all of them never returning got her restless.

"Geist," Major Reese said, bringing his gaze to bear upon her. "You will lead Operation Prometheus. Victory will act as your advisor. Blick, Battery, and Dreamer will make up your team."

"Yes, sir," Geist replied. The only one to reply. Her single voice was followed by a strained hush. Several men glanced over to Victory and then back to Geist.

"*Sir?*" Victory asked, his tone saying everything.

"I've made my decision," Major Reese stated. "It's for the best. Geist has shown remarkable initiative when concerning this magi-tech. We'll need that dedication for the operation to succeed. Everyone part of the Fort Douaumont offensive should head to the arms room for further intelligence and resupplying. You'll be joining the French military in the offensive. You're dismissed."

Vergess gave Geist an odd look before he disappeared into the hall, maintaining his cold manner. Geist watched him go. Vergess had proven himself time and time again to be devastating in combat. Victory, Blick, and Battery weren't even in the same league, and by the looks of Dreamer's dandy posture, Geist assumed he wouldn't be, either.

Tinker slapped Geist on the shoulder as he walked by.

"Good luck," he said under his breath.

With silent nods, the last few sorcerers exited the cramped tactical room, leaving Major Reese, Geist, Victory, Blick, Battery, and Dreamer as the only ones remaining.

The smoke and heat didn't feel quite as oppressive afterward. Geist allowed herself space to breathe and rotated her shoulders to relax.

Before Major Reese said anything about the mission, Blick turned to face Dreamer. "So, you're an Arab, right?"

Dreamer didn't seem to mind. He smiled and replied, "I was, indeed, born in Diriyah."

"You don't look it."

"That's what they keep telling me."

Blick smirked. "Mind if I…" He motioned to his golden eyes and then to Dreamer. "have a look? I see through all sorcery, no matter how strong."

"Blick!" Victory barked. "Now isn't the time."

The word *blick* meant *look* or *sight,* and Geist knew the codename fully explained Blick's abilities. Not only could he see through illusions, but her notes on his magic included heightened sight in *all* regards, which would always be useful for surveillance missions.

However, it was considered a most heinous intrusion among sorcerers to use magic against another, even if the effect was harmless. Asking to use a certain school of magic without first getting consent could be taken as impolite at best—or a threat at worst. Geist sighed. They already had enough trouble between Vergess and Battery; they didn't need to make enemies of Dreamer as well.

"Geist," Major Reese said, motioning her forward. "You and your team will be heading to Germany-occupied Belgium."

She stepped up to his desk and nodded.

"You can't cross the frontlines," he continued. "Instead, you'll be taking the train to the port city, Le Havre. From there you'll be meeting with American shippers who will deliver you to Belgium."

"I understand, sir."

"All information, money, and field codes will be given to you within the next ten hours. Your destination is the German frontline command compound, the OHL. It was mapped out months ago during a recon mission by our boys up north. You'll need that intelligence to navigate your way through the myriad of buildings.

"I hate to be so grim, but if you fail, the Central Powers are sure to advance the timetable of their New Schieffen Plan and Paris will fall, and we'll likely drown in GH Gas. You're the best we've got for the mission. I can't send a backup team, not with the few sorcerers here in Verdun. Getting Dreamer was the best I could do, and even then I had to fight to get him.

"I've put all my eggs in one basket, but I'm banking on it being one damn amazing basket, *do you understand me*, gentlemen?"

They nodded somberly.

Major Reese focused his gaze on Geist. She straightened under his scrutiny.

"Victory will help you strategize, Blick is for counterintelligence, Dreamer will help you infiltrate the compound, and Battery is there to empower you. Your team needs to be sleek and efficient, but is there anyone else you think you would need to complete your objective?"

"Yes," she said. "I need Cross."

"What?" Major Reese balked. "Cross? Our Matron-in-Chief?"

Victory narrowed his eyes, his jaw tight, but otherwise, he said nothing.

Geist nodded. "Yes, sir."

"Impossible. She can't go on this mission."

"Sir, you said the mission was paramount. That it was—"

"Belgium is a hellhole, son," Major Reese said, cutting her off. "The Germans' losses in Calais have prevented them from moving west. They've taken their frustrations out on the Belgium women and killed most of the able-bodied men in the surrounding cities."

Geist gritted her teeth. She *had* heard of the horrors of the German-occupied territories. *The Rape of Belgium,* some called it.

Resistance groups had sprung up in opposition to such brutality, but they didn't stand a chance against Germany's military might.

"If you're caught, you'll be taken to a POW camp," Major Reese said. "But Cross… Well, let's just say, they won't be gentlemen to a captive woman."

Geist ran a nervous hand over the back of her neck. After a moment of thought, she said, "Then Cross should be part of the offensive against Fort Douaumont."

"Why are you so insistent on her participation?"

"She's a talented sorcerer," Geist blurted out. "If these are the turning point missions of the war, we need everyone we can get. Cross is more than willing to be part of the frontline. She may even make the difference between success and defeat."

Major Reese seemed to consider this. Blick, Battery, and Dreamer exchanged confused glances, but Victory took the moment to interject.

"I think it's a good idea," he said. "Cross has proven herself steadfast in the face of danger. She's just as talented, if not more so, than the majority of the medics."

Geist restrained herself from smiling. Cross was right. He *did* take her wishes to heart. A small piece of Geist feared that Victory would have asked for Cross to be kept out of harm's way, but it was clear she'd underestimated him. Cross had wanted to travel with the medics to the frontlines for a long time. There was no better way of stopping the dangers of the GH Gas and enemy magi-tech than with her amazing sorcery.

"Very well," Major Reese said. "I'll assign Cross to the offensive. Anything else you want to say?"

Geist nodded. "I also need Vergess."

Victory didn't chime in this time. He, Blick, and Battery exchanged small glances. Dreamer, on the other hand, perked up and leaned in closer.

"Vergess is a German defector," Major Reese declared.

"I knew it," Battery muttered. "I *knew* it…"

"We all knew," Blick drawled. "You can't hide that sort of thing for long."

Geist shook her head. "He helped me through Fort Douaumont. It's not fair to treat him like—"

Major Reese held up a hand. "That's true, but Vergess was once an Abomination Soldier, and one of the Kaiser's Guard, to boot. He may be recognized."

THE REVELATION of Vergess's past twisted in Geist's stomach. She hated that they judged him, especially since her own past was filled with so many lies.

"Perhaps Vergess can't hide his heritage," Dreamer interjected, smiling. "But I can. That's why I was brought in, correct?" He twisted his hand in the air and a white glove formed across his fingers, the display of sorcery chilling the room. "He won't be recognized under my watch."

"Commander," Geist said, "Vergess is a valuable asset. Our team currently doesn't have much firepower, and Vergess can fill that role. If you trust Dreamer's abilities, there shouldn't be a reason to hesitate. This mission is too important."

She turned to Battery hopefully. Battery looked at Victory, then back to Geist with a furrowed brow and gritted teeth. He said nothing, and his gaze went to the floor.

Fine. I'll convince Major Reese myself.

"We need someone who can think like an Abomination Soldier," Geist insisted. "Vergess worked for the Kaiser. He knows their movements inside and out."

"You're right," Major Reese replied. "Vergess would know the ins and outs of the German High Command, but it would only take one slipup to compromise the entire operation. Are you willing to risk that? To risk the whole war?"

The weight of the question hit Geist the moment Major Reese uttered it. The others in the team were certain. They wouldn't risk that much—not for Vergess, not even for her. But Geist had seen how Vergess handled himself behind enemy lines. And when she had asked him to keep her secret—when she had been falling unconscious on the French countryside—he had been the one to bring her back and keep her safe.

But if I'm wrong…

Geist set her jaw.

"I think Vergess's information is invaluable at this point," she said. "We need him on the team. It would be a mistake to leave him."

"Very well, son," Major Reese said. "I'll inform Vergess. You have your team."

TWELVE

Train Tickets

E ven far from the western front, war left scars across the land. Geist had seen it all a million times. Shy citizens hid in their homes, fields lay barren, and the wreckage from air raids could be seen from miles away. But the trains still ran, delivering soldiers, mail, and travelers all across France, fighting or no fighting.

Geist laced up her boots, her mind preoccupied with distant worries. The white noise of commotion filled the station platform. All manner of people, no matter their social standing, used the trains for travel. She blended with the patient citizens, wearing casual slacks, an undershirt, a button-up shirt, and a frockcoat. A regular gentleman.

The commander didn't want the members of Prometheus dressed as soldiers. No one could know the purpose of their journey. Their instructions included destroying all preparation paperwork before they entered Belgium—a contingency should they be discovered.

Geist stood and smoothed her clothes. Without the heavy tunic of her uniform, she felt vulnerable, but the long frockcoat helped her relax. No one would see her curves under the thick fabric, two shirts, and Cross's wrappings.

With a small rucksack slung over one shoulder, Victory walked through the crowd to stand by Geist's side. He wore similar clothing, but unlike Geist, everything fit him well. *Too* well. Tall, muscular, commanding—his pinstripe vest and dark coat enhanced his already dapper appearance. She stole glances from time to time, though guilt hounded her thoughts. *I need to stay focused.* Ever since Vergess had teased her about shaving, her thoughts had gotten all muddled.

Or maybe this is Cross's doing. She speaks of Victory like a princess speaks of a knight.

Victory's quiet confidence allured even passing women. They smiled and nodded, slowing for lingering looks once they caught sight of him.

For a prolonged moment, Geist allowed herself to think of life after the war—building a home, finding a husband, making a family. Outside of dying, she'd either be dishonorably discharged or ending her service still disguised as a man. In either scenario, it wasn't likely that a man would find her desirable—especially a man like Victory, who stood as though the blood of kings flowed through his veins. He could have any woman he wanted. Cross was a lucky woman.

Victory glanced over. Geist flicked her gaze off into the crowd, hoping the man wouldn't confront her.

"Geist," he said.

She tensed. "Yes?"

"I've been meaning to thank you for bringing Battery back alive."

"Ah. Right. Of course."

"I also need to thank you for nominating Cross to take part in the offensive."

Geist could feel her stress waning. "It's what she's been asking for."

"You spend a lot of time with her."

"Yeah."

"Don't."

She'd dreaded this conversation. There couldn't be rifts between teammates, especially her, the team leader. If Victory thought they were fighting over a woman…

"Look," she said. "You've got nothing to worry about. I'm not after Cross."

Victory sighed. "She told me that there's nothing between you. I believe her. This isn't about that."

"What's it about then?"

"This is about how your actions reflect on her."

"What're you talking about?"

"I know you've never had to worry about your chastity, but it's different for women. When you associate with her late at night, outside the walls of the fort, you're igniting rumors. It might be all fun and games for you, but the mere hint of impropriety could have her discharged."

Geist turned away. Victory was right, and she hated herself for not realizing it sooner.

"I've reassured Major Reese the rumors are groundless," Victory said. "Just keep it in mind. For her sake."

As the train screeched into the station, Geist found herself lost in thought once more. Victory hadn't even raised his voice.

I can't believe the commander thought I would do a better job at running the operation.

Victory must sense it, too.

The blue, red, and white of the French flag waved in the wind and smoke as the train's passengers filed out onto the already packed station. The smell of sweat and coal blanketed the area with a nauseating thickness.

Geist lifted her gaze to meet Victory's. "Do you resent me for being the one in command?" she asked.

"No," he replied. "I understand the commander's concern. I've told him about my sorcery… He's been nervous about relying too heavily on it in the past. I saw Battery's death when he left with you for the zeppelin. I thought it was inevitable. I hadn't even considered Albatross."

"I see," she said.

"Don't worry about me. Keep your focus on the operation, and the others will fall into line." Geist breathed a sigh of relief. Battery had said that his older brother always said the right thing. *It's his sorcery,* Geist reasoned, almost laughing at herself. *It must be. Does he glance into the future just to make hard conversations easier?* She shook her head. *Why not?*

"Besides," he continued, "whenever you need to step down, I'll be waiting."

Could he see when that happened as well?

Blick and Battery made their way through the crowd. Battery's rucksack, twice as large as the others', hung heavy on his shoulders. At a glance, Geist could have mistaken him for a high school student or college freshman—his outfit pressed and fresh, laboring under a load of books and homework. Blick, on the other hand, had a small bag and relaxed posture. His coat was open, his vest unbuttoned, and his dusty brown hair, though combed, swayed in the breeze.

"Pack enough there, did you?" Geist quipped, motioning to Battery's rucksack.

Battery huffed. "As far as I'm concerned, I'm the only one taking this assignment seriously."

"What car are we traveling in?" Blick asked, ignoring his younger brother.

Geist withdrew the tickets from her pocket and passed them over. Blick gave them one quick glance and rolled his eyes.

"Coach? That won't do."

"We're not spending extra money on luxury accommodations," Geist stated. "We've slept in barracks and camped in trenches for days at a time. What're you complaining about?"

"It's *because* we've been out in the fields for so long that we *should* be staying in a luxury car." Blick turned to Victory and smiled wide. "C'mon, brother. Get us into the luxury car. I know you can."

Victory shoved his hands into his pockets. "I won't use my sorcery for that. And we don't need a first-class car, anyhow."

"We'll have more privacy to discuss tactics," Blick replied with surprising quickness.

For a long moment, Victory remained silent. Blick shoved his shoulder, grinning wide, and finally his brother smiled too.

"Ugh… Very well," Victory groaned.

He closed his eyes and exhaled, feigning defeat. Geist straightened herself as the chill of magic filtered onto the train station platform. Faster than she had expected, Victory opened his eyes and motioned Blick close.

The two brothers walked over to the far brick wall of the platform. Victory guided Blick until his back was against the wall and his small bag next to his feet, almost as if Victory were getting his brother ready for a photograph. Once satisfied with his position, Victory placed all six train tickets inside Blick's vest breast pocket. He took several steps back and waited.

Battery turned to Geist with a look of mild annoyance. "They were awful as kids. You should've seen what they pulled on Mum and Dad. They always got their way."

"What's going to happen?" Geist asked, never taking her eyes off Blick.

"I don't know. Something ludicrous, no doubt."

Almost as soon as the words left Battery's month, a train attendant exited a nearby ticket booth to assist an elderly couple with their luggage. It was clear to Geist the couple was moving—to escape the war, she figured—as their trunks were stuffed to the brim and both husband and wife were carrying a half-dozen parcels each in their arms.

The train attendant hefted a bag and stumbled backward from the unexpected weight, bumping straight into Blick at just the right angle to lose his balance. Flailing about, the attendant fell, throwing the trunk onto the cement of the railway platform. It burst open, slinging knickknacks across the concrete, including an elegant glass oil lamp, which shattered upon impact, sending a fountain of oil splashing up onto Blick's slacks and coat.

"I'm so sorry, *monsieur*," the attendant stammered out in hurried French. "Forgive me, forgive me!"

The elderly couple shook their heads and attempted to gather their scattered belongings. Blick stopped them with a wave of his hand and took up the task in their stead. The attendant muttered apology after apology as he gathered an armful of items.

"It was a complete accident," he said. "I should have been paying more attention. I will pay for any broken possessions."

Victory walked up to the scene, feigning disbelief. "Brother," he said, his French perfect and clear. "What happened? Your coat is ruined."

Blick reached up with oil-covered hands and examined his clothing. The oil stains dappled everything. Either out of curiosity or worry, Blick reached into his breast pocket and pulled out the train tickets. Oil had soaked through the thin fabric of his vest, destroying the tickets entirely.

"Those were so we can get home," Victory continued in a scolding tone. "Mother has prepared our homecoming. Now what will we tell her? We're stuck on the frontlines until her *coxcomb* of a son can find new tickets?"

"You're soldiers?" the attendant asked, wide-eyed. "Veterans? Home from the war? How rude of me." The man continued to berate himself as he finished gathering the scattered materials. Once finished, he brushed off Blick and snatched the oily tickets out of his hand. "I will fix this matter immediately. Wait here, wait here." He hurried away into the ticket office, his face red.

The old woman, thin and wan, bowed her head to Blick, careful to keep her wide-brimmed hat in place. "Thank you for your service, young man."

Her husband, hunched at the back, straightened his suspenders and nodded in agreement. "You're doing a great deed."

"It's my honor," Blick replied, effortlessly lifting two of their trunks by the metal handle. "Where do you need these?" He was broader-shouldered than his two brothers—not as tall as Victory, but close enough—and he made lifting the trunks seemed almost effortless.

The couple pointed to the luggage car. Blick and Victory packed away each trunk without incident before the attendant could return. The woman thanked Blick with a hug and a peck on the cheek. The man gave Victory a firm shake of the hand. Together, the couple entered the train with the hundreds of other citizens looking to get to the coast.

"Excuse me, sirs," the attendant said as he exited the office.

"Please accept these front car tickets as an apology. Decauville Railways appreciates your sacrifice."

Geist had observed the entire exchange without getting involved, curious to see how it would play out. Battery, who had given the incident fleeting, disgusted glances, rolled his eyes.

"Did you see that?" he asked with a snort.

She nodded. "Yeah. Clever."

"*Clever?* Ha! You wouldn't say a man cheating at poker was *clever*. You'd call him what he was. And my brother's no better. He cheats at life. It gets insufferable at times."

"Is that so?"

"How do you ever know if he's being genuine?" Battery asked, indignant. He crossed his arms tightly over his chest. "Maybe he's only doing and saying things because he knows it's the best course of action for dealing with you. You never know."

Geist didn't know how she felt.

Victory and Blick returned to Geist's side, Blick flashing the tickets with a confident smile. He handed them over and patted Geist on the arm, splotching oil onto her coat.

"I'm impressed," Geist said, rubbing her arm. "But why not use that magic to win the war?"

"That's what I'm doing," Victory said with chuckle.

She smirked. "I mean, why don't you tell us how this operation will turn out?"

"It just doesn't work that way. I can't see that far."

"How far can you see?"

Victory glanced around. "Imagine it like your own sight. Things up close are clear and obvious. Asking me to see the end of the war is like asking me to read a street sign in the next city over." He motioned down the train tracks to the distant wispy shadows of a town stationed on the horizon. "Everything is all too blurry. Besides, the future isn't written in stone. The more possibilities there are, the harder it is to concentrate on just one outcome."

"Interesting," Geist murmured.

Battery rolled his eyes but remained silent.

"Where are our foreign teammates?" Blick asked, panning his gaze over the crowded station. "The train is half full already."

Sure enough, when Geist returned her attention to the station, she took note of the many passengers cramming themselves into the cars. The back cars were already jampacked—no seats, no boxes, no wasted space—while the front cars accommodated wealthier travelers with tables, cushions, and fine china. The hospital car, separating the low-class from the high, sat in the middle.

Geist spotted Vergess and Dreamer by the weighing scales, a short distance from the train doors and only a hundred feet from her position. "What do you mean, *foreign teammates?*" she asked, careful to keep her voice down so that Vergess and Dreamer wouldn't hear. "Are you saying that because Dreamer is an Arab?"

Blick lifted an eyebrow. "And because Vergess is German."

"Enough," Geist stated. "I'm sick of you bringing this up."

"Why? It's true."

"Listen. As my first order as team leader, I say we drop this nonsense about Vergess. Mentioning it only breeds distrust, and I won't have it. He's American now. End of story."

"Don't you want to know more about his past in Germany?" Victory asked.

Geist straightened her posture and stole a quick glance at Vergess. His blue eyes were set on the scales as he helped Dreamer finish the last of his luggage check.

"What do you know?" she asked.

"His American name is William Black, but he's actually a sorcerer from House Richter," Victory said, his voice low but clear enough to be heard through the clamor of the station. "His German given name is *Wilhelm* Richter, and he trained with the Kaiser and his guard since age ten.

"Nine years ago, he was a special agent and officer fighting the Serbians under control of Austria-Hungary. He was a death agent. A man sent in to kill enemy sorcerers. He's killed dozens of Ethereal Squadron soldiers."

Blick nodded. "Tell Geist how."

Victory took in a deep breath. "He manipulated them.

Pretending to defect until he was close enough to kill them. He was even responsible for murdering some of the Black Hand—the Serbian resistance force."

"How do you know all this?" Geist asked. The paperwork the commander had shared with her had had the names of her teammates, and information on their past operations, but it hadn't had their life stories.

"Word gets around the elite sorcerer families," Victory replied. "Most of the European families mingle at the Paris soirées. House Richter comes up more often than you'd believe."

Geist held her tongue. She'd attended several such soirées herself with her family. She'd heard the rumors, too, about how House Richter had served the Kaiser faithfully since Germany's formation. But beyond the rumors, she had remained in the dark. Political posturing, social gossip—that was her father's world, not hers.

"Still," Geist countered. "There's no need for fearmongering. Major Reese knows all of this too, right?"

Victory nodded.

"And I trust Major Reese even more than I trust Vergess. So there's no need to worry."

"Even though Vergess is a proven turncoat?" Blick asked.

"Until he does something wrong, I won't entertain hypotheticals."

The train whistled. Geist slung her bag over her shoulder. She had to find a way to bring the team together. She had formed a bond with Battery and Vergess on their last mission, and she was determined to treat them like she would treat her old teammates.

Walking over to the train car, Geist handed over the six tickets. The attendant waved her and the others aboard.

The commander said to rely on others when my own skills didn't meet the task…

Geist held Victory back, right at the edge of the train car door. He waited, allowing everyone else to get on before they spoke.

"Yes?" he asked.

"We can't have tension on the team," she said, keeping her voice low. "Fix it."

Victory offered her a one-sided smile. "Yes, sir."

"Thank you."

"We're out on the field, you know. If you don't think you can handle this, I can take over. We don't need the commander's approval."

"That won't be necessary."

"Perhaps you should try some good ol' fashion *conversations* if you want the men to trust each other."

Geist nodded. "Yeah. All right."

The whistle screeched a second time as Victory pulled himself up into the train car. He hesitated at the threshold, however, and glanced back at Geist with a distant gaze. "But Blick isn't entirely wrong," he murmured. The cold chill of magic followed his words, sending shivers down Geist's spine. "There are futures where some of our teammates might not be reliable."

She wanted to ask more questions, but the attendant snapped a crop against the metal plating of the train. His yell echoed throughout the platform:

"*All aboard!*"

Geist hurried up into the train, catching up with the rest of her team as the door snapped shut behind her.

THIRTEEN

Cameraderie

The luxury car's plush lounge area was worlds away from the high-capacity coach cars at the other end of the train. Padded recliner chairs and tables lined the wall of the car with an open walkway down the middle. In between high-class cars were washrooms and—what had once been—diner cars.

"We're sorry for the inconvenience," the attendant said as he made his rounds. "But to help with wartime efforts, all diner cars are acting as storage and transport for the military."

The clack of the train wheels over the steel rails rang out a consistent *ka-kak* rhythm. The incessant noise was muffled by the thick polished redwood walls and deep green carpeting. Geist relaxed in her reclining chair, amused by the heavy curtains tied at the side of the train car windows. The posh and gaudy design reminded her of home.

They had a car all to themselves. The car behind them was full of socialite women—debutantes, the lot of them. Although Geist could steal glances of them through the windows of the cars, sound didn't penetrate. Instead, she focused on her team and Victory's advice.

Get them talking.

Victory and Blick shared small talk over a local newspaper. Battery stayed close, absorbed in organizing and reorganizing his rucksack. Dreamer and Vergess sat on the opposite side of the car, dead silent.

Even though discussing strategy had been the original excuse for acquiring the first-class car, there wasn't much to discuss. Even Victory's future sight couldn't help them until they got closer to the OHL—and until then, they were flying blind.

"We have eight hours until we reach Le Havre," Geist said. "Let's use our time wisely."

The others turned to her.

Blick smiled. "I know exactly what you're trying to say."

"You do?"

"Yes."

"We need to discuss our experience with *the ladies*."

"Wait, what?" Geist asked. "We don't need to discuss women." *Anything but that.* "But I was going to suggest we get to know each other a little more by—"

"Nothing is more revealing than how you handle yourself with the fairer sex," Blick interjected with a snap of his fingers. "As veteran soldiers, it's our sworn duty to teach new recruits how." Blick raised an eyebrow and swirled an imaginary wine glass, speaking with all the class and sophistication he could muster.

For fuck's sake, Geist thought as she held back a roll of her eyes. *He takes things just as seriously as Tinker does.*

"Just ignore him," Battery said as he closed his rucksack. "He's got to stop eventually."

Without warning, Blick wrapped an arm around his little brother and pulled him close. "You went into combat. You're a man now. You heard Commander Geist. We need to use our time wisely."

"Listen, that's really not what I meant," Geist said as she held up a hand. "I was trying to say that we should—"

"We may never get another moment like this," Blick said.

His sudden shift to a serious tone stopped Geist cold and drew the attention of the others.

"You never know in combat," he continued. "Any of us could be next. If we don't seize these moments to enjoy ourselves, when will we?"

The question left everyone speechless. Geist didn't care to dwell on mortality, especially not after losing her teammates. The others shifted positions in their seats as well, casting quick glances to one another as though trying to find the right words.

But before Victory could say something divined through his sorcery, Blick's smile returned.

"Which is why now is the perfect time for Battery to learn how to talk to women!" Blick squeezed his arm around his little brother.

Geist ran an open palm over her face, hiding her smile, amused by how fast Blick could change from serious to preposterous. Then her mirth faded. *Out of all the conversations he could've picked...*

Growing red and frustrated, Battery remained silent. Blick either didn't notice or didn't care—he held his brother closer than ever. Battery appeared tiny when next to his burly brother, more so than with others. He fit under Blick's arm, disappearing into the crook of his armpit.

Dreamer chuckled. "Englishmen are a delight."

"I want no part of this," Vergess drawled.

Blick leaned back in the chair. "We should start by each of us recounting the tale of our first kiss." Blick spoke again with the same faux sophistication as earlier. I shall begin." He closed his eyes and exhaled. "It was a beautiful summer day in Derbyshire."

Victory chuckled and cocked an eyebrow. "*That's* the story you're going to tell him?"

"Hush," Blick snapped. "It's my story."

"All right, then. Fine. Continue."

"It was a *beautiful* day in Derbyshire. My academy chums and I were talking around the trees. A few girls walked by. Pretty, too. Their hair glittered when it caught the light. I called one over, and we got to talkin', of course. She had a foreign accent. French, I think. Something musical-sounding. I stole a kiss and she laughed. So then we did it again."

Battery, red from his chin to ears, gritted his teeth and remained silent. His brother wasn't even looking at him.

"Tell them how old you were," Victory said.

"Well, ten, of course," Blick replied. "Still in academy. What's that matter?"

Victory smiled and shook his head. "And then Father took it out on your hide for showing improper manners to a sorcerer from House Brittany. To this day, they refuse to intermarry because of Blick's bad manners. It was a scandal."

Blick shrugged. "But it was worth it. She had lips like velvet."

"Exactly how does this story help Battery?" Geist quipped. "Or are you just boasting?"

Battery pushed his brother away. "Geist is right. Besides, it only counts when you're grown. Nobody's going to be impressed by a schoolyard peck."

"Oh, I've had a few since I was grown. Do you want those tales as well?"

"O-of course not!" Battery scooted away. "I thought this was a terrible idea to start."

"Have you kissed a girl at all?"

"Never," Battery said flatly. "Are you happy?"

"Hardly," Victory said. "Not after Blick's stunt. Father made sure you stayed in your boys-only academy."

Battery nodded. "And Father and Grandfather never got mad at *you* for anything, of course."

"That's not fair. They scolded me plenty."

"For flirting?"

Victory shook his head, a slight smile about him. "No. But nothing ever serious came of anything until I met Cross. She has an old soul and wisdom beyond her years. I'll never forget our first moments together..."

His tone and distant gaze got his brothers chortling. Geist couldn't help but smile. Cross adored him, and it seemed apparent that he felt the same. Yet they couldn't be together, for duty meant more to them than personal happiness. *Life can be cruel.*

Battery turned to Geist, his brow furrowed. "How do you get

along with women, Geist? Everyone says you're a lady killer, but you're small, just like me. I never get a second glance from a woman, even when I'm in uniform."

Victory set his newspaper down in his lap. "Accounts of Geist's accomplishments are greatly exaggerated."

"Oh, I know a thing or two about women," Geist said, waving airily. *I can give Battery some advice, if that's what he wants. I am an actual woman, after all.*

"Big talk!" Blick said, punching Geist in the arm. "Okay, Romeo. Let's hear it. First woman you ever kissed."

Although Vergess had been sitting on the far side of the car, he slid over to another seat, inching closer and barely concealing a smirk. Geist couldn't believe she had dug herself into such a hole. Her face flushed—this would take delicate phrasing.

What have I done? Should I tell them about my first kiss? If I avoid the details, they'll never guess I was the one getting kissed...

"It was... after my father announced my engagement," Geist muttered, turning her gaze to the floor. She could picture the entire event in her head—the anxiety, the trepidation at meeting a man she would supposedly spend the rest of her life with.

"Your family let you meet your future wife?" Blick asked. "My father didn't meet my mother until three years after their engagement. And it was the day of their wedding."

"Well, *s-she* is... a member of a Royal House."

Just muttering the term got everyone in the train car on the edge of their seats. Most magical families maintained long lineages to safeguard their sorceries, but sorcerers from Royal Houses had sorcery far more potent than anyone else's. Marrying someone from a Royal House was frontpage news.

"Who?" Battery asked, breathless. "And how? Since when did House Weston have the clout to marry someone from a Royal House? Ah! Was it a crown princess from the Royal House of Romanov? I hear they have so many."

"I'd rather not say," Geist said, hoping the other men would fill in the details themselves. "It doesn't matter anyway. I broke off the engagement when I—well, when I went to war."

Geist rubbed the back of her neck while she recalled the event.

"My betrothed introduced herself," she muttered. "And we spoke for a short bit. Then, she… ah, she kissed me."

The others waited for a long moment.

Blick scooted to the edge of his seat. "*She* kissed *you?* She's a daring one. Knows what she wants."

Geist nodded, trying not to shudder. *Leopold*—that had been his name, but he had insisted she call him "*Prince.*"

Like she wasn't even good enough to speak his name.

"Did she swoon?" Battery asked.

"No," Geist replied. "She was satisfied, told my father I would suffice, and left."

"Not very romantic."

"It wasn't."

Blick shrugged. "She sounds like a dynamo." Before the conversation could lull, he glanced over at Dreamer. "Your turn! You've had a dopey smile on your face the entire time."

Dreamer turned a page to his novel, *Le Fantôme de l'Opéra.* He didn't glance up when he replied. "When I was born, my mother kissed me several times, I'm sure."

"That doesn't count," Blick said in exasperation. He threw a cushion and missed Dreamer entirely.

Dreamer never flinched. He turned another page of his book and continued to grin. "Outside of family, I have not had the delight of a woman's company, nor have I sought it."

"There you go, Battery," Blick said. "Someone else on the team hasn't kissed a woman, either."

Dreamer shook his head. "Perhaps your brother would be better served reading the romantic deeds of literature's great heroes? There is much he could learn from these pages alone."

"We don't have time for books."

Dreamer replied with a chuckle, turning yet another page. Much to Geist's curiosity, the disguised Arab withdrew a pencil from his front pocket and wrote some notes directly in the pages of his novel.

What's he doing?

The train car returned to silence momentarily. Blick glanced over at Vergess, and Geist gave Blick a glare and waved him on. Blick replied with a glower. They stared off for a moment until Blick finally exhaled.

"Vergess," he said, a hint of distain in his voice. "C'mon, then. Tell us your story."

Geist gave Blick a smile, but the other man simply rolled his eyes.

The train clacked on the tracks, the only reply.

Victory motioned Vergess over. "Everyone else answered."

"I agree," Battery said. He turned to Geist. "Don't you want to hear?"

She rubbed her cheek with the heel of her hand. *Of course I do.*

"Tell us a story," Geist said.

Although Vergess didn't move closer, he did let out a strained exhale before he said, "And here I heard Englishmen didn't kiss and tell."

Blick scoffed. "No need to be so gentlemanly. There aren't any women here to offend with simple stories. Or is this an excuse? Battery and Dreamer weren't embarrassed by their chastity. You don't have to pretend you've been with women if you haven't."

"I don't need to pretend," Vergess snapped.

"Then tell us. What happened?"

Several seconds passed before Vergess said, "Her name was Isidora. I met her in Serbia. It was there. In Belgrade. We had no common experiences, but we were two pieces cut from the same cloth. A simple conversation, and I knew she was a woman worth fighting for."

Battery nodded along with the words, a smile growing on his face. "Really? That's the kind of story I want to have for my children. Something romantic. Something you'd read about."

Vergess ended his story without another word. Geist held her breath, wondering what had come of their relationship. *Is she waiting for him?* She turned and focused her gaze on the passing countryside. *He's like Victory—of course he would have someone waiting.*

"Okay," Blick said as he rubbed his palms together. "Let's mingle."

"Mingle?" Battery repeated, one eyebrow cocked.

"Yes. The next car over is filled with beautiful women. We'll save them from their boredom. And ours."

"That's a terrible idea."

"Better than staying cooped up here."

Battery grabbed his rucksack and held it close. "What if we offend them? I learned nothing from your stories, other than we're a group of mostly incompetent gentlemen!"

Both Dreamer and Victory laughed.

"You just need practice," Blick said. "C'mon. I'll show you."

Battery gave Geist a sidelong glance. "How would *you* approach women?"

"Well——" Geist began.

Then she stopped short. It occurred to her that while she was a woman, she'd never wanted anything the other girls in her life dreamed of. Even when the war had broken out, she had opted to fight rather than develop her corpus sorcery to heal. Most women involved in the war became medics. She was a soldier.

Think. I should know something. *What would my mother like?*

Even that struck her as a difficult question.

"It's… complicated," Geist said at last. "All women are different. That's my actual advice."

"Nah," Blick said. "I have some universal pointers that I've been saving to pass on. I know what women want. Trust me."

I can't wait to hear this.

Battery lifted both eyebrows.

"First off," Blick said. "Women want men who are gentle with them, but rough with everyone else. You have to be tough on the outside, but soft enough for them to feel like they've *learned the real you.*"

Geist could hardly believe her ears. *Who taught him this?* Even Victory couldn't stifle a smile. Despite Blick's declarations, Battery listened intently—if he had paper and a pencil, she imagined he would take notes.

"Second, you need to make eye contact as much as you can. Across the room. In a conversation. While you eat. *Whenever. You. Can.* Women love it when you stare deeply into their eyes. Lastly, you need to pick a physical feature about them and compliment it as the most beautiful you have ever seen. Her eyes. Her hair. Her complexion. No other girl compares. Got it?"

"Is that what you do, Geist?" Battery asked, a naïve genuineness to his tone.

She answered with a nervous laugh and nothing else. When she snuck a glance at Vergess, he was stifling a chuckle, a slight smile fixed to his face. *I can't believe he's enjoying this.*

"Do you want to join us?" Blick asked, giving Victory a stern stare. "We need to test my techniques."

"No," Victory replied. "I have news to catch up on." He picked up his paper and returned to the headlines.

"Dreamer?"

Although still smiling, the other man shook his head. "This sounds like an activity for brothers."

"C'mon," Blick said. "You've been reading this entire time."

"Trust me when I say I don't have what women are looking for. So there's no need for me to go. And I enjoy my novels. Now, if only the train served tea, it would be a pleasant afternoon."

Geist lifted an eyebrow. *Didn't have what women were looking for?* She had never heard anyone use such a phrase. And what was he talking about? He clearly had the looks, and he spoke with an upper-crust accent. Most women considered those desirable traits.

Blick gave Vergess a fleeting glance before turning his gaze to Geist. "How about you? You claimed to be an expert."

"No, thank you," Geist said. *Mingling with women disguised as a man will be awkward. I needn't risk anything unnecessary.*

Without anyone else as company, Blick grabbed Battery by the upper arm and helped him up. "All right. Just me and you. I'll show you how to be a proper gentleman."

Battery's flustered movements, quick breath, and pink face got Geist smiling. How could he have problems finding someone? The man had a sincerity about him that most lacked. *He'll be happy one day, I know it.*

The two brothers exited the front car and disappeared into the women's car, opposites in every regard. One large, one small, one jovial, one reserved, one confident, one… not so much.

A stillness came over the car. Victory and Dreamer read to themselves, content. Without company, Geist glanced over at Vergess. He stared out the window, his eyes vacant, as if lost in thought. When she was certain no one was taking note of her actions, Geist got up and moved to the seat next to his.

"You're engaged," Vergess said under his breath, never shifting his gaze.

"Not anymore. I was being truthful when I said entering the war ended that."

"Hm."

Geist leaned back and crossed her arms. She wanted to ask about the girl in Serbia, but it really wasn't her business. She and Vergess weren't anything more than fellow soldiers in war, even if the curiosity ate away at her insides.

"She died," Vergess drawled, answering her unasked question. "Isidora. That's the spy I told you about. She was captured and I saw recorded reports of her execution."

"Who caught her?"

"The Austro-Hungarians. She was targeted for assassination as a member of the Black Hand." Vergess shook his head. "I hated working with the Austrians. It was the worst part of my career when the Kaiser ordered me to act as a double agent. It was… ultimately why I left."

Geist refrained from speaking. The one truth Vergess didn't know came back to her.

She was Austrian. Her father hailed from the capital city, Vienna. She had made up the name "Charles Weston" and assumed an American identity because her mother was American and because she had lived in New York for a few of her younger years, gaining an appropriate accent.

I'm American and *Austrian,* she told herself. *Both. I'm not lying.*

But it had been one of the major reasons she had joined the war. Austria-Hungary had committed crimes against other nations, and declared war on Serbia, engulfing all of Europe in a bloody conflict. Germany acted as their stalwart allies, creating a power block against the other nations, but Austria-Hungary was behind the war.

"I'm sorry for your loss," Geist whispered.

Vergess sighed. "No one can change the reality of war. Still, the thought of her dying because of the conflict... alone and without anyone else. It's hard to describe."

"Isidora, you said? What house did she belong to?"

"I don't wish to discuss it," he snapped, his voice louder than before. He took a deep breath. "I'm sorry. Let's just move on. There's nothing that can be done about it now."

"All right."

The clack of the train continued in rhythm. Geist couldn't bring herself to stare at Vergess. *I never meant to open an old wound.* She went to stand, to leave him to his thoughts, but Vergess took hold of her sleeve.

"Stay," he said under his breath. "Please."

She retook her seat and lifted an eyebrow.

"Even if we don't speak, I'd rather not be alone with my thoughts."

Geist nodded, understanding how the weight of the past could crush one's desire to see the future. Anytime she thought of her dead teammates, she felt a crushing ice heavy on her soul.

"Perhaps you can tell me about apex sorcery," she said. "It's in my blood, but I've never practiced it."

Vergess gave her a sidelong glance. "And you want to develop it?"

"Yes."

He chuckled. "Very well. I'll start by telling you the basics. It might take the remaining seven hours of our trip."

"Better than being alone, right?"

They both shared a knowing smile.

FOURTEEN

The Evening Rose

"Apex sorcery strengthens your body," Vergess said as the train clacked on. "You become stronger, tougher, more capable in every way, physically."

"I'm aware," Geist said. "My father practices. He's an expert."

"Is that right? Well, the way I learned is through meditation."

Geist shifted around on the train seat, her eyebrows knit together. "I thought apex sorcery was developed through physical strain. Exercise and such."

"No. Apex sorcery may alter the body, but its strength comes from deep within. I mastered ruina sorcery because destroying things is easy. Mastering your own body—that's what apex sorcery is all about."

"I see," Geist muttered.

She had always imagined her father working hard in a field, pulling a plow with his bare hands. He was strong enough to drag three plows if he wanted, all thanks to his magic.

Imagine what I could do with such an advantage.

So she closed her eyes and tried taking even breaths. Vergess did the same, and the conversation between them died. But Geist didn't know what to think about. What was perfection? How would she quiet her mind when she still had doubts about her place in the world? About failing her team? About her charade?

It all seemed impossible.

The train ride dragged on. Even with Vergess's companionship, Geist was happy when the ride came to an end at last.

Geist exited the luxury car, only to be greeted by the icy winds above the English Channel. The city of Le Havre rose before her—churches, abbeys, and tall villas soared above the cityscape. The city had largely been shielded from the war's destruction. Away in the distance, past the grit of the city proper, was the maritime boulevard, complete with casinos and beach huts. The seaside resort would have been a relaxing sight had the roadstead beyond the port not been filled with British warships.

"Want me to carry your bag?" Blick asked Battery, eyeing his oversized burden.

Red in the face, Battery secured the rucksack firm against his back. "Very funny."

"I'm serious. It looks heavy."

"I'm quite capable, thank you."

Battery marched on ahead. Geist held Blick back, allowing the distance between them and Battery to grow before speaking.

"You can't treat him like a little brother," Geist said, keeping her voice low.

"He *is* my little brother."

"You said it yourself—he's a man now."

Blick scoffed and pushed past her. "Some things never change."

The streets of Le Havre held the bustle of merchants and sailors. News from the western front spread from one person to the next, each retelling more grisly than the last. The death toll was high—higher than any had dreamed, and the fighting had just begun. Whispers of German spies caught Geist's ears, but what she heard sounded more like fearmongering than fact.

The port at Le Havre swarmed with naval types. British reinforcements unloaded from transports, their fresh faces and excited murmurs a hard sight for Geist. She knew they would be different men once the trenches ground them down.

Steering away from the military vessels, Geist headed for the *Evening Rose*, a tramp steamer loading the last of its cargo. Major Reese's information included details of the *Evening Rose's* armament and complement. The captain, Edward Madison, and his first mate, Kevin Kell, were both members of the Ethereal Squadron based out of New York. They ran deliveries for the US and UK under the guise of merchants, bypassing most wartime travel restrictions.

Captain Madison refused to use a codename, according to Geist's notes—thought they were yellow-bellied. His first mate, on the other hand, went by the codename "*Shell.*"

Geist hustled to the loading ramp, an anxious energy fueling her steps. Every wasted moment ate away at her mind like a slow-spreading disease.

She panned her gaze to the line of passengers waiting to board. They were paupers and, she suspected, foreign nationals fleeing the war-torn lands of their birth. Without engaging the mundane populace, Geist made her way up the boarding ramp, passing the throng of passengers waiting to have their things inspected.

When she stepped onto the deck of the *Evening Rose*, a wiry man with a matted, rust-colored beard blocked her path.

"Too good for the line, lad?" he asked, a thick scent of sea salt about him.

"I'm here for Captain Madison," she stated. "I have special accommodations with him."

"You found 'em. You're Geist?"

"That's right."

"Good." He lifted his seaman's cap and smiled, his smoke-stained teeth rough and gnarled. "I'm glad to see you're American. I was afraid I'd be haulin' another Brit."

"Something wrong with Brits?" Victory asked as he stepped off the ramp and landed on the swaying deck of the steamer.

Captain Madison placed a long cigarette in his mouth. "Ah. It seems I didn't get lucky enough. Forgot you brought a team."

"We won't be any trouble," Geist said, taking note of the damp atmosphere and harsh chill wafting up from the waters.

"We'll see. Brits can be awful prissy."

"Did he just say what I think he said?" Battery asked, stepping onto the slick deck of the ship and almost slipping. He straightened himself, brushing off his crisp slacks.

The captain pulled a pack of matches and struck one against his teeth. "Ugh." He motioned with his chin to the bow of the ship. "Bring your men. I'll give ya the nickel tour."

Geist nodded. The *Evening Rose* would be their transport to and from Belgium—knowing its interior better wouldn't hurt. She waited for each member of her team to board and found Dreamer lingering behind, his steps unsteady and his eyes flitting to the edge of the boat repeatedly.

"You okay?" Geist asked.

"I have no love for deep waters," Dreamer stated, his posh voice twanging with nerves.

"Can't swim?"

"I can swim." He ran a hand through his thick, blond hair and forced a smile. "But to me, the darkness of deep water looks exactly the way I imagine the depths of hell. I'd simply prefer not to float above it."

"I see. I suppose you can stay below deck."

"Perhaps I shall."

Geist hurried to catch up with Captain Madison, careful not to slip due to the rocking of the boat. She had traveled on ships many a time, especially as a child when she would travel from Austria to New York, but she had never earned her sea legs.

"The *Evening Rose* was laid down in 1903," Captain Madison stated as he walked out onto the open bow. "She had a different purpose then. Now she carries four 47mm guns—and my favorite, the 57mm there at the front."

The 47mms were heavy naval guns, operated while standing and mounted to the deck with thick, steel bolts. Each ammunition shell, as long as a man's forearm, weighed three pounds and had to be loaded individually after every shot. The 57mm, with six-pound shells and a ninety-inch barrel, sat mounted at the forward deck, a pair of recoil cylinders equipped to the sides in order to reduce kickback from the devastating shots.

Captain Madison exhaled a long line of smoke. "We had 'em installed a year back after the fighting started. We run cargo, mostly; the Germans play nice because we're neutral, but you never know when you might need the firepower."

He turned and motioned to the deck cabin.

"The *Evening Rose* is two hundred and sixty-two feet from stern to bow." Captain Madison glanced back with a smirk. "That's eighty meters for you Brits."

Battery snorted. "Unlike *you Yanks*, we learn both systems."

"I know you have a plot to replace one with the other."

"One is objectively better."

"Feh. If somethin' works well enough, you leave it alone."

A chill drizzle settled over the port. The lines of passengers shivered through the cold, unwilling to look for shelter and lose their places in line. Puddles of water appeared across the deck of the *Evening Rose* as crewmen hustled to get everything tied down and secured. Geist observed a family devoid of menfolk—a grandmother, a mother, three teenage daughters—huddling together as they waited their turn to descend into the bowels of the ship.

"Ever wonder how many widows this war is making?" Battery murmured.

"No," Blick said, his serious tone returning. "And neither should you. Think too long like that, and you'll be putting a bullet in your head."

Geist glanced to Vergess, his gaze still hard and unwavering. He'd been quiet since exiting the train. Geist assumed it had something to do with returning to Germany, but now she figured there must have been more to it than that.

I guess war affects everybody differently, she thought. *The sooner we hurry up and win, the better.*

Captain Madison led them into the main cabin and down to the passenger holdings. The conditions below deck were as cramped as trying to squeeze forty men into a broom closet. Even the forts around Verdun had more space and ventilation. The cold gray steel of the ship creaked with each gentle wave upon the hull.

"Our first stop is Dover," Captain Madison stated. "We'll be dropping off passengers then. Afterward, we cross the Channel again to head into Belgium's port city of Antwerp. From there it's a two-day hike to Spa. Half a day, if you get horses." He motioned to a steamer trunk chained down to a bunk cot. "Major Reese wanted you resupplied. There are SMLEs in the trunk, along with some gasmasks."

Victory popped the latches and threw back the lid. The Short Magazine Lee-Enfield was a bolt-action repeating rifle, the main firearm for the British Empire. The six in the trunk had a pristine shine, and the Mk. III variant had man-stopping power Geist had come to appreciate over countless battles.

The gasmasks, on the other hand, were large and bulky. The eerie, dead-circle eye sockets and long canister filter that hung off the mouths gave them a haunting, almost nightmarish appearance. Geist hated looking at them. Their skull-like faces reminded her of the horrors gas could wreak during warfare—especially the GH Gas.

The captain sucked on his cigarette and finished it off, snuffing the butt on the floor of the ship. "I'll be in Antwerp for a day and returning fourteen days after. After that, I'll be trading throughout the Netherlands. If I see you, I'll take you back to Le Havre. If I don't, I'll wait ten days before returning. No more. Got it?"

"What if we're stopped by German warships?" Battery asked.

"The Brits up north have that covered," Captain Madison said with a chortle. "The North Sea is under blockade. German warships haven't gone anywhere for years."

"And we're to stay here? In the hold? With the... others?"

"Too prissy for the mundanes?"

Battery glowered silently. The standard procedure was to separate sorcerers from non-sorcerers, but the convoy to Belgium would last no longer than fourteen hours. For the short period, Geist was certain they could keep their nature a secret.

Geist nodded. "We can handle it. Take us to Dover."

⸻

THE PERSISTENT RAIN numbed Geist and the rest of the passengers of the *Evening Rose*. The hold, filled to the brim, felt gloomier than a funeral home. Further bad luck: the fleeing passengers' soggy clothing thickened the air with a foul musk that stung Geist's nose.

Dreamer, unwilling to go above deck, stationed himself on a cot and gripped the edges with white knuckles. The Hamilton brothers entertained themselves like only brothers could, recounting stories from their childhood and exchanging barbs.

After seven hours of musky, sweaty, *soggy* travel, Geist locked herself in the lavatory. She undid the buttons of her clothes and loosened her bindings. The ship had showers, but Geist couldn't risk it. Instead, she stripped and used the washbasin with a single cloth to scrub the grime from her body.

Changing into a fresh set of clothes proved difficult in such cramped conditions. She twisted and turned in the tiny lavatory, laughing at herself out of the absurdity of her situation, wondering what the others would say if they saw her.

Geist packed her rucksack and exited the lavatory. Their storage room containing their luggage and guns sat empty—the only place under the deck with clear air. The groan of the ship on the waves of the English Channel echoed throughout the corridors. She threw her bag down next to the steamer trunk and glanced up to spot Vergess standing in the shadows of the corner. She nearly jumped.

"Vergess," she muttered, meeting his stare. "What're you doing here?"

He looked her up and down and then walked over, glaring. "You really should pay more attention to your disguise." He grabbed the buttons of her shirt and fastened them the rest of the way. "And you should loosen your belt. When it's tight, it adds curves to your body."

Vergess abandoned the buttons and slid his hands from her shoulders to her hips, emphasizing the curve in question. Geist suppressed a shiver and stepped away, avoiding his gaze. Her hands shook as she undid and redid her belt to accommodate her figure.

"Like this?" she asked.

Vergess gave her the once-over, his eyes scrutinizing for a long moment, lingering on places that got Geist's palms sweaty. Finally, he nodded, and Geist found it easier to breathe when he looked away.

His gaze stirred Geist's imagination. *Why? Does he just feel obligated since he knows? Or is there another reason?*

The ship quaked and trembled, testing Geist's balance. She stumbled and corrected herself, leaning on the nearest wall. Vergess snapped his attention to her.

"What was that?" he asked, urgency in his voice.

She shook her head. "I don't know."

The ship shuddered again. Panic gripped Geist as she remembered the plummeting zeppelin. She wanted off the ship, and every second aboard was one too many. Deep breaths didn't help and she gulped down air at an uneven rate.

"Get it together," Vergess said. "We need to get to the captain."

He ran past, his determination infectious. Geist took in a single steadying breath and chased after him, but their progress was halted by the crowd of passengers attempting to flee onto the deck. Crewmen at the doors blocked the halls.

"Stay calm," a crewman shouted, his voice echoing off the metal. "Stay below deck. The ship is in no danger. It's only a storm."

Vergess pushed through the crowd and made his way up the stairs. The crewmen tried to stop him, but they were no match for his strength. Geist followed in his wake, exiting onto the rain-drenched deck before anyone could stop her.

The morning sun couldn't penetrate the dark gray storm clouds blanketing the sky. Heavy rain whistled in at a diagonal slant, pelting the *Evening Rose* with raindrops like bullets. Vergess entered the boat's center cabin and turned for the helm. Geist squinted through the storm. No land in sight.

When she entered the enclosed safety of the wheelhouse, Geist spotted the captain at the helm and his first mate at the binnacle. Vergess stared out the far window, his gaze on the shifting waters.

"What's going on?" Geist demanded.

"The weather's been queer for some time now," Captain

Madison said, wrestling with the helm. "Don't fret. We're goin' around."

"You've seen this before?"

"A few ships have capsized in waters like these. I try to save their crews when I stumble upon them. Not much luck."

Blick burst into the wheelhouse, his clothes soaking and his hair slicked back. Geist caught her breath—his eyes were a bright gold, damn near bioluminescent. She had never seen something so striking on a sorcerer before.

"It's enemy sorcery," Blick stated between heavy breaths. "The whole fucking storm."

Vergess snapped his attention to the other man. "What?"

Blick hustled to the window and pointed out into the dark waters, his gold eyes focusing on something no one else could see. His pupils dilated into a wide spot of black. "There's something under the water. A ship? It's not moving."

"Did you just say a *ship?*" Captain Madison asked over the crash of rain outside of the windows. "*Jesus, Mary, and Joseph!*"

Victory and Battery entered moments later. Shivering and unsteady, Battery ran to Geist's side and gave her a questioning look. The small wheelhouse had become crowded.

"It's definitely a boat," Blick murmured. "There's powerful sorcery inside—I can feel it."

The captain shook his head. "A damn German U-boat. I can't believe it's been in the Channel this entire time. I should've known." He turned the helm hard to starboard. "We're right on the edge of it. Hold on and we'll be out of this storm soon."

Vergess turned on his heel. "Head toward it. We'll end this here."

"My guns can't hit a target that far beneath the surface. Heading for it is suicide."

"Victory," Geist said. "What do you see? Can we handle the U-boat?"

Wiping water from his face, Victory shook his head. "We should sail around the storm."

"Why?" Vergess asked. "Did you see a downside if we pursue?"

"No. All I see is a blur. It's too difficult to say. So I still say we sail around."

Vergess punched the metal wall of the wheelhouse, denting it under the force of his blow. The room flinched at the show of power, but Victory and Vergess stared each other down with steel resolve.

"Are you serious?" Vergess growled. "You want us to *allow* them to sink ship after ship? We're right here. We can solve this problem."

"We can't handle a U-boat."

"*You* can't. Get me close, and I'll get the submarine to surface."

"The *Evening Rose* is full of civilian passengers," Victory said, his voice rising. "If we start a fight, their lives will be in the middle of it. One torpedo will be all it takes to put us neck-deep in corpses."

"And what of the other ships that capsize?" Vergess retorted, his voice rising above Victory's. "You don't think they're filled with corpses at the bottom of the Channel?"

"This isn't a part of our operation!"

"This is war! We have to adapt to the situation or risk defeat!"

Captain Madison coughed out a bark and drew everyone's attention. "*Ladies!* Enough of your pissin' match! I hate the Germans enough to fight 'em, but you'll have to do the heavy liftin'. We need to turn or we need to continue on."

"The torrent is out of control," Battery said, turning to the captain. "Can you get the steamer through the storm without capsizing?"

"I didn't get to the position of captain because my magic can control songbirds, mate. The sea is my bitch."

Everyone in the wheelhouse turned their attention to Geist. She stepped back and clenched her hands into fists. "Victory—you've never failed a mission. Don't you think you can see your way through this?"

"I succeed because I avoid risks," he said. "And even if we get through this, I can't see how this will affect the outcome of our operation. It'll certainly slow us down."

"Well?" the captain demanded, looking Geist in the face. "It's now or never, Commander."

FIFTEEN

The English Channel

Geist looked from one face to another and back. Both men were right. Fighting a U-boat could harm their chances of success, but she couldn't bring herself to leave such a dangerous enemy vessel in the middle of the English Channel. It would kill so many, and harm not just *their mission,* but all of the allied powers.

Then again, if she failed, they could lose the war. And millions more would die.

You took the position, Geist. Now do the job.

"We should destroy the U-boat," Geist stated.

"Good!" Captain Madison shouted.

He nodded to his first mate and slammed the helm to the side, turning the steamer into the oncoming waves.

The first mate, Shell, a fresh-faced Yank with a fisherman's knit cap, punched in commands to the engine order telegraph, sending information down to the engineers in the engine room. A wave crashed across the deck and shook the *Evening Rose* like a blow from a fist. Everyone stumbled to keep themselves upright, but the captain's enthusiasm didn't wane, nor did the first mate falter in his transmission.

Where lesser boats would have had difficulty, the English

Channel swirled to accommodate the *Evening Rose*. The captain's sorcery rippled through the water, taming it enough for the ship to keep upright.

The rain intensified the closer they got to the U-boat, the chill of the weather and magic mixing together in the air.

Geist hated elemental sorceries. They were the most common and easiest to learn—and they cropped up in almost every bloodline. The schools of tempest and ignis sorcery were especially common, given advantages of fire in trench warfare and storms in naval combat. Before the war, tempest and ignis sorcerers would have been dismissed as inconsequential, their magic relegated to party tricks—but in combat, these sorceries became mighty forces of nature. They gave even average sorcerers devastating power that left lingering horror in Geist's mind.

"Over there," Blick said, pointing into the darkness of the storm. "Maybe twenty feet below the surface."

Captain Madison held firm on the helm. "Keep your lighthouse eyes on our target, then. You're my navigator." He gestured with his chin, pointing to his first mate and then the door. "Shell, get to the guns and stand ready. We're engaging."

Shell ran out of the wheelhouse and clanged the deck bell. The chime cut through the cacophony, summoning a small group of crewmen from below deck. They clawed their way to their battle stations dressed in lightweight armor, fighting against the squall.

Vergess turned to Geist, his hard gaze the definition of determination.

"You can get the submarine to surface?" Geist asked.

He replied with a curt nod.

"Then do it."

Vergess ripped off his coat and vest and threw them to the floor. He kicked off his shoes, and, still dressed in a shirt and slacks, entered the storm as though the rain and wind didn't affect him at all.

The rock and sway of the ship on uneven waves had everyone bracing themselves against the walls for support. From the wheelhouse, Geist could see the bow deck. The crewmen shivered through the rain to load the guns and steady them for attack. The men were confused—there were no targets in sight, after all—but they followed commands regardless.

"We're coming up on it," Blick stated.

Through sleet and ice, the ship sailed over the U-boat's location. It didn't rise to meet them, nor did it fire. Why would it? The deadly submarine was camouflaged by the storm and fighting the *Evening Rose* without endangering itself in the slightest.

Vergess stepped up to the railing of the deck and leapt overboard, plunging into the dark, stormy waters of the English Channel.

"He's mad," Battery said. "What if he drowns?"

Victory ran a hand over his face. After a long moment, he let out a strained breath. "Turn the ship around. Vergess will make good on his word."

"He will? How?"

"I see him rising out of the water on the U-boat. That's when we strike."

Geist half-smiled. The Major had put this team together well. Blick saw the targets, Victory gave her the odds, Vergess played the heavy—all the puzzle pieces fit neatly in place.

And I'm leading them, she realized. *I'm actually doing it.*

"It'll take time to turn back around," Captain Madison grunted, his focus clearly divided between his men, the ship, and his sorcery. "The *Evening Rose* isn't a small lass, that's for sure."

Geist kept her eyes on the waves as the *Evening Rose* began its slow, looping turn. Only when lightning struck could she see anything beneath the water.

"It's surfaced," Blick announced, his gold eyes shining. "Right there!"

"Off the port side!" the captain shouted as he rang his bell.

The gunners hesitated, and the captain turned to Blick. "My men still can't see the damn thing. Do you know how to operate a forty-seven?"

"I can manage."

"Get out there! I've got the U-boat's location."

Blick rushed from the wheelhouse and jumped to one of the big guns on the port side. The crewmen let him take aim, but the wind and unsteady waters made everything difficult, even for someone who could see. The punch of gunfire cut through the howl of the storm as Blick opened fire. Another shell, loaded by hand, was hoisted into the 47mm seconds later.

Return fire echoed immediately.

German U-boats, designed to submerge beneath the water, were narrow, tiny vessels. Made of thin metal and outfitted with the lightest of armaments, the enemy ship didn't have the same fire-power of the *Evening Rose*, but it had deck-mounted guns and cannons only a little smaller than the 47mms.

Torpedoes rushed beneath the surface, creating waves as they hurtled toward the boat.

Shell ran to the side of the ship and held out his hand. The torpedoes surged forward, but instead of striking the ship, they exploded mere yards from the hull.

I guess that's why he's called "Shell," Geist thought. She could feel the first mate's magic blanketing a portion of the ship; his sorcery prevented the hull from taking damage, but he trembled and shook after each attack, as though each explosion were striking him instead. He hung onto the edge of the deck, his breathing ragged and his hand outstretched to guide his magic.

Enemy shell after shell exploded off the bow, sending plumes of water high into the night sky. But Shell's magic couldn't cover the entire length of the two-hundred-foot ship. Several shots slipped by his magic and made impact—shrapnel clipped the wheelhouse windows, shattering glass within the helm room.

Geist covered her face and ghosted, allowing the glass splinters to sail through her body without harm, but it ripped small holes in her clothing. The captain never released his grip on the helm, despite the cuts across his knuckles and forearms. Battery and Victory both fell back from the hit, a shard of glass striking Victory across the right eye.

"Battery!" Geist shouted. "Get out there and help Shell!"

Shaken, Battery got to his feet and stumbled out of the shattered wheelhouse. He slid across the slick deck, fighting the downpour, and only stopped once he reached Shell.

Blick fired round after round. Geist could have sworn she saw the U-boat shudder, but she couldn't be sure. Return fire continued regardless.

As Geist braced herself for another hit, she caught her breath the moment she felt Shell's sorcery empowered by Battery's. The shield that had once protected only a small portion of the *Evening Rose* had grown to encompass the entire vessel. From stern to bow, the powerful magic covered the craft like a bulletproof blanket. Captain Madison craned his gaze up and around, a look of confusion on his face.

"What sorcery does your boy practice?" he shouted. "What is this?"

Rain swept in through the broken windows, coating the ship's controls in water. Geist picked herself up and stepped close to Victory. Even through the storm, she could see the man had multiple lacerations and shards of glass embedded in his arms and legs. He remained sitting on the wheelhouse floor, his hand over his injured eye to stem the flow of free-flowing blood.

She held on to his shoulder. "Will you be okay?"

"I won't die from this," he stated. "As far as I can tell."

The ship tilted, and Geist leaned into the turn. Crashing through the waves, the *Evening Rose* headed in close to the surfaced submarine. She stood and saw the dark gray of the U-boat deck, a series of silent lightning strikes illuminating the hull long enough for her to see the damage.

But where is Vergess?

There were four holes—two bore the distinct burst markings of exploded 47mm shells. The last two were rusted, rotted holes that reminded Geist of centuries-old metal left to neglect. The frail carbon steel hull around the gaping entrances gradually disintegrated, as though the rot were slowly spreading to the rest of the U-boat like a disease.

Vergess's ruina sorcery.

But the thin hull of the submarine gave her pause. Before she could piece together the mystery of the rot, Geist turned to the captain. "Ram it."

"What?" the captain balked. "Ram the U-boat with the *Evening Rose?*"

She turned to Victory. "Will it work?"

"I…" He closed his other eye and held his breath. For a moment, it seemed as though he wouldn't be able to focus, but despite everything, he exhaled and calmed himself. "It'll work."

Captain Madison, an unlit cigarette dangling from the corner of his mouth, cocked a smile. "Heh. The *Evening Rose* is a big girl. I knew she could handle it."

Geist helped Victory over to the corner of the wheelhouse, bracing against the bulkhead for impact. He pressed himself up against the wall, still quite capable, and motioned for her to return to the captain. "Don't worry about me. Watch over the others."

The captain rang his bell in a series of hurried strikes. The frantic nature of his message translated to the others on the ship. The crewmen ran for the rigging or to get below deck and the first mate returned to the wheelhouse. Blick and Battery, following the lead of the others, also returned, their attention drawn to their older brother. They went to Victory's side and gave Geist a questioning glance.

"Hold on!" the captain shouted.

Before Geist could fully comprehend the situation, the *Evening Rose* crashed into the half-submerged U-boat. She lost her footing and fell to the floor as the whole ship shook. The crunch and screech of metal on metal was like the blood-curdling shriek of nails on a chalkboard. It lasted for the length of the steamer traveling over the submarine, shivers rolling across Geist's spine the entire time.

The final shudder of the ship dismounting the U-boat punctuated the end of the terrible noise.

Another round of salt water waves washed onto the deck and into the wheelhouse. Blick shielded Victory as best he could. The chill of the waters pierced Geist to the bone. Once free of the waves, she stood and craned her head to get a better look at the wreckage. The submarine took in water at a frightening rate. It wouldn't last long enough to reach the shore.

"We have to get Vergess," she said. "He was on the U-boat."

Blick shook his head and wiped the water from his face. "He already disembarked. He was on the deck of the U-boat last I saw him."

Geist glanced back as the final bits of the submarine sank beneath the raging waters. Seeing anything else through the ill weather was impossible and she returned her attention to the immediate. Captain Madison dialed down to the engine room using the telegraph, but after a few grunts of irritation, he pulled Shell over.

"You have the helm," he said.

The young first mate hopped over to the controls, his fisherman's cap lost during the naval battle. He ran a hand over his disheveled reddish hair and nodded to his captain. "Sir, are we whole?"

"I'm going down to the engine room now. Handle everything up here till I get back."

"Yes, sir."

The captain exited the wheelhouse with a singular focus. Geist would have been concerned about losing his sorcery if it hadn't been for the storm suddenly dissipating. Within minutes, the rain died and the wind dwindled to a gentle breeze. Rays of sunlight broke through the black clouds in pillars, shining spotlights down onto the swirling waters of the English Channel.

"I'll be all right," Victory said.

Geist glanced back. Both his brothers fussed over him, trying to get Victory to remove his hand from his eye. He refused, his clothes half-soaked in blood, and stood despite the shallow cuts across his leg.

"At least get under some good lighting," Battery insisted. "We should remove the glass and patch you up."

"That's fine. Let's just do this quick."

Leaving the brothers to themselves, Geist jogged out onto the bow deck and ran to the railing. Shell's magic had done wonders in protecting the majority of the *Evening Rose* from attack, but the impact with the submarine had been a different story. Dents and jagged lines marked the bow just beneath the surface of the water. The sturdy ship had held together as far as Geist could see and she breathed a sigh of relief.

Geist removed her attention from the boat to search for Vergess. She ran from the bow deck back to the stern, passing the steamer stacks, busy crewmen, and flag mast without stopping. The steady waters made it easier to run, and she took advantage by sprinting all the way to the back guardrails. She leaned over as she ran and searched the dappled waters, hoping to spot Vergess among the waves.

Where are you? Come on… Something like this couldn't have done you in.

To her relief, Geist spotted Vergess on the side of the *Evening Rose*, his arm twisted through a line of chain that had broken loose during the storm. He yanked himself from the water despite the weight of his soaked clothes and clung close to the hull, above the waterline. Geist jogged to the edge of the boat and gathered a coil of rope to help him climb aboard. She tossed it over and secured the other end to the rigging mast.

Once Vergess had dragged himself aboard, he rung out his clothing, water streaming from bullet holes in his slacks and shirt. Geist gave him the once-over. Despite the state of his clothes, there wasn't a scratch on his body. From his pocket he pulled out a handful of enemy tags and dropped them into her hand.

"The submarine was part magi-tech," he stated.

Geist caught her breath. "How could you tell?"

"There were no Abomination Soldiers aboard."

Geist sifted through the tags. They were German naval officer ranks—engineer officers, torpedo officers. One sported the blue of a medical officer. None bore the marks of sorcerers.

They're experimenting out in the English Channel?

The news didn't surprise her. The battleground of Verdun was no place to test naval magic. But the rate at which the Germans were accelerating their advances frightened her. Even if she brought back the information for magi-tech, would it be in time to counter the enemy forces?

Geist handed the insignias back to Vergess. "We can't fail this mission."

He took the cloth pieces and pocketed them without answering.

"And, thank you," she continued. "You did an excellent job."

Vergess stared down at her for a long moment, his emotionless gaze something she couldn't decipher. Then he said, "I have a question. You have apex and specter sorcery in your blood. What other schools of sorcery can you learn?"

Wind rushed by, carrying with it the smell of salt and ammunition.

Geist floundered. Sorcerers could only ever learn the sorcery they had inherited, and nothing else, making tracking family lines the utmost importance. Most sorcerers and their families kept their abilities hidden. Some made their living stealing information from others and selling it off to the highest bidder. Wars had been fought over legacy and rights. Selling children who contained the link to powerful magics was forbidden, but it happened nonetheless.

This was why so many sorcerers in the military went by codenames. Geist knew Victor, Bernard, and Percival were all from the Hamilton family, and so did the other members of the Verdun Ethereal Squadron, but their official records never revealed their true surnames. Even their assignments and packets of information addressed them as Victory, Blick, and Battery.

Vergess's hard stare persisted.

Just as Geist was about to give up on her wait, Vergess spoke. "You're afraid of revealing your true identity."

She nodded.

"As you should be. That's the right instinct for any good spy."

"I'm sorry."

He stepped closer to her and lowered his voice, almost to the point it was lost to the waves crashing against the hull. "Do me one favor."

Geist glanced around, taking careful note to make sure the crewmen were preoccupied with their work before returning her attention to Vergess. When certain no one would hear, she lifted an eyebrow.

"What is it?"

"Tell me your name," Vergess said. "Not your family name. I know you want to keep that hidden. And not *Charles*. Your real name. I realized I didn't know it when I was under the water."

Her mouth went dry. *He thought of me. In the middle of a fight, he thought of me.*

The question hung between them. Vergess cleared his throat. "Does this bother you?"

"No. I just—I'm surprised."

"Then you'll tell me your name?"

Geist wanted to tell him, but she stopped herself short when she thought of the consequences. Could he possibly learn her identity from just her given name? No. Her name was common enough.

"Florence," Geist replied.

"It suits you." He raked his fingers through his wet hair, combing it back and slicking the water away. "But not as well as Geist."

Geist smiled.

"Where are the others?" Vergess asked. "We should rejoin them."

She contained her musings and pointed toward the bow. "Dreamer never came up from the hold. The other three are on the forward deck."

Vergess answered with a nod and made his way to the front of the ship. Geist followed him, allowing herself to relax after the stress of the ordeal. The feeling didn't last long, however, as she came to the bow of the ship and spotted Victory still soaked in crimson. Battery and Blick hovered close, but their twisted expressions of concern didn't put her at ease.

"What's going on?" she asked.

Battery motioned her over. "Victory needs a medic. We spoke to the doctor aboard, but he says he needs tools or… or else he's going to have to take Victory's eye."

"What do you mean?"

"There's glass there." Battery motioned with unsteady hands to the corner part of the eye, just into the socket. "It's deep."

Geist turned to Victory. "Let me see."

He removed his hand—his good eye closed in pain—and Geist's heart seized in her chest. A long shard of thin glass had wedged itself between the soft flesh of the eye and the hard curve of the bone socket, cutting in through the corner of the eyelid. The blood wept in copious amounts, bleeding out as though a long line of red tears. The injury wouldn't have been as much of a concern anywhere else on his body, but the vulnerable eyeball left Geist nauseous.

"Geist, please do something," Battery said. "I don't know if Victory will be able to use his sorcery if he loses his sight."

"I'll be fine," Victory interjected.

"You said you *see* the images."

"I see them in my mind's eye. There's no need to panic."

"But will that be the case if you lose your vision? You don't know. We shouldn't risk it."

"What do you want me to do?" Geist asked. *Send him back to Cross? We need him for the operation. Even his contribution to the U-boat fight had been invaluable.*

Battery fidgeted with his restless hands. "Didn't you say your family made you study corpus sorcery? Like Cross?"

"Body alteration. I don't know how to heal."

"Try to remove the glass at least."

I haven't practiced corpus magic in years, Geist thought, anxiety gripping her thoughts like a fist. *I could be making this situation a whole lot worse.*

Vergess gave her a sidelong glance. "You have apex, specter, *and* corpus sorcery in your blood?" He stood off to the side, watching the exchange with a critical eye and glower.

At this rate, he'll figure out everything, Geist thought.

"It'll be fine," Victory said, confident despite two inches of glass protruding from his face. "Everything will work out."

Hearing Victory's reassurances put Geist's fears to rest before they could cripple her into inaction. He could see the future. If he said everything would work out, who would deny it?

Geist motioned for him to sit against the deck guardrail and tilt his head back. Victory complied and remained stable even when Battery and Blick both looked as though they would explode.

Geist placed a hand on his face and dragged her finger along the skin. Corpus sorcery unwound or re-stitched the very fabric of flesh. Her nail acted as the center point for her ability, and she "cut" a short line from the corner of the eyelid to the temple just before the ear. The boat rocked, making the line uneven, but her touch never went deep.

With the shard loose, Geist used her other hand to pull it out. A good inch of glass emerged from his socket coated in blood.

Geist turned to Blick. "Get me some gauze and cotton. I'll wrap this up."

"Right," he replied, taking off for the hold.

She threw the shard overboard. "That was crazy."

Battery let out a long exhale, his hands still shaking as he wiped them off on his shirt. Even Vergess took in a long breath, as though he had been holding it in the entire time.

"Not bad," Vergess muttered.

Victory laughed, then grimaced for the effort. "Thank you, Geist."

"Cross would kill me if anything happened to you. Besides, it's a lot easier to be confident in your actions when you know they'll succeed."

"What do you mean?"

"I mean, I could have fucked up your eye just now. I'm glad you knew I wouldn't."

Victory smirked. "Well, you shouldn't assume I'm using my power one hundred percent of the time. I had no idea this would work."

Geist gritted her teeth, on the verge of shouting. "You told me everything would work out!"

"I didn't want anyone else panicking for my sake."

She stood and stepped away, incredulous. "Why wouldn't you use your magic?"

"How well would you be able to focus if you learned you had a piece of glass the length of your finger in your eye socket? Not very well, I imagine."

Battery glanced between them, a look of exasperation clear on his face. "How are you two so calm about this? Unbelievable."

The crash of water against the *Evening Rose* rang out in natural rhythm as Blick approached the group. He handed over the gauze and medical supplies, his attention focused on his older brother.

Placing cotton over the injury, Geist wrapped a diagonal bandage around Victory's head, giving him a makeshift eyepatch of white linen. She smiled to herself realizing that everyone had come through the battle with the U-boat in one piece—unlike the GH Gas and zeppelin. Hope swelled in her breast despite herself.

I haven't let anyone die yet. We're going to do this. We will.

"Land!" the first mate yelled out. "Dover off the port side!"

Once finished, Geist patted Victory on the shoulder. "C'mon. It won't be long now until we're in Antwerp."

SIXTEEN

Antwerp, Belgium

With the other passengers gone, the hold of the *Evening Rose* had all the warmth of a graveyard. Geist and her team were all that remained; no sane person wanted into German-occupied Belgium.

The slosh of waves echoed along the steel walls of the passenger quarters. Geist, lost in her thoughts, stared at the ceiling as she attempted to sleep. It wouldn't be long before she would be needed again and the constant pressure to perform was already fraying her reserves.

And I haven't even gotten to Belgium yet. God give me strength to make it through alive.

"Geist."

She rolled over and spotted Battery staring. He shifted from one cot and moved himself closer. He held a scrap of paper and a long pen, a half-composed message written out in his neat handwriting.

"This is the last chance you'll have to write home," he said. "Everyone else is taking the time to pen a letter. Captain Madison even said he would ensure their safe delivery."

Geist exhaled. "Everyone?"

"Even Vergess."

Geist kicked her one foot over the other and laced her ankles together. Her clothing felt stiff after drying, but she refused to change. Vergess's point about apex sorcery detecting faint scents left her needing to disguise her natural aroma, just in case any nearby Abomination Soldiers would sniff her out. Salt water and blood worked wonders.

"I have no one to write to," she muttered.

Battery rubbed at his neck and frowned. "I know you said your father was a harsh man, but do you really hate him so much that you wouldn't write him on the eve of your most important mission? There's a good chance we might not make it back."

"I know that."

"Every father is concerned about his son."

Geist gritted her teeth. *Oh, I know.*

"Listen," she said, "we had many disagreements. From my magic, to my place in life… to the war."

"What do you mean?"

Although Geist didn't want anyone to discover what family she was from, the thoughts of her father put her on edge. She wanted to talk. She wanted to explain everything. And Battery had been there for her before. Even if she told him details, she suspected he would never betray her trust.

They were Team Teensy-Weensy, weren't they?

"My father wanted to support Austria-Hungary," Geist said. "And he wanted *me* to support them as well."

Battery's eyebrows shot up. He glanced over his shoulder, scanning the room and taking stock of everyone's location. For all intents and purposes, they were separated enough to be considered alone. When he turned back, he lowered his voice regardless. "Are you Austrian?"

Yes. And no.

"I was born in the United States," Geist stated, not a lie, but not the whole truth. "But my father is Austrian."

"I had no idea House Weston hailed from Austria."

Geist crossed her arms over her chest. "House Weston," as far as anybody in the squadron knew, was a family of total recluses. It was usually the perfect cover, but Battery's thoughtful expression reminded her that some sorcerers took linage and house politics serious enough to study.

"You were going to marry into the Royal House of Habsburg-Lorraine," Battery muttered. "Weren't you? The Austro-Hungarian royal family."

"I never said that." Geist sat up on her cot, her chest tight.

Battery shook his head. "It's okay. I won't tell anyone. But that's pretty shocking. They're the family behind the whole war."

"I know." Geist turned away and exhaled. "Trust me. I definitely know."

"Who were you going to marry? A princess? A duchess?"

Geist couldn't reply.

The crown prince, Leopold Habsburg-Lorraine.

"Well, if you're not going to tell me who, could you at least tell me why you didn't go through with it?"

"It was a multitude of reasons."

"Such as?"

"I hated the fact Austria-Hungary had started the war and was more upset that their ally, Germany, had invaded Belgium. I tried talking my father into joining the Ethereal Squadron, but he had pledged his services, and consequently, our whole family, to the Royal House of Habsburg-Lorraine."

"He never listened to your input."

Geist exhaled, allowing her breath to take the last of the lingering resentment. It had all happened a year and a half ago. The yelling, the arguments, the rift that had formed in a once-united family.

My father would never listen to his children. Geist grazed the ribbon on her wrist. *Not me. Not my brother.*

"I still don't understand how your father managed to get a wedding arrangement for you," Battery said, starting at the edge of the cot, his eyebrows knit together. "House Weston must have rare sorcery running through its veins. Or maybe that was your father's attempt to apologize? Setting you up with a favored marriage?"

"Perhaps. But that's not like my father. It was… probably for his benefit, in the end."

Her voice faltered for a brief moment and Geist coughed to conceal it. Memories of her father and mother brought back emotions she'd rather not relive. Her father's disappointment in her magic—and his anger when she hadn't wanted to marry the crown prince—made him a frightening figure in her memory. He wanted obedience and nothing more. Joining the Ethereal Squadron after running from the house was her final *fuck you* to the man who had raised her.

Her younger brother had been the only one not to harass her for her decisions, though he hadn't intervened when their father had scolded. Still, she missed him. Out of everyone she could write, it would be her kid brother, but their father would never see the message delivered.

"Is that from your sister?" Battery asked, staring at the ribbon.

Geist chuckled. "Yeah. My sister."

Battery brooded. "You could've been a prince, or a duke, or even a king. And your children would have been powerful sorcerers."

Queen, Geist corrected in her mind. *Marrying the crown prince meant I would've one day been Queen of Austria-Hungary.*

But what kind of queen would she have been?

"Some titles aren't worth the price," Geist muttered.

"But still. Hapsburg-Lorraine sorcery is unique. No other family has ever accessed it."

"It doesn't matter. I refused."

Battery narrowed his eyes. "Was your bride mulish?"

"Mulish?"

"You know. Ugly."

I know what it means. Geist let the words sink in as she gave herself the once-over. *Oh God…* Her shoulders slumped.

"My bride was far handsomer than I am," she said begrudgingly.

"But you didn't feel anything for her?" Battery asked. "No? A shame." He leaned back on his cot and stared at the far wall, his eyes unseeing. "I hate the thought of the war ending and you having no home to return to. Maybe someone in my family wouldn't mind marrying a member of House Weston. I mean, the Hamilton name doesn't carry as much weight as the Habsburg-Lorraine, but we're influential enough."

His offer caught Geist off guard. Battery was so earnest she found herself genuinely considering the matter. Marrying into House Hamilton wouldn't be as repulsive as joining the Hapsburg-Lorraines, surely—even if she ended up with a second cousin.

And the Hamiltons do have access to a bevy of rare sorceries.

"I'll think about it," Geist said.

"Really? Brilliant!" he replied, beaming. "I'm sure someone in my family would be interested in specter magic. From what I read, it's rare. And very useful. People thought it lost to history at one point."

"Yeah, my father would say so quite often." Tired of the conversation, Geist stood and walked around Battery's cot. "I'm going to check on the others. Finish up soon. We should be there within the hour."

"Of course."

The tiny passenger area, cramped, was still an impressive length. Geist weaved between cots until she reached the other end, finding Victory and Dreamer wrapped up in their own quiet discussion. They ended their dialogue once she drew near. Their letters, finished and folded, sat on the nearest cot.

"Battery told me you were all writing loved ones," she said, staring at the motionless paper.

"You could say that," Victory said, grazing the bandage over his eye. "I wrote Cross to tell her I got injured just so she could care for me."

"That mush work for you?"

"She's a classic romantic."

"She's joining in on the assault against Fort Douaumont. Are you worried for her?"

"Of course," Victory said. "Just like I'm worried about Blick or Battery. But I try not to think too much of it."

"I think she'll make a difference there," Geist said.

"And she'll impress her family," Victory added with a knowing smile. "House Moreau has been keeping track of her service record, after all."

"You know about all that?"

"Intimately. Cross's mother denied my marriage proposal so that Cross could marry a proper French gentleman rather than an English one. I tried to explain our courtship, but my letters were returned after postmark, unopened."

"You haven't written anything to Cross about our mission, right?" Geist asked, hoping to change the subject.

"Of course not. Nothing about the mission. Do you want to review my letter?" He handed over the paper and Geist gave it a quick glance. She saw the first three sentences and turned away, red in the face.

My dear Mattie,

Already, I miss you. Forgive me for being weak, but my thoughts turn to you whenever I am alone. It's your gentle touch and mellow voice I crave above all else.

"It's fine," Geist said, unwilling to read the rest. "Perfect. I'm sure she'll love it." Did they know love so deep, they no longer felt shame? Desperate to exit the conversation, if only because the feelings it brought up confused her, Geist turned to Dreamer. "Who did you write?"

"A widow in London," he replied with a polite smile. "I write her before every mission."

"A random widow?"

"One particular widow. A woman with the lovely name of Evelyn. She appreciates the correspondence."

Geist cocked an eyebrow, but Dreamer offered no further information. She had a million questions—*Why? How did he know her? Wasn't he an Arab? How had it begun?*—but she kept them to herself. Perhaps it was best not to pressure people about their past. *Lord knows I wouldn't divulge everything, even if they asked.*

"We should be arriving soon," she said. "Make sure you're ready."

Both Victory and Dreamer replied in nods. She left them to their writing, pushing the love note from her mind. A small piece of her wished she could go home to find letters of such passion in her locker, but another part of her knew it couldn't be so.

Geist felt a twinge of jealously as she imagined Cross reading an armful of Victory's letters. *Don't be childish,* she thought, scolding herself as she walked. *You should be happy for them.*

It didn't take Geist long to find Blick. She entered the galley of the ship to find two crewmen and her large teammate drinking from the stock of rum. They laughed and joked as they filled up another round of jugs. Geist approached and glanced between them, surprised to see their flushed faces. How much had they been drinking?

The dark substance they poured between them had a strong odor. It was the type of rum that made men's eyes water.

"You want in?" Blick asked, offering up his jug. "It's damn good. Better than the stuff in the trenches."

"No, thank you."

"You're not a teetotaler, are you?"

"I drink. On occasion. But not before an operation."

The two crewmen exchanged cringes. They placed their jugs back in their cubbies and exited the room with due haste. Geist suspected they had sensed her scolding tone.

Blick shrugged. "I'm a big guy. I can hold my liquor."

"I thought you were writing home."

"I was. That's why I need a drink."

"Most men *enjoy* the thought of writing loved ones."

"I'd rather be thinkin' about women and good food than writing loved ones that I might not return home," he said with a forced laugh. "You ever write someone about somebody who died? It makes you hate letters."

Geist recalled her own letter to Little Wick's lover. The few words she had managed to write had drained her of all her determination. His death still haunted her, but her lack of courage to write the woman haunted her worse.

"I know the feeling," Geist murmured. "Just make sure you've got your wits about you when we get to Antwerp." She turned to leave, but Blick held out a hand, stopping her.

"Thanks for keeping Battery safe," he said.

"No need to thank me."

"No, I don't think you understand." Blick downed another gulp and exhaled. "I've already lost one brother. I feel like losing another might cost me my sanity. And writing about it… just gets me sick."

"It weighs heavy on all men."

"Not Victory," Blick snapped. "Not you." He took a short sip and frowned. "Look, forget it."

"Blick, I—"

"I said, *forget it.*"

He took a seat on the galley countertop, turning to face away from her and stare out the porthole. Geist stood silent for a moment, mulling over the conversation. Blick had been so energetic and happy on the train, but the dark shadow of his depression always lingered. She didn't know how to deal with it, besides allowing him to flirt with women or drink himself into a confidant man, and they didn't have the luxury of stopping for rest or therapy.

Geist exited the room without another word. She would let him cope in his own way.

SEVENTEEN

Inspection

The ringing of the deck bell could be heard throughout the ship. Geist paused when the clang reached her ears, surprised at the clarity. She ran back to the passenger hold and straight for her bag. The SMLE rifle hung off the side, but she knew that wouldn't fly during port inspections.

"Dreamer," she called out. "It's your time to shine."

Dreamer regarded her with a smile. "Of course. Once everyone has gathered, I'll handle the problem."

The others reconvened in the hold. Vergess alone entered from the top deck. He threw his letter down with the others and joined the group, his rucksack already slung over his shoulder. Geist secured her gasmask to her bag and attempted to steady her heart.

Maybe I should've taken a drink, she thought. *Anything to calm the nerves.*

Dreamer motioned for everyone to gather. His sorcery chilled the room as he ran his hand across their rucksacks and clothing. Magic wove itself into the fabric of their clothing and the metal of their weapons. Illusions spread across them—rifles became walking sticks, coats became crewmen's uniforms, complete with ratty loose threads and sun-bleached jackets—concealing their true purpose to anyone looking for enemy soldiers amongst the crew of the *Evening Rose*.

Battery grabbed at his clothing and gawked. "Amazing. This is way better than I thought it would be."

"I'm good at what I do," Dreamer replied, motioning to his own pale English face.

Blick snorted. "Nothing *I* can't see through."

"Then you'll see through enemy disguises, too, no doubt."

"The enemy isn't going to sneak up on us anytime soon."

"How reassuring."

The deck bell rang a second time and Geist waved her men to the stairway up. "Let's go."

They walked out onto the open deck and into the full brilliance of the afternoon sun. Even the light didn't penetrate the illusions. Geist ran her fingers over her disguise and wondered how long Dreamer could maintain such detailed sorcery. She stared at him for a long while, realizing that everything about him had been an illusion, right down to his blue eyes. And he had never dropped it. Not once. Not even during the storm.

Amazing. He puts Battery's concentration to shame.

I wonder what they could accomplish together.

The Port of Antwerp sat on the River Scheldt, deep in the heart of Europe. The massive docks could accommodate cape-size ships, the largest of dry cargo sea vessels, too large to pass through even the Suez Canal. Small rivers, railroads, and major thoroughfares all connected to the Port of Antwerp in one way or another, making it a hub of trade and activity.

The port defenses reeked of German "contributions." Cement bunkers with mounted machine guns lined the entrance to the docks, built on the edge of the city or in the rocks that lined the river. Soldiers manned the weaponry at all times, focusing in on each new ship that came to call. The German flag—red, white, and black—waved on the river winds, signaling to all who controlled the territory. The black, yellow, and red of the Belgium flag was nowhere to be seen.

The *Evening Rose* sailed into port at a leisurely pace. The United

States, technically neutral in the conflict, could sell to the Belgians and Germans alike so long as they cooperated with Germany's strict inspections and regulations. Weapons weren't allowed to the Belgians, nor were propaganda or wartime materials.

And, most important of all, the Belgians were not allowed to leave.

Victory stood next to Geist and lowered his voice. "Once we dock, a German inspection crew will board. They won't see through our sorcery, and as long as we don't make a scene, they'll allow us to leave the ship and enter the city."

"You've seen all that?" Geist asked.

"Yes. No need to worry."

"I wasn't worried."

"You've been stiff for some time."

With some effort, Geist relaxed the muscles in her neck and shoulders and allowed herself a few easy breaths. Antwerp was in the heart of enemy territory. She knew the risks, even if she didn't dwell on them.

"Can you see our success yet?" she asked.

"Not yet."

"Let me know."

He chuckled. "You'll be the first to know."

Captain Madison and Shell strode from the damaged wheelhouse, leaving the helm to another officer. The captain signaled his crewmen to secure the ship as it made its way into port.

"I hardly recognized you," Captain Madison said as he walked up, his eyes panning over each member of the Prometheus crew. "I dare say you'll make it through enemy territory just fine. And you'd better."

Geist lifted an eyebrow. "We better?"

"Major Reese gave me a couple of details. You better not let Paris fall. Let's just say, I do business there, and I don't want to do more business with… Germans."

Shell stepped forward and held out his hand for Battery. "I've been meaning to thank you. Your sorcery, it's unlike anything I've felt before."

Battery took the hand and shook it. "It was nothing," he said with a nervous laugh. "It was your sorcery that protected the ship. Potentia only enhances what's inherent to the other sorcerer, you see."

"I've never heard of potentia sorcery. I'll keep an eye out for it."

Geist wanted to stop Battery from talking about the specifics of his magic, lest he reveal too much information, but she couldn't bring herself to stop a moment of praise. Battery needed the recognition more than anybody else on the team—maybe more than anybody she knew.

She moved closer to Victory and whispered, "Have you used Battery's sorcery before? To help you see the future?"

"I have," Victory intoned. "It was a nightmare."

Geist recalled what Cross had said about Victory's magic, how he'd seen his brothers' deaths and his own in more than a few visions. With the ability to see further in the future—to see more possibilities—it only stood to reason he would see more terrible fates.

"We're comin' into port," Captain Madison stated, pointing off the starboard side. "You fellas will stay here on the deck while they do their inspecting."

Vergess glowered at the city, his gaze lingering on the German flag. When the *Evening Rose* got deeper into the port itself, Geist watched him stare down at the German soldiers waiting on the docks. They stood in lines, some still wearing trench coats from their time on the frontlines.

The docking process was entirely too long. Even with Victory's assurances, Geist hated every second she had to stand and wait. The staring German soldiers brought back painful memories of No Man's Land. Their dark green uniforms rang alarms in her skull. They would not hesitate to kill them on sight if the squadron's true identities were discovered.

The *Evening Rose* slowed. Crewmen scrambled to prep the ship and throw down the gangplank. The crew lined up along the far railing; Geist and the others followed suit, taking places among them. Dockhands from Antwerp attached the gangplank and tied down the *Evening Rose*, securing it in place.

The enemy soldiers didn't waste time boarding. They came up in an organized line, ten men, fully armored, along with one officer. Captain Madison walked forward with Shell at his side. The German officer, *Max Krause* stitched above his lapel, stepped up to the captain with a hard-set expression. His face reminded Geist of Vergess—Officer Krause didn't look like a man who smiled much.

The officer walked across the deck and stared at the damaged wheelhouse, his gaze intense and his scrutiny apparent. He wore a cape over his left arm—a habit for some Abomination Soldiers— and Geist wondered what his sorcery might be. His belt buckle, larger than most, read: *Gott mit uns.*

God with us.

"You have a small crew and your helm is damaged," Krause said. "Tell me what's happened here."

Captain Madison snorted. "I don't speak that gut-cough you call a language."

Krause turned on his heel to face the captain, his expression never changing, though his eyes lit with interest. "American arrogance," he said in equally perfect English. "You're the only people in the world so proud of your own ignorance."

"If that's all you've got to say, you can switch back to German."

"Tell me what happened to your ship."

"There was a storm," Captain Madison said with a shrug. "It happens."

Krause snapped his fingers and four men jumped to his side. He spoke under his breath, issuing fast commands and pointing to the hold and wheelhouse. The German soldiers broke away and searched.

With a purposeful gait, Krause walked among the *Evening Rose*'s crewmen. He glanced between each man, taking note of the rucksacks and personal belongings. When he came to Vergess he stopped and met his gaze dead on. Though she tried not to stare, Geist couldn't help but fear that Vergess might be recognized.

Krause never said a word. He moved on to Blick, gave him a

quick once-over, and went to Battery, obviously dismissing the smaller man without a second thought.

Blick and Dreamer both allowed their sacks to be inspected, but the contents remained hidden under illusion. Krause stepped up to Geist and stared down at her with expressive ice-blue eyes. Geist refused to speak as he inspected her. Once finished, he moved on without a second wasted.

Victory, on the other hand, caused Krause to pause.

"Your bandage," the officer said. "Are you injured?"

Victory shook his head. "A souvenir from the storm."

"The English Channel can be treacherous."

"Especially these days," Victory drawled, glancing around to the German fortifications.

Krause refused to reply and instead turned his attention to the first mate. With a sneer, he motioned to Shell's reddish hair.

"Irish?" he asked.

Shell nodded. "That's right."

"Another immigrant fleeing the war, I assume? Too yellow to fight for your homeland?"

"Hey," Captain Madison said, cutting in. "I didn't go around flirting with *your* subordinates. Check my boat and be done with this. I don't have all damn day."

Krause pursed his lips and narrowed his eyes. "You tramp steamers—sailing into every port you can, jumping whenever someone waves money under your nose. Just like your country."

"I didn't see you complaining. Your port is spread wide, just askin' for as many tramps as can fit."

The two men glowered at each other. One crewman snorted. No one else made a noise.

Krause waved to the remainder of his men. "Search the rest of the ship. Confiscate all ammo and shells. And *take your time.*"

He said this in English, making sure everyone on board understood.

His men got to work, but not too fast, and Captain Madison pulled a cigarette from his pocket and lit it up.

"You can stay in port for the next two days," Krause stated.

"Your men can go anywhere they want in town, but they cannot leave Antwerp." His tone made it abundantly clear this was not a suggestion—and with that, Krause left the ship in a few quick steps, his shiny black boots clicking the entire way down the gangplank.

Captain Madison shifted his attention to Geist. "You heard the man. You've got run of the place."

EIGHTEEN

Occupation

Geist stepped onto Antwerp's shore with a heavy heart. The once-thriving city felt somehow deadened, desolation reflected in the charred trees, empty streets, and frigid wind. The buildings lining the main road had sealed shutters and locked doors. Parks and outdoors cafés sat forgotten and empty. German propaganda covered every wall and lay soaking in rain-filled gutters. Even the colors of spring felt muted under an invisible, stifling umbrella.

Most horrible of all were the small shrines on windowsills and street corners. Some had been trampled, the pictures of the deceased stomped into the mud. The longer Geist stared, the more she saw. No building was free of tributes to those who had passed during the war. No doubt the Germans forbade such shrines—but the citizens kept them up regardless.

Victory shoved his hands deep into his coat pockets. "We should get off the streets."

Geist lifted an eyebrow. He pointed to one of the many posters. It was an ordinance, written in Dutch, French, and German that read: *No more than four people may gather on the streets at a time.*

It wasn't the only one.

Posters with artwork depicting hardworking Belgians included demands such as fixing the price of beer, giving the streets new German names, and requiring that each household post the ages and occupations of all inhabitants. Other posters depicted men in chains with demands to "keep the peace, or else"—and to follow all orders by German soldiers.

Geist wondered how the Germans dealt with rule-breakers.

"Belgium was neutral in the war," Battery said, propping the collar of his coat up past his chin. "What have they done to deserve all this?"

"They were between France and Germany," Vergess huffed.

Geist bit her tongue. She had traveled to Belgium many times in the past and had fond memories of romping through the lush countryside. This all felt *wrong* to her—like a piece of her childhood was being turned over a spit.

They veered off the road and into one of the pubs that serviced the docks.

The two-story pub had a small entrance room and a long hall of tables in the back past the bar counter. Dark wood tables lined the walls under the windows, though no light shone through the thick curtains drawn over the glass. A combination of oil lamps and electric lights provided visibility, but the lack of airflow created a thick atmosphere of muggy musk. The lit fireplace in the backroom didn't help the matter.

No decorations adorned the walls or corners. The only bit of character came from the framed photograph of a man hanging above the establishment's front door. He had smiled as he had posed for the picture—but the candles and flowers draping the frame belied the unpleasant end he'd met.

A young woman at the bar, a week over eighteen at the oldest, glanced up at Geist and her team as they walked into the tiny front room. She frowned and observed them with a reserved stance.

"Good day, ma'am," Blick said, pushing his way past Geist and walking up to the bar counter. "We just got in from sea, and we're looking for refreshments." Blick spoke his French with the refinement of an upper-class education, nothing like a sailor.

I need to speak with him. He can't go flirting with every girl we run across.

Geist did find it funny how the man went from the blackest moods to exuberance within an hour. *Or perhaps he's just burying his feelings. I should have Victory deal with this. They're brothers. He'll know what Blick needs to stay sane.*

"We have bread and soup," the young woman said with a forced smile. "Potatoes cost a bit extra."

Geist put down a handful of notes, Belgian francs, and nodded. "For all of us."

The woman took the paper money and counted it with trembling hands. Once finished, she motioned to the back room. "You will sit in there, sirs."

Blick patted the counter. "Call me 'Blick.'"

"A-all right."

"And what should I call you?"

She held her breath, hesitating, and Geist couldn't help but feel her reluctance. The woman didn't want to speak to Blick, but she visibly steeled herself with a shallow exhale and answered regardless.

"My name is Sofie."

Blick, moving away from the bar, gave her a slight nod. "Nice to meet you. Thank you for your hospitality."

Walking past the bar and into the back room, Geist took note of the surroundings. Only two sailors sat in the pub, and they kept to themselves, quiet and wary. They gave Geist a quick glance before focusing on their food as though it required every ounce of their attention to consume.

Geist sat at the far table, but the tiny chairs made seating cramped and awkward, especially when everyone threw their bags underfoot. Blick hung over his seat, his body well beyond the recommended size for the piece of furniture. The wood creaked under his muscled weight. Vergess sat with stiff posture, his discomfort plain in his rigid back and balled fists, hidden just beneath the lip of the table.

Keeping his voice low, Victory addressed the rest of the group with a stern expression. "You've all read the mission packet. We need to scout the city, find a way out, learn how the Germans are controlling travel, and get transportation to Spa."

"The Germans will be checking each individual's *Ausweis*," Vergess stated. "Or they'll be issuing travel passes."

"What's an Ausweis?" Blick asked.

"An ID card. It's standard procedure."

His information got the table nodding in agreement. Geist knew she had made the right decision in bringing him along. *Traveling through Germany won't be easy, but it'll be far easier with him than without.*

"Then we need to find out what these ID cards look like," Victory murmured. "It's imperative we don't alert Abomination Soldiers to our presence. If they suspect we're here to infiltrate Spa, they might move their research or send assassins after us."

Geist leaned forward and cleared her throat. The others gave her their full attention. "I've played recon plenty of times," she said. "I'll scout the city. Blick, can I trust that you'll ferret out Abomination Soldiers? You said you can see their magic."

"Of course," he replied. "I'll let you know when they're around, but my sorcery is rather… blatant. I can't go using it unless we're somewhere secluded."

"I'll keep it in mind."

Geist stared at Dreamer, and he returned her gaze. He had *illusions*. How could she put them to the best use? She wanted to suggest he disguise himself as a German officer and lead them through the checkpoints. But his accent was too thick—he'd give them all away the moment he spoke, no matter how convincing a mask he conjured.

Geist glanced over to Vergess, but his attention was drawn by the bell that rang at the front door. Three German soldiers stepped into the establishment.

Tension rippled through the pub. The two sailors finished their sad meal and stood to leave. The girl at the bar stepped back and hovered near the kitchen door. Her long, hazelnut hair, loose and flowing, covered most of her face when she hunched forward and bunched her shoulders close to her thin neck.

"We're here to collect requisitions," the lead soldier stated as he sauntered up to the counter. "Are the goods ready for pickup?"

Sofie banged on the kitchen door with a loose fist. An older woman emerged with a box of brown potatoes and hefted them up onto the counter, straining to hold the weight the entire time. The soldiers took the box and placed it on the floor, but they didn't leave.

"Where's the rest?" the soldier asked. "This isn't enough."

The older woman went back into the kitchen and returned with a container of white eggs and crooked carrots. The soldiers stacked the new container on top of the potatoes and examined the offerings with deep frowns.

"You know the rules. Sixty pounds of food. This is barely thirty-five. We know you have more."

"We need food for ourselves," the older woman said, wiping her blistered hands across her dirty apron. She had the haggard look of a hard worker coming off her second shift in one day. Women didn't typically run pubs or restaurants, but war forced everyone into new roles.

The soldier snorted and leaned heavy on the bar counter. He pulled out his sidearm, a Luger P08, and held it loose in his hands, tapping the narrow barrel on the hardwood.

"Hunger is all in the mind," he drawled. "You can stand it for a short while. Ships come in every day."

"Ah… I never thought of it that way." The woman heaved a sigh and turned for the kitchen. "I'll pack another box of potatoes." She shuffled into the back with a nervous energy.

Geist watched the scene with clenched teeth. Interfering would jeopardize their presence. She wanted the interactions to end before anything terrible happened, and a small piece of her hoped the German soldiers would be satisfied once the last box was brought.

The soldier motioned to Sofie. "It doesn't have to be this way, you know. We offer reprieve to… cooperative young women."

Sofie didn't answer.

"You wouldn't have to work too much. Maybe dry some apples between entertaining a few soldiers. The other girls don't complain. We'll treat you well."

Still, she said nothing.

"What's wrong? Not even a *no, thank you?* Do you think you're too good to speak to me?"

Sofie shook her head. "I'm sorry. No, thank you."

"Come here. Talk to us like a hostess should talk to her customers. We've had a long day and don't deserve this kind of disrespect."

With an exhale and a small step, the girl moved a few inches closer, though her body kept the same stiff, unreceptive posture. The German soldier stood straight and glared. Sofie shuffled closer a second time.

The man grabbed Sofie's forearm and yanked her half onto the counter as his two comrades leered. "I thought you Belgian girls were known for your courtesy."

"This one's always been stubborn, Keller," the second soldier commented. "I don't think she knows how to act."

"Leave me alone," Sofie said through shallow, shaky breaths, her language slipping to Dutch.

"Speak to me in German," Keller snapped. "And don't go making a scene. We just want some attention." He held his Luger close and Sofie stiffened like a board. She closed her eyes, unwilling to meet the man's leering gaze.

"Let me go," she said in forced German. "Please, *no more.*"

"Calm down. No one likes loud women." He leaned in close to her, smiling wide. "Why don't you give me a little kiss and I'll let you go?"

Geist had been so disgusted by the unfolding scene that she hadn't even seen Vergess get out of his chair. By the time Vergess was on top of the soldiers, it was too late.

He grabbed Keller's Luger and smashed it up into the man's face with enough force to send him stumbling backward. Blood gushed from Keller's nose and mouth as he fell over, dazed.

The other two soldiers, taken aback, took too long reaching for their sidearms. Vergess punched one square in the jaw, his knuckles busting a gash across the man's chin. The soldier hit the bar counter and then collided with a stool on his way to the floor, unconscious.

The last soldier stepped back, but Vergess shoved him against the wall and punched into his gut. The man gasped and whimpered, unable to form words.

Geist leapt from her seat and grabbed Vergess by the back of his tunic. "*Vergess,*" she hissed. "Enough. This isn't worth it."

Vergess held the man by the shoulder, pinning him to the wall. He said nothing.

"Let him go," Geist commanded.

Everyone in the pub stood motionless for a moment. Even the other soldier looked too stunned to move. Finally, Vergess sneered and released the man he had pinned.

Keller rolled to his side and ran an unsteady hand over his bloodied face. He staggered into the upright position, bracing himself with the counter.

The one man on the floor shook his head and staggered to his feet, befuddled and wobbling.

"Take your supplies and leave," Vergess commanded, his German clear and forceful.

Sofie watched, wide-eyed, never moving from her position right behind the bar. A small smile crept onto her face as one frightened soldier half-tripped in his haste to comply with Vergess's demand.

Keller lifted his handgun, but Geist was too quick. She ripped the weapon from his hand. Keller flinched back, shielding his face with an arm. Geist unclipped the magazine, allowed the bullets to fall to the floor, and threw the lightweight Luger back at its owner. It struck Keller in the face, busting open a gash across the eyebrow.

Keller grunted and wobbled back, unsteady. He turned and fled the pub with the last remaining soldier, half-doubled over and bleeding.

Another moment passed in silence. Vergess, looking satisfied that the soldiers wouldn't return anytime soon, walked back to the long table, his expression set into forlorn contemplation. Geist joined him, though she knew their time was short. They hadn't killed the soldiers, so someone would report the incident soon.

Victory held the bandages over his eye in place as he glared. "What do you think you're doing? Don't you know you anything about German laws in occupied countries? It's a crime to interfere with the military's business—*attacking* soldiers is all the more worse."

"What should I have done?" Vergess growled. He pulled out his chair and took a seat, reeking of anger. "Should I have done nothing?"

"You don't think the soldiers will harass the pub more now that you've attacked them? Think! You won't be here to protect this place when they come calling a second time."

"I'm not going to sit back and watch them torture some girl just because they *may* come back in the future. Perhaps they've learned their lesson. Perhaps they'll be too embarrassed to return."

"The girl was in no danger. Or did you forget I could see that? If I had seen her hurt, I would've intervened."

"Is that right?" Vergess snapped. "Or would you have avoided the trouble, like with the U-boat? I'm starting to think your sorcery has made you a coward. Am I the only one here with the guts to fight the enemy when they're digging their claws into our necks?"

Blick slammed his hand on the table, shaking the oil lamp and nearly toppling it to the stone floor. "Enough of this shit. You've got a bloody problem. I don't know what's going on, but—"

Blick cut himself short.

Sofie walked into the room with a tray of drinks—a full glass of water for each person at the table. She passed them out with relative speed, nodding and smiling to everyone she made eye contact with, despite the tension in the room.

Not too many people challenge the Germans, it seems.

Blick cleared his throat and changed his tone to one of pleasantness. "Ah, just what we need."

When Sofie reached Vergess, she stopped and combed her fingers through her hair. "Thank you."

Geist didn't appreciate the admiration in her tone, or the way she took in Vergess from head to toe. But she forced herself to remain quiet.

Sofie placed a hand on his shoulder. "I appreciate what you did."

Vergess jerked away from her touch. "Forget it," he said, his voice a low growl. "Bring us our food and pretend like you never saw us."

Geist's eyes widened.

Sofie stepped back, her lips in a tight line. "I'm sorry," she murmured. Before anyone could say anything further, she trotted back into the kitchen, her pale skin awash of red.

"What's gotten into you now?" Blick demanded.

Vergess scoffed. "Don't lecture me on etiquette."

"You're only making things worse," Victory said. "She could have been useful later, a local girl like that. And now our chance is ruined."

Vergess stood, knocking the chair to the floor in his haste. "Keep your future-sight out of my business. Maybe you should stay focused on your own problems before you lose another goddamn eye." He stormed out of the room, past the bar, and out the front room to the street. The others watched him go with varying levels of visible relief.

"Is he *ever* reasonable?" Dreamer asked. "I've yet to see him friendly since we began this trip."

"He's reasonable," Geist said. "He hasn't been himself since—"

Since heading back into the German Empire.

"It's because he's back in German territory, isn't it?" Blick guessed. He leaned back in his chair, resting his weight on the two back legs and kicking a foot onto the table. "Remember who said bringing him would be a bad idea? He's a liability—and this only proves it."

Geist stood. Battery stared up at her in confusion. "What're you doing?" he asked.

"I'm going to speak with him."

"You are?" Battery held out his hand, palm up. "At least let me lend you a little of my power. You never know what's going to be out there."

"I'll be fine. The rest of you can determine the path we take to Spa. I'm sure the locals will know the roads best for travel. Speak to the girl and apologize for Vergess."

"All right."

Geist exited the pub, her eyes on the scuffed hardwood as she made her way by the bar and out the heavy oak door. She ignored the ominous feeling she got from Victory—like he was paying attention to the future a little more for a reason—and instead contemplated how she would deal with Vergess's behavior.

Ever since stepping foot on Belgium soil, Geist had been absorbed with thoughts of the nation's continuing downfall. The thoughts left her cold and numb all over. *We all deal with suffering in different ways,* she thought, spotting Vergess in the afternoon shadow of a nearby building. *I try to ignore it, but maybe Vergess needs something else.*

He had a lit cigarette hanging in his mouth as he leaned against the bricks. Geist approached warily, trying with all her might to seem casual.

"Hey," Geist said.

Vergess exhaled a long line of smoke. She met his gaze as she slipped into the shadows next to him. Where had he found that cigarette? The smoke stung her nose and she knew it to be some European brand. It reminded her of her father.

"What's going on?" she asked, cutting straight to the point. "You weren't like this in Fort Douaumont. I know this is difficult for you, but you need to pull it together."

"Shh," Vergess replied, motioning with a jut of his chin.

Geist gritted her teeth, half-ready to yell. *Is he even paying attention?* She followed his gaze down the main road and all her anger disappeared. German soldiers lined the sidewalk in front of a tailor shop. Two inhabitants were dragged out by their arms and hair—a teen boy and a forty-something man, their blood relation apparent in their shared copper-brown hair and dark complexions.

The boy sported a black eye, busted nose, and bloodied shirt while his father stood straight in a clean white-collar vest, slacks, and coat. Geist eyed the soldiers. One, his tunic smeared in crimson, had a bright red ear and swollen cheek.

Was the boy fighting the soldiers? How foolish. He's worse than Vergess.

But that wasn't all she saw. Keller and the two soldiers from the pub were amidst the group of Germans. Keller pointed down the street, urging the other soldiers to follow, and Geist knew what they wanted. Fighting a squad of Germans was the last thing on her list.

"We should get inside," Geist whispered. "We'll get the others and exit out the back."

Vergess threw down his cigarette and snuffed it out under his boot. "I can handle them."

"No. We're not here to fight every enemy soldier we see."

"Fine. Whatever you say."

There it was again—something in his tone nearly driving her to frenzy.

Geist turned to the pub and froze. The door was open and Sofie stood at the threshold, her eyes locked on the soldiers down the street. The teenager and father were pushed and pulled, forced to their knees like dogs in the mud. Sofie retreated into the darkness of the pub, her gaze flitting over to Geist and Vergess for but a second.

In that moment, Geist could see the teen girl weighing the consequences of her actions.

Sofie locked the pub door with a heavy click of the metal latch, leaving Geist and Vergess to the soldiers on the street. Geist caught her breath, shocked that Sofie would lock them outside, but she realized right away why. Sofie was giving them to the soldiers. There would be no need to scour the pub if their targets were already on the streets.

Geist crossed the cobblestone road and hit the front door of the pub. She attempted to pass her hand through the thick wood. Pressing her palm up to the solid object only burned her skin when she attempted to pass through it. She pulled back and bit her lip. *Damn. I can't do it on my own yet.*

She motioned for Vergess to join her: he could dislodge the door, if needed, but it was too late.

"Halt!" a German soldier shouted. "By order of the German Empire, you will surrender and place your hands atop your heads!"

NINETEEN

The Resistance

Geist placed her hands on top of her head, lacing her fingers together through her curly hair. Vergess followed suit. He stood still, keeping his gaze down and his posture relaxed.

The soldiers approached with Mauser rifles at the ready. They surrounded Geist and Vergess, jittery, casting their commanding officer frequent glances. Keller, his uniform tunic splattered with his own blood, muttered warnings and curses under his breath. He pointed to Vergess.

"They attacked us," Keller stated. "And he consorted with the Belgians."

Geist straightened her posture. "We're citizens of the United States. We'll return to our ship."

Perhaps her statements would have allowed her to return to the docks unmolested, but Vergess destroyed all chances when he spat on Keller, his saliva arching to hit the soldier on the jaw. Geist had heard stories about the Germans. Always serious. Taking every offense to heart. If she could, she'd shake Vergess by the collar of his jacket—or strike him for his foolishness.

The enemy soldiers shouted among each other and brought their bayonets to bear on Vergess's neck and Geist's back.

"We're in charge here," a soldier stated. "We're taking you both into detention."

With a few quick shoves, the soldiers pushed Geist together with the Belgian father and his teenage son. They gave her sorrowful glances, both a mix of pity and frustration. Vergess joined them, but not until one soldier struck him across the face with the butt of his heavy rifle. The force of the blow sounded as if it would hurt a normal man, but Geist knew it couldn't have done much to an apex sorcerer. To her amusement, Vergess stumbled back and played into the blow, his black hair disheveled and hanging across his face.

Soldiers wrestled him into the group of detainees. Vergess kept himself close to Geist as he scanned the soldiers, his gaze lingering on their guns and ammunition. Geist kept her wits about her, knowing that normal men could still kill a sorcerer quite easily.

If an opportunity presented itself to attack, she would take it. But revealing their sorcery here in Antwerp would blow their cover.

But the moment we're alone…

Civilians peeked out from behind wooden shutters and thick curtains, but when Geist met their gaze, they hid away. Doors locked and shops closed.

"God, forgive me," the father muttered under his breath in hasty statements. "Watch over my family. Let my wife know I love her. Protect my unruly son."

The teenager, sullen, stared at his feet. Blood dripped from his nose and lips, spilling in droplets across his leather shoes.

"March," Keller commanded.

Geist walked where the soldiers told her to walk, biding her time, her mind racing. The Germans steered her toward the edge of Antwerp.

The old stone walls of the city stood in shambles. Debris from the German siege littered the outskirts. Barbed wire filled in the holes in the wall and shreds of clothing caught on the sharpened metal told a desperate story Geist didn't care to think of.

A terrible odor of decay hung on the air with the fog once they exited the city. Geist glanced around, her gaze drawn to the bloody furrows in the earth, shallow trenches not used for war, but for corpses. Bodies lay in piles in all states of decomposition. Flies feasted, but the carrion birds dared not venture too close to the hungry men and their guns.

The soldiers forced the father and son to their knees on the edge of the trench, a good three hundred feet from the wall. Geist and Vergess were pulled and pushed to join them. Mud soaked into Geist's slacks, sending a cold shiver from her legs up to her spine. The foul stench stung her eyes.

Although Geist had always known of the Belgian's plight, she didn't fully comprehend their wretched situation until she glanced up at the rifles.

The Germans didn't keep detainees. They dragged them to hastily dug graves and filled them efficiently. Anyone who argued—anyone who showed signs of rebellion—would find no mercy, only charnel houses.

Geist gritted her teeth as the men lined up behind them and steadied their rifles, ready for the execution. *I hope we're far enough away. I'm not going to wait any longer.*

She jumped to her feet, steady and without fear. The startled soldiers pulled their triggers on her, bullets flying through the air with a few cracks from their rifles. She shimmered and shifted, her body untouchable, and ran for the nearest soldier, who stood no more than twenty feet away. The shots pierced and tore her clothing, but Geist didn't care.

Geist pulled the Luger pistol from the belt on one soldier and shot another, gore splattering across the uniform of the next man in line. Amidst the confusion, the men attempted to reload, but Geist was far too swift. She fired again, pointblank, killing another soldier by running a bullet through his temple.

Vergess stood. When soldiers fired upon him, the bullets cut his clothing, but they slammed into impenetrable flesh and fell to the ground. Vergess shielded his eyes and ran to the nearest soldier with impossible speed. He slammed a knee into the man's gut and ruptured organs. Coughing up a mouthful of blood, the soldier hit the ground with a voiceless groan.

Geist shot twice more, making sure to take aim and not hit the civilians. She struck one soldier in the chest and another in the jaw, sending them both to early graves, though neither would die for some time. They would bleed out, here in this field of death—*and they got what they deserved,* Geist thought.

When the remaining soldiers fired upon her, they hit nothing. When they fired upon Vergess, they hit a stone wall. Their panic took their aim, and bullets went flying off into the woods or into the walls of Antwerp. But the firefight would surely attract more attention, and Geist knew they had to end the conflict as soon as possible.

Vergess grabbed a soldier by the neck and held him up off the ground, his supernatural strength a terrifying spectacle for the other three Germans. Putrid rot emanated from Vergess's fingertips, spreading across the soldier's body and eating away the skin, muscle, and membranes like only a wicked disease could.

The soldier tried to scream, but his breath was lost to the rot and his voice died to a wet gurgle. He went limp in Vergess's grip, his neck a mass of blackened flesh on the verge of ash. Vergess released the corpse, and the rot continued to spread—down the chest and over the skull, even to the uniform. After a few horrid moments, the body lay with no head and half a chest, the rest crumbling and caving in.

"*Demon,*" Keller muttered under his breath.

They stared at Vergess with wide, panicked eyes, never noticing Geist as she took advantage of their gaping. She rapid-fired her last three bullets, striking each man in the head and downing them before they could retaliate.

"We need to go," Geist said.

Vergess nodded.

"W-wait."

Both Geist and Vergess stopped before they had gotten more than two feet toward the city. They turned and saw the father and teen standing near the trench, their expressions bordering on disbelief. Despite the blood and busted nose, the boy approached with his head held high.

"What are you?" he asked, his voice just above a whisper. "Are you really demons? Or something else?"

"Don't talk to them, Lucas," his father pleaded. "It's a godsend we're alive. Don't test their wrath."

Vergess tensed. "If you know what's good for you, you won't talk about what happened here, understand?"

Before the youth could answer, bullets struck the earth all around them. German snipers lined the broken wall of Antwerp, no doubt drawn by the sounds of fighting. The fog hindered their aim, but each shot was closer than the last.

"Take cover!" Geist shouted.

She ran for the wall, knowing the city would be the far safer than the open fields around it. Bullets rained down, one clipping her boot and causing her to stumble.

Vergess doubled back. "Stay behind me."

The snipers posed virtually no threat to his impenetrable skin. Geist stepped up close, thankful for the size difference between them. Two of her could hide behind Vergess with little problem.

The boy, Lucas, ran to his father and offered his shoulder for support. His father, though spry, moved with arthritic stiffness. Together, they ran a short distance until the crack of a rifle echoed in the field. His father slumped and Lucas, confused, attempted to help him stand.

"Get up, get up!"

But he couldn't.

Blood wept from the entrance wound on the man's forehead, but it gushed out the larger exit wound in the back near the spine. He hung as deadweight on his son—a son who refused to believe he couldn't stand.

"Get up! *Get up!*" Lucas dragged the body, attempting to hold it upright. "*Come on!*"

"Vergess," Geist said. "Get him."

Vergess dashed from Geist's side. He ripped the corpse from Lucas' grasp and wrenched the child away, despite his loud protests. When Vergess returned to Geist's side, they ran together, the boy flailing to free himself, only to be yanked by the arm into Antwerp.

"Stop!" Lucas cried. "We have to go back! We have to get him!"

Vergess slammed his back against the wall of the city and shook the boy hard. "Don't be a fool. He's gone."

Shouts from confused German soldiers echoed above them. The snipers had lost their targets' position through the fog and chaos. While they had cover, Geist motioned to a nearby alley between brick buildings. Vergess shielded them the short distance it took to run. Once safe between the buildings, they stopped to catch their breath.

Vergess released Lucas. "Go."

The boy, shaken, shifted his gaze between Vergess and Geist. After a moment, he glanced down to the red on his shirt—a mix of his and his father's blood—and took a deep breath. He ripped his attention away from the horror and returned it to Geist.

Lucas rubbed at his eyes, smearing crimson across his cheek. Each word he spoke came out terse and reserved, as though he held back a flood of emotions. "Take me with you. I want to fight them."

"You won't survive," Vergess stated, not bothering to look at the youth.

Lucas turned his attention to Vergess and stepped closer to him. "I don't care!" he cried out. "I don't want to survive. I want to *fight.*"

He was younger than Battery and smaller to boot, almost smaller than Geist herself. Sunken cheeks and protruding collarbones spoke volumes. Determination shone in his eyes, but a body couldn't sustain itself on revenge alone.

Vergess shook his head. "You can't help us, kid. Protect what little family you have left."

"You don't understand! I'll do whatever it takes! I don't care if you're demons or wizards—I'll give you whatever you want if you take me with you."

Vergess grabbed the teen by the shirt and jerked him close. The boy gasped and trembled, taken aback by the other man's sudden assault.

"You're weak," Vergess drawled. "You're not like us. You can't stand against the enemies we fight. Stay home—in a realm you understand—and do what you can there." He shoved the teen back, sending him to the ground with little effort. Dirty street water splashed onto Lucas's soiled clothes and the boy glowered up at Vergess with a wet sheen to his eyes.

Unfazed, Vergess strode away, his back to the boy and his expression nothing but ice. He walked past Geist, intent on entering the heart of Antwerp. Geist's chest seized up with indecision. Vergess wasn't wrong. The boy couldn't even fight normal soldiers, let alone sorcerers.

But…

You're weak. You're not like us. Stay home. Do what you can there.

They were the arguments used against her—the very reasons she hadn't been allowed to be a soldier or join the Ethereal Squadron as a woman. If Geist followed Vergess and left Lucas, she would be a hypocrite. She would be using the exact same excuses on another person. She would be judging him unworthy without testing —tacitly saying that she knew him, and what was best for him, without his input or capabilities taken into consideration.

Geist exhaled and walked over to Lucas, her pace quick and her mind dwelling on the enemy soldiers who were sure to arrive any second.

Lucas stood and met her gaze with his own. She sensed his grit.

"Our foes may be insurmountable," Geist murmured.

He squeezed his hands into tight fists. "If they are, we've lost anyway. I'd rather say I fought than say I did nothing."

Geist smiled. That was exactly how she felt.

She handed over the Luger pistol. "If you mean what you say, you'll find passage to Le Havre. Speak to the BEF soldiers there and ask for the 2nd E Squadron. Tell that squadron what you saw here, and no one else."

"Le Havre?" Lucas repeated in confusion. "You're not with the resistance in Liège?"

"No. Go to Le Havre. They'll know who sent you."

Holding the Luger with both hands, Lucas stared at it in deep contemplation. Geist turned on her heel and ran to catch up with Vergess, who had already traveled down the long road and waited in the broken shadow of a nearby building. She didn't know if Lucas would make it to Le Havre, but a piece of her hoped he would.

When she joined Vergess, they walked together into the main district of the city, avoiding everyone along their way. Through controlled breaths he said, "You've sent the boy to his grave—you realize that, right? The non-magical men in the Ethereal Squadron don't last the year."

"I'm not so arrogant as to say I know what's good for everyone," Geist said with a huff. "Maybe it's best he's ruled by his own foolishness, rather than someone else's wisdom. Lord knows that's what I wanted at his age."

But Vergess was right. Non-sorcerers did join the Ethereal Squadron from time to time. They were men who had discovered magic or had been born to sorcerer mothers and non-sorcerer fathers. They chose to help in the fighting—in the secret war between magic-wielders—but their limitations gave them little opportunity to do much in service of their new comrades. Still, their bravery impressed everyone. Those who didn't die won the respect and care of the sorcerer families they fought alongside.

Perhaps Lucas will find solace fighting his enemies—at least for a little while.

Vergess slammed his back to a stone wall across the street from their pub. The roads were filled with patrols of soldiers running to the walls. The soldiers ran in lines of ten, some in groups of thirty, and the citizens of Antwerp knew not to venture outside. Geist wondered if Lucas would fare well enough to escape. If caught, the soldiers would surely blame him for the death of the men beyond the walls.

Geist slid close to Vergess and glanced around. The pub sat unmolested, and she wondered if the rest of the team remained inside.

"Is this how Victory always operates?" Vergess asked, staring at the locked wooden door.

"What do you mean?"

"I mean, the city swarms with the enemy, and we've been gone for some time, yet your advisor did nothing."

"He waited, as he should. We aren't a team of lone wolves. We have to work together."

"There's no cooperation if some members aren't invested in cooperating."

Geist glowered up at him. "If you have something to say, out with it."

Vergess ground his teeth loud enough for her to hear. He met her glare with one of his own, cold fury in his eyes.

When he remained silent, she continued. "Why are you acting like this? Is it because we're approaching Germany?"

"Of course," he snapped, rage behind his words. "I never wanted to return. And here I am, standing on the precipice."

Geist caught her breath. She had never considered that Vergess wouldn't want to be a part of Operation Prometheus. Forcing him to venture so close to his homeland might have been more painful than leaving had ever been.

"I'm sorry," Geist said. "I was the one who asked that you be moved to this team."

"I know." He snorted and turned away.

"I didn't think we could do it without you. You've already done so much, from the U-boat to the IDs. Please understand it wasn't to hurt you. We need your strength." She took in a deep breath. "I… I feel more secure when you're around."

"I've lost people here. In Germany. In Austria. In Serbia."

"Is this about Isidora?" Geist asked. "The woman you loved?"

Vergess gritted his teeth. "You don't understand what it's like to return to a homeland filled with painful memories."

"I do. I swear it."

When he returned his gaze, it had softened, but not fully.

Geist exhaled. "My father is Austrian. We're getting close to my homeland as well. I hate to see Belgium like this. I came here as a child."

"What?"

"It's true, all right? No one else knows." Geist shook her head. "Well, I told Battery. But no one else outside of you two knows."

Vergess stared for a long moment, his eyes widening until he stared at Geist as though seeing her for the first time. "You're a

Cavell," he drawled. "I can't believe it. The house of assassins. The kingkillers."

The shock lasted a full second. *He pieced it together that quickly? How?*

"House Cavell has access to specter, apex, and corpus sorcery. That has to be the house you're from. I'd stake my life on it. They serve the Royal House of Habsburg-Lorraine." Vergess narrowed his eyes. "Are you… working for them? Is that what this is?"

"I have nothing to do with my house," Geist blurted out, desperate to stop his line of thought. "I wasn't lying when I said I ran from them. I swear it. My father tried to marry me to Leopold and—"

"The crown prince?"

"Yes, and—"

"Why would you keep this hidden?" he asked. "If you aren't involved with them, it should be common knowledge to avoid suspicion."

"I told you. I have nothing to do with my house." Geist spotted a group of enemy soldiers heading down the street in their direction. She grabbed Vergess by the coat and pulled him farther into the shadows, her knuckles white and her heart pounding. "Do you think anyone would've taken me into the Ethereal Squadron if I had told them who I was?"

"I told them when I defected," Vergess said. "If you had been truthful—"

"Don't," Geist snapped. "How can you stand there and say *if I had only been truthful from the beginning* that everything would have worked out?" Her nails dug into her palms, even through the fabric of Vergess's jacket. "They wouldn't have accepted me. Not as a woman. Not as a defector of House Cavell. I had to keep it hidden. Changing a few lines on my registration was all it took to remove the doubt—to remove the barriers—to allow me a chance to prove myself…"

It took all of Geist's willpower to keep her frustration in check. She never let go of her vise grip on Vergess's jacket, dreading what he would say next.

"The Verdun general doesn't know you're a woman, does he?"

"Cross knows," Geist forced herself to say.

"I see."

The silence that followed twisted Geist's stomach into knots. They didn't have time to bicker about her past. They had a mission, but it would never be accomplished with doubt plaguing them at every step.

"I've wanted to know your name for a while now," Vergess said, breaking the stagnant atmosphere. "Florence Cavell."

She held still, waiting.

"You trusted me, even when the others said I would betray them. I know they didn't want me on this mission—I could hear it through the walls anywhere in Fort Belleville—but you insisted." He took one of her hands in his and rubbed at her knuckles, relaxing her grip. The simple motion took her by surprise. "I'm going to offer the same trust in return. If you say you have nothing to do with House Cavell, then that's what I choose to believe."

Geist stared at his hand, her fears melting away despite the echo of marching boots and the sound of distant gunfire. "Thank you," she murmured.

"We both want to do right in this war," he continued, his voice low. "I'll try to keep some perspective as we get closer to the German Frontline Command."

The soothing Belgian breeze washed between them. Geist could see Vergess relax: his posture loosened, and his breathing returned to normal. No more words were needed.

When Geist attempted to reenter the pub, Vergess held her back, keeping his hand on hers.

"I hope you were serious when you said you were no longer engaged," he said.

Geist locked up, her thoughts grinding to a halt. After a belabored moment, she found her breath and shook her head. "I—uh…"

"It would be trouble for us if they're looking for you. I'd hate to have to kill a prince."

Geist went to speak but stopped herself short. She hadn't given that situation consideration. *They won't be looking for me here… right?* And Vergess's statement almost sounded like a promise.

Then he brought her knuckles up to his lips and gave them a light kiss.

"What're you doing?" Geist whispered, unwilling to take her hand away but trembling from the contact. No one had ever done this for her, not even the Crown Prince of Austria.

"I'm making my intentions clear," he said. "As any gentleman should. Now would be your chance to deny me."

"But—I'm not—I mean, look at me." She gestured to her body, her curves dulled, her clothes splattered with blood, and mud on her knees and hands. "I'm not like the others. The women. I'm—"

"We're cut from the same cloth, you and I," Vergess interjected. "And you're terrible at hiding your beauty."

"I…" Geist took in a breath, at a loss for words.

"You won't deny my advances, will you? If you want me to, I'll stop now, before it becomes serious, but I want the chance to win your affection."

"Vergess, I… we're in the middle of an operation," she said. "We'll talk about this once we're back at Fort Belleville. Please. We need to go."

"Yes, I know. But promise me we'll speak afterward."

There was a long silence. Then: "I promise."

Geist gave a curt nod and urged him toward the pub, desperate to leave the conversation. *I can't do this. Not here, not in the middle of Antwerp.*

Once convinced soldiers had left the street, Geist returned to the pub and slammed her fist on the heavy wooden door. It remained locked, much to her frustration. Vergess ran up and motioned her to one side.

He placed a hand on the handle, and after a moment, rot spread from his palm to the door. His ruina sorcery broke down and aged anything, from flesh to metal. Blackish rotting power degraded the copper handle, unraveling it to dust.

Vergess pushed the door and stopped his ruina power from consuming the rest of the entrance. They walked in together, Geist avoiding all eye contact, and found the front room empty. Victory, Blick, Battery, and Dreamer sat in the back room at their table, bowls of soup and slimy bread sitting before them.

Geist hustled over and took her seat, her breathing still shallow. Battery scooted close and tilted his head. "We heard some commotion outside," he said. "But Victory said everything would be okay. He was right, wasn't he?"

"Is that why you all stayed inside?" Vergess asked, taking a seat between Dreamer and Geist. "You put a lot trust in him. Imagine the consequences of a misprediction."

Victory smirked. "Well, fortunately, you've returned at just the time I saw you returning." He rubbed the bandages over his face. "And while you were away, the owners of this fine pub have provided us with examples of ID cards. Dreamer believes he can make us look like citizens or soldiers, depending on the need."

"You knew what was going to happen to us?" Geist asked. *He knew we would be attacked by soldiers and he said nothing to me?*

"I apologize," Victory replied, glancing over to her. "I don't fully know why, or how, but I saw that if you and Vergess went out alone, you would return with valuable information. You would know where we should stop before the city of Spa."

"Where?" she asked, raking her mind for such information. Her thoughts went straight to her interactions with Lucas. He *had* mentioned a city. A city where the "resistance" dwelled.

"Liège?"

"The city of Liège?" Victory repeated. "I see."

Dreamer ran his thumb and pointer finger down the edges of his mouth. "Interesting. And now we have an advantage over our enemy. Vergess, do you know of any sorcerer families in the German Empire with this future sight ability?"

"No," Vergess said. "I was taught it died off with Anhalt."

"That's what I thought. The sorcerers of the Najd believe those with destiny sorcery in their blood are descended from the prophets, and that they died out long ago."

Victory shook his head. "Any of my brothers could develop the same magic if they focused. I studied the school of destiny magic to aid the Ethereal Squadron, but I'm afraid my inexperience limits its usefulness. I still cannot see our victory in Spa."

"You're still the team's most valuable asset," Dreamer said. "We've got a destination and a clear way to avoid soldiers now. This operation will certainly be a success."

Battery rolled his eyes. Blick nudged him with an elbow and shook his head. Still, the younger man turned away from the conversation and glared at the table. He pushed his half-eaten bread around while Dreamer continued his compliments.

"You better now?" Blick asked, staring down Vergess. "Or are you going to have another tantrum?"

Vergess snorted. "I'll shape up once you stop acting like a wild dog around every woman we encounter."

"Gentlemen," Dreamer said, holding up a hand. "If I may? Perhaps we should eat and be on our way without further discourse. If that's all right with everyone?"

Everyone in the team murmured agreements.

Geist turned her attention to the food awaiting her on the table. The soup, mostly broth, contained goat meat, onions, carrots, and cabbage. The smell didn't invite consumption. *But better than bread,* she thought with a chuckle under her breath. She had seen the type of bread before in France—they called it "K bread"—a brick of foodstuff made from a mixture of potato, rye, and flour. The crust was tough as a rock and the soft, slimy insides tasted like wet mold. Doctors advised to eat as little of it as possible, but sometimes food for the soldiers was scarce.

Vergess ate his meal without word or complaint. First the bread, which he downed easily, and then he continued to the soup. Although the thought of speaking to him returned her to a flustered state, Geist knew she couldn't keep quiet much longer, especially not in front of the others.

I have to maintain myself and act as though nothing has changed.

"So," she said, her voice strained. "Which was easier to learn, apex or ruina sorcery?"

A random question, she knew the moment the words had left her mouth, and Vergess responded with a narrowed gaze.

"Ruina. It's a simple magic."

"Oh? Why is that?"

He laughed and picked up his bowl of half-consumed soup. "It took a man several years to raise the animal that died to give its meat for this meal. It took another man several months to grow the crops. It took yet another man several hours to cook everything together."

Vergess tossed the soup to the floor, spilling the room-temperature broth across the wood panels.

"It took me two seconds to ruin it," he stated.

Geist stood and stared at the mess. The others at the table followed suit, confusion on their faces.

"What're you trying to say?" Battery asked, flailing an arm at the soup. "Use your words, for God's sake."

"It's far easier to destroy than it is to create," Vergess replied, giving the group a long stare. "Everyone who practices ruina sorcery, right down to the children, pick it up with ease."

Geist's thoughts lingered on the discarded soup.

"I hope you understand," Vergess continued. "Because, without a doubt, there will be Abomination Soldiers in Spa with the same destructive power as my own."

TWENTY

Liège, Belgium

"Why didn't we fly in?" Battery asked. "Not that I wanted to use a parachute again, but it might have been faster."

"The British Empire controls the seas, but Germany controls the skies," Vergess stated. "Fighting through a fleet of zeppelins and triplanes would have been suicidal."

Geist sighed. The roads of Belgium did not cater well to travelers: German soldiers stood in groups of ten to twenty on all the major thoroughfares, their rifles ready, some with machine guns, others with motorcars and explosives. At checkpoint after checkpoint, they demanded IDs and barked dozens of tricky questions, even with Vergess disguised as a German NCO.

The only other travelers made their way across the country with carts and pack animals. Geist, perched on the backend of their own wooden cart, glanced over at their toiling horses. The animals hadn't come cheap, but the Belgians had been more than willing to sell the property for a fistful of bills. A motorcar would have been ideal, but the Germans had long since requisitioned all such vehicles.

A great deal of Belgium's landscape had been devastated in the fighting. When the Germans had marched through the country, they had sieged and sacked big cities and small towns alike. Geist could see the shadowed remnants of buildings and homes far in the distance. Black fields marked the location of devastating fires and craters smoldered in the wake of artillery bombardments.

Most disturbing were the babies left in irrigation ditches along the side of the road. Dead infants—some a mere three days old—abandoned with nothing, not even a blanket. Their shriveled bodies and sealed, sunken eyes sent sharp chills through Geist's body every time her gaze fell upon them.

"What happened here?" she whispered, unable to look away.

Vergess, walking alongside the cart, kept his attention forward, never glancing to the ditch of child corpses. "*Boche* babies," he said. "Children of native women and German soldiers."

"The mothers commit infanticide out of spite?" Battery asked, his face drained of color and his hands shaking.

"Such conditions drive even the sanest among us to extremes," Dreamer chimed in, mounted atop the lead horse. "I'm sure it wasn't a mistake that the babies were abandoned on the main road for the German soldiers to see. I pray the children find shelter in the arms of the saints in the world after this." He stroked his nickering horse and calmed the creature despite the smell of rot that lingered on the air. He rode with the grace of a nobleman as Geist pondered the fate of the children.

Blick, walking alongside the cart, motioned to the corpse-infested ditches with an outstretched thumb. "Any of these yours?" he quipped to Vergess.

Vergess tensed but didn't answer.

"*Blick*," Geist snapped. "You've had your fun. Now shut the hell up."

Blick gave her half a salute. "Yes, sir."

The exchange left a sour taste in Geist's mouth. She kept her eyes on Vergess, and he occasionally glanced up and met her gaze. Something about his blue eyes kept her staring at him. Did he feel guilt for the children? Would he one day want them? Would he want them… with her?

Geist shook her head, unable to dislodge the confusing thoughts.

I don't know if I can wait until we return to Fort Belleville, she thought. *Could we be together? Would we continue in the war? Could we elope? What kind of life could we lead, two estranged sorcerers running from their houses?*

"Anyone here know sorcerers from the Royal House of Habsburg-Lorraine?" Vergess asked aloud, breaking Geist's train of thought.

Battery whipped his attention to the other man but offered no commentary.

"I've met a few of them," Victory said, almost disinterested. "Why?"

"Have you ever met the crown prince? Leopold?"

"Yes. On occasion."

Blick chuckled. He placed his hands on his head while he continued to walk, a smirk on his face. "You think *I'm* a wild dog? You should meet Leopold. That guy thinks every woman wants him."

"Is that right?" Vergess asked, sneaking Geist a sidelong glance. Geist looked away, clamping her lips shut.

"That's not the most important thing," Victory interjected with a wave of his hand. "It's his new proposal that worries me. Many sorcerers believe it's he and his father who started the whole war."

"Oh?"

It didn't surprise Geist that Victory considered them the root cause of the war. The sorcerers of the Royal House were famously power-hungry. They had even stated, on multiple occasions, that ruling over all Europe was their right by birth. That they were the last true kings and queens, the only sorcerers left with a bloodline that traced back to the first sorcerer—and the only ones capable of wielding the ultimate school of sorcery.

The magic they called *The Final Argument of Kings.*

"Do you think they have magi-tech technology?" Battery asked.

Victory nodded. "No doubt in my mind."

Geist knew Austria-Hungary had to be behind the fighting. They were an older nation, more established than the fledgling Germany, and they shared a common language and border. When Austria-Hungary wanted war, they called in their allies to attack—

that was how it had always worked. It was the same on the front-lines. If Germany had a devastating weapon like the GH Gas, Austria-Hungary would have it as well.

Victory whistled, cutting the discussion short.

"Pay attention to the road," he intoned. "Something's coming."

Blick nodded once, then his eyes lit up with a golden bioluminescent glow. He peered into the distance, his pupils widening.

Geist scooted back down the cart to join Victory and Battery. They pressed themselves against each other and slumped their postures to maintain the ruse. Dreamer glanced over his shoulder: his sorcery had transformed their clothing into bloodied German uniforms, complete with bandages and pus stains. Geist, Battery, and Victory were disguised as wounded soldiers returning to the nearest base while Vergess, Blick, and Dreamer acted as their soldier escort. No German patriot would stop wounded men heading to a wartime hospital.

"Three men coming," Blick said to the group in a low voice. "All Abomination Soldiers." His eyes still gleaming yellow, he turned to Dreamer and grimaced. "Ah," he grunted, taken aback. "I knew you were hiding your real face from us."

Dreamer lifted an eyebrow. "Surprised by what you see?"

"I guess it makes sense. But do you actually *know* how to use those all those knives—or are they heirlooms?"

Dreamer responded with a smug smile, piquing Geist's interest. How much did they really know about this man?

Victory closed his one good eye and took a deep breath. "Vergess. When the men ask you how we were wounded, tell them it was from fighting rebels."

Then the sound of heavy hoofbeats approached.

Geist craned her head back and saw the sun glint off the chestnut coats of the soldiers' sorrels. Their horses, beautiful beasts, closed the distance in good time, trotting up to the cart with powerful strides. They pulled to a stop in front of Dreamer and his horse, preventing the cart from moving forward.

Vergess stepped up and straightened his posture. "Sir."

The lead German, a tall man with a gray cape over one shoulder, stared down at Vergess with squinted eyes. He wore the rank of lieutenant but held himself with the pomp and condescension of an emperor's spoiled child, his nose up in the air, his expression judging them with obvious disgust. His coat bore the name *Graf* stitched on his tunic, over the heart.

"Soldier," Lieutenant Graf said with a sneer. "Have you seen a group of five Belgians on the road within the last hour?"

"No, sir," Vergess replied.

"Are you positive?"

"I think I would have remembered seeing five people, *sir*."

Lieutenant Graf kicked his horse into a canter and walked around the cart, giving every detail the once-over. Geist kept her back and shoulders slumped over, feigning pain, but her sidearm was tucked in her lap, ready for use.

"Three soldiers to escort three wounded men?" Lieutenant Graf asked.

"We're escorting a staff captain and his right-hand men," Vergess stated. "Top priority, sir. We're to get him to the hospitals in Spa."

Lieutenant Graf scanned the back of the cart and stopped once his gaze found the illusionary insignias of rank on Victory's uniform. "Staff captain?"

Vergess nodded. "Staff Captain Wolff."

"Is that so?"

"Yes, sir."

"And how were Captain Wolff and his men injured?"

"Rebel attacks," Vergess replied with the ease of a pathological liar. "We never saw it coming."

Lieutenant Graf frowned. He yanked on his reins and jerked the horse back toward the road with little regard for the animal's comfort. "Those *dogs*. They never learn their lesson." He rode out a short distance before glancing over his shoulder. "If you see anyone on the road from here to Liège, shoot them. If they run, herd them north."

"North, sir?"

"Toward the wire."

The wire.

Geist's chest tightened. She had heard the stories: a German-constructed electric fence, ten feet tall and a hundred and twenty-five miles long, on the northern border of Belgium and the Netherlands. Six barbed wires charged with two thousand volts ran all along its length. Those who attempted to climb died instantly. Those caught within five hundred yards of the fence posts were summarily executed.

News didn't travel in Germany-occupied Belgium like it did in the rest of the world. While she knew of the wire, most Belgians would think only of escaping to the neutral Netherlands, a country virtually untouched by the war. But that was just what the Germans wanted.

The wire was a thing of evil, a true terror weapon. The line between war and peace. Between life and death.

"I shall endeavor to do so, sir," Vergess said.

"Good," Lieutenant Graf huffed. "Come, men!" He kicked his steed and set off at a canter. The other sorcerers followed suit, vanishing into the night.

Blick shoved his hands deep into his pockets. "Belgium is locked down. I'm surprised we've gotten as far as this without incident. At least we've secured an exit."

"Don't jinx us," Battery muttered, pushing away from the side of the cart. "We had an exit plan for the zeppelin and look what happened. Let's just focus on what's ahead."

"You didn't have your brothers with you on the zeppelin. Things will be different here."

"You tempt fate."

"If Fate is Lady Justice's mysterious sister, I don't mind tempting her."

Battery rolled his eyes. Victory and Geist shared a chuckle, Victory going so far as to swing an arm over her shoulder, brotherhood camaraderie in every regard, though Geist couldn't help but tense as he touched her.

"You three don't have to sit so close anymore," Vergess said, his stern voice reminiscent of the German soldiers, as though they had been purged of humor at birth. "We're almost to Liège. I'll cover you in the sheets when we get close."

"No need to risk discovery," Victory said, unmoving. "We'll lie here until then."

Vergess glared but offered nothing else in return.

It's fine, Geist thought, wishing she could reassure Vergess. *We're just two wounded soldiers on the back of the cart. That's all.*

The silence that followed was better than any quip Battery or Blick could dream up. Geist could only hope they were getting accustomed to each other's company.

They needed all the advantages they could get.

THE CRACK of gunfire rang out, and Geist's hair stood on end. She wanted to sit up, throw off the blanket, and glance around, but she continued to lie on her back, playing the part of a dying soldier to the hilt. Battery fidgeted to her left, but Victory made no move, holding still enough to make her worry. Was he even awake? *Of course he is. How could someone sleep at a time like this?*

Wind swept over the cart and agitated the horses. The evening chill brought Geist to the edge of shivering. The blanket and her heavy breathing kept her warm enough, but her feet were locked in icy boots that hung out the back of the cart.

The gunfire intensified.

Vergess threw back the blanket, and the cool night air wafted over Geist. The cloud-covered sky above offered little light, but the street lamps and distant fire kept the city visible.

"There's fighting," Vergess stated. "The Belgians are swarming the streets."

"What's going on?" she asked, knowing they were in the heart of Liège with no easy escape.

"The Germans were executing rebels and burning buildings. The Belgians didn't like that."

"Can we avoid it?"

"I think the fighting's gonna find *us.*"

A blast and tremor shook the cart, agitating the horses and setting Geist's nerves on edge. The sounds of war swirled all around them: screams and cries and sudden bursts of gunfire. Whatever had happened descended upon them in one lightning-fast moment, as though they had found themselves in the middle of the storm.

Geist sat up and glanced around, her eyes frantically panning over the commotion. Liège was torn apart by a cacophony of violent flashes and bombastic sound, waves of heat following behind artificial booms of thunder. Civilians, men and women alike, were rent apart by explosions, gore and offal flung in every direction.

A board with dynamite tied to it, no doubt a handmade weapon from the Belgians, landed next to the cart. On instinct, Geist hauled Battery up by his collar and pushed him out the back. In the second moment she had before the explosive followed through with its damage, Geist yelled, "Get out!" with her voice no more than a hot rasp.

Victory, perhaps already knowing, leapt out the front of the cart and sprinted away. Dreamer produced a dagger, seemingly out of nowhere, and cut the leather strap holding his horse back before kicking his animal into motion.

Blick and Vergess were outside of her vision, the only two not confined to the cart.

Time slowed as Geist flung herself from the vehicle, sensory overload filling her brain with static. The roar of the world died away as the dynamite blast deafened her. She staggered and swayed, but all she was capable of achieving was a half-crawl as she clambered away from the destruction.

German soldiers answered with suppressing fire. They opened fire onto the crowds of Belgians, mowing down anyone and everyone in their path. One in three bullets hit their targets while the rest shredded buildings, shattered windows, and struck animals. Geist kept her belly to the ground, struggling to focus.

In the fleeting moments of clear thought, she noted that Dreamer's illusions had disappeared, leaving her dressed as a civilian. Then her thoughts flew to Vergess.

Where is he?

Undeterred by the machine guns, the Belgians continued their bombardment. Grenades, dynamite, Molotov cocktails—anything was fair game. The blasts mutilated and burned the frontline soldiers while the grenades thrown behind them tore up the men hiding behind cover.

Battery grabbed Geist by the shoulder and shouted something she couldn't hear. Instead, Geist took his hand and squeezed hard, needing his sorcery more than ever.

Time snapped back into place as Battery's power flowed through her, restoring her hearing and even clearing her head in spite of the chaos that surrounded them. Battery tried again to yell something to her, but his own throat was hoarse and his words came out in broken fragments.

"Stay with me!" Geist commanded.

She jumped to her feet and cloaked herself in a shroud of invisibility. Through the black smoke and red flashes of fire, Geist could only make out silhouettes. She grabbed Battery by the arm and dragged him through the street, running as fast as her body would allow, coughing back the smoke with each ragged breath.

When soldiers stood in her path, Geist didn't hesitate. She released Battery and lunged forward, using her incorporeal form to slide into the men and become physical, scooping out a chuck of innards with a swipe of her hand. She tore through their uniforms and the blood splashed across the cobblestone streets in cinematic splatters. The crimson that remained on her body became invisible with her.

Battery pulled out his grandfather's Lancaster pistol and shot at oncoming soldiers too confused by their teammates' sudden deaths to notice his presence. His pistol shots were nearly silent amidst the rage of sound and destruction swirling around them. Some soldiers, struck in the arm or side, carried on as though they hadn't been hit, blind adrenaline fueling their assault and numbing the pain of their wounds. Those struck in the head and chest crumpled, limbs continuing to spasm as if the body didn't understand yet that the brain was dead.

"Get back!" a man's voice yelled, his voice muffled by gunfire.

Geist spotted Victory amidst the smoke, Blick standing by his side and his glowing gold eyes piercing the darkness to match her gaze. They motioned for her and Battery to move.

"Get back!" Victory repeated.

A thick line of flame lit up the night, fifteen feet long and oozing black smoke. German stormtroopers wielding flamethrowers stepped through the haze, their faces covered in thick, leather gasmasks with glass over the eyes that reflected the demonic glow of the fire belching from the mouths of their weapons. They turned the flame in an arcing wave, the lit petrol and pressurized tanks spreading the heat over the streets of Liège. The gates of hell billowed in their embers.

When the fire came, Geist gritted her teeth. *I'll never make it.*

She willed herself ethereal, shifting as fast as she could, allowing the chthonic heat to pass through her body. The surreal sensation of standing in a blaze meddled with her courage. Every fiber of her being told her to run, but she stayed rooted in place, aware the stormtroopers couldn't see her.

But they could see Battery.

Frightened and ungraceful, Battery stumbled back when the fire came his way. The flames licked across his arm and chest, scorching his uniform and filling the air with the stink of burnt flesh.

His sorcery shut off. Geist appeared—seemingly out of nowhere—and shot forward, rushing the stormtroopers before they knew what had hit them. Pulling out her Bowie knife, she plunged the blade into the tubing of the flamethrower. The odd device was nothing more than a backpack full of flammable fuel, a hose, a nozzle, and a pressurized tank. Severe damage would lead to deadly malfunction, if only her aim was true.

Sure enough, the stormtrooper wheeled on her and pulled the trigger. It clicked several times as petrol spilled over his trousers and tunic, coating him with a foul-smelling liquid. Geist kicked at the ground, sparking embers to jump into the air. The soldier caught fire and screamed, his voice muffled by the gasmask. He frantically attempted to pull off the backpack, but it was too late. Soon, his entire body was covered in billowing flames, and Geist left him to his fate.

A German officer on horseback galloped onto the street. The soldiers pointed their guns elsewhere, but Geist caught her breath the moment she knew the German to be her ally. He wielded a scimitar—a curved saber from the Middle East, a sword not found anywhere in Liège.

Dreamer.

The horse barreled through the enemy line, scattering ammunition and sending the soldiers tumbling. Dreamer, disguised with a new illusion, slashed a stormtrooper on his way through, slicing open the man's neck and spilling blood across the man's flamethrower hose and nozzle. He continued on into the smoke, narrowly avoiding gunshots from the few soldiers who had realized he was an enemy.

Vergess grabbed her by the shoulder. Geist hadn't realized how cold she'd gone until that moment. She couldn't feel his grip, only see his hand shaking her.

"Battery," she said, high and loud enough to cut through the cacophony.

"His brothers have him."

"We need to disengage."

"Victory's seen a safe place."

Geist coughed a mouthful of smoke. Bullets whistled by, and she stepped back. "Let's go."

Vergess pulled her arm up onto his shoulder and Geist jerked back, half-stumbling. Her legs weren't as sturdy as she had expected. She stared down and found shrapnel embedded in her hip and thigh; she felt no pain, but her heart beat hard and fast.

Vergess grabbed her arm again and hefted her up onto both of his shoulders in a fireman's carry. Her stomach pressed against the back of his neck, Geist tensed, but allowed him to carry her. He ran without getting winded and the burning particles in the air couldn't sting his eyes or inhibit his movement.

Geist stared at the bleeding wounds on her leg in disbelief. When had they appeared? Had a grenade struck her? The heat of battle was confusing, and discovering injuries afterward was not unheard of. Despite this logic, terror still gripped her.

I can't fail before we make it to Spa. I can't be the one who holds the team back. I have to push through this. I can't let this slow me down.

Stunned Belgians, seemingly entranced by the carnage, stood in the streets, pawing at mutilated bodies or holding the charred corpses of children. Vergess weaved through them, his grace and speed boosted by his sorcery. He restrained his haste, unwilling to break the illusion of normalcy, but he lifted his arm when the bullets came, protecting Geist as the gunfire pinged off his unbreakable skin.

They broke through the smoke and Vergess ran for a tall, square building. Geist gleaned, from the Dutch on the sign and her own limited understanding of the language, that it was a heritage museum, a hall of records and a glorious monument to the past. Large barrels of petrol lined the museum's base, tied together with thick, oil-soaked rope.

The building is set to burn, Geist realized.

To her surprise, Vergess sprinted toward it, his pace never slowing.

"No," she grunted. "It's a trap."

"It's Victory's location," Vergess replied.

Fuck. "The fires——" Geist coughed and cleared her lungs of grime. "It'll go up fast! We need to hurry."

"Right. So let's go."

TWENTY-ONE

Museum

Vergess broke into a sprint, reaching the museum within seconds. The lack of smoke and explosions allowed Geist to see her surroundings. German soldiers were holding off the Belgians, preventing them from reaching the museum. There were soldiers at the door, but most had left their posts around the perimeter to join in the fighting. When Vergess reached the west side of the building, out of sight from the front door, Blick rounded the corner from the back and took aim.

For a brief second, Geist tensed.

Blick fired, his glowing gold eyes only requiring half a second to aim down scope before he pulled the trigger. Geist felt the shift of wind as the bullet flew by her face, striking a soldier who had turned and seen Vergess.

"Were you aiming for him?" Vergess asked as he glared over his shoulder.

"He was going to sound the alarm," Blick said with a half-smile. "Good thing you weren't in the way, right?"

Vergess huffed and the men regarded each other for a long second before turning back toward the building.

Victory, Battery, and Dreamer stood at the back corner of the building, their backs to the wall and their weapons at the ready. Vergess jogged over and slid Geist off his shoulders. She hit the ground with an unsteady leg but managed to keep herself from stumbling about by leaning against Vergess. He kept a hand on her shoulder, holding her close.

"There are barrels of fuel," she said, taking in deep breaths to clear the smoke from her system. "The Germans are going to burn this place to the ground. We should take the opportunity to leave while they're fighting."

Victory shook his head. 'There are Belgian sorcerers inside the museum."

Geist stifled a gasp. *The resistance. That's what Lucas was talking about. These are the rebels fighting the occupation.*

"Can we save them?" Geist asked. "Have you seen it?"

"It's likely," Victory replied.

"Is this why your magic brought us here? To rescue these people?"

"My magic doesn't have a will of its own. It doesn't lead me places on purpose. Don't think we *must* do something just because my power suggested it."

Geist gritted her teeth. The school of destiny sorcery was so imprecise. *But it hasn't failed us yet,* she reasoned. *If Victory thinks we can save these sorcerers, then we should.*

"Vergess," she said, glancing over her shoulder. "Can you make a hole through this wall? We should get in and out as fast as possible."

She turned to the others and took stock of their condition. Battery had splinters through his clothes and in his hands, not to mention the red and black charred flesh on his chest and arm. The flamethrower had consumed the skin but left the muscle intact. Battery would carry a scar for the rest of his life, but that was a small price to pay for escaping the stormtroopers.

Victory, besides his eye, seemed unscathed. Dreamer, however, had long lines of cuts down his right shoulder, side, and leg—deep and torn enough that Geist recognized the damage of barbed wire. Dreamer's horse was nowhere to be found, but the cruel twists of the wires had ensnared hundreds of creatures attempting to cross the trap-laden battlefields in the past. The animals had all died slow and painful deaths. Geist pushed the haunting memories out of her mind and instead focused on her team.

Blick, too, seemed unharmed. He stood vigilant, his golden eyes scanning in every direction, his vision empowered by his magic.

"Battery, I need your magic," Geist said, turning to face him. "Can you focus enough to use it?"

Despite his raw burns—the red flesh that peeled along one arm and charred shoulder—he nodded. "Yes. Count on me."

"Good. I'll go in first and signal the rest of you to follow."

Dreamer reached out and touched each member of the team individually. The mind-bending cold that heralded his sorcery hung on the air as everyone's illusions knit themselves together, hiding their injuries beneath layers of magic. Although Geist could still feel the shrapnel in her leg, nothing showed on the surface. The enemy wouldn't know she wasn't at her fullest.

Unless they see me limping.

They once again appeared as German soldiers, dressed in head to toe in dark green.

Vergess kept his hand on the wall of the building. The rot spread from his touch, eating through the brick façade like oil through brown paper. He stared at his progress, his brow set in a hard glare, and Geist wondered how difficult it was to use so much ruina sorcery at once. Within a few seconds, a hole appeared in the wall as ash piled at Vergess's feet. Pipes and wooden beams curled into themselves like the legs of dead spiders, warping under the force of his magic.

Geist wrinkled her nose in disgust. The terrible stench from the black rot of wood could churn the stomach of a corpse.

"Go on," Vergess said, glancing over to her. "I'll continue here while you scout."

Battery held out his hand. Geist took it, eager for the added strength of his sorcery. The moment she felt his power coursing through her, she breathed easy and fell invisible once more.

Geist felt safer in this state, almost invincible. Battery's powers complimented hers so well. Together, they were unstoppable.

Slipping through the two-foot-wide hole, Geist stepped into the museum's restrooms. Her boots clicked on the tile, but there was no one in the tiny space to hear her movements. She opened the door and walked out into the museum's main display hall.

The display cases were shattered and torn apart. Valuables had been stolen and carried away. Dead bodies—likely the museum's curators—were strewn about the floor. The checkerboard tiles were stained with blood. Even the finished oak of the walls had been scratched and singed.

The echoed crack of a gunshot made Geist jump. She whipped out her handgun, cursing herself for not having drawn it sooner, and wildly glanced around. She calmed herself, remembering her magic. *Keep it together, Geist.*

On the far side of the massive room—past a labyrinth of shattered glass, overturned bookshelves, and signs—sat a group of individuals huddled in the dark, bound hand and foot and gagged. POW sorcerers, separate from the non-magical men and women who fought outside.

A German officer stood over them, pointing a pistol at one of their heads. Next to him stood two Austrian soldiers, their gray-blue informs and black helmets more ornate than the Germans'. The Austrians' black gloves and gold chain fasteners for their capes marked them as members of the *Magischen Jäger*—the Austro-Hungarian version of the Abomination Soldiers or Ethereal Squadron.

Magischen Jäger.

Magic Hunters.

A corpse lay between them, still bound and gagged, bleeding from the neck and chest.

The second crack of the handgun sent a splatter of brain matter and blood across the wall as the German officer executed another Belgian sorcerer. The eight remaining captives flinched and turned away, their white faces and trembling bodies a hard sight.

Geist leapt from her position and ran across the large showroom, her boots crunching the glass beneath her feet with every step. The Abomination Soldier and the two Magic Hunters turned toward the sound, their eyes darting around, looking through her but never at her.

Geist brought her gun up and fired on the first Magic Hunter, her aim square between his eyes.

The Magic Hunter shimmered and faded and the bullet passed through his body without harm, striking the far wall. Geist caught her breath—*another specter sorcerer, here!* She almost lost her focus when she got a good look at him.

It was like looking in a mirror. His dark curly hair, narrow frame, and androgynous features were utterly unmistakable.

He was none other than Dietrich Cavell, her younger brother.

No! Geist shook her head as her stomach tightened in a painful knot. *Anyone but him!*

The ribbon on her wrist burned in her mind—Dietrich had never had the stomach for fighting, only crafts. Even in the split second she had to stare directly into his eyes, she could sense his overwhelming fear.

But here he was. On the wrong side of the war. And she had almost shot him.

"Don't stand there," the German snapped. "Do something!"

He waved his hand in an arc and telekinetic force blasted everything around Geist back with tremendous strength, including the busted display cases and bookshelves. Geist hit the floor on her back several feet away, her invisibility dropping as thoughts went black and the room went to pieces around her.

The enemy soldiers stared at her in confusion. Surely, they saw only a German soldier—perhaps they thought her a turncoat—and the revelation had rocked them into inaction. Geist took the moment to jump to her feet and move under the cover of invisibility, her body stiff and not as quick as she'd like it to be.

"Traitor!" the Abomination Soldier roared. "Show yourself!"

Dietrich ran an unsteady hand over his face and backed away. His fellow Magic Hunter whistled, the sound laced with potent sorcery. Harsh clicks on wood caught Geist's attention. Five dogs—

beasts turned monstrous by magic—lurked in the darkness and stepped out of some void as though they had been waiting there.

The canine brutes stood four feet at the shoulder, their heads wide and their jaws lined with double rows of teeth. Their shiny black coats had a distinct sheen, even in the low light of the museum prison, shards of opals embedded into their hides. Bulging, red eyes stared outward with an undead sheen that gave them an almost demonic appearance. Every time the dogs exhaled, the room filled with the stench of decay.

The Magic Hunter panned his gaze between his beasts. "Find him. Kill him."

All five animals sniffed the air and turned toward her with freakish precision, despite her invisibility. She froze and caught her breath.

They could see her.

Fuck.

One dog lunged for her, teeth bared in a soundless snarl, and would have thrown Geist to the ground had she not ghosted. The beast flew through her, but it didn't pass through her harmlessly like the stone wall—it *stung* for the half second they had been connected, like her magic had rejected the intrusion. The dog collided with the museum equipment, rending it apart with little effort. It stood, unfazed, and wheeled around with a ravenous growl.

Shaken, Geist dodged the second animal that came for her, stumbling back and half-slipping on the droplets of blood that bled from her shrapnel wounds.

The third dog crashed into a toppled display case after it flew through her body.

The Abomination Soldier wheeled on Dietrich with a fierce glare. "What is this? A specter sorcerer? Another Cavell?"

"I don't know," Dietrich said, his back against the wall, his palms pressed against the wood.

"Weed him out!"

"I—"

"That's why you're here! *Get out there!*"

But he stayed against the wall. Geist knew he could ghost

through it, if he needed. Unlike her, their father had beaten his magic training into him. He was younger, but his specter magic was fully developed—especially for fleeing.

Then Vergess stepped out of the restroom and into the main museum hall. His German bloodline did him well. At first glance, Geist thought him to be the enemy, especially with Dreamer's perfect illusory uniforms. The others must have thought the same thing as they smiled upon seeing him.

"Brother," the Abomination Soldier called out. "Careful! An enemy specter sorcerer is among us!"

"I'm here to help," Vergess replied, his eyes darting to the dogs.

The swarm of beasts had Geist preoccupied. She ghosted through support beams and display cases, keeping the dogs from "connecting" with her.

Vergess hustled across the room. Upon reaching the German, he smiled. "Perhaps ruina sorcery will end this."

"Ruina?" the enemy asked, confusion and realization striking him at almost the same time. Before he could voice his alarm, Vergess grabbed the man by the face. The next moment, dark rot consumed flesh, but the Abomination Soldier placed his hand on Vergess and shoved him back with a blast of telekinetic force. Vergess tumbled away and crashed into a bookshelf, sending papers flying.

"Traitors!" the German sputtered through his damaged lips and cheeks. "*Traitors!*"

"Kill him as well!" the Magic Hunter shouted as he gestured to Vergess.

The rot on the Abomination Soldier spread regardless. Within seconds, it became impossible for him to yell and the man struggled to gulp down air, his face strained red with panic. No matter the man's thrashing, his body caved to the destructive magic.

Three dogs stormed for Vergess, but Geist ignored the fight, instead turning her focus to the Magic Hunter who had summoned them. *If he dies, his damn dogs might all go with him.*

She ran forward and brought the barrel of her gun to the man's temple before firing. The bullet ruptured his skull and he collapsed to the floor.

But the monster dogs didn't disappear.

They barked—deep, echoed grunts with unnatural timbers—and flew into an unrestrained frenzy. Each animal went for the closest thing to them, smashing wood furnishings and eating shards of glass from the floor. One hit Vergess and toppled him, but even its razor-edged fangs couldn't pierce his flesh. Instead, it shook him like a terrier, tearing his shirtfront to pieces with its teeth.

Two more leapt at the bound sorcerer hostages before Geist could act. The first dog bit down on a man's shoulder, right where it joined with the neck, and ripped through muscle and veins. The other dog latched on to a woman's face and crunched through bone, chewing through the screams.

Even amid the chaos, the gore and terror formed crisp memories in Geist's mind. She knew she would never forget this horror—the twitch of the dogs' muscles and the prisoners' agonized screams would sting in her memory forever, a nightmare unending.

Gunshots rang throughout the building in volleys of three. Geist glanced over her shoulder and spotted Blick, Dreamer, and Battery on the other side of the room, their rifles in hand. The bullets pierced the dogs, but it did not kill them. Instead, the enraged animals shifted their attention to the newcomers and ran toward them, leaving the remaining hostages behind.

Through sheer reflex, Geist jumped for the closest hellhound and plunged her ghosted arm straight through the center of its chest. When she released her sorcery to pull to out, white-hot agony shot up her arm. For a brief second, her whole *being* felt tainted—the same taint and burn she had experienced from the GH Gas—and the feeling sent shivers through her body.

Despite the pain, Geist jerked her arm back and ripped out a fistful of lung. The dog choked and gurgled black blood as it collapsed into the fetal position, its feet kicking feebly as it bled out.

Vergess touched the dog ripping his clothing to shreds, his fingers grazing its maw and nose. Vergess's rot took hold, not as fast as with the German sorcerer, but enough that the animal could sense its own impending doom. The beast leapt off and slammed its face against the floor, almost as if trying to rub off the corrosive magic eating through its hide and bones.

While the other monster dogs ran at the team, Vergess got to his feet and dashed to the opposite end of the room. He rushed for Dietrich, no doubt looking to finish the fight. She held her breath and ran for her brother, using all of her's and Battery's combined power.

Dietrich—flee! For the love of God, flee!

Trembling, Dietrich pressed himself harder against the wall. Had his focus failed him? Couldn't he use his sorcery to ghost through? Geist had seen him accomplish this many times before. But all he did was stare, wide-eyed, as Vergess closed the distance.

Geist reached Dietrich the same moment Vergess went for her brother's throat.

"Stop!" Geist shouted.

She ran her ghosted hand through Vergess's shoulder, startling him. He gritted his teeth and jerked his hand away from Dietrich, rubbing at the spot where Geist had made contact.

Dropping her invisibility, Geist stood between Vergess and her younger brother. She couldn't let him die. Even if he *was* the enemy. "The dogs!" she snapped. "Kill the dogs! I'll take care of this one."

She sounded crazy, she knew—it was plain to see on Vergess's stunned face—but in the brief moment of conflict, Dietrich found his focus. He ghosted backward, shifting through the wall of the museum, escaping before Vergess could destroy him.

Vergess stared down at Geist, his pale blue eyes piercing her.

"Why?" he murmured thickly.

"He's my brother," she replied, shaken.

The cacophony of war sank away with each heartbeat.

Ice ran through her veins, but Geist didn't look away. Vergess already knew everything. Her secret, her family… But she knew she would be branded a spy and a traitor for allowing an enemy sorcerer to escape, no matter who he was to her.

The punishment for such an act was death.

The gunfire stopped. Geist glanced over and saw the rest of her team standing over the corpses of the last three dogs—Blick with his rifle, one boot poised on a corpse. The beasts decayed and melted away, their bodies slipping back into the void from whence they had come.

Vergess took her by the shirt collar and shook hard, forcing Geist to meet his gaze.

"You said you weren't a traitor," he growled under his breath. "You said you didn't have ties to your family."

"I don't," Geist said, staring up at him, pleading with her eyes to impart the truth. "I didn't know Dietrich would be here. I swear. It was instinct, me protecting him, and—"

"What's going on?" Blick asked, his voice loud enough to echo throughout the room.

Blick and Dreamer jogged over and went to the hostages, but their gazes stayed glued to Blick.

The hostages hollered through the gags and flinched away.

"We're not Germans," Battery said, untying the first man he came across. "We're with the Ethereal Squadron. We're here to help you."

The mere mention of the Squadron seemed to relax the captives. They moved to allow their hands and feet to be unbound and those with the energy began to speak.

"Please," one man said, an acute desperation in his voice. "There's a chateau outside of town. Chateau Coppens. We must make it there. We must—"

"Not until we handle this," Blick stated, cutting the man off.

The hostages fell silent. Battery stood and glared, his gaze shifting between Vergess and Geist. "We need to get these people to safety. Vergess, what're you doing to Geist?"

"Vergess let one of the enemy sorcerers escape," Blick said, his gold eyes fixed on the confrontation. "And then he started manhandling Geist. I'll say it one more time. *What's going on?*"

Geist's mind raced. So Blick had seen everything, but hadn't heard her orders to Vergess. What could she say to save herself? She was safe for now, but the moment Vergess opened his mouth, she'd be found out.

"Vergess wouldn't let the enemy escape," Battery said. "He wouldn't do that."

The other men just stared.

Victory appeared, heading straight for the men and women hostages and helping with the last of their bindings. He withdrew a serrated knife from his tunic and sliced through the restraints with ease, calming those who shook and offering his jacket to one of the women.

The hostages murmured *thanks*, but their voices were strained and their faces pale. When Victory attempted to get them to stand, most shook their heads and revealed their bare feet.

Nails had been driven through the arches of each foot, hobbling the Belgian sorcerers and preventing them from using their magic. Focus through torture—it was impossible without a well-trained mind. In this state, all but the most powerful sorcerers would be no better than a civilian.

"We need to help these people leave," Victory said.

"Then I'll make this quick," Blick replied, hefting his rifle. "Explain what's going on, *Wilhelm*, or so help me God, I'll kill you myself."

Vergess kept his hold on Geist's collar, his gaze never leaving hers. She had nothing to say. Her claims were made. All Vergess had to do was tell them everything and her career and life would be over.

I'm not a traitor to the Ethereal Squadron. If Dietrich had attacked us, I would've retaliated, but…

But that doesn't change what I've done.

"Vergess has got nothing to say," Blick said. "He's a traitor. We knew it all along. He's here to help the Austrians."

Geist shook her head. "It's not true." Her voice faltered, shaken through frustration. The fighting had been intense and horrific, straining her mental state.

"Then what happened?"

"It—"

"It was an accident," Vergess stated. He released Geist's collar and

stepped back. "In the heat of battle. Geist and I went for the same target, and I almost killed them both."

His words hung over the group like fog.

Geist stumbled back and gave a weak nod, grasping the opening Vergess had provided her. "It's true. I was caught up in the fighting. I almost attacked Vergess and he reacted instinctively."

Blick stormed up to Vergess and grabbed the man by the arm. "You expect me to believe that? That you just let a Magic Hunter *go* by accident?"

Unfazed by Blick's indignation, Vergess shoved him aside, almost sending him to the floor. "Don't be a fool. You think the Kaiser would send one of his guards into the Ethereal Squadron to save one Austrian sorcerer? It only took the deaths of several powerful German sorcerers to complete. What a master plan."

His unmitigated sarcasm served its purpose. Blick stood down, but he continued his glower.

He trusts me like my old team, Geist realized. *Cutter, Little Wick, and Buttons all would have done the same thing.* Her chest tightened, almost ashamed she couldn't reciprocate the show of loyalty.

"Gentlemen, we don't have time for this," Dreamer said, his presence almost forgotten amidst the argument, his upper-crust accent lending a mollifying effect to his voice.

"Why don't we just put this to rest?" Blick asked. He gave brothers hard glares. "We all know Victory can determine whether Vergess is a traitor or not. Settle the doubt so we can move on."

Then Geist smiled. *Here's how I'll reciprocate.*

"Do you trust me, Blick?" she asked.

"Yes, but—"

"Then leave this alone," she snapped. "Your constant doubting and suspicion are only hurting us. Hell, it's hurting the *whole goddamn mission.*"

Leaving the side of a shaken Belgian sorcerer, Victory stood. "I agree. Blick, this isn't the time. We can't prove it one way or another, and it's best we trust our teammates."

"We *could* prove it," Blick muttered.

"Whatever we do, we must do it soon," Dreamer said.

He jogged to the nearest barred window of the museum and shook his head. The foggy glass was stained with black smoke. The fires that consumed the city danced in the distance, creeping closer with each mismanaged second.

Vergess growled. "Well? What's it going to be?"

"I already made my decision," Geist said, stifling the urge to shout. "Blick, there have been several times Vergess could've turned us over to the authorities. When the boat was inspected, when we were caught in town, *right now*—obviously Vergess hasn't done that. He's one of us."

He was. Geist knew it in her core. Just like her old team.

The next few moments occurred in absolute silence. No one moved. Not even the hostages.

TWENTY-TWO

Chateau Coppens

"For the love of Mary," Dreamer said. "I believe it. Vergess is one of us. Now can we leave? Or should we allow the enemy to regroup and swarm us again?"

Battery nodded. "I think he's a friend as well."

Vergess gave him a sidelong glance.

At least Battery came around, Geist thought with half a laugh.

An explosion outside the northern wall cut the conversation short.

"Help the Belgians," Geist commanded. "We're leaving. Right now."

"We might find we have difficulties," Dreamer said, his eyes reflecting the bright red of flames just beyond the window.

Heat engulfed the room as though summoned by the statement. The barrels surrounding the museum had been lit. Geist knew there was a good possibility it had been Dietrich who had lit the flames. *But I can't think of that now. We need to focus on escaping.*

Geist stared at the back wall. They could avoid the Germans if they stayed off the main streets. She shifted her gaze to Vergess and he met her stare with one of uncertainty.

"Vergess," she said. "Make an exit."

"Right," he said.

The Belgian sorcerers, some so weak, they could barely keep their eyes open, allowed Geist and her team to help them up. Blick and Dreamer shouldered three while Geist and Battery managed the rest.

The Belgian hostages left bloody smears across the floor as they walked together to the far wall, but everything became difficult to see with the dark smoke billowing in from all seams of the building.

Vergess destroyed a wall and kicked out a large portion, enough for three people to walk through. Fire swooshed into the museum, flaring up once the wall fell upon it. The barrels that lined the building had erupted into pillars of flame, blocking their escape. Vergess stepped forward, and without hesitation, kicked over a red-hot barrel, sending it tumbling into the street. The narrow opening would allow for people to pass one at a time without harm, though speed would be the key.

With the exit made, Vergess jogged back and took two sorcerers off the hands of Blick and Dreamer. His strength was enough to carry two full grown adults at a dead run, and he leapt through the flames in a single bound.

Geist and the others shadowed his steps. Embers burned holes through their soiled clothes, but they couldn't stop, nor could they panic. They ran into Liège, leaving the museum to its fiery fate.

"We can't carry these guys forever," Blick said as they stepped onto a cobblestone street.

The Belgian woman on Geist's shoulder stirred. Her face, caked in dried tears and blood, scrunched up as she strained herself to breathe deeply. "Please," she murmured. "Chateau Coppens. We should head for Chateau Coppens."

"A chateau?" Geist asked. They had mentioned nothing else since the arrival of the Ethereal Squadron.

"Yes. We'll be safe there. Please. Before the Germans find us."

Geist paused. She didn't know this place—but the woman she carried sounded so certain, so *desperate*. Geist rolled her neck in frustration. Another decision only she could make.

"Blick, Victory," Geist called out. "Get us to Chateau Coppens."

They nodded in unison.

Geist clawed at her clothing. Heat pulsed through her with each beat of her heart, not heat from the flames, but the dreamlike burn of fever. She felt a twisted sickness taking hold of her body, and she cursed her own weakness.

I need to hold it together until the end of the operation. Just a little while longer.

The chateaux of France and Belgium were large palatial estates, so massive that foreigners sometimes confused them with castles. They had stone walls around the property, some hundreds of acres within. They could rest safe within a chateau—so long as the Germans and the Austrians didn't get there first.

We'll have to risk it.

<hr>

CHATEAU COPPENS HAD ONCE BEEN an elegant manor on the edge of Liège. The U-shaped building, complete with a red stone façade and steepled roofs, stood in the center of the multiacre property, surrounded by a row of trees and a tall, brick wall. Gardens lined the estate, but the flowers lay dead and the bushes had been mowed down to stumps.

There was no sign of German forces around the edge of the chateau, much to Geist's great relief. And as they approached the front gate, they were welcomed with open arms, the servants taking the Belgian sorcerers into the safety of the private estate.

The entire estate had been converted into a hospice. The servants delivered letters, running around the manor in a blind panic as they attended to so many wounded and injured Belgian citizens. House Coppens, the sorcerers who owned the chateaux, oversaw the medicine and supplies.

Geist and the others were given two private rooms and access to the pool, garden, and west ballroom, their parts of the manor secure from individuals who didn't know of the family's occult leanings. The opulent rooms, furnished in green and white, hadn't been touched in months.

While most beds had been used for injured soldiers, much remained untouched, including soft couches, bookshelves filled with hundreds of novels, and dining rooms complete with polished wood tables.

While Blick, Victory, and Battery went straight for their room, Geist focused on her injuries. She walked the long hallway with Dreamer and Vergess on either side.

The shrapnel in her leg and hip twinged and pinched with every movement, and her fever burned hot behind her eyes.

She rocked on her feet, stumbling down the wide hall of the chateau. Vergess caught her shoulder, his teeth gritted. "You need to be looked at."

Dreamer pointed to the far door. "She could stay in the hospice area."

Never, she thought. *Where is Cross when I need her?*

"I'll see to Geist's injuries myself," Vergess said.

"You two? Alone?" Dreamer asked, a smile on his face and in his voice. He reached into his pocket and pulled out his sole book— the one he claimed to be *Phantom of the Opera*. But then he wrote in it, as if keeping notes.

That's exactly what he's been doing, Geist realized. *Keeping notes. But on whose orders? Major Reese's?*

"You've been watching us," she said. "Why?"

"I pay attention to a great many things," Dreamer replied. "I'm a spy, after all. But I can't remember everything. So, to better write reports, I take copious notes."

"Tell me," Vergess said, "as the watchful one in this group… do you honestly think me a traitor?"

"No," Dreamer said.

"Then why did it take you so long to say something in the museum?"

"I observe first, then make decisions after. I was on the fence at the time. But seeing how you've acted since, I'm convinced you're not."

"Since?"

Dreamer glanced to Geist, then Vergess, then back to Geist, a smile widening on his face. Geist didn't understand—but she smiled back anyhow. *At least he's one less person I have to convince.*

Dreamer turned and walked in the opposite direction.

"Where are you going?" Vergess asked.

"I'm going to observe the sorcerers here in the chateau. We should have information about this place..." He stopped and glanced back. "We shouldn't stay here more than twenty-four hours, but we need to recover our strength. So, whatever you're going to do to help our commander, do it now."

Geist placed a hand on her face, holding back the pressure that built behind her nose and cheeks. Thoughts came like dynamite, bursting through what concentration she had.

"All right," Vergess said.

With quick and quiet movements, Dreamer disappeared down the hall, leaving Geist and Vergess to the stillness of the gigantic chateau. The moment they were alone, Vergess took one of Geist's arms and threw it over his shoulder. He guided her to the ballroom antechamber. The cozy room had two couches and sets of accompanying chairs, each upholstered in jade, complementing the off-white of the wallpaper and dark browns of the carpet.

"You're sick," Vergess said as he took her to the nearest couch.

"It's not bad," Geist muttered.

"You're wrong. Something happened to you during the fighting. You haven't smelled the same since."

Chills washed over her body in waves.

Where had her illness come from? She grabbed at her left sleeve and pulled it up, revealing her arm. The sight sickened her, and she caught her breath, unable to think. Her gas-damaged skin had splotches of black that ached like deep bruises all the way up to her elbow.

How?

The dogs.

The *monster* dogs.

It must have been them. The moment she had plunged her hand into the beast's chest, she had felt their terrible corruption. Her arm trembled with each breath she took. Geist held it close, trying not to think of the all the men she'd known who'd lost limbs to war. Trench foot, bullet poisoning, shrapnel lodged into the bone… all amputees now.

"You're still bleeding," Vergess said, pulling her back to reality.

Geist glanced to her hip and leg. Bleeding could be fixed. Could her arm ever recover?

"I need to remove the metal."

Without much fuss, Geist lay down on her undamaged side, wishing she could disappear into slumberland and wake up with all of her problems fixed. Her team. Her body. Everything.

"You said you wanted to develop your apex sorcery?" Vergess asked.

Geist nodded.

"Then stay awake. Apex sorcery is the mastery of one's own body. It improves strength, endurance, toughness—and protects you from illness."

She took in a ragged breath, a pulse of pain running through her body. *Protects me from illness?* She wondered if she could use the magic to fight the pox on her arm. "Didn't you say I needed to meditate?"

"Yes."

"How can I do that when I'm sick?" *Thinking hurts sometimes.*

"When I was young, the Kaiser's Guard forced me and the others to endure infection after infection. They got us sick on purpose, breaking down our bodies until there wasn't much left."

The details of his story played in her fever-stricken mind. "They hurt you?" she asked.

"Yes. But those of us who overcame it never got sick again."

"So I should…"

"*Stay awake.* That's how the magic takes hold. You need to be conscious and fight against it with an iron will. Meditation helps with that."

"All right," she murmured. "I will."

Vergess examined her leg, his fingers grazing the tiny holes on her pants. Blood made everything sticky, and the stiff fabric got in the way of the injury. He took a deep breath in and out.

"I'll need to remove your…" He took a prolonged second to finish. "Your trousers."

There was no one else to do it. Cross couldn't be summoned, and the medics of Chateau Coppens would report her for being a woman.

"All right," Geist said. Her heart beat fast, but she knew it could be a side effect of the illness. Even the heat in her face was likely just fever.

Vergess's hands shook as he undid her belt and zipper. He exposed the flesh of her injured leg, keeping the clothing half on and then pulling her button-down shirt to cover anything that he didn't need to work on.

"You needn't worry about your… chastity," he said in an unsteady voice.

"I trust you," Geist said in a light breath.

He pulled a knife out from his belt and examined the puncture wounds from the stray metal. Pieces of grenade remained lodged in her muscle, and Vergess took his time examining each scratch and gouge to find the source of the injury. The bits of jagged copper and brass were tiny, smaller than a fingernail, but Vergess found them regardless.

Each one he plucked from her flesh made her gasp. But Geist didn't complain. She had gone through worse, but she clutched the edge of the couch with a white-knuckle grip just the same. Vergess used the knifepoint to loosen the metal, never slicing.

He tossed the scrap onto a nearby table, splattering the pristine oak with dots of crimson. "I'm sorry," Geist said as Vergess examined another wound. "I shouldn't have risked the operation to save my brother. It was selfish."

Vergess didn't look up from his task. "It's done. Just make sure you know where your loyalties lie the next time it happens."

"The others still think you were trying to save him."

"The others can believe whatever they want to believe, but I didn't leave my nation and my *home* behind to risk it all over this operation. I don't care what Blick thinks."

His tone—his overpowering *seriousness*… Geist enjoyed the conviction. There could be no more doubt.

"If my brother is here, my father isn't far off," Geist whispered, her thoughts set to the future. She gritted her teeth as a large bit of shrapnel came out of her leg.

"Your father…" Vergess narrowed his gaze. "First Lieutenant Markus Cavell."

"You know him?"

"He's a special agent for the Royal House Habsburg-Lorraine. An assassin. A dangerous one, too."

"Th-that's right."

Vergess threw the brass bits onto the table and took a moment to meet her gaze. "Will he try to stop you if he finds out you're here?"

"Yes," Geist said, no hesitation in her answer. "He'll try to take me back to Vienna. I can already hear what he'd say."

He'd say I was worthless. He'd say I was a disappointment. And then he'd force me back into submission. Like always.

Geist continued. "I know he forced my brother to fight. Dietrich… he's never had the fighting spirit." She touched the ribbon on her arm. A craft he had made when their father hadn't been looking.

"He reeked of fear," Vergess said. He pulled a small roll of gauze from his pocket and wrapped it around Geist's leg, his eyes somehow on the couch cushions, operating from the peripheral.

The way he acted—the restraint, the almost hesitant nature to his touch—Geist couldn't help but notice it, even through the pain.

"Do you have any family?" she whispered, needing to know more about him.

"House Richter sends their young sorcerers to join the Kaiser's Guard. There's no expectation that they'll ever come back."

"You were given away?"

"Yes. So I would be less likely to betray the Kaiser. I haven't seen or heard from my mother and father since I was eight." Vergess finished his work, his jaw tight. "That's why I would never betray the Ethereal Squadron. Where would I go after that? I have no one else."

"We have each other," Geist said. "You have the squadron."

Vergess locked his gaze with hers.

"Don't look at me like that," Geist said. "We'll convince them. Dreamer and Battery already believe. And Victory is a man of reason. And once both his brothers agree, Blick will change too. No one will doubt your loyalty."

Geist spoke quietly but earnestly, and Vergess kept his focus on her, his face neutral, but Geist saw a passion in his blue eyes she hadn't seen before. For a long moment, she waited, counting the beats of her heart.

He leaned closer, his breath on her chin.

And then she couldn't count the beats.

"Florence," he said, his voice low, speaking in German, the gruff language softer than anything she had heard before. "I prayed for years to find someone who could understand. When I'm with you, when I imagine us together, life is worth infinitely more than it was before."

Vergess slid a hand behind her neck, weaving his fingers through her curly hair.

"When the Abomination Soldiers subdued me in Verdun, when I became a POW, I didn't care if I died. But then some brazen soldier broke into the bunker and took a bullet for me. Some soldier who knew honor like she knew the breath she took. A woman without compare."

"Vergess…"

His lips pressed against hers for a moment, testing her, warning her; his motions smooth and controlled.

Geist grabbed his shirt collar and pulled him closer. Leopold might have kissed her years ago, but there was nothing to remember about it. Vergess—his taste, his hunger, the way his tongue slid along her lower lip, as if asking to take the intimacy deeper—she shuddered, knowing she could never forget such sensations.

But she pulled back, taking a deep breath before meeting his confused stare.

"I want you," she whispered.

Vergess said nothing for a full second. Then he offered the room a short glance. "Here?" He reached for the top buttons of his shirt, his control waning as his fingers shook.

"No," Geist said.

"Do you want me to—"

"Please understand. We have to finish the operation."

He nodded, slow and hesitant. "Yes," he murmured. "I apologize. I… might've been too eager."

Geist shook her head. "No. Not too eager." She slid her hand to the base of his neck, her grip weak. "Because I really do want you."

So many contradictions. If there was no war, if she could do whatever she wanted, then she would stay with Vergess and melt away in his arms until they were one.

But duty came first. Duty always came first.

Vergess took her hand and rubbed at her knuckles. She sat up and brought her lips to his, needing—just one more time—to experience that heat again. Vergess gave what she wanted and more, his hand running along the side of her body, feeling the curves she kept hidden, setting her skin on fire. Or perhaps she was still very sick. Geist couldn't tell, and she didn't want to find out. All she knew was the fervor of the moment, and she enjoyed it.

Vergess broke away, his breathing ragged and his tone husky. "Don't," he said. "If we must wait, you can't tempt me like this."

Geist rested back on the couch, her body awash in a million sensations. Her stomach twisted, and she knew she had to focus on recovery.

When Vergess stood to leave, she held out a hand. "Stay," she whispered. "I'd feel safer knowing you were close."

Although he hesitated, Vergess took a seat on the edge of the couch, his breathing still heavier than before. He avoided looking at her straight on when he replied, "I'll watch over you while you rest, but you have to promise me you'll focus on that and that alone."

She chuckled. "I'll try."

TWENTY-THREE

Regroup

Geist's fever broke when the sun set. The ache of a long-fought battle remained, but Vergess had been right. Staying awake helped. When she was awake and silently meditating, it was as if her body forged itself into something tougher. It was a battle—her will over the sickness—and the longer she fought, the more the fever waned. At the end, she breathed easier, a cold magic lingering in her blood, killing the last of the sickness.

If I master this further, I may be like Vergess one day. Strong and unbreakable.

Sitting up on her couch, Geist winced as she ran a hand down her leg. The shrapnel had been removed, but the wounds remained painful. Her arm, on the other hand, retained a bit of dark bruising, but the coloration had faded. Did the apex sorcery help her with that as well?

"Are you ready to speak to the others?" Vergess asked. "They'll want to discuss the future of the operation with you. They'll want to discuss… me."

She nodded, ready for Blick.

Vergess helped her to her feet, and she secured her belt back around her waist, making sure to keep it loose enough to hide her curves. Together, they left the ballroom antechamber and made their way to one of the designated bedrooms for their team.

Geist stepped in, Vergess right behind her.

Free of fatigue, Geist noticed everything. The four men in the room, Battery, Blick, Victory, and Dreamer, had all taken baths. They waited around in their undergarments—or nothing, depending on the man—like they were waiting in a locker room back at Fort Belleville. Geist had seen such behavior before, and she had avoided any long stares or conversations, but this moment felt different, especially after her intimacy with Vergess.

"You look like shit," Blick said.

She opened her mouth to give Blick a piece of her mind, then stopped short. The man was wearing nothing but his ID tags. His chiseled form, freshly washed, rested back on his bed, one leg kicked up and the other tossed off to the side. The view left Geist flushed and flooded with guilt. *He probably wouldn't be happy to hear I'm a woman. And Vergess—it feels like a betrayal to even glance at the other men now.*

Of all the times, she thought, cursing herself. *These kinds of thoughts are why I shouldn't be fraternizing in the first place. Fuck.*

Vergess stepped into the room and glared, his hands curled into tight fists at his sides. "Get dressed," he barked. He positioned himself between Geist and the others, a slight redness to his face.

The others tensed, each giving him a long stare. Geist wanted to motion for him to stop—there was no way to explain away *this* behavior now—but all she could do was give him a pleading look.

Now isn't the time for jealousy!

"Our clothes are being washed," Blick finally said.

Vergess stepped back, his jaw clenched. Dreamer lifted an eyebrow, a smirk on his face, like he was in on a private joke.

Battery fidgeted on the edge of his bed. Unlike the others, he sat around in his long johns. They were for school boys, but Geist knew why he wore them, despite his age. It was easier to hide the opals lining his spine—and all the hideous scars—in long underwear.

"We should discuss what we're doing." Battery glanced over to Geist. "Are you feeling any better?"

"I'll live," Geist said, her voice little more than a rasp. "I need water."

Battery reached for a silver pitcher perched on the edge of the nightstand and grimaced. He instead grabbed the pitcher with his left hand, the side spared from the flamethrower's deadly touch, and passed it over to Geist. She took the container and, without pouring a glass, chugged liquid from the spout. The coolness opened her senses, waking her all the way.

"Thank you."

The guest room in Chateau Coppens, one of many, had the comfort of its occupants in mind. There were wide beds, though the mattresses had been taken, cushioned chairs on par with thrones, rugs made of vibrant cloth, and electric lighting hanging from the ceiling. A fire crackled in the fireplace at the far end of the room, keeping the place warm.

"We need to clear the air," Victory said as he stood over the washbasin. He still wore the eyepatch from the battle with the U-boat, and he seemed to be avoiding getting it wet. Instead, he ran a damp cloth across his bare shoulders, lines of water dripping down his chest and soaking into the waistband of his drawers. Geist averted her gaze, hating how naturally her eyes followed the path of the water downward.

I wouldn't be a lady if I stared at Cross's man when he was half-dressed.

Vergess took a seat on the edge of a chair, his body tense and his glare lingering. He couldn't say another word about their clothing, not without explaining, but it was clear he hated the situation. He glanced to Geist every few seconds, never meeting her eyes, but obviously watching where they went.

Dreamer waved his hand and clothing appeared across his body before Geist could see what lay beneath. His illusions were a wonderful thing, and Geist almost asked him to dress the others. Instead, she remained quiet—fascinated with the ceiling above her.

"I agree," she said. "Let's clear the air, then."

The others gave her their full attention.

Geist continued. "We can't charge a man with a crime he didn't commit. Vergess has done nothing wrong."

Blick scoffed. "He has motive to betray us. See bloody reason."

"I agree with Geist," Dreamer interjected. "Vergess's treachery is but a possibility—a possibility, I should point out, that is available to all men involved in this operation. House Hamilton has ties to Germany through marriage. And I am but a man from the desert. My loyalty has always been in question."

"Where're you going with this?" Blick demanded.

"I'm saying our doubts must be set aside to accomplish our mission. Vergess's situation is not so unique that we must throw all trust to the wayside."

Geist smiled. *I need to remember to thank the man.*

Battery scooted to the edge of his seat. "Look, I've worked with Vergess before. And so has Geist."

Blick stood. "So you're all against me, is that it?" He turned to Victory. "What about you? You're always telling me you see horrible futures with that sorcery of yours. Does Vergess betray us in any of them? Huh?"

"I can't tell for certain," Victory said. "It's too blurry. Sometimes I die. Sometimes you die. Sometimes the whole operation fails. But there are many instances where we win, which means he must be trustworthy… at some level."

"Look, I'm not saying we have to kill him." Blick threw an arm into the air. "We send him back to Verdun. We tell the commander he let an enemy sorcerer go free." He glanced over to Geist. "That's the safest bet, isn't it? Then he can't betray us."

To her surprise, the conversations in the room ceased. The others turned to face Geist with hard-set gazes and intense looks. She was, after all, the one in charge of the operation.

"I agree with Dreamer," Geist stated. "Vergess has done nothing wrong—sending him away now would be folly. Besides, if Vergess *were* planning to betray us, it would be easier to do so once he left us. He could ambush us in the dead of night or pick us off from a distance. It'd be better to keep him with us at all times."

"He can't attack us if he's dead," Blick snapped.

Battery tucked his hands into his armpits. "We aren't killing one of our own. What's your problem?"

Before anyone else could speak up, Victory gave a curt nod. "I second Geist's decision. We can't charge people for crimes before they commit them, and we sure as hell don't kill our own. You're out of line, Blick. If anything, we should send *you* home. You're too quick to anger."

Blick gritted his teeth and turned away.

"My decision is final," Geist stated. "Vergess stays—and we'll have no more traitor talk."

Blick ran his fingers through his hair. He paced the small space between beds, each footfall a stomp.

Finally, he stopped. "Fine. I'm a man of the Ethereal Squadron. I'll live by my commander's order."

Dreamer, Battery, and Victory nodded, each giving Geist a quick glance before relaxing back on their seat.

Battery hung his head and ran his palms across the tops of his legs. "Geist," he murmured. "We're going to make it through this, aren't we?"

She wasted no time in answering. "I'm going to do everything in my power to make sure this operation is a success."

Battery let out a sigh. "Thank you."

The others in the room gave a quiet *hear, hear.*

Geist let herself relax. *We can come back from this,* she thought.

The door to the guest room opened slowly, revealing a man dressed in humble attire. He wore the dirt-caked tunic of a farmer and the chaps of a horseman.

"Pardon me, gentlemen," he said, his French an odd dialect. "But the lady of the house will speak to you once everyone is ready."

He held a stack of clothing in his arms, clothing far nicer than anything he wore. He placed them down on the nearest dresser and left with a simple bow of his head. Geist wondered if the man knew they were sorcerers as she watched him retreat. Those few "in the know" were often either in awe of magic-users or utterly terrified of them.

"We shouldn't dawdle," Victory said as he rose from his seat.

"The sooner we finish this mission, the sooner we can celebrate our success."

GEIST STARED out the foyer window. Germans had taken supplies from Chateau Coppens and fortified the roads to allow for motorcars. It was a mystery as to why they hadn't requisitioned the entire property. Geist knew they had in France and other parts of Belgium.

Backing away from the thick glass, Geist rejoined her team in the center of the room. The soft yellows and whites of the furniture gave the room a sense of welcoming warmth that Geist had thought she had forgotten. It had been close to two years since she had sat in the luxury of a fine manor house.

Lucie Coppens, the lady of the house, entered and greeted them with a smile. She walked to the far end of the room, every movement proper and precise. Her sleek, meadow-green dress and light ash-brown hair matched the environment, almost as if she were a tree aglow in the light of summer. Geist admired her subtle beauty and wide, expressive green eyes.

"Gentlemen," Lucie said. "It's an honor to meet sorcerers from the legendary Ethereal Squadron."

Geist straightened her new outfit, uncomfortable with the ill fit, and stepped forward. She bowed her head. "Thank you for offering us shelter within your estate."

"Anything for the sorcerers of Britain and the United States."

"If you don't mind me asking," Geist said, glancing around the room. "Why is it the occupying forces haven't seized control of this manor and quartered their soldiers here?"

Lucie replied with a reserved smile. After a moment, she said, "I am the wife of General Gustav Becker and a distant cousin of Alfred von Schlieffen. When I requested that my family home be left as intact as possible, the military complied."

"I see." *Then she has ties to the enemy.*

Geist had wondered how the Belgian resistance had lasted so long inside occupied territory. Lady Coppen's explanation helped, but Geist couldn't help but doubt. Something about the woman's tone left her uneasy. And why would the Belgian wife of a German general be allowed to reside in her family's estate? Why wouldn't she be in the safety of Berlin, far removed from the fighting?

"I'm lucky you were passing through Liège," Lucie said, taking a seat on a cushioned chair and motioning for everyone to join her. "The occupying forces have taken to drastic measures quelling the resistance." She smiled wide. "My fellow countrymen tell me that you fought the sorcerer soldiers of both Austria-Hungary and Germany and won."

Geist shook her head, declining to sit, indicating her team would stand as well. "Luck had nothing to do with our passing. We're headed for Spa."

"Spa? It's a nest of Germans soldiers, and highly fortified. And the Abomination Soldiers on guard there are some of the most powerful in the entire military."

"I'm aware."

"Then why travel there?"

"That information is classified."

Lucie raised a perfect eyebrow. "You believe a woman wouldn't understand the importance of such missions."

"No," Geist said, stifling a laugh. "It's simply not up for discussion. It really is classified."

"I see."

"But I would enjoy the lady's help, if you have any means to aid us."

"Is that so?" Lucie asked. "It's hard to give you assistance when I don't know what you're doing."

"We need to find the *Oberste Heeresleitung*."

For a moment, Lucie was speechless—but only for a moment. She brushed her hair back and replied, "You've picked a terrible time to try to infiltrate the German frontline command. If you think Spa will be dangerous to infiltrate, than the *Oberste Heeresleitung* would be suicide."

"Can you help us?"

The look on Lucie's face surprised Geist. A tight smile, knit eyebrows, narrowed eyes—an odd blend of fear and anger. Why fear? Geist doubted the woman worried for the members of the Ethereal Squadron.

She's afraid we'll get caught, Geist realized. *And that we'll reveal our connection to her.*

"It's a gathering of sorcerers," Lucie said. "A grand ball, if you will. Generals and their families will be there, their sorcery more powerful than the Ethereal Squadron."

Geist caught her breath, dreading the answer to her own question. "Sorcerers from Austria-Hungary will be there?"

"Yes. I've seen the invitations. They invited me as well, but I declined."

"Will the crown prince be there? Leopold?"

"Yes. And the Crown Prince of Germany. The son of the Kaiser."

Geist exchanged worried looks with the others, but only Vergess met her eyes with a knowing gaze. If the crown prince was attending the ball at the OHL, her father would also be there, and likely her brother as well.

"Perhaps… it would be in everyone's best interest if you waited to infiltrate the frontline command," Lucie stated, her words slow and deliberate.

The shift in temperature gave Geist a shiver. She ran a hand over her prickled skin and shook her head to dispel hazy thoughts. A small piece of her began to think as Lucie did—perhaps it *would* be better to wait—but another piece of her screamed against it.

"You can always stay here," Lucie continued, "under my protection. Just until the talks at the *Oberste Heeresleitung* have concluded. Once the soldiers have returned to their fronts, it should be easier to infiltrate."

Without prodding or invitation, Blick stepped up to Geist and nodded. "I think that would be for the best. Lady Coppens has been rather hospitable."

"I agree," Battery said. "It would be safer."

Victory nodded. Vergess frowned, caught in Lucie's gaze but offering no other reactions.

Their words left Geist confused. Their mission was too important to wait. Why did they all want to stay? She couldn't seem to rationalize their behavior, nor the part of her that wanted to stay as well.

But she couldn't.

"I'm afraid… we can't," Geist muttered, practically forcing each word out of her mouth.

Lucie tilted her head. "What was that?"

"I'm afraid we can't stay."

"It's dangerous to approach Spa at this time. Don't you agree?"

Geist nodded. "But I can't stay." Repeating the phrase strengthened her resolve. She couldn't stay. No matter what. No matter how much she wanted to.

Lucie stood from her chair, growing redder with each passing moment. "How foolish! Perhaps you didn't hear me right. You should stay here. It's in everyone's best interest."

"I agree," Victory said, chiming in. "It's in everyone's best interest."

His parroted speech bothered Geist more than his agreement. Something was wrong, but her mind erased each thought after the next when she attempted to discern what. *Is this the work of sorcery?* Geist already knew the answer. Of course it was. But how would she fight it?

"Enough," Dreamer stated, his tone dry. "You dishonor yourself, Lady Coppens. There's no need for such deceit among allies."

Taken aback, Lucie brought a hand up to her shoulder. "How dare you. My craft is meant to comfort and soothe, nothing more." When Dreamer didn't reply, she offered him a scowl. "Most sorcerers appreciate my methods. I am your ally, I assure you. What I do, I do for everyone's best interest."

"You disgrace yourself further. I am not as easily confused as my cohorts. Your sorcery has no sway over me."

Geist turned her head from one side to the other. Vergess, Victory, Blick, and Battery all stood around as though the conversation were irritating. They didn't glare at Lucie, however, but at Dreamer, as though he had begun screaming and foaming at the mouth. Even Geist felt a slight twinge of anger at him for interfering, but she managed to suppress it. The fog in her head lingered, however. It stifled, like packed cotton.

Dreamer displayed no such indication of addled thoughts. He merely leveled his stare at Lucie, waiting for her to speak.

"Both of you?" Lucie asked, shifting her gaze from Geist to Dreamer. "I didn't think they allowed such men into military service. It's a sin against our Lord."

"You cannot dig your talons into the carnal desires of a man who has none," Dreamer stated. "Nor can you control the iron will of our commander. I suggest you allow us to leave and we'll separate on neutral terms."

"I'm trying to help you."

"And we're declining your aid."

Lucie made eye contact with Geist.

With a short exhale, Geist nodded. "Allow us to leave. We won't reveal you to the enemy. We're soldiers, not untrained civilians."

Lucie backed away, pressing her body up against the fireplace. Her gaze shifted to the doors of the parlor, and Geist knew there would be Belgians waiting in the halls.

"We're all on the same side," Dreamer said. "Let's not do the Germans' work for them by fighting amongst ourselves."

Lucie glowered. "Very well. Leave. I hope, for all our sakes, that the Ethereal Squadron is as effective as they say."

"Thank you for your hospitality," Geist muttered.

She fortified her mind as she turned on her heel to leave. The woman's sorcery was impressive. It was also hard to stay mad at her—her magic seemed to suppress her anger as well as her will. Geist marched through the chateau, attempting to keep her thoughts focused while glancing back to make sure her team still followed. To her surprise and good fortune, they did, though their eyes were still glassy and their jaws still slack. It looked to Geist like they were sleepwalking in one big flock.

All except for Dreamer.

As they made their way out the front door, he turned to her with a tight smile. "I'm impressed. You fought her influence better than our compatriots. You've experienced the school of *amor* sorcery before?"

"No," Geist replied. *Amor sorcery? Is that some sort of mind control?*

"I see. Interesting."

"Have you experienced it before?"

"Yes."

"So much so that it no longer affects you?"

"*Amor* sorcery preys on the lust of those affected. But if you feel no attraction to the casting sorcerer, then the magic has no effect."

"She *was* beautiful," Geist said, half-answering the unspoken question. She glanced back at Vergess. He had been the least affected of the men, never parroting Lucie's words. With each passing moment, her thoughts cleared and sharpened, and it warmed her heart to think, even under the influence of sorcery, he had remained loyal to her.

"That she was," Dreamer said. "But such appearances have little impact on a eunuch."

Geist caught her breath.

Eunuchs were commonplace in Saudi Arabia—all slave men had to be castrated, after all. Her stomach turned. She hadn't thought stately Dreamer had come from such a brutal place.

"I'm sorry," Geist murmured.

"Think nothing of it."

"I will think of it," she said. When he gave her a questioning glance, Geist sighed. "It's impressive to come from such a place—to overcome it. I refuse to disregard such an accomplishment."

As they left the last of the garden walkways and stepped out onto the street, the other members of their team shook their heads and rubbed at their temples. Dreamer ignored their perplexed stares and instead smiled.

"They said Arab crows such as myself could not understand the complexities of combat." Dreamer stared at the war-torn road ahead. "They told me that slaves were only good for milking goats and serving masters. But each time they whipped me, I knew I would always dream of more. I did not fit the role they wanted me to play. I had to leave, no matter the cost, lest I lose myself."

You must learn your place, her father would say.

You must do as the family tells you, her mother would add.

You have a role to play, for the betterment of House Cavell.

"You look as though you understand," Dreamer murmured, his smile a knowing one.

"Oh-ho," Geist said with a chortle. "We're more similar than you think."

"All men grow to think differences separate them. It's only through wisdom do they see we were all made in God's image."

The way he said it—for a brief instant, she considered that Dreamer might know who she was. What she was.

No, she thought. *He couldn't.*

But maybe…

Geist again reminded herself to thank Major Reese for building this team for her. At first she had wondered why a man from the Middle Eastern Theater needed to be pulled for her operation, but Dreamer was clearly the best possible choice.

A messenger boy, no older than twelve, ran from Chateau Coppens clutching a small stack of parchment. He wore a peaked cap, much like the soldiers in the trenches, and it slid around his small head with each energetic stride. He huffed as he came to a stop in front of Geist.

"Lady Coppens sends her apologies," he said through hasty breaths. "She offers you this information. Please, take it."

Geist took the parchment from the soot-covered hands of the messenger boy. A slow smile spread across her face as the others gathered around to see: a detailed map of Spa and a list of the military personnel in attendance.

TWENTY-FOUR

Spa, Belgium

S pa was a resort city, a playground for the wealthy. Its large estates, landscaped parks, and sparkling hot springs made it a destination to behold, even while under the occupation of Germany. But not everything stood as it once had. Archways over the roads had been wrapped in ribbons to symbolize Belgium's neutrality and plea for peace. The tattered strands of cloth hung like ghosts off the neglected wooden posts.

I guess that shows what the Germans think of peace.

The stress of a single hour behind enemy lines took ten years off any soldier's lifespan. But the dark of night made the trek easier. Geist managed to keep her heartrate below the panic threshold as her men slipped through the moonlight shadows.

Nobody spoke. *At least they're not arguing about Vergess anymore.*

To her surprise, no one on the team mentioned Lady Coppens or her attempts to manipulate them. All four men carried on as though it had never happened. Either they had forgotten somehow or were just too ashamed to admit they had been so easily swayed.

Geist feared Lucie's sorcery more than most others she'd experienced in the past. Magic that could affect the mind was the most dangerous kind she could imagine, more so than Vergess's bulletproof skin or Dreamer's illusions or even her own ghosting. *Such influence can do more damage than the wielder realizes*, she thought. *Especially if they manage to control a particularly powerful sorcerer.*

The breezy night air brought with it a deep chill. Geist found herself missing her usual insulated uniform. The soft civilian outfit offered little defense against the weather.

"There it is," Blick whispered, his eyes as bright as stars.

He pointed into the distance.

"You sure?" she asked, holding up the map and pointing to the OHL. "It has to be this one."

"I'm sure. There's way too much security there to be anything else."

Indeed, the streets hummed with the music of marching soldiers and tired horses. Despite the late hour, men swarmed the block, some with storm lanterns that flashed like eyes in the night.

Geist and her team stayed within the foliage of the Spa park, nestled in the shrubs not ten feet from the road. Victory's sorcery kept them alert for nearby soldiers, and Dreamer's illusions kept the team camouflaged.

"What's the plan?" Battery asked. He crouched down low and cursed under his breath. "Our supplies were lost in Liège."

"We'll need to improvise," Geist said. "Lucie gave us some supplies, but we don't have anything for a second run. We've only got one shot at this."

"I don't like going in without a contingency."

"We don't have the luxury of contingencies."

Battery replied with a short exhale. "Then let's hope we get it right the first time."

Through the fog and darkness, Blick scanned their surroundings, careful not to stay up too long or stare in the same direction twice. "There are checkpoints at every entrance. One at the gate, one at the door… They even have a checkpoint for the supplies brought in through the back."

"Who are they letting through?" Vergess asked.

The others turned to face him. He hadn't spoken since the chateau and the sound of his gruff voice caused them to flinch.

"Officers," Blick said. He kept an eye on Vergess as he motioned to the southern road. "And occasionally women. They ride in at different points."

"That's standard practice," Vergess said. "They'll have the military personnel go through separate checkpoints than the civilians."

"Good to know."

"They're checking IDs on everyone and comparing them to a master list. Weapons won't be permitted unless authorized. And there'll be sorcerers posted to sniff out foreigners."

Victory nodded. "That's all well and good, but we need to move. Follow me."

Weaving through the park's benches and fountains, Geist followed Victory as best she could. The dewy night fog made it almost impossible to navigate the city, but Geist hoped what hindered her and her team would hinder their enemies as well.

Geist stopped behind Victory once they reached the edge of the market street. A small bakery stood on the corner, pale light emanating from the front windows. No doubt the baker and his family were within, preparing for the new day.

Victory motioned them to the backside of the building. "What's wrong with your arm?" Battery asked, motioning to the dull patch of bruises that ran up to Geist's elbow.

Geist grimaced. Her shirt had rolled up in the running, and she smoothed it back into place. "I'm fine. Nothing I can't handle."

"Are you sure?"

"This isn't the time, Battery," Blick said with a groan. "You can't even lift your arm over your head—maybe you should focus on yourself."

Battery tried to lift his arm but winced before his hand got higher than his shoulder. The flamethrower had done more than Geist had suspected. She hoped Battery would be able to recover.

Or maybe I should take my own advice. Geist pulled back her sleeve and peeked at the skin. The edges of the bruise were a wash of deep reds and purples, like a deep battle wound.

Geist shoved the sleeve back down her arm.

"We should stake out the far civilian road," Dreamer said. "If we subdue some of the guests, we could take their IDs and passports and slip into the OHL in disguise—with my illusions to assist, of course. From there, we can search the building for the magi-tech research."

"Good plan," Geist replied.

That was all they needed. Notes, journals… anything to start their own research of magic-infused weapons, like the GH Gas.

Or, Geist thought, *at least a way to counter it.*

"How long do we have?" she asked.

Victory sighed. "According to the information provided by Major Reese, the OHL meetings will last five days, but we don't have the luxury of waiting. I've been using my sorcery since we arrived. We have two days before we're discovered. Someone… turns us in. I think it'll be a hostage we're likely to take in the future, but I'm not certain."

"We'll act as though we only have a few days then," Geist said. "Anything is better than getting caught. With Battery's help, my sorcery should be strong enough to help me find what we need once we infiltrate the command center."

The others murmured agreement, and for a brief moment, Geist allowed herself a flicker of hope.

All we have to do is get in.

THE RISING SUN brought an unexpected opportunity.

Geist ignored the roar of triplanes as her eyes locked on to the first horse-drawn carriage to approach without a motorcar escort. The double-headed black eagle insignia engraved on the door told her the occupants were from Austria-Hungary: no doubt civilian sorcerer nobles invited to partake in the war talks.

Unlike mundane civilians, sorcerers were included in major state decisions. Abomination Soldiers and Magic Hunters came from noble families, after all, and generals often had to convince the young sorcerers' parents to agree to send their children to war. A particularly stubborn patriarch might be promised a favorable marriage for his soldier son, or even a captured enemy sorcerer to add to his family's bloodline.

Not only that, but grudges between sorcerous families often spanned whole generations, even whole centuries. Some families needed only the opportunity for deadly revenge against a rival house to be persuaded to join up—an opportunity the generals were more than happy to provide.

An ornate carriage trotted toward them, its windows covered by thick curtains. Vergess and Blick stepped out from the sidelines and took positions on the opposite sides of the road. They wore the official garb of the German checkpoint soldiers thanks to Dreamer's sorcery, and the driver of the carriage pulled on his horse's reins.

They stood a half mile from Spa, but the curves of the road and the lush trees provided a fair amount of cover. Vergess and Blick had no stand or paperwork station, leaving the driver of the carriage glancing around.

"Papers, please," Vergess said, stepping up to the side of the vehicle.

"I have them here," the driver replied, unfolding crisp papers from the bench atop the carriage. He handed them down with hands red and swollen from the cold. Geist suspected his gloves had been requisitioned by German soldiers many checkpoints ago.

Vergess snapped the papers straight and scanned through them. "Count Ernst Mittrowsky and his two sisters, Countesses Margarethe and Berta Mittrowsky?"

"That is correct."

Geist, hidden behind the low branches of a magnolia tree, gritted her teeth. She had been hoping for a carriage full of men. Disguising her team would be far more difficult if she had to accomplish it with women's clothes.

Blick walked up to the carriage door and knocked.

The door opened to reveal the three nobles within. The man, Ernst, leaned out and frowned. "Another one? I daresay, these stops are getting ludicrous. It'll be midafternoon before we arrive, mark my words." He tugged at his wax-sculpted mustache and flattened it into place under his nose. "Go on then. We're done here, are we not?"

"We need you to exit the carriage," Vergess stated, the authoritative tone of his voice harsh and uncompromising. He handed the paperwork back to the driver.

Ernst stepped out with a huff. "What's the meaning of this?" He stood tall and proud in his dress slacks, coat, and button-up silk shirt.

Without warning, Blick lifted his rifle and struck the man hard across the face. The crunch of bone startled the driver and the two women in the carriage, all three gasping in chorus.

Vergess grabbed the reins of the horse and pulled the driver from his seat before anybody could react. The older man, his hands shaking as he attempted to stand, tried to call out, but Dreamer leapt from his hiding spot and grappled him to the ground. He wrapped an arm around the driver's neck and yanked back, strangling him into unconsciousness with savage expertise.

Opening the second door, Vergess held up his handgun and motioned for the two countesses to exit. Both women glanced over to their brother lying motionless on the road before stepping out with tepid movements.

The two women wore enough wealth on their bodies to feed a small town. Each dripped with pearl-and-diamond necklaces, accentuating the low cut of their long, flowing dresses. They pulled their thin shawls tightly across their bodies, their shoulders shaking in the cold.

Geist, Victory, and Battery stepped out from their hiding places. Geist drew her weapon, and Battery gave her an odd glance.

"There's no need for that," he said. "You'll frighten them."

Geist considered this. She didn't blame them for not wanting to fight six strangers in the middle of nowhere, especially with their brother incapacitated. Even if they were sorcerers, not all had practiced magic in combat.

"All right," she said with a groan, holstering her weapon. "But stay on guard."

"Thank you."

Dreamer dismounted the driver's unconscious body and brushed himself off. "Every moment on the road is a risk. We should hurry."

Everyone turned to Victory. He shook his head. "Don't worry. We're not in any immediate danger."

"What're we going to do with them?" Blick asked, kicking the count. The unconscious man gurgled.

"If we leave them here, they'll be found before we're finished inside," Victory said, rubbing at the bandage over his eye. "We can secure them down by the nearest stream. No one will find them in time." He spoke in English, and neither of the countesses seemed to react. Geist assumed they couldn't understand.

"We have papers for three people," Dreamer announced. He grabbed the paperwork off the bench and waved it around. "If we're to use these as our disguises, only three of us can go."

"We can't use these," Battery said as he motioned to the Austrian noblewomen. "Two of them are women. That means only *one* of us will be going in."

"You underestimate my sorcery, good sir. I assure you that, with the right tools, I can disguise a like-sized man."

"As a woman?"

"Of course."

The count on the ground moaned. He stirred but made no attempt to stand. Vergess pulled the rope from the side of the carriage and bound the man. When he reached for the women, he handed Blick the tools and stepped back. Blick regarded him with a sneer and continued, treating the women delicately as though trying to woo them with his knots.

"You're in good hands," he said with a smile—though again, neither seemed to understand him.

Battery glanced from person to person, sizing them up with his gaze. The women were short—the same height as Geist and Battery. It became apparent what Dreamer meant.

"Does it look like I visit molly-houses?" Battery asked, flushing mightily.

Dreamer shook his head. "Of course not. But you are the right size."

"Why don't you conjure a woman around me? We can get the same effect."

"My sorcery doesn't work that way. Illusions are like paint. They need a canvas."

"W-well, maybe coupled with potentia sorcery, you can craft something from nothing."

As he spoke, Battery kept shifting his weight back and forth, occasionally throwing apologetic glances over his shoulder at the two women.

"You can only empower one person at a time, right?" Geist asked. "I'll need your help once we're in the OHL. Empowering Dreamer might work, but it's a luxury we can't afford."

"They're wearing dresses," Battery said, ignoring Geist's observation. "If your illusions are paint… I mean, well, does that mean *me*—er, *I*—would be wearing…?"

Blick snorted. His chuckle spread to Victory and, to Geist's surprise, Vergess. The three struggled to bite back outright laughter, which only seemed to make Battery madder. The younger man looked like a ripe tomato ready to burst. Geist almost joined in, but held herself back—barely.

"What will it take for you to disguise us?" she asked Dreamer. "Will we need to wear the dresses?"

Battery bunched his shoulders to his neck.

"Take the shawl," Dreamer instructed. "I can affix my magic to them."

Geist took one from a countess, much to the countess's shock. Before anyone could comment, Geist wrapped the cloth over her shoulders and allowed it to drape down to her ankles. The thin material was soft to the touch and there was plenty of it, practically a cloak when secured shut. It swayed with any movement, and Geist took the opportunity to twirl. The shawl fluttered outward in an elegant circle. It had been so long since she had actually worn a dress.

Dreamer touched the fabric once it settled. His illusions stitched themselves into the garment, transforming it into a lovely, albeit simple, cotton gown. With the shawl over her shoulders and arms, Geist appeared to be covered from neck to toe.

You will wear a dress for all formal occasions, her mother had said, scolding her every time she had attempted to wear her brother's outfits. *You will act like a lady at all times, do I make myself clear?*

She shook the words away. There had been a time when she'd enjoyed wearing women's clothing—but those days were long gone.

While the others nodded in approval, Vergess stared, his eyes lingering on her curves.

"What're you staring at?" Blick asked with a laugh, almost smirking. "Haven't seen a woman in that long, huh?"

"There's ample room for handguns under the shawls," Vergess said, turning away. "But I doubt it'll hide our rifles."

"Is that what you were looking at?"

Geist rubbed her cheeks, hoping nobody saw her blushing. Every bit of attention she received from Vergess was like the first time all over again.

When she let the shawl fall off her shoulders, the illusion shimmered and faded, returning the shawl to its original state. A perfect disguise that could be easily discarded. Geist couldn't ask for anything better. Even their short hair wouldn't prove too much of a problem. It was an acceptable practice for women to cut their hair short to help with the war efforts, either as a show of solidarity or for resources needed for the injured soldiers.

Dreamer rewove the illusions as Geist fastened the shawl back in place. But, unlike last time, he wove illusions into a dress far more slimming than before, even going so far as to duplicate the necklaces the countesses were wearing.

Blick lifted both eyebrows. "You look good."

Vergess shot him a glare. "Keep your eyes to yourself."

"Calm down. I'm not about to forget he's a man. I'm just taking the piss."

"It's fine," Geist said, waving away the comment. "I know I look good."

Blick chuckled. "Careful. Some men inside might mistake you for breeding stock."

"They'll be in for a surprise."

Forsaking restraint, the others laughed aloud. She spun again, this time admiring the intricate detail of Dreamer's illusions—the jewels embedded in satin. The dress fluttered outward, and if the shawl stayed over her shoulders, it appeared to be a normal functioning outfit, covering her civilian clothing underneath.

The Austrian noblewomen watched in total bewilderment, unable to understand the conversation and observing Geist's team with furrowed brows and wide eyes.

Even Geist had to laugh.

And it felt good to experience something other than battlefield emotions. She could sense the members of her team needed levity.

Battery uncrossed his arms as the red drained from his face. "Geist, you aren't embarrassed?"

"*Me?*" Geist retorted. "I think all the other ladies will be embarrassed once they realize they've been doing it wrong this entire time." She fluttered her dress a second time.

Battery stared at her. "You're a regular joker, aren't you?"

"Better than a blushing virgin."

"H-hey! I'm just, well—*you don't have your brothers here!*" His blush returned in full force, and he hid his face in his hands.

Victory and Blick couldn't contain themselves. They shook their heads and snorted. Battery flounced back and forth, their merriment dulling his anger with each passing second.

"You know I've operated as a spy for some time, right?" Dreamer asked.

Battery lifted an eyebrow. "What of it?"

"I've disguised myself as a woman on several occasions. Trust me, it's actually easier to fool soldiers with this disguise than any other."

"Really? Even you dressed like this?"

"You cannot conceal your true nature from the eyes of our Lord. Clothing is temporary."

"Fine," Battery groaned in exasperation. "Give me the damn shawl."

TWENTY-FIVE

Ohl

The bump and rock of the carriage irritated Geist's stomach. She hadn't eaten a full meal for days on end, and her whole body felt like it would fall apart at any moment, but she silently pleaded with it to wait until the operation concluded.

Victory, acting as the carriage driver, rode on the outside and controlled the horses through the roads of Spa. Blick and Dreamer hung off the side of the carriage and played out the roles of door-men, neither man saying a word. Geist glanced between Battery and Vergess, her only companions in the carriage.

Vergess offered Battery a one-sided smile. "You look cute."

"Shut it," Battery snapped.

"Tsk. That language isn't very becoming of a young lady."

Both Geist and Vergess got another round of chuckles as Battery sank back into his seat. The carriage compartment was large enough that Battery could squirrel away in the farthest corner—his shoulder up against the door, his back to the others. His blush matched the shade of pink Dreamer had made his "dress" exactly.

Dreamer's illusions had done the trick. Battery would never be recognized, not with his girlish face, short, golden hair, and long eyelashes.

Geist's stomach growled.

"I'm sure there'll be food in the OHL," Vergess said.

Then he pulled her close.

Geist offered him a smile and happily leaned against his side. Battery glanced over and glared. "What are you two doing?"

"Acting the part," Geist replied with a chuckle. She took the moment to fantasize, if only because the opportunity had presented itself.

Battery continued his icy stare. "Aren't we supposed to be siblings? We don't have to pretend to be lovers or mistresses."

Vergess snapped his fingers. "Damn. And you're both such a catch."

Again, Battery threw himself into the corner of the carriage, his face burning. "I'm trying to be serious! Siblings don't *cling* to one another."

Geist released Vergess and sat up.

"We're almost to the OHL gates," Vergess said, staring down at her. Then he smiled and added, "You look beautiful, by the way. I daresay you've worn something similar before."

His playful tone got her blushing faster than anything he had done before. *Since when did he get so flirty?*

"Thank you, my lord," Geist said, forcing herself to use her normal, feminine voice.

Vergess flushed, turned away, and shook his head. "Enough games. And don't ever call me that again."

"Not in public, at least."

Vergess pursed his lips but said nothing else.

He wore the outfit of a count, his styled suit the height of modern fashion. If it hadn't been an illusion, Geist would have said it was worth more than some houses. Vergess had the poise of a king.

The carriage came to a stop.

The mood shifted in an instant. Battery sat up in his seat, proper and dutiful, staring forward without a hint of discomfort. Geist did the same, her body stiff and her veins filled with ice.

They had arrived at their destination: the *Oberste Heeresleitung*. The frontline commander for the German offensive. The OHL.

Victory spoke loud enough to hear, but the thick, wooden walls that surrounded Geist, Battery, and Vergess muffled his words. More voices rang out in response until the doors on both sides were thrown open.

The OHL gate guards glanced around with expressionless faces. They held their rifles in both hands, using the bayonets to shift fabric and prod empty space. Their coats hung heavy and damp in the thick fog.

"This everyone?" one guard asked. "No others?"

"No, sir," Victory replied.

"Any weapons?"

"None."

"We'll be searching all trunks regardless."

"As you wish."

Blick and Dreamer opened the trunks and allowed the Germans to inspect every inch of the carriage without fuss. No words were exchanged until the gate guards had finished their search.

"Enter," the one guard said. "And turn to the left."

"Yes, sir."

The doors shut, but Geist kept her guard up. The carriage moved forward, past the iron fence that surrounded the OHL. Men with rifles stood every twenty feet around the perimeter and Geist peeked through the curtain in an attempt to get a good count.

Hundreds.

There were hundreds of soldiers standing guard.

Victory took the left path and found a space cleared for carriages. The right turn in the driveway was occupied by motorcars —Geist assumed the horses didn't like the roar of engines.

Although they could have stopped their carriage near the front, Victory urged the horses to take them behind the thirty other carriages that stood idle. Footmen and drivers shared cigarettes while waiting for their noblemen; some even had tins for coffee and soup. They regarded the incoming carriage with little interest, some never bothering to look up from their own conversations or card games.

Once the vehicle stopped, the doors opened and Blick, Victory, and Dreamer piled into the compartment. The space allowed for it, but it was a tight squeeze. Geist leaned heavy against Vergess, pressing herself against him to avoid touching the others. He clenched his jaw, his grip on his pants tightening, but he otherwise made no fuss.

"There are doors that lead inside, just around the western wall," Victory whispered once the door was shut behind him. "They lead to the kitchens. Three of us can enter as waitstaff while the other three go as nobles."

"We're *all* going inside?" Blick asked in a whisper.

"Only those of us who can speak and read German should bother," Geist said. "Anyone else would be deadweight as far as searching for our information goes."

The group glanced between each other.

Dreamer cleared his throat. "Of the West Germanic languages, I'm afraid I've studied English and English alone."

"I'm not very good at German, either," Blick admitted.

Battery regarded his brother with a disappointed frown. "What did Mum say about your studies? She knew you shouldn't have signed with the Ethereal Squadron when Victory did. You lost out on two whole years."

"In that dress, you nag just like her."

"Well, I never—er—that's just—"

"Quiet," Victory said as he held a hand out to distance them. "This isn't the time. Blick stays outside." He glanced over at Dreamer. "You can illusion me to look like one of the help, correct? I'm fluent."

Dreamer ran a hand over his face—right where Victory's bandages would lie—and shook his head. "I cannot hide that injury. I'm sorry."

Geist cursed under her breath. Having a driver with an eyepatch —especially during wartime—was no strange occurrence. But a nobleman with such an injury? Or one of the high-class waitstaff? It would draw attention, even from halfway across a room. People would ask questions.

Geist had seen it a hundred times in the past.

Then again, Victory had proven time and again he could handle himself in even the stickiest situations. Geist didn't doubt his abilities, but did she want to take the risk?

"Vergess, Battery, and I will go inside as nobles," she intoned. "You three will secure us a safe means of exit while the rest of us search."

"Do you think that's a good idea?" Battery asked. "Victory's sorcery could help us navigate the building."

"We have a layout of the estate thanks to Lady Coppens. And I'll be able to search the place with ease as long as you're empowering me."

"But still. He could help us avoid trouble."

Victory shook his head. "My insights don't always provide a solution. Sometimes I see a situation, but no way to correct course. I think you can still do well without my aid."

"It's better this way," Blick said. "While you get a lay of the land, Victory can focus on using his sorcery to find an escape route."

Geist nodded. "That's true."

Everyone shared a collective nod.

"Be quick," Dreamer said. "And be safe."

He waved his hand, adding a few extra details to his illusions, including a few minor adjustments to their facial features—the slope of an eyebrow, the jut of a chin, the point on a nose. When he was finished, Geist was certain: even their own mothers wouldn't recognize them.

Good.

Geist, Vergess, and Battery slipped from the carriage. The cold Belgian air sent shivers down Geist's spine, but she ignored the urge to return to the cramped warmth of the carriage compartment. The other two shrugged off the cold with ease.

She took two steps forward and Battery came to a halt. "I have a bad feeling about this," he murmured.

"Well, we can't go back," Geist replied.

"Wait a moment."

Battery turned back and opened the carriage door. He withdrew his Lancaster pistol. "You should keep this," he said, handing the weapon butt-first to Victory. "Just in case."

"I have my own sidearm."

"I know. I'd just feel better if you had this one. Just take it."

Victory took the weapon and turned it over in his hand. "Ever thought about studying destiny sorcery? It's in your blood too, you know."

Battery whirled around on his heel. "Don't be ridiculous. That's what *you* do. There's no point in competing."

Victory chuckled. "Lucky me."

"Come off," Battery said with a huff. "We'll be back soon." He shut the door and hustled back to Geist and Vergess, his face flushed all over again. Geist lifted her eyebrow. He pushed past her. "He doesn't mean it."

Without further comment, Geist headed for the entrance to the OHL.

The frontline command was once a two-story Belgium manor. Ivy grew up the stone walls—trimmed neat around the windows and entrances—and the roof came to points at the corners and in the center, mimicking the silhouette of an old-world castle. The white-and-black flag of Germany, as well as the yellow and black flag of Austria-Hungary, waved from every flagpole and hung over all major entranceways.

Servants catering to the soldiers rushed to and fro, gathering food from newly arrived shipments and rushing them to the kitchens. Geist didn't bother examining them for long. She walked past, her gaze set to the large double doors of the front.

Vergess stepped up to her side and they entered together.

The gaudy halls of the Belgium manor seemed to bleed wealth. Fine rose porcelain vases sat atop solid birch wood stands accented by twenty-four karat gold-plated studs. The rich red hall runner carpets and high dove white walls could make a giant feel small. Geist understood why the highborn generals and staff officers preferred the comfort of the royal life over the grime and disease in the trenches.

It's unfair, she thought. *All those young men dying on the frontline, and the men giving the orders get to hide here in these palaces—palaces stolen from a conquered nation.*

Generals, ladies, dukes, duchesses, and all manner of people in between lingered in the hall. Fine dresses and expensive jewelry were on display from one wall to the next.

Geist turned to Battery and held out her hand. "Please. I need your power."

He placed his hand on hers. "Right." His sorcery flowed into her, giving her both additional strength and confidence.

"Remember to stay close," he said. "I don't think I could keep this up if you were on one side of the manor and I was on the other."

"We'll go together," Geist said. "We're sisters, after all. Vergess, you can search the west wing."

When Geist went to turn away, Vergess grabbed her arm. "Wait. There's no reason to split up yet. It might be safer if we stay as a group and search for places of interest. Then you can break away and investigate with us nearby."

"You're worried?"

Vergess motioned to the end of the hall with a jut of his chin. Geist glanced over her shoulder and caught her breath. Abomination Soldiers stood by the far doors, their eyes glowing gold, just like Blick's.

Of course they would have sorcerers to weed out intruding magic-users, she thought, gritting her teeth. *If we're discovered…*

"Don't panic," Vergess said, his voice low. "And act natural. As long as we avoid the Abomination Soldiers, we should be fine."

"Yes. We'll be fine. They're rather noticeable, after all."

The front doors opened and a waft of cold air rushed down the hall. Servants ran to straighten the rug and move guests aside. A man stepped inside, and to Geist's great horror, she knew him. There was no mistaking that face.

One of the men at the very top of the Austria-Hungarian high command.

A man responsible for waging war against the rest of the world.

The Crown Prince of Austria-Hungary... *her ex-fiancé*... Leopold Habsburg-Lorraine.

TWENTY-SIX

The Magic-Technology General

Leopold wore the uniform of a general, a cape on his shoulders with a black cross, a military merit stitched straight into the fabric. He looked as any prince should—tall, perfect posture, dark hair slicked back and clear eyes scrutinizing the crowd with an intelligent gleam. It had been years since Geist had met him, but he had been the same then. Arrogantly confident, almost to the point of boredom.

He's here already? Geist shook her head. *Fuck.* She'd hoped to avoid the more high-profile nobles by arriving early—part of her wondered, perversely, if Leopold had had the same idea.

"This way," Geist whispered.

She hustled down the first hall off the main entrance, desperate to put as much distance as possible between her and the man she'd once been betrothed to.

Vergess and Battery followed, but once they rounded the corner, Battery stopped and knit his eyebrows together. "Geist, what's wrong?"

"Leopold Habsburg-Lorraine," she muttered. "He's here."

"Right now?"

"Yes."

Vergess cursed under his breath. Then he glanced to the doors in the hallway and pointed to the kitchen. "What's the plan now? Return to Dreamer and look like one of the help?"

Geist shook her head. "I'm going to scout ahead. Alone. You two stay within this wing of the OHL."

"What? Why?"

"There are too many variables. One wrong move, and we'll fail the whole operation. It would be safer for me to go alone, with you two on backup. Maybe you can find something here."

"Military secrets aren't typically kept with the stew."

"Maybe you can find something else of use," Geist said. Then she deeply inhaled. "But I'm safer by myself."

Battery nodded. "I agree. Wholeheartedly."

Vergess shot him a glare, but the younger man ignored it.

"We're at a terrible disadvantage," Battery continued. "If we're caught, I doubt we'll be able to escape. You and Vergess are tough, but I've already counted twenty Abomination Soldiers, and that's not including the other sorcerers here. Vergess was right about one thing—he's not the only one with *ruina* sorcery—and you won't be the only one here with specter sorcery, either."

Catching her breath, Geist turned to face him. "Who are you worried about?"

"House Cavell, of course. They're bound to be here. We need the magi-tech information before any of them can find us. Please, go scout ahead. Vergess and I can stick to the shadows."

"Good. Just stay safe until I can find something."

She nodded and left the pair in the hallway, avoiding Vergess's gaze. Disapproval was stitched into his features, but there wasn't time to argue the point now.

There were too many people about to use her sorcery right away. Instead, Geist walked to the nearest washroom and locked the door. Staring into the mirror mounted on the wall, Geist watched her body shimmer and fade until she was completely invisible.

Once ready, she left the room without opening the door. The

compound didn't feel so intimidating when no one knew she was there. Still, her invisibility didn't mask the sound of her footsteps on the hardwood floors, nor did it protect her from the enemy sorcerers with Blick's golden searchlight eyes.

She maintained a normal walking pace as she slipped through the OHL, glancing down each corridor and taking note of the occupants. Then she inspected the rooms. Bedroom after bedroom, study after study.

Geist took special note of any door with soldiers posted outside of it. *They wouldn't post guards outside a broom closet, after all.*

Much to her curiosity, the west wing of the manor had been cordoned off, and only sorcerers were allowed in. She followed a group of Abomination Soldiers inside, making sure to keep her distance. They marched with spring in their step and spoke with energy.

Something important was about to happen.

That's why Leopold is here. There must be a meeting before the actual social gathering. But what're they going to discuss?

Heavy black curtains covered every window in the west wing. Electric lights lit the way, and Geist couldn't help but feel as though she were walking into a dungeon. The crimson rugs, black statues, and dark oil paintings only added to the gloomy atmosphere. And the waitstaff had been replaced with buffet tables and an open bar.

There wasn't a single non-sorcerer anywhere in sight.

"Did you see the reports?"

Geist turned to face two Abomination Soldiers standing near a tall wine rack. They smirked and swirled their glasses, careful not to spill on their dress uniforms.

"What reports?" the other asked, his German laced with an Austrian dialect.

"The Ethereal Squadron has been steadily increasing their numbers."

"Ah, I saw."

"We might get what we were promised, after all." The man took a sip from his glass, his expression almost giddy.

The other chortled. "It'll change the game forever. I'm hoping sorcerers from their most powerful houses come out to face us first."

Geist listened, but their conversation left her baffled. *Why would they want more sorcerers against them? What could they possibly hope to gain?*

The men with glowing golden eyes walked through the open dining hall. Their gazes swept over the participants and Geist ducked behind a large banquet table. Fortunately, they couldn't seem to see through solid objects. She crept around the room, keeping quiet and out of sight.

The next room over, the west wing conference hall, had an entire audience worth of sorcerers. Geist stutter-stepped to a halt. They numbered close to two hundred strong. Mostly civilians, yes, but the number was still staggering. There weren't many times in her life she had seen so many in one place at one time.

Everyone in attendance wore military formal garb, complete with medals, shoulder capes, and tassels. Civilian women wore long, flowing sleeveless gowns and gloves past the elbow. The shine of polished boots and the glitter of high heels reflected the giant electric chandelier hanging from the ceiling. Soft classical music played from a Victrola in the corner of the room.

But Geist's heart dropped to her stomach the moment she saw *them*: Dietrich and her father walked by, heading straight back for the main table.

Father.

There was no mistaking it. *First Lieutenant Markus Cavell,* stitched in golden thread above his breast pocket.

Perhaps it was her nerves—but her father seemed taller than she remembered, more imposing. Like Vergess, he was an apex sorcerer, and it showed in his every movement. He strode through the room without acknowledging anyone else, barely taking heed of his son, who trailed behind him.

Dietrich said something to their father, and Geist broke away from the wall to follow them.

"Shouldn't we be out looking for them?" Dietrich asked, his cowed tone and slumped shoulders the exact opposites of their father's.

"We have specialists for that," Markus said, an irritation and boredom to his tone. "Besides, you had your chance and you fled. Best not embarrass me a second time."

"Forgive me," Dietrich muttered. "What if they've come here?"

"Then it won't be long until we have them."

Geist's heart beat against her ribs. *Dammit,* she thought. *I never should've allowed Dietrich to escape. He reported our presence in Liège! Now there are enemy sorcerers searching for us. I need to inform the others as soon possible.*

She stepped back and a single wooden floorboard creaked beneath her weight. Markus stopped and turned, his gaze instantly falling to her location. Geist froze, her breath held hot in her chest, but her father's eyes darted around without seeing.

"Is something wrong?" Dietrich asked.

Markus waited a moment longer, his dark brown eyes seeming to stare straight into hers. Geist had hated his stare as a child—always scrutinizing, always judgmental, always *disappointed.* Nothing had changed about him, it seemed. By now, he was in his early forties, though it didn't show. His dark hair wasn't graying, nor did his skin wrinkle at the face or neck. Geist could only assume apex sorcery was to blame for this supernatural youthfulness.

"We should have the sentries sweep this area a second time," Markus drawled, turning away from Geist and continuing his path to the back of the room.

"I think they already scoured the room."

Markus spared his son a single, half-second glance.

Dietrich wilted. "I'll go get the sentries." He hurriedly shuffled away.

A part of her wanted to follow Dietrich and speak to him, but she knew it was folly. Dietrich would never follow her over their father, not when he was already on such a tight leash. And Geist couldn't risk explaining to the others why she had to save a Magic Hunter—the same soldier whom Vergess had allowed to escape days before.

And yet…

She turned to watch her father. Even though the mission had nothing to do with Markus, Geist almost wanted to confront him. And she wanted to know why they were gathering.

It would only take a moment.

Staying near the wall, she slunk around to the corner and then along the back, under the heavy-curtained windows. Her father had taken a seat at the longest table alongside the other decorated officers and their dazzling wives. As Geist drew close, slinking behind the men at the table, a mere arm's length away, she saw one stand suddenly. Crouching, she waited.

"Ladies and gentlemen," the man said, his German formal enough for a textbook. "The highest echelons of the German military command would like to thank you all for your attendance. Unfortunately, the Kaiser could not attend, but the crown prince himself is here in his stead."

A rousing round of cheers and claps filled the massive room. Geist kept her head down. She knew what the Crown Prince of Germany looked like. The playboy sorcerer had made a name for himself, after all. It surprised her he was even here.

As the clapping waned, the man continued, "And I would like to thank the heir apparent to the Crown of Austria for his attendance as well."

The round of cheers that followed was louder than the last.

Geist couldn't resist. She stood, keeping her head up for a few seconds, and caught a glimpse of the commotion.

Leopold walked through the crowd, offering a tight smile to the officers. He held a glass of wine and raised it to a few young ladies, their giggles lost in the applause. Geist ducked back down as Leopold took a seat at the table, only a few feet from her.

When Prince Leopold spoke, his voice rang out clear and filled with authority. "You're too kind, General von Moltke. But please, dispense with the pleasantries. We're all curious to see if your claims are true."

Sorcerer-General Joseph von Moltke!

Geist stole another glance. Here was the man in charge of the

Abomination Soldier division for the German Army. Unlike her father, however, who seemed cut from steel and hardened from a lifetime of fighting, General von Moltke was long past his prime. His white hair and paunchy belly didn't match the physical prowess of the sorcerers he commanded, but Geist had read many reports about his brilliant tactical abilities.

General von Molke chuckled. "Everything is true."

Three words silenced the room. Geist narrowed her eyes.

What are they talking about?

"All of our toil and research has led us to unprecedented success," General von Moltke proclaimed, his gleeful voice booming off the walls. "We finally have it! The solution to a problem that has plagued sorcerers since the very first users of magic. Gone are the days when our bloodlines restrict our sorcery. Today is the dawn of a new future, one where we can mix the blood of one sorcerer into another and give them access to a whole new host of magics he never had access to."

Murmurs rippled through the room in a wave. Even Geist couldn't suppress a gasp. This went well beyond combining sorcery with technology—this broke a cardinal law of magic itself.

"We no longer have to think about the magic we'll be passing on to our children," the general continued, his excitement never waning. "Now we can add the sorcery *to ourselves*—and we'll be taking it first from our enemy!"

Again, gasps and whispers. The room buzzed for a few moments before the general continued.

"Men who join us will have first pick of Ethereal Squadron sorcerers," General von Moltke stated with a laugh. "The sorcery of the Americas, French, and British will be ours for the taking. Imagine what you could accomplish with the added magic of House Hamilton, House Chambers, or House de Viennois? Their sorcery mixed with your own will make our combined might unstoppable."

Applause erupted throughout the room. Geist took the opportunity to take a step forward. She was a whisper away from her father and the sorcerer-general, but she didn't care.

How?

General von Moltke held up a hand and quieted the room. "I have someone here to explain, but first let me share more news. I am pleased to inform you that for their tireless efforts in service of our great nation, the Kaiser has approved a brand-new magical-technology division of our military high command. Our plan to syphon sorcery from our enemies would never have come to fruition without their research. And today, here before you, I wish to confer the first ever title of Magic-Technology General to Heinrich von Veltheim, our lead researcher on the project."

The general placed a hand on the man sitting next to him as the room fell into another round of cheers. The new magic-technology general, however, jerked away from General von Moltke's touch. He glared at the older man and clenched his jaw—Geist was so close, she could almost hear his teeth grinding together.

Heinrich von Veltheim, unlike the soldiers in the room, wore thin-framed spectacles and a suit without any military decoration at all. "How dare you," he said, almost inaudible amidst the clamor. "I told you *very plainly* that I intended to resign."

"And I told you that wasn't an option," General von Moltke replied in a whisper, never breaking his smile. "Your house agreed to keep you on the project until the end of the war, and you'll keep that promise."

"My work was never meant for this," Heinrich said. "I don't approve of this… this butchery!"

"It was *always* meant for this, boy. Now stand up and accept the damn position like a good soldier."

Heinrich stood, his gaunt frame taller than the general's. He straightened his spectacles and allowed his face to smooth. He was young, Geist realized. No older than twenty-five.

No older than herself.

The room grew quiet. When Heinrich turned to face the other sorcerers, they gave him their full attention. The entire room seemed to hold its breath.

"I respectfully decline," Heinrich stated, his voice loud and clear enough to carry.

Murmurs again swept across the room. Even Geist knew it was

tantamount to treason to publicly shame a high-ranking military officer. *He means it,* Geist thought.

And they'll probably kill him for it.

Heinrich shot General von Moltke one last glower before turning on his heel and storming from the table, his dress shoes clicking heavily on the polished wood floors.

Leopold placed a hand on General von Moltke's shoulder. "I thought you said you had him under control."

"Forgive me, Your Highness. I can—"

"No." With a glare, Leopold focused his attention on Geist's father. "Markus. Notify the sentries. Tell them we need a *handler* for our new magic-technology general."

Markus stood and replied with a curt nod. "Consider it done."

"And don't let him leave the estate."

"Of course."

Markus shimmered and faded—until he suddenly vanished from view.

Damn. He's far better than me at specter sorcery. He doesn't even need a Battery of his own to become invisible. Geist took a few steps back, hoping the noise of the room would cover the sound of her steps.

She still didn't know *how* the enemy was going to steal magic from the Ethereal Squadron. Geist had never expected to discover such a monstrous scheme. All she could think of was returning to the others. They needed to know. Major Reese needed to know. Everyone had to be prepared.

But first I have to find out more.

With the speech concluded, the music started back up, and men and women paired off and danced to the pleasant melodies, celebrating their future victory. Those not participating lifted glasses and offered toasts.

Leopold stood behind the table, observing the party, General von Moltke at his side.

When Geist turned to leave, she bumped a flagpole affixed by the wall. The flutter of the German flag drew both the general's and Leopold's attention, and Geist moved behind the fabric, thankful it fell all the way to the floor.

"Who's there?" General von Moltke asked, his voice harsh. He reached for his sidearm and Leopold narrowed his eyes, his gaze fixed on her location.

"Reveal yourself," Leopold commanded. "We know you're there."

TWENTY-SEVEN

Defector

Geist held her position, her breath caught in her lungs, her heart pounding in her ears.

Fragments of flame swirled around Leopold, the chill of magic crawling up Geist's spine.

There was a reason the sorcerers of Royal Houses had kept their political power for so many years. They were the only practitioners of *ultima ratio reguma* sorcery in the entire known world.

The magic known as *The Final Argument of Kings.*

It gave them an advantage no other sorcerer had. When they improved one school of sorcery, they improved *every* school of sorcery they had access to in their bloodline. Where Geist had had to learn *apex* sorcery separate from her *specter* sorcery, Leopold had only had to learn one—*any* one—and he would suddenly be a master of hundreds. And over the generations, through careful breeding, the royal family had accumulated a vast array of magics. No normal sorcerer stood a chance against anyone within the royal bloodline.

Leopold could burn the whole building down with *ignis* sorcery, and Geist didn't doubt he had *apex* sorcery at his disposal as well, perhaps even *ruina*—and a hundred more. Maybe even some she had never heard of.

What if he can see through my invisibility? What should I do?

Gripped with a single, terrible plan, Geist allowed her invisibility to drop and stepped out from behind the flag.

Both men lifted eyebrows at her appearance.

"Who're you?" General von Moltke growled. "What're you doing here?"

"I—" Geist kept her gaze down and clasped her hands together in front of her. "I just wanted to get closer to the prince. To, er, see him in person."

She didn't sound convincing, but Geist wasn't banking on her subterfuge, just on the two things she knew about Prince Leopold.

His arrogance—and his lust.

The flecks of flame ceased and Leopold offered her a slight smile. "Ah. I see. Stand down, General. I'll handle it from here."

Leopold stepped forward and held out his hand, palm up. Geist took his hand, wishing with all her heart to end the interaction as quickly as possible. She had Dreamer's illusions, and her hair had been long when she had met Leopold years ago, but...

There's always a possibility he'll recognize my voice or sense my magic. If he attempts to keep me by his side, I don't think I'll be able to get away. I just have to hope he lets me go without suspicion.

"You're not the first woman to hide in my presence," Leopold said as he led her to the dance floor. "And I like to reward those who admire me."

"Th-thank you," Geist said, focusing her gaze on anything but him. *He'll grow bored and discard me. Then I can get back to the others. Eventually.*

He slid his hand down her side and around to the small of her back, his other hand holding her up as they joined the dance. Geist held herself as far away as possible, her feet falling into place with the slow tempo of the music. She had studied dance for ten years and the rhythm came naturally, but she could not bear to press her body against the prince.

While everyone on the sidelines stared, the other couples

dancing gave them ample room. No one wanted to be the fool who bumped the crown prince. Geist gritted her teeth, hating the taste of fear that ran through the crowd.

"You dress is rather… dowdy," Leopold said as they circled around. "Not very flattering for a woman of your age."

Geist forced herself to nod. "Forgive me." *I think you said something similar the first time we met.*

With each step, Geist tried to lean away, but Leopold pulled her close after a spin and trapped her against his chest. He was muscular—like Vergess—and carried the clean scent of the outdoors. His skillful dancing came, no doubt, from years of study; he never missed a beat.

"For someone so desperate to meet me, you're not doing much to endear yourself to me," Leopold said, his voice low. "I don't share my time idly. You shouldn't waste this opportunity." He leaned down close, his mouth by Geist's ear. "Impress me."

"Aren't you engaged?" Geist whispered.

"Is that what you're worried about? Think nothing of it. I've yet to take a wife, but you could always be my mistress."

Lucky me. Geist stifled a sarcastic laugh, but Geist couldn't help but asking, "But weren't you engaged? Before, I mean."

Leopold seemed to consider this, his hot breath washing down her ear. "Now that you mention it," he began, "I suppose I was. I had almost forgotten. But that's long over and she was of no consequence anyway. I just needed her for her blood. You understand."

The knowledge didn't surprise Geist.

He's not going to recognize me. I could be standing in front of him, no illusions whatsoever, and he probably wouldn't even remember who I am.

The music stopped, and Leopold ended their dance. He stepped back and shook his head. "You really weren't much of anything, were you? There are a hundred girls ready to take your place, most with better looks and younger to boot. You should've tried a little harder. You'll be forgotten by dinner at this rate."

Geist gave the prince a curtsy and then muttered, "You'll remember me."

The prince narrowed his eyes, but otherwise said nothing.

She knew she should have kept her mouth shut. But she was going save Paris from their New Schieffen Plan, and it would be *his* arrogance that allowed it to happen. A part of her wanted him to know he'd let her slip by—that he could have stopped her, if he'd only kept his head.

If only I could tell him who I really am, she thought.

But then again, he still might not remember me.

Geist made her way out of the room and hustled back through the west wing entrance and into the main OHL compound to rejoin Battery and Vergess. But when she rounded the corner into the main hallway, she froze. Vergess and Battery were nowhere to be seen. She glanced back and forth, confusion blossoming into panic. Where were they? Geist hid behind a pillar and became invisible before rushing along the hall and peering into every room, dodging the busy servants who hurried this way and that.

Relief flooded her being the moment she caught sight of them in a nearby pantry doorway. *Thank God.* She dashed over as they entered and took position in far corners, their backs leaning against the empty shelves.

"Some scholars say excelling in *ruina* sorcery is a mark of poor self-esteem," Battery said.

"I've got enough self-esteem for the both of us," Vergess replied.

Battery crossed his arms over his chest. "What's that supposed to mean? I'm plenty confident, thank you very much."

"That's why you keep saying it, right? Because it's so true?"

Geist allowed her invisibility to drop, ending their conversation when they spotted her. Both men straightened their posture at her sudden arrival.

"I'm glad you're okay," Battery said, uncrossing his arms. "Did you find anything?"

"No," she murmured. "But I did see the sorcerer-general and the newly appointed magic-technology general. We need to—"

The screech of a door cut Geist's speech short. She wheeled and spotted an Abomination Soldier standing in the doorway, his hand on the butt of his holstered Luger. His angled German face scrunched in bewilderment.

"What's going on here?" he asked.

Vergess stepped forward, no hesitation. "Oh, well, we're sorry but we needed a moment to catch our breath and—"

"This is for servants only."

"Yes. Forgive us. Come, sisters. We should be returning to the festivities."

Vergess went to step around the man, but the soldier blocked the exit. The two men regarded each other for a long moment.

"What're your names?" he asked.

"I'm Count Ernst Mittrowsky. There are my sisters, Margarethe and Berta Mittrowsky."

"Siblings snooping around a pantry? Do you take me for a fool?"

Geist and Battery glanced to one another, each offering a short nod.

Vergess took a deep breath. "Well, you've caught me in an awkward position. You see, these aren't my sisters… Perhaps we can leave it at that?"

What a lie, Geist thought, almost smiling as Battery's face went beet-red. *At least he's playing the part.* Geist feigned embarrassment by fretting with her dress and huffing a few breaths, but a piece of her wanted to laugh as well.

The Abomination Soldier smirked. He relaxed against the doorframe and hooked his thumbs through his belt loops. "Oh, I see. Well, maybe I'll keep quiet about this… if there are marks involved."

Shit. Dreamer had given them illusory clothing, but no money in the pockets. Geist had never imagined they'd need it. If the Abomination Soldier gave them too much trouble, it wasn't like they could go to the authorities. Out of the corner of her eye, she saw Vergess's fists tighten. So it would be a fight, then.

"How dare you," Battery said, his voice rising an octave. He glared at Vergess. "My father will hear all about how you tried to trick me and my fair cousin." Then he turned to the soldier. "Do you know who my father is? *Karl Richter*—the right hand of the sorcerer-general. I can't wait to see the look on his face when I tell him about the dishonorable soldier who also tried to extort money when he should've been doing his job and—"

"Wait, please," the Abomination Soldier said with a forced smile. He stepped aside and motioned to the hall. "There's been a misunderstanding. It was all a jest, my lady. I assure you."

Battery offered a haughty huff before storming off down the hall, his head held high.

Vergess and Geist followed close behind, Geist still on the verge of laughing aloud. Battery had all the pomp and sass of a debutante, though she would never tell him so.

When they reached the main hall, Battery turned for the front door. "Where are we going?"

"Back to the others," Geist said. "I need to speak with Victory and Dreamer before we move forward."

"THEY'RE GOING to steal magics from Ethereal Squadron sorcerers?" Victory asked.

Geist nodded.

The cramped carriage wasn't her ideal base of locations, but since they had nothing else, it had to do. Blick, Victory, and Dreamer sat on one side while Geist, Vergess, and Battery sat on the other. Their heavy breathing added to the temperature, and Geist hated the amount of sweat coating her body.

"How are they going to do it?" Blick asked.

"I don't know," Geist replied.

"What about Paris?" Dreamer asked. "Did they discuss the New Schieffen Plan?"

"No. They were too busy congratulating themselves on new technology. And appointing that new general." Geist moved to the edge of her seat, her mind raking over all the information she had. "Victory, can you use your magic to see this man? He's distraught. And the other German high command officers weren't pleased with his defiance. They were calling for a *handler* to control him."

"I've been using my sorcery since we've been here," Victory

said. "In a few of my visions, I see a defector who helps us get the information we need."

"Who is it?"

"I don't get their names from my sorcery, only faces."

"Was he wearing spectacles?" Geist asked. "And a civilian suit?"

Victory also moved to the edge of his seat, his eyes wide. "Yes. He was."

"That's him! I saw him inside the OHL. If we go back inside, perhaps this evening, perhaps I could approach him."

"Why would he defect?" Vergess asked. He narrowed his eyes and lowered his voice. "When I… was thinking about leaving Germany…"

Blick snorted. "Finally admitting it."

Geist shot him a glare.

"*Listen,*" Vergess hissed. "Months before I defected, I thought everyone was spying on me. I assumed every person I spoke to was an Abomination Soldier sent to weasel out my plans. I was more guarded than I ever have been. If this new magic-technology general is looking to defect, he may be cagey. He won't believe a member of the Ethereal Squadron is here to whisk him away to safety. I wouldn't have believed it."

"But Victory said he helps us," Battery interjected. "So it must be true."

Victory shook his head. "Only in some of my visions. That means there's a chance he doesn't. And I've seen plenty where we all die as well—much more of those, actually."

Dreamer took out his book and penciled down a few notes. Blick slammed his back against the seat of the carriage, his gaze on the ceiling, his jaw clenched tightly.

"If there's a chance of succeeding, I have to go," Geist said. "I'll approach Heinrich when he's away from the others and offer him safe transport from Belgium. In exchange, he can provide us with whatever information he's got on the New Scheiffen Plan. He was a lead researcher, after all. He'll know what we need to know."

"But we still don't know how they intend to attack Paris with the

GH gas," Battery said. "Or how they're going to steal our sorceries."

"You and Vergess will go back inside with me. You two will search for that information while I deal with Heinrich. Got it?"

"What about us?" Blick asked.

"You three get us a car," Geist said as she snapped her fingers. "Steal a set of keys from the drivers. Something fast—in case we need to make a quick getaway."

Victory, Dreamer, and Blick nodded.

Geist lifted the curtain over the window and peeked out. "We'll wait a few hours, then we'll make our move. If we coordinate, perhaps we can leave under the cover of darkness."

TWENTY-EIGHT

Revelation

Even more sorcerers and mundane citizens filled the OHL for the evening talks. Geist snuck in with Vergess and Battery through the servants' entrance but quickly detached and mingled with the attendants in an effort to find Heinrich.

Although she hadn't gotten a good look at the man early in the morning, the young general was one of the only sorcerers in attendance wearing spectacles. Geist went from guest to guest, avoiding the golden-eyed guards, glancing at the faces of each man. But she couldn't find him. Room after room, person after person—nothing.

With each wasted minute, Geist's heartrate increased until the beating became white noise that deafened her to the music and chatter around her.

Where is he? If I can't find him, what're we going to do?

No. I mustn't think like that. It can't even be an option.

Geist took a deep breath, closed her eyes, and meditated. To her surprise, the scents of the room intensified. The stew and grilled vegetables two rooms over filled her nostrils. When she focused, she could detect the scents and perfumes of each individual in the room, mentally separating each distinct odor from the next.

Apex sorcery, she realized happily. *I'm improving.*

She opened her eyes and hustled toward the west wing, the section of the OHL only for sorcerers. Once in the main hall, Geist made her way around the room, all the way to the back table, where she had first seen Heinrich and Leopold. The table sat empty: even the sorcerer-general was nowhere to be seen.

Geist walked up to Heinrich's seat, closed her eyes, and inhaled. So many scents—it almost overwhelmed her, but she focused and separated out five individuals in her mind. Although she had no way to know which was Heinrich's, Geist half-smiled when she recognized the cologne of her father.

He always wore the same damn one.

She snapped her eyes open and followed the trail. He had been ordered to watch Heinrich, hadn't he? Her father would lead her straight to him.

Geist hurried to her destination, keeping her father's scent fresh in her mind. It took her to the other side of the OHL, the East Wing, and she had to slow when she realized sorcerers were living in the rooms, much like an inn. Most of them were men, all thin and gaunt and without military uniforms.

Researchers. But why are they here?

Geist slipped by open doors, still invisible, until she reached a short hallway and came to an abrupt halt.

Her father paced at the opposite end, his hands behind his back, his face set in a glower. Geist held her breath and stepped back. Then she waited, watching him wear a line in the carpet with his heavy footsteps. He grumbled and cursed, and while Geist weighed her options, considering creating a distraction, he turned on his heel and walked straight in her direction.

Geist ducked behind a vase, the breath in her lungs burning.

Without giving the vase in front of her a second glance, her father marched down the hallway, passing her in a matter of moments.

She still waited a minute before moving. *Better safe than sorry.*

Then she scampered down the hall and came to the sole door.

Heinrich has to be here.

She ghosted through the oak of the door until she emerged

inside an ornate bedroom. A huge bed, adorned with a scarlet canopy, sat in the corner, while a large dresser and armoire stood opposite.

"Did you think I wouldn't notice?" a man asked in German.

Geist whipped around, her focus almost broken, but she maintained her invisibility.

Heinrich stood by the bathroom door, his long sleeves rolled up to his elbows, his suit vest unbuttoned. He held himself with a rigid posture and offered Geist a sneer as he said, "You know I can sense your magic."

Seconds ticked by in silence as Geist raked her mind for an answer. She hadn't planned on *him* being the one to confront *her*.

When she offered no reply, Heinrich walked over to the dresser and opened the top drawer. "You weren't satisfied guarding me like a dog in the hall? Our commander's trust doesn't run deep, I see."

Then it hit her.

He thinks I'm my father.

"You don't have to stay here," Heinrich said, his voice growing louder with each word. "I'm not going anywhere—where would I go?"

This charade won't last long. Geist stepped back and patted at her belt. She hadn't taken a weapon—there hadn't been many to take—but she cursed herself regardless. Even a sap or a blackjack would have been better than nothing. What if she needed to subdue Heinrich when he realized who she was?

Heinrich turned around, his eyebrows knit together. "Are you pulling a gun on me?"

Geist froze. How did he know? Was it the sound of her clothing? Or, God forbid, could his sorcery detect her thoughts?

"I can't believe it," Heinrich whispered. He turned away again and grabbed at the contents of the drawer. A pristine Luger sat between two piles of sheets, and he lifted it up with an unsteady hand. "I... always suspected this would happen... but I didn't think it would come to this so soon. And here, of all places. Or is that why you came into my room? Were you hoping for a quick and quiet kill away from the guests?"

He won't be any use to me if he's dead… and if we fight, we'll draw every single Abomination Soldier in the compound! Geist gritted her teeth.

"Wait," she said in German.

Heinrich glanced in her direction, his wide eyes betraying his shock.

"I'm not Markus Cavell." She allowed her invisibility to drop. "I'm a member of the Ethereal Squadron." Then she held up her hands, hoping her smaller stature worked in her favor.

He said nothing as he stepped toward the bathroom door.

Fuck, she thought. *I can't mess this up. I need to convince him, no matter what.*

"I've come to help," she blurted out. Then she forced herself to lower her voice. "I've been watching you for a while now."

"Is that right?" Heinrich asked, taking another step.

"It is. I saw when you rejected the office of magic-technology general."

He stopped and lifted an eyebrow. "What of it?"

"Is this…" She took in a deep breath. "Is this all really what you want? Having your work stolen from you—used to take innocent lives?" She lowered her hands and then motioned to the Luger. "You thought they sent someone to kill you. Is that the way you want to spend the rest of the war? Looking over your shoulder, wondering when you'll outlive your usefulness?"

Heinrich caught his breath after the last sentence. He lowered his weapon, his hand still shaking. "You said you've come to help me?"

"That's right," she said. "Me and my team."

"How many of you are there?"

Geist hesitated. She couldn't risk telling him specifics like that, not yet. Victory said he would defect, but what if she failed to get him out of the OHL? If Heinrich was recaptured, her father would make him talk, and she and her team could be captured as well.

"I have enough people to get you out of Belgium," she said. "We'll take you to our headquarters in Paris. From there, you can—"

"Paris? It'll be a warzone."

"Are you talking about the New Schieffen Plan?"

Heinrich placed his Luger back in the dresser. Then he opened a second drawer and tore through the contents, his breathing becoming faster and shallower. "So the Ethereal Squadron knows about that, do they? You have talented spies. But listen—information about the timing of the attack has been misleading. Germany intends to launch the attack at the end of the OHL meeting."

"What?" Geist balked.

"That's right. Six days from now, all of Paris will be smothered in gas."

Geist ran a hand through her curly hair, fighting for breath. *Major Reese needs to know. They all need to know.* "We need to leave," she said. "Right now."

Heinrich glanced over his shoulder. "Your team has an extraction plan ready?"

"Yes." *Not really, but we'll have to improvise.* "If we waste much time, we risk the enemy discovering us. It's now or never."

"And I assume you'll want my research in exchange for safety."

"I'm glad you understand wartime tactics," Geist quipped. "Yes, that's exactly what we'll be hoping for."

Heinrich stopped searching and straightened his glasses. "I won't give the Ethereal Squadron my research. Not now. Not ever."

"Now isn't the time for negotiation."

"I can't allow another military to use my weapons."

"It's in the hands of our enemy. And you've seen what *they* do. How are we to fight them if we don't have the tools?"

"More destruction will come of this," Heinrich snapped. "If I surrender my research—if everyone knows—then they'll *all* use it, don't you understand?" He pushed his long sleeves down with a quick and forceful motion. "And it'll all be on me."

"What does that mean?"

"It won't stop at protection. Once the instruments of war I've created are... *loose* in the world, there's no stopping other world powers from using them. Nothing but destruction and death will come of this. How am I supposed to sleep at night knowing that it's my doing?" He walked up to her, a few inches away, and shook his head. "Well? How can I?"

Geist pressed her knuckles against his arm and shoved him back a step. "This isn't about *you*," she said, her voice low. "Look at the big picture. The enemy *already has* these weapons. We can't change that. And they're *using* those weapons. We can't change that, either. But if we use your research against them, we can force them to stop. Or, we let them continue—and fear of your creations control the world. Those are our options. What's it going to be?"

Despite the bite in Geist's words, Heinrich didn't flinch or back away. Instead, he stared down at her, his dull, green eyes shifting back and forth. He exhaled twice, his stern expression melting into something melancholy.

"I'll go with you," he said. "But I still reserve the right to discuss this with the commander of the Ethereal Squadron."

"Fine." Geist motioned to the door. "We need to leave." She shimmered and shifted until invisible. "I'll follow behind you."

"I need my notebook," Heinrich said. "It's not here. I probably left it in the basement, with the research and… *the specimens.*"

The specimens. The way he had uttered the words… the chill in his voice had been like the chill of magic.

Heinrich grabbed the door handle. "I should also grab a few other things. Meet me at the eastern end of the basement, in the room with windows to the outside. We can leave there."

"How long do you need?"

"Less than twenty minutes."

"Make it ten."

"Very well," Heinrich said. He buttoned up his vest before opening the door. After a quick glance down the hallway, he strode forward, his head held high. Geist shadowed his movements. Heinrich had long legs and walked so fast that she almost had to jog to keep up.

Once they reached the main hall, Geist broke away from Heinrich and headed back to meet with Battery and Vergess. She watched Heinrich go for some distance and even held her breath when Heinrich wished a couple of Abomination Soldiers *good evening* before he disappeared around a corner.

I hope Victory is right about him.

Geist reached the servants' hall and found it empty. Her nerves singing, she leapt to each door, glancing inside, searching with all the frenzy of a hive of bees. It didn't take long for her to stumble upon a parlor with Vergess and Battery conversing with two Abomination Soldiers. Geist caught her breath the moment she entered the room, her gaze darting between her allies and the enemy.

"Nothing compares to the Berlin Palace," Vergess said as he swirled a glass of wine. Battery and the Abomination Soldiers nodded along. "The incorporation of baroque architecture is simply stunning."

Battery lifted a delicate feminine eyebrow. "I'm surprised you even know what *baroque* means, *sweetie.*"

"Why is that, *darling?*" Vergess asked.

"Oh, you know. You struck me as a simpler sort of man is all."

"You don't say."

The Abomination Soldiers chuckled and exchanged glances.

Geist crept behind Vergess and leaned in close to his back. "I'm here," she whispered—so quiet, she almost couldn't hear herself, but Vergess turned his head for a moment before refocusing on the conversation.

"I prefer Gothic architecture, myself," Battery continued. "It has more personality."

"The Germans are planning to launch their attack on Paris within six days," Geist continued in a whisper. "Heinrich has agreed to go with us. He's gathering information in the basement. We're to meet him and leave."

Vergess took a sip of his wine. Then he said, "Well, gentlemen, it's been pleasant."

But before he could finish his speech, the illusions on him and Battery dropped, revealing the shawls and Belgian clothing underneath.

For a moment, no one said anything.

Fuck, Geist thought as she stepped back. *Dreamer and the others—*

something's happened to them!

"*Vergess*," she snapped. "Kill them. We need to go."

Vergess nodded and threw a punch at the nearest Abomination Soldier. But the blow never connected. The man shifted his weight slightly, then vanished, reappearing instantaneously in another part of the parlor as the chill of magic filled the room. Without hesitation, Vergess leapt for the second enemy soldier, his hand open, and he grabbed the man's uniform. His *ruina* sorcery ate through his clothes and left a permanent rot that crawled through the fabric of the khaki uniform.

"*What the fuck's going on?*" the German soldier roared.

He lashed out at Vergess, his fingers leaving a trail of rot along Vergess's shirt.

He's a ruina practitioner, too!

The first soldier appeared next to Battery and pulled out his Luger from his side holster. Geist leapt to his defense, thrusting her hand into the man's neck and allowing her body to reform, her fingers curling around membranes and the cylindrical tube of the trachea. She pulled back, rupturing the skin and crushing the man's windpipe. The man tried to yell as he stumbled back, but all he managed was wet gurgles. He fell to the ground, his blood soaking the carpet crimson.

Vergess and the other soldier wrestled back and forth until they tripped over a cushioned chair. They both tumbled to the floor, the soldier's hands flailing about, rotting everything they touched. Vergess had a tight hold around the man's neck, preventing him from shouting again, but the damage had been done.

More are coming, Geist thought, her hands shaking. *We need to leave right now!*

She ran to the door and barred it with a spare chair.

Battery gasped. "G-Geist!"

Geist whipped back around. The teleporting soldier had used his sorcery to get back to his feet. He grabbed Vergess on the shoulder and "blinked" away a layer of clothing and flesh, all the way down to the muscle. Vergess bit back a shout of agony, his eyes going wide.

Without thinking, Geist ran forward and ripped another chunk of flesh from the injured soldier, this time from the gut. In her haste, she'd forgotten the *ruina* sorcerer. The man broke free from Vergess and then grabbed in Geist's location, hitting her shirt and spreading his rot onto the collar with a mere grazing touch.

Vergess sucked in breath through his teeth, jumped to his feet, and then grabbed the man's head and twisted it sideways, breaking his neck in one motion.

"Fuck," Geist hissed. She allowed her invisibility to drop as she attempted to tear away the rotting clothing. It spread to her flesh, disintegrating portions of her shoulder and bicep.

"Give it to me," Vergess commanded, panic rising in his voice. "Let me see."

Geist forced herself to peel away her shirt to expose the skin. Vergess placed his hand on it. Although he couldn't reverse the decay, he stopped its spread, his cold magic neutralizing the black rot in an instant. He then reached for her shirt, but Geist pulled away on instinct. The rot ate away the threads and she knew it would soon seep through to the wrappings underneath.

"Take it off," he said as he removed his own affected clothing.

She glanced at Battery. "I... I can't."

"Just give it to me!"

"I..."

Vergess wheeled on Battery. The younger man stared with wide eyes as Vergess leapt at him. Before Battery couldn't even form words, Vergess slammed him to the ground and pinned him to the floor, effectively trapping him.

Geist took the moment to rip off her shirt and bindings. She threw herself to the floor and covered herself with her arms, her breath coming easier now that she didn't have anything constricting her.

"What's going on?" Battery asked, muffled by the carpet.

Vergess didn't reply, and he kept Battery's face buried beneath him.

The two Abomination Soldiers lay motionless. The room was still, which only compounded Geist's dread.

What was she going to say to Battery?

"Are you… actually betraying us?" Battery asked in a small voice.

There was no explanation. No lie she could use to justify her actions. No untruth that could shield her from what was coming.

Then the truth would have to do.

She walked to one of the corpses and pulled off a bloody shirt. "Vergess. Let him up."

"Are you sure?" he asked.

"Yes."

He stood, and Battery leapt up, glaring. He immediately turned his attention to Geist. She kept her back to him as she slung the shirt over her shoulders.

"Wait," he muttered. "What's going on? Geist, your back… there's nothing there. I thought—"

"I'm a woman, Battery," she said, almost inaudible.

She trembled, knowing she could never take those words back. The cool air of the parlor brought goosebumps to the skin of her back, but she ignored them, waiting for Battery to reply.

Battery shook his head. "Impossible. That can't be."

"It is," Vergess said.

"There's no way Geist is… well… It's impossible. Someone would have known by now."

Vergess walked over and placed a hand on Geist's shoulder. She suspected that he wanted her to speak, but no words could escape her lips. She shied away from his touch, anger mixing in with her confusion. *We don't have time for any of this—the enemy will be on us at any second, and we need to flee!*

But another question froze her in place. What was the rest of the team going to do when they found out?

"What's your name?" Battery whispered. "Your real name."

"Does it matter?" Vergess snapped. "We have an operation to finish."

"You knew? For how long?"

No answer. Again, a terrible silence descended.

"Florence," Geist forced herself to reply. "My name is Florence."

Battery stepped toward the parlor door. He shook his head and gripped his shirt tightly. "I can't believe it. Are you even from House Weston? I mean…" He took a deep breath and then stared, his eyebrows knitted. "You're from House Cavell. Aren't you? That's how you can use specter sorcery."

Geist inhaled. "I have nothing to do with my house," she said, her words slow.

"I… I can't believe this."

"Something happened to Dreamer," Vergess interjected. "That's why our illusions dropped. We don't have time for this."

"I thought…" Battery took another step toward the door. "I mean, I… I trusted you. I *idolized* you, Geist. I thought we both had been operated on, and that we were truly brothers in arms. But… you're a traitor and… and a liar."

"Stop," Geist pleaded. "I know what you're thinking, but—"

Battery withdrew his empowerment.

"I need to speak to Victory," he murmured. "He always knows what to do." He turned and threw the chair away from the door before rushing out into the hallway, heedless to the danger beyond.

Vergess went to follow but stopped halfway, cursing under his breath. He wheeled back to Geist, conflict scrawled across his features.

"I'll go after him," he said, glancing between her and the door. "I'll bring him back. But…"

But I can't leave you.

Geist nodded, half-drowning in her own thoughts. "Go. I'll be fine. I can handle this."

"Are you sure?"

"I said *I'll be fine.* Please. Get Battery. If he gets caught, the mission's over."

There was a long moment of silence before Vergess stepped up to her and pressed his lips against hers. The quick touch left a fire on her skin, and Geist wished he could stay, but Vergess had already turned and dashed out of the parlor.

TWENTY-NINE

Abomination

Geist waited, listening to his boots pound down the long hallway. Alone with two Abomination Soldier corpses, she stared at the wall opposite her, unseeing.

Her chest was tight. Agony throbbed from her upper arm. More than just her body—without Battery's empowerment, everything hurt.

The dim lighting of the parlor blackened her thoughts.

I lived through trenches, artillery bombardments, and deadly gas, she thought with a smirk. *This can't kill me. Or if it does, I'm going to be furious.*

Biting down on her lip, Geist tasted copper. She pushed away from the wall and pulled her shirt tightly closed, hiding the bloodstains. Her injured arm—twisted by the GH Gas, weakened by the corrupted dogs, and now rotted through *ruina* sorcery—could barely move. Her hand was a claw, her fingers unable to extend, and it hung at her side like it belonged to somebody else.

Taking one step after the other, Geist exited the parlor, her hair disheveled, her face red and her strength drained. She didn't know how Vergess and Battery had made it through the hall undetected, but she gave it no thought. Instead, she stumbled forward, heading straight for her destination.

Without Dreamer's sorcery, it was clear she was a woman and she made little effort to hide it, but no one wandered the hall. Perhaps servants would walk by, but she also didn't care about them. She could hear shouting in the distance and she suspected an alarm had been sounded.

Geist continued, her mind buzzing. The manor layout was still fresh in her mind. She pictured the room she wanted and turned down the hall without seeing. Once at the door, she opened it and slipped into the opulent bedroom, clicking the lock behind her.

Geist couldn't wait a second longer. She ripped off her clothes, the seams tearing noisily in her haste.

This isn't about me. Not about my pain. Not about my secrets. I can't let anything stop me, not even my own team. I'll do it myself. I'll find a way.

Like I always do.

She walked to the closet and tore open the doors. The women's apparel that hung before her came in every color. Garments of pastel pink and dark velvet and delicate patterned embroidery—the closet of a princess. Geist didn't care. She grabbed the first gown and discarded her old outfit in a few quick motions.

Once dressed, Geist fought through the pain to slip into a pair of long gloves—anything to hide her damaged arm.

She entered the adjoining washroom and glanced at the mirror above the sink. Her mind played tricks and, for a brief second, she thought she saw her mother in the reflection. Choking on a laugh, Geist sifted through the makeup on display and selected a few products. Applying what she could with one hand, she could not help but remember her father had once had to hold her down while her mother had painted her face—*like a proper lady*, she'd said.

Everything would be better if you weren't so difficult.

Geist smiled darkly. "She was probably right."

Satisfied with her work, Geist pushed away from the washbasin. She walked back into the bedroom and plucked a large-brimmed hat from the display rack next to the closet. Before she left, she slipped into a pair of heels.

She exited the room and strode through the manor with her head high.

No one attempted to stop her. No one questioned her presence. Geist walked among the mingling sorcerers as one of them, even as they muttered rumors and exchanged gossip. She offered a smile and a royal nod as she continued to the eastern side of the compound to the basement entrance.

The sentries—the men with glowing gold eyes—gave her the once-over, but they no longer worried her. Geist had no illusions to see through. She was a sorcerer of House Cavell. Was she the belle of the ball? No. But she belonged, and that was all that mattered.

Even when the soldiers began searching rooms, they ignored her. A woman wasn't whom they were looking for. She was invisible again, though without the use of sorcery this time.

"So many soldiers rushing to the courtyard," one noblewoman said.

"I heard something dreadful," another replied.

"Well, don't keep me in suspense."

"Enemy operatives were found outside. Spies, most likely. Or assassins."

"Oh, my."

"Come to kill the crown princes, no doubt."

Geist refused to let her mind wander to her comrades. Battery and Vergess had already gone to deal with the situation. They would make sure the others were safe.

Geist entered a small stone-walled room once used for storage, but it had nothing of interest except for a door leading to the subterranean levels of the manor. She ambled in and met the gaze of the lone guard.

Don't falter, Florence. Only fools trip on what's behind them. Finish the operation.

"I'm sorry," the man said in formal German. "But you'll need to return to the festivities. This is off limits to civilians." The operatic music in the room over was muffled by the thick stone and wood walls.

Geist fanned her face. "Oh… I'm so sorry. I've had so much to drink. I thought this was a washroom."

"No, ma'am."

"Do you mind showing me to one? I'm so turned around."

"I'm not to leave my post, but the washroom is on the other side of the dance floor."

"Oh, thank you." She crossed the room and smiled up at the guard. No doubt he was an Abomination Soldier. "Do you mind if I stand here for a moment longer? It's much cooler here than in the commotion of the dance floor."

The man nodded, his stance relaxed. She got up close and giggled, the sound foreign to her ears, but the soldier seemed to enjoy it. He offered a one-sided smile.

Geist replied by stepping up in front of him and running her fingers over his dark green uniform tunic. She couldn't feel anything from her injured arm, but that didn't matter. The man's smile widened and he leaned in close.

With a smirk of her own, Geist reached around and opened the door, driving her shoulder into the man's midsection. Caught off guard, the soldier fell back and plummeted down the stairs, his grunts and cries trapped in the stairwell. Geist stepped in and shut the door behind her before taking the steps four at a time to reach him. Her stolen hat fell from her head and fluttered to the ground behind her, forgotten.

To her surprise, the soldier had his trench knife ready by the time she had reached his side. He slashed at her, but Geist let the long blade pass through her body without making contact, though he did slash the stomach of her gown.

Geist lunged and took the knife. The man attempted to stand, but the fall had twisted his leg. Geist fell upon him, using her strength and weight to plunge the point of the trench knife deep into the soldier's chest. The man writhed and choked out a whimper of agony, but it was too late.

House Cavell. The house of assassins.

Vergess's words echoed as she watched the man's life fade, his eyes full of pain and terror as they stared up at her. She was an assassin. House Cavell had cultivated specific schools of sorcery to make their sons and daughters efficient killers. Geist could run from her past—from her home, from her family—but she'd still used their sorceries to kill hundreds of men.

Once the man was dead, Geist retrieved the handgun from his belt and tucked it into the brassiere of her dress. She knew she was running on borrowed time—once the corpse was discovered, soldiers would swarm the basement like termites. Either she would get her information, or she would die here. There were no other options.

Stepping over the warm body, Geist opened the door to the basement floor. She shivered. Magic lingered in the air. *So much magic.* The click of her heels sent chills down her spine. Geist discarded them on the first few steps and continued barefoot.

The largest room of the basement had once been a wine cellar. Empty wooden casks lined the walls and glass bottles sat on racks scattered around without rhyme or reason. Electric lights provided enough to see by, but not enough to illuminate the corners or the shadows under every step. Geist's eyes played tricks on her, seeing forms lurking in every dark corner.

Several doors and hallways led from the central chamber, most of which looked to have been made recently through additions to the house and impromptu mining. It was a true labyrinth, not documented by Lucie Coppens's detailed maps.

But where is Heinrich? He said something about a room with windows…

Geist walked to the far door and opened it with slow, cautious movements. She took three steps in and froze. More rooms. More hallways. More areas to search. How large could one basement be? How long would it take to search it all?

An arm wrapped around Geist's body, its steel grip trapping her against the chest of a man. Her heartrate jumped as the barrel of a pistol pressed into her flesh—right where the jaw met the neck— and she locked up, her whole body seizing in sudden terror.

She hadn't been paying enough attention. Her dread had blinded her.

So this is how it ends.

Geist waited—for the bullet, for the agony to shatter her neck and jaw—but it never came.

"I know you," the gruff voice of a man muttered into her ear, his hot breath running down her neck. "I've met you. More than once."

Her heart stopped. She knew that voice. She could never forget that voice.

First Lieutenant Agustin Fechner. The man she'd thrown to the GH Gas the night her team had died—the night she had saved Vergess.

The arm around her body tightened and Fechner stepped forward, pushing her forward as well. Geist's mind raced. Last she had seen Fechner, he'd been broken beyond even Cross's ability to heal, lying on a medical table with his body half-melted by the GH Gas. A dead man, clinging to life through force of will alone.

So how was he here?

"You were different before," Fechner said, his voice echoing along with his boot steps in the dark halls of the basement. "You were the nurse I couldn't get out of my head. Imagine how surprised I was when I sensed you here. I couldn't believe you'd have the audacity to infiltrate the *Oberste Heeresleitung.*"

Geist wanted to turn to face him, but the pistol at her throat stopped her. She kept her eyes open, calculating the path of the bullet in her mind. Fechner came to a door and kicked it open, walking in with Geist still pinned against his chest.

There were no lights. None whatsoever.

"And then I remembered where I first met you," Fechner drawled. "And I realized why I couldn't stop thinking about you. You're that soldier I met in the trenches. *You're the one who pushed me into the gas.*"

He drew her into another room, one somehow darker than the last and filled with stagnant air. Geist couldn't see, but she didn't need to. Fear hung in the air like pollen.

No. It can't be.

That chill, that unmistakable crawling dread… it had to be GH Gas. It was all around her. She couldn't see it, but the terror singing in her bones told her it was close.

Geist brought her good hand up to Fechner's arm. "If you're going to kill me, get it over with." Anything was better than death at the hands of the gas.

Fechner chuckled, a rough, hollow sound. "You spared me on the operating table. I figured I would extend you the same courtesy."

He shoved her farther into the darkness. Geist stumbled forward, her eyes wide, but not a single drop of light alleviated her blindness. Somehow, Fechner moved through the shadows with certainty, never once tripping or fumbling in his trek around the room. When he stopped, and before Geist could react, he slid his hand down her gown and withdrew her handgun. With her disarmed, Fechner pushed her onto the edge of a metal table. He strapped down her good wrist, trapping her to the equipment.

When he grabbed her second wrist, she cried out pain.

"Please," she said through clenched teeth. "It hurts."

Fechner released her damaged arm and left it free. Then he walked away, leaving her attached to the table. Geist focused in on her hearing, tracking Fechner's movement through the gloom of the underground room.

"I couldn't believe you were a woman," Fechner said, continuing his musings. "I fought myself over the fact for some time. But here you are. In the flesh." He touched a few things—metal things that clinked when they collided—and then went still. "Now that I know for certain, I think I understand you. I had a lot of time to dwell on the subject as I lay strapped to that table."

Electric lights flooded the room.

With each blink, Geist found her vision returning. She squinted through the pain and glanced around the room. Large duralumin gas tanks—some the size of motorcars—sat stacked one atop of another until they reached the ceiling. The pressurized contents could hold thousands of gallons of gas, and Geist didn't need to read the labels to know what was inside.

GH Gas. *All* of it.

So much, Geist thought, unable to look away. *One shell on the battlefield killed hundreds. The gas here could fill thirty shells, at least.*

She panned her gaze around the room, taking in the details one at a time. Gas grenades sat on the metal tables scattered around the middle of the large room. Geist stared down at her own table, shocked to find bloodstains near the leather straps for the wrists. By the far wall stood a wooden shelf filled with bottles of thick blackish-red liquid, each with its own label. Tubes and nozzles hung off a few fire-extinguisher-sized gas containers, some with mouth attachments and IV needles.

This wasn't just a storage facility. It was an operating theater.

"I knew I would see you again," Fechner said as he crossed the room to the wooden shelf. "It would just happen, given our professions. And I asked myself, *What would I do once I found you?* And after some thought, I knew the best solution. One that doesn't involve killing you. Snuffing out magic like yours is the last thing I want."

And then he turned to face her.

Geist quickly turned away, her stomach in knots. He wore clothing—a pair of uniform slacks and a belt—but his "shirt" was nothing more than tight leather bindings that kept him together, spanning all the way down his arms, covering every inch of flesh beneath the neck. The once-open sores and mutilated parts of his body were covered and held in place, the leather attached to his skin directly with small metal hooks.

Geist remembered Fechner's arm had melted into his gut, becoming one solid mass. His arm, cut away from his body, had been reshaped through braces and wire. Black opals, shattered into fragments, traced his bones, and a gauntlet armored his mangled hand. He moved it through magic: even Geist could sense the power, and she knew his whole uniform was some sort of magi-tech miracle, giving him the ability to function once more.

But his neck, face, and head still retained their waxy sheen. He didn't have eyes—Geist could even see the bone of the sockets—and his mouth stretched farther back than any mouth should. She could see the points of opals emerging at the tip of his spine, and she knew they must have been lodged all down his back, just like Battery's.

Whoever had crafted him had created a monster.

"Don't like what you see?" Fechner asked, his back to Geist as he ran his fingers over the bottles. "I don't blame you. I'm not... what I used to be."

"What are you?" she asked, breathless.

"An abomination."

Not an Abomination Soldier. Just an abomination.

"Can you see?" Geist barely got the words out.

"I see magic," Fechner said. "And sorcerers. And anything they touch. I didn't know this before, but magic, it hangs in the air like a fog. Sorcerers like you are vibrant, while others are dull and hard to discern... But I see. I see just fine." He pulled a bottle off the shelf and searched for another, running his fingers over the glass as though reading braille.

"Fechner," Geist began, but she cut herself short.

"What's your name?" he asked. "I've wanted to know for some time."

Geist held back a laugh. So many people wanted to know. She had gone nearly two years without revealing it, and now a whole handful of individuals knew. What was one more? Once Battery told Victory and the others, she would be discharged from the Ethereal Squadron eventually.

"Florence."

"No. Your true name. The one your allies know you by."

She looked up at him, surprised at the question. "Geist," she whispered.

"Fitting," Fechner said. "I also have a true name. They call me *Amalgam.*"

Amalgam. Geist couldn't unhear it. The name rang like a cracked bell in her ears. It would never have suited Fechner, but it fit this slumping, monstrous creature perfectly.

Amalgam plucked a second bottle from the shelf. "I don't like seeing you like this, Geist. I won't lie, I was excited when you decided to come down to the basement, to enter my domain, but you're so distraught. Something is wrong."

"Your domain?"

"I was one of the first they made with the GH Gas, you see. I'm one of their specimens. One of the first to survive."

Amalgam turned around and walked back, his terrible, misshapen face unable to convey the weight of emotion his voice carried. "The magic whispers things. I couldn't hear it before, but now it's as clear as church bells. When you came to me as a nurse I could hear the song and see the colors—your magic came through bright, but now it's suffering."

There had never been stories of men hearing magic before, but Amalgam was right. He was right about it all.

"I'm—" Geist took in a breath and exhaled. "I'm failing my operation. My teammates. They need me. Right now."

"Is that so?"

She pulled on her restrained wrist. "I have to go. You said you weren't going to kill me, but if you keep me as a captive, that's exactly what'll happen. I know too much. I know about the plan to attack Paris."

"I'm not going to keep you restrained," Amalgam said. "Not for long. But I am going to change your destiny."

"What… does that even mean?"

"The doctors used it to fix me." Amalgam stepped away. "When they told me that I would be gathering sorcerers from the Ethereal Squadron, all I could think of was you. I knew if I found you first that I could save you from the fate that awaits your compatriots." He grabbed a small canister of gas and filled an IV bottle with a mix of the blackish-red liquid from the shelves.

Blood. Geist could smell it the moment Amalgam had opened the bottles.

"Not everyone lives through the process," he said as he mixed his vile concoction. "I've seen a few sorcerers simply *give up* once they changed. But that won't happen with you. Your will is too strong for that."

"Amalgam. Do you know why they want sorcerers from the Ethereal Squadron? How they're… how they're going to add schools of sorcery to their bloodlines?"

"Yes."

"Tell me."

With the canister of GH Gas and the IV of blood, Amalgam walked back over to the table and set them down. "Once, I only knew the school of *aversio* sorcery. Then, after I pulled myself from the trench and they scraped up my body, the scientists found traces of others on the battlefield and mixed them together. The GH Gas… it *fuses* things. Flesh, and the magic within it. It makes everything one. Now I'm not some no-named sorcerer from a family with just one school of magic. Now I am more."

Amalgam snapped his fingers and a spark of flame appeared in his hand.

Geist couldn't breathe. Even here, she recognized Little Wick's fire.

And suddenly, it all fell together.

The Germans and Austrians had discovered a way to add magics to a sorcerer—not through bloodlines or dynastic legacy, but with *GH Gas*. They could melt the body of one sorcerer into another to create a new superbeing capable of different magics, with more sorcery.

Like the mutilated deer in the forest. Like Amalgam.

Geist glanced back at the bottles of blood and then returned her gaze to Amalgam's fire.

Little Wick. He fused with the blood of Little Wick.

Geist forced herself to gulp down air. *They're going to liquefy sorcerers in the Ethereal Squadron to strengthen themselves. Vergess… Battery… Victory… Me. All of us.*

That's why they're attacking Paris. That's the Ethereal Squadron headquarters for all of Verdun. They want us all.

Amalgam held the fire in his palm; it shifted and twirled, eventually changing from orange to a sickly shade of green. He grabbed at his forehead and allowed the *ignis* sorcery to fade. The sound of his breathing filled the room, his body shaking.

"What's wrong?" Geist forced herself to say, her mind still reeling.

"The gas," he muttered. "I can hear it whispering when it's this close… It's enough to drive you mad. Can you hear it, Geist?"

Amalgam walked over to a nearby table and picked up a gasmask. It was made from the same material as the leather of his shirt, but the visor, unlike that of most gasmasks, was fully reflective, like a small mirror. When he pulled it on and secured it to the rest of his uniform, Geist could see her reflection in the glass lens as clear as day.

"Don't worry," he said, his voice both muffled and mechanical through the mask. "I won't use enough to kill you. The doctors figured out a way to administer it in small doses. Enough to change you without breaking you. All you have to do is stay sane."

Amalgam picked up the canister of GH Gas, and Geist recoiled. The strap of the table kept her from fleeing.

"Amalgam," Geist pleaded. "Listen to me. You don't have to do this. You can stop. You can help me. We can leave together."

"I don't think so."

"You know this is wrong. And I think the GH Gas is something far worse than just a tool." She held up her arm. "Look, it's corrupted. Something's wrong."

"There's no escaping this, Geist. If I use the GH Gas on you, they won't kill you. It's the only way to save your life."

"No, wait. I'm here with others. Together, we can—"

"Others?" he interjected. "No. They already captured your teammates. They're here, in these dungeons past these research rooms. They're having their blood drained as we speak."

For a second, Geist's heart stopped beating. *Draining their blood?*

Of course. To fuse them into the enemies. To steal their magic. To empower German and Austrian soldiers.

God, I failed them again. I should have done something… I should have…

The door to the room opened, revealing an Austrian Magic Hunter. The man scanned the room, sweeping his gaze over Geist to rest on Amalgam.

"Lieutenant?" the man asked.

Amalgam turned and faced the newcomer. "What is it?"

"Lieutenant Cavell wants you to, um, *handle* the new magic-technology general."

"Don't fret. Heinrich's already down here. He's not going

anywhere."

"Yes, s-sir."

"Now leave us."

"There's one more thing," the man said, his nervousness on display with each word he stuttered. "Lieutenant Cavell also wants you to s-search the grounds for hidden members of the Ethereal Squadron. He thinks there may be more."

Geist pulled on her restraints. When she couldn't slip out, she took a deep breath and focused. It was harder without Battery, and she yearned for his strength, but hearing about her teammates had hardened her determination. Her arm shimmered and shifted, allowing her to ghost through the leather strap.

"I've already taken care of that," Amalgam said. "But tell Cavell I'll search the place again once I'm finished."

"Y-yes, sir."

The Magic Hunter shut the heavy door as he left. Amalgam didn't bother turning around when he spoke. "You remember I can see magic now, right, Geist?"

Geist leapt across the room and slammed into the table that held her handgun. She brought it up and pulled the trigger, the soft click of an empty magazine her only reward. She cursed under her breath. Of course Amalgam had unloaded it under the cover of darkness.

"I'm not going to let you do this," Geist said, tossing aside the weapon.

"I don't think you understand. It's either let me help you or die." He kept his back to her, unmoving. "Don't make me kill you. Your magic has such… luster. Like a night full of stars."

Geist moved around the room to another table and picked up one of the GH Gas grenades. The icy metal of the weapon left her hand numb. She held it at arm's length, well aware of the deadly power contained within.

"I'm going to give you one last chance," Geist said. "I'm going to leave this place, one way or another, and then I'm going to rescue my teammates. I can take you with me. We don't have to be enemies."

"No. No one will accept what I've become beyond these walls." He waited a moment, breathing heavily in the gasmask. "You saw that man just now. Even the men who created me find my form… distasteful. I've accepted it. I'm a monster."

"I'm sorry," Geist murmured. "You don't deserve this."

"You made me this way."

"I didn't make any of this. Your country did. Please, Amalgam. Come with me."

For a moment he said nothing.

"You'll never make it," he muttered. "Your plans for escape are mere fantasy."

"I have to try."

Amalgam laughed, his voice echoing inside the mask. "You've always been defiant. Ever since when we first met. I like that—but it's not going to do you any favors here."

Geist lifted the grenade, her fingers wrapped tight around the pin. "Stand. Aside."

He turned to her, the reflective eye pieces of his gasmask leaving him utterly faceless. "You don't know what you're doing. That won't affect me. Not while I'm wearing this."

"I don't believe you."

"It's true. You'll only destroy yourself."

Despite her doubt, Geist pulled the pin and hurled the grenade. Amalgam jumped back as the gas poured out of the canister, filling the room with an evil hiss. Yellow-greenish fog wafted up, and Geist took the moment to grab a bandolier of four more grenades.

Amalgam stood amidst the cloud of gas. Although he did not melt, he grabbed at his head, his fingers curling around the seams of his mask. "The *voices*," he rasped. "So terrible. They *burn*."

Geist could almost hear it too. The gas had always seemed more than mere vapor—almost sentient, pursuing its victims across the battlefield. And now it wanted to whisper something to her…

But she didn't have time to listen. Geist leapt around the room and hit the door hard. She burst into a dark hallway and collided with the opposite wall, fighting through her dress to stay upright.

THIRTY

Flight

The gas followed.

She ran for the next room over and grabbed the door without a second thought, throwing it open and rushing inside. It was an armory, complete with lockers. A soldier, half-dressed and smoking, finished fastening his belt just as he glanced up to spot Geist. Her attention didn't linger on him long. She took stock of the room in a matter of seconds.

Rifles on the far wall.

A box of mining dynamite in the corner.

"What're you doing here?" the soldier asked, his words coming out in indignation as he pulled the cigarette out of his mouth.

Geist picked up the bottom of her dress and crossed the room. She took a rifle, checked to see if a round was loaded in the chamber, and then glanced over to the box of explosives.

They were underground. Using the dynamite would be a terrible risk.

"Hey," the man barked as he pulled on his tunic. "You can't touch that! It's dangerous!"

She hefted the rifle and aimed, using her bad arm as a post to rest the barrel on. "Stand down," she commanded.

The man froze and held his hands in the air.

"Get on your—" Geist stopped the moment she saw the GH Gas slither into the hallway outside the door. *I don't have time for this!* She grabbed the man's cigarette and lit a long fuse on a stick of dynamite. "You need to run."

She picked up the explosive. *I have a little over sixty seconds before this explodes.*

Before the soldier could muster an answer, Geist ran from the room, leaping over what little gas had sifted down the hall. She wheeled around and watched as Amalgam stumbled out of the operating room, his hand still on his head, his heavy breathing labored and desperate.

Using her good arm, Geist chucked the dynamite over Fechner. It landed inside the operation room doorframe, near the first tank of pressurized gas. Geist didn't wait for a countdown, or even to watch what happened. She knew she had to be as far away from it as possible. She ran in the opposite direction, her bare feet barely touching the stone floor in her haste.

"Gas!" the half-dressed soldier shouted the moment he got into the hall. "Gas! Warn the others!"

Amalgam stepped out of the GH Gas unharmed and sprinted down the hall, heading straight for Geist. The half-dressed soldier didn't moved fast enough. His ankles and feet, caught in the vile mist, caved under his weight as though made from melting candle wax. The dark corridors of the basement filled with screams.

Like in the grip of a nightmare, Geist ran from her pursuer, unwilling or unable to glance back. She could hear Amalgam gaining as she rounded a corner, her breathing ragged and her mind soaked in adrenaline. Geist half-registered the four soldiers who stepped out of rooms on either side of her. She pulled the pin on another gas grenade and tossed it back, hoping beyond hope that she wasn't trapping herself in the underground labyrinth.

The dungeons. Amalgam said they were past the research rooms. I need to get there.

Gunshots rang out all around her. Geist tried to ghost, but she couldn't focus enough to access her magic. A bullet pierced the meat of her calf and she collapsed to the floor. She dropped her rifle, but she couldn't take the time to retrieve it. She forced herself to stand, only to be hit by Amalgam as he tackled her back to the floor.

The GH Gas swirled nearby, consuming the four soldiers. They tried to flee, some covering their mouths to avoid the deadly vapor, but nothing saved them. More screams. More panic. Geist could hear dozens of others rushing through the corridors.

Amalgam struck her across the face with a heavy fist, his actions sloppy and imprecise, nearing frenzy. The impact rocked her to her core. Geist felt her vision fade for a brief moment, long enough for her mind to flash back to the first night she had seen the GH Gas. The screams sounded exactly the same.

"Stop," she pleaded. "*Stop*."

To her surprise, Amalgam, halfcocked for another swing, grunted and sat back. He clawed at his gasmask, hissing words that Geist couldn't discern. He was suffering… the voices of the gas, the magi-tech suit he wore—*something* was scrambling his brains.

But she knew the gas wouldn't wait for her to figure it out what was afflicting him so. Geist attempted to free herself, but Amalgam was too heavy and strong; his weight kept her pinned. In desperation, Geist reached up and unhooked part of Amalgam's suit, exposing his twisted flesh to the elements. He jumped off her, grabbing at the hooks, fumbling to reattach them.

Geist leapt onto her feet and half fell back to the floor, her wounded leg buckling beneath her. She felt no pain, but she knew her body was slowly coming apart at the seams. Limping forward, Geist fled the GH Gas and continued through the underground maze, taking turns—one left, one right—to avoid running in circles. Twice more, she threw grenades when soldiers appeared in her peripherals. She could barely think over the shouts and commands and panicked screams.

A loud boom followed by a rumble sent Geist tumbling. She hit her knees on the hard floor and shock paralyzed her body. The dynamite had exploded. Another boom, another rumble. Dust and chunks of stone fell all around her. The pressurized tanks must have ruptured. The whole basement would be flooded with gas, but hopefully the collapsed halls would give her enough time.

Geist stood on unsteady legs and hobbled forward. She glanced into the first room and her heart fluttered.

Victory! Dreamer!

Both men were strapped to tables, two German researchers standing next to them. Dreamer and Victory's shirts were removed and tubes were inserted into their arms, crimson with blood that flowed into glass jars. The researchers stepped back, both glancing from Geist to the door.

"Gas," she hissed. "It's been released. Get out while you can."

The researchers didn't question her—they simply ran, sweat dappling their skin. Geist let them go. They were the enemy, but she was in no condition to fight them.

She hobbled over to Victory's table and reached for the leather restraints holding down his arms, legs, and neck. He bled from open gashes and his body was covered in deep bruises: he'd been beaten badly, but he was alive. For now. After releasing his arms, Geist shook his shoulder.

"Victory," she said.

He opened his eyes and squinted. "Geist?"

"You're free. Can you stand?"

"I… I feel weak."

Geist gritted her teeth. She helped him up into a sitting position and glanced around the room. His blood jar sat on a wire rack, half-filled. She grabbed the container and smashed it against the concrete floor, the crimson splattering all the way to the far wall. *That's one sorcery they'll never steal,* she thought.

Without wasting any time, she hobbled over to Dreamer's table. He didn't look like the man Geist had always known. He was dark of complexion, slender, with black hair. He had described himself as an *Arab crow*—an African slave—so Geist knew he wasn't what he had previously presented, but she hadn't been expecting the same terrible scarring Battery had.

He, too, had opal shards and scars all over his body.

Dreamer's eyes were sunken, but he opened them regardless.

"Dreamer," Geist whispered. "Are you okay?"

"Geist," he said.

"We need to leave."

She undid his restraints and smashed his jar of blood in similar fashion. Both men removed the tubes in their arms, and at Geist's urging, applied pressure to stop the bleeding.

Shouting in the halls grew louder and louder, followed quickly by gunshots. What were they fighting? Was it Battery or Vergess? And what had happened to Blick? Geist didn't know, and she didn't have the luxury of investigation.

A man ran by the door, skidded to a stop, and then turned back.

It took Geist a moment to recognize Heinrich. He jogged into the room, a handgun tucked into the waist of his slacks.

"What's happening?" he asked.

"I set off the gas," Geist replied.

Heinrich ran both his hands through his dark hair, his eyes searching the floor. "All right. Please, follow me. I know how we can get outside without going through the OHL."

Victory and Dreamer threw their legs off the edge of the table. Victory got up first, wobbling on his feet, but he stayed upright. Heinrich ran to Dreamer and offered a shoulder, seemingly realizing that Geist would not leave without him.

Heinrich led them out of the research room and through the long, twisted halls of the basement. He turned a corner, froze, and then backed away.

Gas. In the hall. It wafted in their direction, chasing them like a malevolent specter.

Heinrich took another hallway, running as fast as Dreamer would allow. Victory was steadily regaining his strength, but Geist was falling behind, her leg and arm slowly hurting more and more as her adrenaline waned.

Light—*natural* light—caught her attention from an open door. Heinrich stepped into a large cellar room with crescent windows near the ceiling and shut the door once Geist got inside.

Geist fidgeted with the last gas grenade on her bandolier. "We don't have time…"

"Everything will be okay," Heinrich said, his shaky tone unconvincing.

He stared at the door, watching as puke-green and yellow mist seeped under the crack between it and the floor. Geist turned away. It was too late. They couldn't go back the way they had come.

He guided Dreamer toward a stack of empty casks and left him at the base of the pile. "Here," he said. "We can climb out. One at a time." Then he muttered something under his breath, his voice too low for Geist to hear.

Victory huffed and climbed the first cask. He helped Dreamer up and waited a moment to gather their strength.

She turned to Heinrich. His hair and forehead were soaked with sweat, and his hands were trembling. Geist sometimes forgot how poorly civilians handled battle stress.

"Give me your Luger," she said. Heinrich handed the firearm over without a word of protest, almost as if he didn't want the responsibility of having it.

The door to their cellar ripped open, allowing a wave of GH Gas to pour inside. Amalgam strode through the fog, his magi-tech clothing coated in blood—Geist didn't know whose. His breath came in rasps, his voice a mere animal grunt behind the mask. He lumbered through the door, his boots leaving dark red footprints on the floor behind him.

Geist moved back, away from the gas, and pulled herself up onto the nearest cask. The GH Gas, heavier than air, spread across the floor in long tendrils, traveling to the farthest corners before heading upward. Victory and Dreamer rushed up to the window and slammed on the glass, but the latch had long since been rusted in place, sealing it shut. Geist went up another cask, fearing the wobbly unsteadiness of her perch.

"Heinrich," she said. "Get up!"

"I'll be fine," he muttered. "I'm going to try to calm him down."

"The gas!"

"*I'll be fine.*" Then he turned to Amalgam. "Listen to me, not the gas—you have to ignore it. I know you're still a reasonable man. Please, Amalgam."

Geist stared down from atop the island of casks, Victory and Dreamer still fumbling with the window. Amalgam stumbled forward, straight for Heinrich, wading through the fog like a drunken, blood-soaked shark.

Heinrich, much to Geist's shock, stood among the greenish-yellow vapors without harm, his bare skin exposed yet unharmed. He held up both hands, approaching Amalgam as though he were a wild animal.

The gas doesn't affect Heinrich?

"Please, Amalgam. I know it's difficult to focus, but—"

Amalgam backhanded the other man, shattering Heinrich's glasses and sending him crashing into the brick wall of the cellar. Amalgam returned his mirrored gaze to Geist.

Snapping out of her daze, Geist faced the window and raised her Luger. "Get down!"

Victory and Dreamer leaned away. Geist fired twice, and the latch exploded into splinters of wood and metal. Victory didn't wait for a command—he shoved the window open and pushed Dreamer through. With the window open, the fresh air washed over Geist like a cool splash of water on a hot summer day.

Once Victory crawled clear, Geist reached for the sill, but a powerful grip on her ankle sent a shiver across her body. She gritted her teeth as Amalgam pulled her back, foot by foot. She flailed and clung to the sill, keeping herself above the deadly gas almost through sheer force of will.

Amalgam stood on the first set of casks, looming over her, his grip tight enough to bruise.

"*Amalgam,*" she said, forcing herself to speak. She stared up at her own terrified reflection in his eye lenses, her mind racing. "I—I've changed my mind. Please, listen."

To her shock and amazement, Amalgam stopped pulling, but he didn't release her ankle. Holding himself in place with a hand on the wall, he stared down at her, his breathing just as ragged as ever.

"The gas is lying to you," she continued. She could feel breath of the GH Gas inches from her leg. It wanted her. "I want to help you, but—but you're hurting me." She prayed the pattern would hold—that he would avoid harming her at all costs as he had before.

Sure enough, Amalgam released her ankle, and Geist placed it down on the cask, the bridge of her foot landing on the discarded Luger.

Heinrich forced himself to stand. He wiped blood from his face, the twisted, glassless frames of his spectacles still resting on the bridge of his nose. When he glanced up, Geist kicked the Luger off the cask, and the weapon hit the gas-covered floor with a loud clack.

He met her eye, and a half-second of understanding passed between them. Amalgam either didn't notice or didn't care. He wrapped his gauntleted hand around her shoulder, his heavy breaths coming in even intervals. His grip was like a steel vise, his touch cold. "Amalgam—"

Heinrich snatched up the Luger, took aim, and fired. The bullet struck Amalgam in the ribs, penetrating his suit. The gas slithered all around him, as if it could smell the blood. Amalgam grunted and placed a hand over the hole, protecting his flesh from the gas.

Geist kicked him, driving her heel into the bullet would, sending him stumbling back. He disappeared beneath the surface of the gas, and Geist didn't bother to wait for him to reemerge.

"Come on!" she shouted to Heinrich, slipping into English out of sheer panic. "Hurry!"

As he crossed the room to the casks, Geist lifted herself back out of the window and crawled out along the grass, only stopping once she was fully outside.

Then a German soldier grabbed her by the forearm and hauled Geist roughly to her feet.

Her stomach dropped.

No! I'm so close!

THIRTY-ONE

The Wire

Geist bit back the urge to scream in frustration. *I should've known we couldn't escape. Not like this.*

"Stand," the German commanded, his voice familiar.

Through her frustrations, Geist craned her head back and stared up at the man. Relief washed over her, and she couldn't fight the smile. Vergess's German uniform wasn't an illusion; it was the real deal, no doubt stolen from the corpse of the enemy. He looked German, *sounded* German—and no one questioned his presence in the middle of a crisis.

"Vergess," she whispered.

"Get up," he said, his tone gentler. "We don't want to make a scene."

When four enemy soldiers rounded the corner of the building, Vergess motioned in the opposite direction.

"The others fled that way," Vergess called. "After them!"

They nodded and hurried away. Geist didn't blame them. She could still sense the gas billowing behind her, searching for where its prey had escaped to.

Geist used what little energy she had to stand. She had never been so happy to see someone from the Ethereal Squadron in all her life. With a sigh, she wrapped her arms around Vergess's torso in a weak embrace. "Thank goodness."

Vergess pried himself from her grasp and held her at arm's length. "Not now. Keep it together." He lifted his Mauser rifle, his face red, and motioned her away from the building. "Careful. The gas."

Geist leapt away from the building with all the speed her injured body would allow. The GH Gas billowed out of the cellar, gushing forward in thick clouds as the basement filled completely. Two gunshots rang out, then Heinrich clambered out of the busted window, his body still unharmed by the corruptive vapors.

Vergess pointed his rifle. "On your feet."

Heinrich scrambled to comply, his dark hair disheveled and clinging to his face with sweat.

"This is Heinrich," Geist said. "The magic-technology general. We need him alive."

"Amalgam's not dead," Heinrich rasped. "That'll only slow him down. He—"

Geist gritted her teeth. "We need to leave. Right now."

"What's wrong?" Vergess asked.

As the gas spread across the lawn, Geist pulled Vergess away. "We can't stay here. Where is Victory? Dreamer? Blick?" She forced herself to add, "Battery?"

"They're heading to the motorcar."

"Motorcar?"

"That's what you wanted, wasn't it? A motorcar? To escape?"

Geist glanced over to the basement window vomiting gas. She took several steps away, knowing if she got too close, it would find her. Her gaze lingered on Heinrich.

"Is this how the Ethereal Squadron always conducts an extraction?" he asked.

"Shut up and follow us," Vergess snapped.

Geist unclipped the last gas grenade. "If we need a distraction, throw this."

"Right." Vergess took the weapon and offered his shoulder.

Together, they hobbled to the edge of the long driveway, the swarm of soldiers rushing around the outside of the building itself. When a group of men spotted Vergess, they shouted for him to stop. He didn't, and the soldiers lifted their rifles.

Vergess tossed the grenade.

Only screaming followed. It was all Geist needed to hear.

"Let's go," she commanded.

They ran for the vehicles parked on the edge of the long driveway. Each vehicle was the same—dark ocean-blue paint that shone in the light of the midafternoon sun. A few mundane men, unaware of the scope of the disaster unfolding within the compound, sat in the driver's seat of their vehicles, watching the sorcerers scurry this way and that.

Vergess rushed between the motorcars, his gaze swiveling from one to the next until he stopped, his focus set on the far vehicle. Blick was in the driver's seat, Battery at his side. Victory and Dreamer sat in the back, and the middle row of seats were left empty. Vergess ran over, helped Geist into her seat, and then grabbed Heinrich by the collar of his shirt and unceremoniously threw him in afterward.

"Drive," Geist ordered.

Blick stared at her for a prolonged moment, his gaze locked on her dress.

"Drive!" she repeated. *"Now."*

"Right," Blick said as he gunned the motor. "Tsk. I hate these blasted things."

The motorcar jerked forward and back as Blick wrestled with the controls. Geist held her arm close and her leg tight against the seat. She barely saw the driveway, soldiers, and fleeing civilians as Blick managed to pull the vehicle out of its parking space and onto the road out of the OHL. She shivered as the wind whipped around the single pane of glass mounted to the hood of the motorcar.

But there were five soldiers between them and the southern gate. And not just any soldiers—Geist spotted Leopold's white cape the moment the breeze picked up—they were Abomination Soldiers. They stood in a group by the gate, obviously interrogating the guard, but turned as Blick sped toward them. Leopold pushed a few of his men aside and stepped forward.

"Watch out!" she shouted, almost reaching out and grabbing Blick. "He'll—"

A tempest broke out in the middle of the courtyard, swirling around Leopold as if he were the eye of the storm. The icy chill of magic tainted the wind. The Abomination Soldiers shielded their eyes and backed away from him. Flames sprouted up around Leopold's feet and mixed together with the squall to create a firestorm, bright enough to rival the sun in the sky.

Fuck.

"Hold on," Blick said, punching the gas. "The southern gate is our only option."

Geist gripped the seat. "He'll destroy the motorcar."

"We'll see."

To her surprise, Blick angled the car straight for the prince—straight through the fire. Vergess positioned himself in between her and the worst of the flame, shielding her as best he could as the temperature drastically increased with each passing second.

Although flames wiped around the side of the front window, Vergess soldiered through the heat. Blick increased speed. He lifted his pistol, and with his golden-eyed sorcery, aimed in a fraction of a second and fired.

The bullet pierced Leopold's left eye, shaking the man and disrupting his focus. The firestorm waned, but didn't disappear. When they charged Leopold, his eyebrows lifted and he dodged the vehicle as if by animal instinct. And as the motorcar passed, Geist watched her former fiancé whiz by, her gaze meeting his for a fraction of a second.

His dark eyes were alight with passion. His lips twisted up in a cruel grin.

Leopold was enjoying himself.

Even his eye was stitching itself back together—so fast and so smoothly that Geist figured it would be completely intact the moment their vehicle cleared the southern gate.

He'll remember this, all right.

The motorcar slammed through the wood of the southern gate, splintering the oak across the road as Blick kept his foot heavy on the gas pedal. Soldiers fired at them from afar, but Blick took the first turn around a building as soon as he could, breaking their line of sight. Geist exhaled, not even aware she had been holding her breath the entire time.

"Where are we heading?" Blick asked.

"To the border," Geist said.

Heinrich sat up in his seat. "We'll never make it. There's the wire—it'll kill us if we even try to ram through!"

"Magi-tech?"

"Of course," he said.

But they had no choice. They had to get back to Major Reese. Paris was in danger, and he had to know about the plan to use the gas on Ethereal Squadron sorcerers. If they waited—if they slowed or hesitated, even for a moment—they would never make it back in time.

We're not out of the woods yet.

"Head to the border," Geist repeated. "We'll get past the wire. I'll think of something."

The motorcar continued forward at ridiculous speed. The vehicle shook and tilted when it hit a dirt road, threatening to shake itself apart. Still, their velocity impressed Geist. She could imagine them crossing all of Belgium in a few short hours.

Blick turned the vehicle on the first western road. The empty battle-torn fields that surrounded them were left covered in the dirt kicked up by their vehicle as the winds came in from the east. Geist swore under her breath as she ran her hand down the side of her calf. It didn't bleed much, but the pain came in slow amounts as her body relaxed. She bound the injury with shreds of her stolen gown.

So many enemies, Geist thought, trying to focus her thoughts. *My father, the prince, the abominations, the gas…*

And Amalgam. Wherever he is now.

They'll come after us for sure. We won't be safe until we're back in France.

THE BUMPY ROADS north didn't offer much comfort. For brief moments, the ride would be smooth enough to sleep, but when the vehicle jerked and jostled, Geist snapped awake, sweat coating every inch of her skin.

I need to stay awake, anyway, she thought, fighting the weight of her eyelids. *I need to master apex sorcery. Then I could recover from these injuries on my own.*

Every second they took getting home was another second the enemy had to prepare and plan their attack. No matter how fast Blick drove, she still felt they weren't making good enough time. Once, while younger, she had met a sorcerer who could speak to people in their minds, even at great distances. Geist wished she knew such sorcery now.

Hell, even a messenger pigeon would do. Anything to warn the others.

The ride passed in relative silence. Besides Blick asking for directions every once in a while, no one spoke. The evening winds and dark skies made it hard to see much, but Geist could sense the tension in the car, even if she couldn't see her teammates' faces. Dreamer re-cast his incredible illusions over his own body, becoming a white Englishman once more.

"Thank you," he said, leaning toward her in the dark.

Geist lifted an eyebrow. "Me?"

"Yes. Thank you. Victory and I were searching out the OHL grounds when we were spotted by an Abomination Soldier. I apologize if my illusions failing caused you any trouble."

"Don't think about it. We're a team. I would never leave you behind—not if there's still air in my lungs and blood in my veins."

The others in the car nodded. The conversation died out again.

Heinrich sat up in his seat and reached up to his ear with a shaky hand. Although he didn't have any lenes in his spectacles, he didn't remove them. He lightly tugged at the frames and flinched. A rivulet of blood ran from Heinrich's ear down onto the vest of his disheveled gray suit. The hook at the end of the earpiece—a thin metal wire—had twisted when Amalgam struck him and punctured the earlobe. Geist was surprised the frame had remained intact.

Heinrich left his broken spectacles alone.

"So," he said in German. "You're *actually* a woman in charge of this military unit? Or are you just some nancy confused about his station?"

Vergess grabbed Heinrich by the vest and slammed him back in the seat. Everyone else in the vehicle flinched at the sudden act of violence. Everyone except for Battery.

Battery turned around and glowered. "Never mention that again, if you know what's good for you. Do you understand me? *Never.*"

Both their reactions took Geist by surprise. What had Battery told the others? Had he forgiven her? Would Vergess continue to go out of his way to protect her secret, even though so many people now knew? And what did Dreamer, Victory, and Blick think? Her chest tightened just thinking about it all.

Heinrich, trembling, took a moment to regain his composure.

"Let him go," Geist said. "He's not our enemy."

Vergess released Heinrich with a dissatisfied grunt. Heinrich took the moment to dust himself off and straighten his soiled clothing, regardless of how damaged they already were.

"I have another matter to deal with," Dreamer said. "If we don't all make it back to the base, would one of you please request that my belongings be sent to 161 New Bond Street in London?"

"Does Major Reese know about this?" Victory asked.

"No… I never told him. I've never told anyone."

Geist committed the address to memory, but shook her head. "You'll see your home in London again, I swear to you."

Dreamer closed his eyes and smiled. "Oh, I've never seen London. And at the rate this war is going, I doubt I ever shall."

"Don't say that," Geist said, her voice strained.

"A kingdom eternal awaits me once I'm finished. I have no need to fear."

"Then why have your belongings sent to 161 New Bond Street?"

Dreamer took in another long breath. Then he slumped down into his seat, the pain of his words etched into the furrows of his brow. "They caught me, once," he said. "When I ran from my masters. They caught me."

Geist waited and listened, picturing the harsh suns of the Arabian deserts. Where would slaves run to escape their masters? The vast wastelands around the plateau of the Najd were virtually uninhabitable.

"They knew I would run forever," Dreamer continued, "so they flayed my flesh and left me to the death of the desert. But I didn't die. Instead, a man by the name of Oliver Evans pulled me from the maw of hell."

Vergess, Battery, and Victory turned their attention to Dreamer. All of them stared as though they had never seen their teammate before. Blick focused on the road, and Heinrich watched with narrowed eyes. Even though Dreamer spoke English, it was clear Heinrich understood in the way he nodded along with the words.

Dreamer paused, regaining what little strength he had, and then resumed his story. "There are some men in this world who are angels in disguise. Evans and I became good friends. He saved me in more ways than one. But when death came for him… I wasn't able to repay his kindness."

Even the clouds wept. Rain spotted the cloth cover of the motorcar. Geist huddled close, shivering involuntarily, though not from the cold.

"They told me slaves cannot hold debts or honor," Dreamer murmured. "That slaves do not understand what it means to fulfill a duty greater than the orders given to them. But a free man… His duty and honor are his alone. So when Oliver died, I swore I would protect the two things he cared about most in life. I made an oath as a free man, and that's why… that's why you must send my belongings to his wife."

"What's the second thing you're going to protect?" Blick asked.

"The United Kingdom, of course," Dreamer replied with a weary smile.

Geist said nothing for a long moment. There was one part of Dreamer's story that didn't figure.

"In Verdun…" she whispered. "In Verdun, you said *your* name was Oliver Evans."

Dreamer continued to smile. "I asked him… I asked Oliver to

give me a new name. A different name than the one my old masters had given me. He said, as my own man, I should pick a name for myself. A strong name. A name to remind me why I forged my own destiny. After he died… I knew then what my new name should be."

The rain pounded. Geist allowed it to drown out her thoughts.

"What's that?" Battery called out.

Heinrich didn't have his glasses, but he stared out across the rain and darkness regardless. "It's the wire," he said.

The storm couldn't hide the ten-foot-tall wall of barbed wire that separated Belgium and the Netherlands. Once the motorcar got close, Geist could hear the hum of electricity and feel the aura of magical power. It was magi-tech of the worst kind, and she knew every rumor she ever heard had to be true.

If they attempted to climb the fence, they would die, just like the thousands of Belgians who had come before them.

Blick stopped the vehicle five feet away.

"Where are the German soldiers?" she asked.

"Down the road in guard posts," Heinrich replied. "There aren't any gates around here. We'd have to travel ten miles east before we found anything."

Battery, Victory, Dreamer, Blick, and Vergess turned to face Geist. She stared back at them, weighing their limited options. Then she stepped out into the rain, curious to get a better look at the fence before deciding what they would do.

Battery and Vergess joined her, all three soaked by the time they reached the barrier. The droplets that hit the electrified barbed wire popped and turned to steam. The whole fence seemed to bleed mist, half-shrouded from view.

"Can you destroy this?" Geist asked, motioning to the thick, wooden post the barbed wires were circled around.

Vergess reached out to touch the wooden post, but Victory shouted, "Don't! You'll be shocked."

"Oh, yeah?" Vergess asked. "By what, the wood?"

"That's right. In every one of my visions, you're hurt if you touch the fence. And the electricity breaks your focus. You never destroy it."

"Then what should we do, *soothsayer*?"

Victory didn't reply.

Battery turned his attention to Geist. She stared at him and narrowed her eyes, water dripping over her eyelashes. "What makes you think I can handle this problem? I've never seen a fence like this. No one has."

"You're in charge," he muttered. "You said you'd have a plan."

"I'm—" She stopped herself with a deep breath. "I won't be in charge once we make it back to the commander. One of you can make the call."

"Because you're a woman?"

Geist let her gaze fall to the dirt. "Because I'm not who I said I was."

She couldn't look at Battery, fearing the expression she would see.

He said nothing, allowing their unspoken words to hang between them. The howl of the wind worsened their condition, dropping the temperature even further.

She gritted her teeth. "Look, I'm sorry. I should've… I mean, if I could do everything over again—"

A host of unspoken words hung between them. *He must hate me.*

Battery stepped closer, closing the distance between them to half a foot. "If you could go back in time and do everything over again, you should have told me."

She nodded.

"No. You're not listening. You should have told me the moment we landed behind enemy lines, on the very first mission we were together." He glared, but his lower lip also quavered. "I mean, I can't believe you trusted *Vergess* over me!"

Geist snapped her gaze up to meet his.

"We went through everything together," Battery continued, his hands balled into fists. "You gave me my codename. You saved me from the falling zeppelin. You always had my back, no matter what happened. I trusted you. Why couldn't you trust me?" Then he motioned to Vergess with a flick of his hand. "What does he have that I don't? Why tell *him*?"

Vergess gave him a sidelong glance. "What's that supposed to mean?"

"You *know* what it means." Battery shook his head. "And you lied to me about having the operation. That was the worst part. I know why now, but I wish it had never happened. I don't want you to think you can't trust me. I… I don't think I could stand that."

"It's not just that I'm a woman," Geist whispered, the rain almost drowning out her words.

"You're a member of House Cavell," Blick said from the car.

"Yes."

"I don't care," Battery declared. "You've obviously proven your dedication to the Ethereal Squadron. More than once. More than a hundred times."

"But that's why you let that enemy live, isn't it?" Blick asked as he leaned forward on the steering wheel.

Geist nodded. "Yes. That was… my brother. I made a mistake in the heat of the moment. I'm sorry."

"Younger or older?"

"Younger."

Blick shrugged. "Well, then I can sympathize."

She rubbed at her face, clearing away the water. "You… forgive me? You would trust me after everything I've done?"

"I'm with Battery. You've proven yourself a hundred times. And you've protected Battery at every turn. I won't reveal your secret."

Geist glanced over to Victory and Dreamer.

"You know *my* secret," Dreamer said. "And I've technically always known yours." He tapped at his temple. "I'm a master spy, after all. Your simple disguise didn't fool me."

"You *always* knew?" Blick asked with a chortle.

"The conversations we had on the train were very amusing. It took all my strength not to laugh."

Heinrich lifted an eyebrow, left out as everyone else chuckled.

"I won't betray your secret, either," Victory said. "I had a vision while you were inside the OHL. Things went bad, and you threw yourself on a grenade to save us. We all lived because of you. You're one of us."

"We're a team," Battery said. "Nothing will ever change what we've overcome together."

"Thank you," she murmured. When she turned to Vergess, he replied with a smile and a nod. Had he known what the others would say?

Blick rubbed at the back of his neck. Then he cleared his throat. "I, uh, want to apologize. I never knew you were woman, ya know, when I was spouting off and making an arse of myself. Especially on the train." He shot Dreamer a dirty look.

"It's fine," Geist said with a smile. "And you shouldn't change your ways now. I don't want anyone else finding out." *Too many people know already.*

Battery wiped his face. "We won't tell Major Reese. So, please, stay in the Ethereal Squadron. We need you."

"Of course."

Battery motioned to the wire and Geist looked it over as if seeing it for the first time. She had almost forgotten why she had exited the vehicle in the first place.

"What're we going to do?" Battery asked. "We have to make it back before the enemies launch their assault on Paris. We don't have time to drive around."

I know. Time is our enemy as much as the Central Powers.

Geist held out her hand. "Help me," she said.

The solution came to her in a moment of clarity. With Battery, her specter sorcery reached new heights. If she could make her clothing incorporeal, perhaps she could extend that power to other objects she touched. She would ghost the fence and allow them to drive into the Netherlands.

Battery took her hand. The feeling Geist had when they worked together reminded her of everything being a part of a team was. She felt confident with his strength at her command and appreciated the trust on his part—on everyone's part. She would get the job done.

She was their commander, after all.

"Blick, get ready to drive through," she said. "Don't stop until you're on the other side."

"All right," he called back as he started the vehicle.

Battery hustled back to the motorcar, a spring in his step that hadn't been there before. Vergess placed a hand on her shoulder before returning to the car as well.

She walked up to the wooden fence post, ignoring the popping and humming, and instead lifted her hand and got it as close to the wire without touching it as possible. An arch of power stung her palm, but she gritted her teeth and worked through it.

Focus.

Channeling her sorcery, Geist stared at the fence. The raindrops still hit the metal, colliding with the fence and proving it to be solid. She bit her lip and tried again, but the fence remained stubbornly intact.

Is it the magi-tech? Is it preventing me from doing this?

Geist could almost hear her father's voice berating her, but she pushed the memories from her mind before ever hearing a word. She closed her eyes, envisioning him at the OHL. He could become invisible and incorporeal without Battery's aid. Could *he* ghost the fence? There was no doubt in her mind that he could.

But that didn't matter. *He* didn't matter.

The headlights of the car shone on her back. Geist redoubled her efforts, squeezing her eyes shut and focusing on her sorcery. The vehicle got close, and its engine let out a terrible roar, but she could still hear the fence. The popping stopped. The rain passed through it without making contact.

And the motorcar passed through as well. Geist shuddered. It felt odd—like not being part of the world—and for a brief second, Geist thought she might lose her focus because of it. She calmed herself, however, and held her concentration until the vehicle made it to the other side of the fence. When her comrades were safe, she opened her eyes and stepped through the wire herself. The powerful current of magical power that traveled the barbed wire gave her a jolt almost as bad as the electricity itself, but she shrugged it off and shouldered through.

They had made it to the Netherlands. Neutral territory.

Freedom was just beyond the horizon.

THIRTY-TWO

The New Schieffen Plan

Nothing matched the beauty of a moon reflected on the sea.

There had been something different in the air when they had arrived back at the Evening Rose. Captain Madison hadn't hassled Battery for being British, nor had he made his usual jokes around Vergess. He and Shell had allowed Geist and her team a space on the ship separate from others, letting them recover in peace.

She rubbed at her leg as the ship rocked back and forth on the English Channel. She hoped Cross would be able to save the limb before it was too late. *I don't need any other problems*, Geist thought, staring at her corrupted arm. She pulled her sleeve down and covered the black spots so she wouldn't have to look at them anymore.

Every minute they spent traveling was one minute too many. Only a few more hours and they would arrive in Le Havre and take a train back to Verdun. Vergess sat next to her on the deck of the ship, his vacant gaze set on the distance. Only Blick remained with them, his arms crossed over his chest as he leaned against the ship's railing. The silence between them was comfortable, and it was nice to see Blick and Vergess getting along for once.

"How long has he known?" Blick asked, out of nowhere.

"Well, er, since I rescued him. From the Verdun trenches."

"That isn't *that* long ago." He huffed and kicked one boot over the other. "Battery made it sound as though Vergess had known for years or something."

"No," Geist said. "Not that long."

"Did he figure it out, or was this all a big accident?"

"An accident," Geist said, remembering how she'd had to remove her tunic to deal with the bullet injury. She touched her side where Cross had healed her. "But he's conducted himself like a gentleman."

"That's good. I'd hate to have another reason to hate him."

Vergess glared.

"Don't give me that look. I'm putting two and two together now. All that time you two are giving each other odd glances? Yeah, I noticed. Nothing gets by these eyes." Then he turned his gold gaze to Geist. "Hey. You don't have to settle for the first man who discovers your secret."

"I'm——" Geist stopped herself for a second, considering his words. "He's a good man. I'm not settling."

Vergess huffed. "Do you have something to say, Blick?"

"No." He held his hands up and pushed away from the railing. "But, Geist… if you ever realize you've made a mistake, you'll let me know, right?"

"Get out of here!"

Blick chuckled as he strolled away, heading straight for the ship's wheelhouse.

Vergess scooted closer, muttering curses under his breath. Geist let herself enjoy the moment. It could be fun, thinking about something not quite as dire as war. Soon they would have one more battle. Soon they could all die in service to their cause. But for right now, Geist would enjoy the comforts only a jealous lover could provide.

GEIST HAD THOUGHT, at several points during her journey, that she might never see Fort Belleville again. Seeing its silhouette rising in the distance and knowing she was safe in ally territory took a weight from her heart.

They were home.

The French midmorning air, sweet with the scent of flowers, coupled with the familiar hoofbeats of their horses, lifted everyone's spirits. Geist sat at the front of the cart, Vergess by her side, her mind on the future. Victory and Dreamer had recovered enough to move without difficulty, and they both sat in the back, chatting animatedly. Blick and Battery walked along the outside, and Heinrich sat off to the side.

The moment they reached the outer wall, Geist leapt from the cart, stumbling on her injured leg in the haste, motioning for Heinrich to follow. The stone walls, clouds of gunpowder, and the sweat of men had never been as welcoming to Geist as when she passed beyond the front gates. The soldiers at the gate checked her identification tags before allowing her in.

"Second E Squadron?" they said. "Welcome back."

She nodded but didn't stop to offer them the same pleasantries.

With Heinrich in tow, Geist headed straight into the main building and down the southern hall to Major Reese's office. She knocked on his door, her eyes lingering on Buttons's blood stains, which still remained in faint traces on the dark wood. Black memories lurked beneath her thoughts like a shark beneath the surface of the water, but she took a breath and pushed them down. *Not now. Not when I'm so close.*

"Enter!" she heard the major shouted through the door.

Geist opened the door and stepped into the narrow office. The major's desk sat at the far end of the room, and he stood behind it, his back to the door and his eyes locked on a map of Europe. Red lines had been drawn from Luxembourg to Paris.

"Sir," she said, saluting.

Major Reese turned around, his gut hitting part of the desk in his haste. "Geist," he replied in disbelief. "You're back."

"Sir, I've completed my operation. I'm here to give my report."

"Then give it, man, give it."

Geist refused the offered chair, her legs restless. She motioned Heinrich forward.

"This is the first German Magic-Technology General, Heinrich von Veltheim. He's one of the original magi-tech researchers. He's cooperated with me in escaping German-occupied Belgium, and I believe we have a mutual goal of ending this conflict as soon as possible. He may know more than anything physical I could have brought back."

Major Reese glowered at Heinrich. When he spoke, he did so in a deliberate manner, as though the words pained him at each syllable. "You're the son of Karl von Veltheim?"

"He's my uncle," Heinrich replied, unfazed.

"Our old intelligence said that Karl would be the first magic-technology general. Where is he now?"

"He's… indisposed. I was forced to accept the position on his behalf."

"House von Veltheim would never share their secrets unless they were forced to."

"And I'm sure I won't be welcomed back after this." Heinrich exhaled and shook his head. For a moment, it looked as though he would laugh, but instead, he said, "This war needs to stop, and I'm not clever enough to think up a better way than helping my uncle's enemies. I tried speaking to the Emperor of Austria, but he wouldn't listen. He's only concerned with ensuring his many sons and nephews will be empowered by Germany's research. And Kaiser Wilhelm has ears only for his generals. They see the products of my research as weapons and nothing else."

"I'm surprised." Major Reese grunted. "I can't believe I've lived to see the day a von Veltheim has come to the world with his secrets in hand. I guess the source of magi-tech makes sense now. Only a von Veltheim could be so inventive."

"Sir, there's more," Geist said. "It's about the New Schieffen Plan."

"Don't worry, son. We've got intelligence on the attack. Our sorcerers will be——"

"Your information is wrong," Heinrich said, cutting in. "The attack will begin in a few days. I know the information you've been given. You're expecting zeppelins, aren't you?"

"That's right. They'll be carrying the GH Gas."

"No. They won't. That was a deliberate ploy by the Germans to throw you off the scent. The zeppelins will be carrying false bombs to distract the Ethereal Squadron. The real gas bombs will be fired from superguns behind fortified lines."

"Superguns?"

Heinrich gave a cut nod. "They call them the 'Paris Guns.' Six in total to fire gas shells into the city proper."

"And the Germans are using the gas to steal sorcery from dead soldiers," Geist continued. "They're going to take the blood of every sorcerer they kill on the battlefield and fuse it into themselves with the gas. They're going to gain access to other families' schools of sorcery and use it against the Triple Entente."

Major Reese listened, his eyes darting and his face growing redder with every word. He made no comment as Geist walked up to his desk and spread her hands on the surface.

Then she remembered Amalgam.

"They're altering sorcerers with their magi-tech, sir," she said. "They're making *monsters*, and they're giving them to the Royal House Habsburg-Lorraine. If we don't stop this soon, he might have his own army of abominations by the time we get to Austria-Hungary."

"You're sure of this?" Major Reese asked. "This information will need to be heard by the highest orders of the Entente. It'll change everything, do you understand? So you've got to be certain."

"I'm certain," Geist replied.

Major Reese ran a hand over his gut, his gaze lowered. "We'll have to evacuate. We've got no counter to the GH Gas."

"I can help," Heinrich said.

"No offense, but the word of a traitor isn't much to go on."

"I decided long ago that this is worth being branded a traitor."

Major Reese replied with a curt nod. "I see." He returned his attention to Geist. "Then I'll send this forward to all our generals in the area. Thank you, son. This may have saved us all." He walked to his office door and threw it open. Then he bellowed down the long hall, his boisterous voice carrying to every inch of the fort. "Caveat! Big Wick! I have an assignment for you two!"

Within moments, the two men appeared at the door, huffing and puffing. Big Wick, ducking to enter the room, glanced over to Geist and offered her a half-smile. Then he returned his attention to the major. "You called, sir?"

"Take our guest to Tinker in the arms room."

"Yes, sir."

"And you're both to keep an eye on him."

"Sir?"

"That's an order," Major Reese stated. "Now, off with you."

Both Caveat and Big Wick nodded. They escorted Heinrich from the room, and when the door closed behind them, Geist turned to face the major.

"Charles," Major Reese said. "I know you've just returned, but can I count on you to help with the attack? Even if this Heinrich dreams up a way to counter the gas, the fighting could still get brutal. Can you handle that on such short turnaround?"

She held herself as straight as possible. "I can, sir."

"Good. We need every man we can get."

THIRTY-THREE

Anti-Gas

"Wake up. *Wake up.*"

Geist snapped awake, her body tense and adrenaline dumping into her veins. She jerked up and threw the blankets off her cot, ready to fight.

Tinker stared back at her, his face lit by the dim oil lantern he held in his hand. The odd half-smile on his face told her they weren't under attack. She groaned and rolled her eyes. The enemy forces could move out at any moment, and they would need to be ready to meet them. She didn't have time for Tinker's shenanigans.

"Tinker," she said, her voice groggy. "What're you—"

"Come with me," he whispered. "And be quiet. People are trying to sleep."

Geist held back a string of rebukes as she pulled her uniform on over her long johns in the dark. "What's this about?" she asked.

"Shh!" someone a cot over hissed.

Tinker put a finger to his lips and winked. Geist rolled her eyes. Then, much to her surprise, Vergess rolled off his cot and stood.

"What're you two doing?" Vergess demanded.

Geist stared. Vergess slept shirtless, and his drawers were rather tight, evident even in darkness. She averted her eyes, blushing.

"This doesn't concern you," Tinker replied with a dismissive wave of his hand.

"It does when it wakes me in the middle of the night."

"We've got business," Tinker said, motioning to Geist. "Go back to sleep."

Vergess turned to her, his expression questioning. Geist smirked.

"We're fine," she said. "I'll be back in a bit."

"All right," he replied with a groan. He walked back to his cot, giving Tinker a glare. Tinker lifted an eyebrow.

Once Geist and Tinker had left the barracks, Tinker snorted. "That guy. I'm surprised you managed to suffer his company for so long."

Geist shrugged. "I know him better than you do."

"Too serious, that one. Did you see the way he walked over? Like he was going to thrash me right then and there."

"Tinker. What is this about?"

"Oh, right. Our traitor German."

Geist stared up at him, narrowing her eyes. "You mean Heinrich?"

"Yeah, that Hun you brought back. I've been working with him —we made a breakthrough, but he keeps mumbling to himself in German. Anyway, you need to see what we've made."

"What is it?"

"An anti-gas. It neutralizes the GH Gas completely on contact. It's a kind of opal mist—I guess it's a kind of magi-tech, too. Never thought I'd get to work on something like this."

Geist almost tripped over her feet. She came to a halt and grabbed Tinker by the arm. "You've done it, then?" *Please! Please don't be joking!*

Tinker glanced at her grip and then back to her. "Yeah. I wanted to show you."

"H-how? What did you do to it?"

"I don't know," Tinker muttered. "That's why I need you. Someone has to talk to Heinrich and get him to cooperate. We made some of this anti-gas, but it's nowhere near enough to save all of Paris. We need to make more, and this *boche* asshole isn't talking."

"Take me to him."

They picked up their pace and half-ran to the storage rooms under Fort Belleville. Geist relished the feeling of movement on a healthy leg. Cross and her miracles.

Cross.

Geist hadn't spoken to her friend for longer than thirty seconds since returning, and it looked as though they might not have time until after the fighting was over.

I hope she's okay, Geist thought. *I hope she's gotten to talk to Victory, at least.*

Tinker led her down the stairs to the arms room and motioned her in. The underground facility had once housed cannons and ammunition, and at another point, had functioned as a hideaway for sorcerers fleeing the war before the real fighting had started. Geist could see the history on the walls from the stacks of Napoleonic era weapons to the tally marks engraved on the wall that indicated the passage of time. Someone had been stuck in the cramped room for over thirty days. Geist didn't envy them.

Tinker nudged Geist, motioning to Heinrich with a jut of his chin. The German researcher stood by a table, hunched over with his face as close to the surface as possible. He was grinding opal fragments into dust using an old-fashioned mortar and pestle. Geist couldn't help but notice how pale the man looked, far sicklier than he'd been at the OHL. If Geist didn't know better, she'd think Heinrich was dying.

"Heinrich?" Geist asked.

The man didn't look up from his work. He grabbed at his face as if to adjust his glasses, but when his fingers met nothing, he sighed and squinted. "What is it?" he asked in German.

"See what I'm talking about?" Tinker muttered under his breath.

Geist walked up to the table. A handful of opals littered the surface. Most were white, but a few came in other colors: grays, reds, oranges, blues, and a few magentas. Geist touched a few, curious as to how they felt, and was surprised by the chill of power contained deep within.

"Careful with those," Heinrich snapped. "The Ethereal Squadron doesn't keep many in stock."

Geist snatched her hand back. "What's going on? Tinker says you made some breakthroughs, that you can counter the GH Gas."

"That's right. We've been testing them on the supplies that were seized from Fort Douaumont." Heinrich waved his hand to the side, motioning to another table on the opposite end of the room.

Geist's whole body tensed the moment she got a good look at the supplies atop the table. GH Gas grenades. At least twenty. She shook her head. "What are those doing here? They could kill us all!"

"It's okay." Tinker shrugged. "We have everything under control. Here, let me show you." He walked over, set his lantern down, and picked up a grenade. Geist watched as Tinker grabbed a second container, this one smaller and carrying all the trademarks of his own craftsmanship, and carried them both to the center of the room.

"What're you going to—"

Tinker threw down the grenade and his own homemade device at the same time. A terrible hiss filled the room. Geist jumped for the door but stopped at the staircase, watching in amazement as the second canister spewed black vapor that instantly consumed the GH Gas. The yellow-greenish cloud swirled with the black, transforming both into a dull gray mist that hung in the air like smoke.

Tinker reached down and touched both grenades, his sorcery switching them off before they had released their full contents. He stood and laced his hands atop his head. "See? We're safe."

"Would you keep what little anti-gas I've made secure?" Heinrich said, switching back to angry English. "We'll need all we can get!"

"This would be easier if you told me how you made it. I could start producing more. It's no good to us if only one guy has all the magi-tech knowledge."

Heinrich didn't respond. He kept with his work, his hand red and white from the strain of crushing gemstones.

Tinker walked over and pushed Geist toward Heinrich. "Get him to talk. I'll be back after I speak to Major Reese about our breakthrough." Then he strode from the room, leaving Geist alone with the German.

"What's this all made of?" she asked, cutting straight to the heart of the issue.

"Opals." Heinrich answered.

"What else?"

He didn't reply.

Geist met his gaze with a glower. "I thought you were here to help us."

"I am."

"Then tell me."

Again, he said nothing.

Tinker flew down the stairs, interrupting the silence. "We need to pick up the pace," he said between huffs as he jogged into the room. "Something is happening outside. The barracks are swarming with soldiers."

"*Why* won't you tell me?" Geist asked.

Heinrich gritted his teeth. "The destruction the magi-tech will bring… It'll be on me. Every weapon—every death—will stain my soul no matter who makes them."

Geist clenched her fists. "Is the alchemist who discovered gunpowder responsible for every man gunned down on the battlefield?"

Heinrich stopped his work, but he didn't look over.

"Is the first man who sharpened a stone responsible for every death at the end of a sword?" Geist continued, her voice growing louder. "Stop thinking about yourself, goddammit! This isn't about *you*! This is about countering the destruction already in the world! We talked about this in the OHL—trying to keep this knowledge contained is a fool's mission. You're only allowing more people to die by keeping this all—"

"It's blood," Heinrich interjected.

Geist stared. In a calmer tone, she asked, "What?"

"Blood is the key. Sorcerers draw their magic from their blood and opals can tap into that same strength."

"Opals can?" Tinker asked as he walked over to the table and examined the supplies. "How?"

"They're like sponges. They can hold the sorcery for prolonged periods of time. That's why the opal operation for sorcerers has been so effective. The magic contained within makes it easier for the sorcerer to tap into their strength."

"How are you making material that cancels out the GH Gas?"

"I study nullis sorcery."

"Really?" Tinker asked, disbelief written across his face. "You aren't affected by magic *at all?*"

"That's right."

Geist was taken aback. Everything made sense. Heinrich was immune to the GH Gas because he was immune to magic itself. *Which is why he could study and experiment with such terrifying substances.*

Tinker stared at the opals longer. "Then… you've been using your own blood?"

Heinrich rolled up his long sleeves and revealed the partly healed slashes down his arm. His pale complexion said what he could not. That every bit of anti-gas they had was part of him.

Memories of the magi-tech floated through Geist's thoughts. Every instance of magi-tech had actually been someone's lifeblood poured into the technology. A sorcerer had given part of themselves to make it reality. From the zeppelin, to the U-boat, to the dungeon in the OHL. Geist could barely believe it.

And the GH Gas… The sinister near-sentience of the gas left her wondering. *How is it made? Is it just blood? Or is it… more?*

Bells rang out throughout Fort Belleville. Geist knew the sound well. It was a call to arms. The German army was moving into Luxembourg and preparing to attack Paris.

"So we can't mass-produce this on a huge scale?" Tinker asked, ignoring the summons. "Because we need to, and I don't know of anyone else here capable of using nullis sorcery."

Heinrich motioned to the crushed opals. "Once I've made enough, the sorcery contained in the opals can be spread to the others."

"Like a disease?"

Heinrich glared. "Yes. Like a disease." His distaste almost made it funny, but Geist couldn't bring herself to laugh when her heart was beating so fast.

"Then we need to keep this up. Tell me how to help."

Geist turned for the door. She knew she wasn't needed in the arms room. She wasn't a scientist or a researcher or a test subject. She was a soldier needed for the frontline.

This is it. We either save Paris and fight back, or we lose Paris... and surrender.

THIRTY-FOUR

The Paris Guns

"We don't have enough counter-gas to cover Paris," Major Reese said.

The transport motorcar shook and jostled with every bump on the road. The Verdun sorcerers sat packed together, shoulder to shoulder, holding their rifles between their legs. Geist held a cigarette and match in her hand, fumbling thanks to the shake of the vehicle. She didn't smoke often, but the eve of battle seemed as good a time as any to indulge in a vice or two.

Major Reese steadied himself with a leather strap that hung from the metal frame of the overhang. "Our plan—our only hope—is to neutralize the GH Gas shells before they're fired. We know there are six guns. Each team will get to a gun and disable the shell before it launches. Afterward, you'll take out the gun itself, preventing any further attacks."

The soldiers nodded, but no one spoke.

"Victory's sorcery tells us we can be successful, but don't let that kind of fool confidence get to your head. If we fail, Victory's seen a hundred nightmares' worth of horror. That's what's at stake, men."

Geist struck a match as the vehicle lurched and she lost her last light. Before she could ask around for another, Big Wick held out a large hand and a flame sprouted from a fingertip. Geist gave him a lopsided smile and lit up.

The harsh whistle of bombshells and bullets made its way into the motorcar. The frontline was mere yards away, and everyone knew it.

"Once boots hit ground, make your way through the enemy lines in any way you know how," Major Reese shouted over the din. "There will be enemy sorcerers in your way, but they don't have the moxie we do. We're fighting for innocent women and children. Let that strengthen your hearts and harden your resolve. I say we push these monsters back all the way to the dark forests they crawled out of."

Geist took a deep drag of her cigarette as the men in the truck slammed the butts of their rifles into the floor, whooping in agreement.

The truck stopped. Everyone stood. *Showtime.*

Geist's boots hit mud. The smell of gunpowder and copper mixed in equal amounts on the air. The rattle of machine gun fire nearly deafened her, but the rest of her senses were razor-sharp, attuned to every detail. In a way, Geist preferred the chaos of a largescale battle like this to the fierce focus of single combat. The battlefield had a music that guided her forward: the drumroll of gunfire, the percussive beat of mortars striking, the shouts of the men around her… She looked left and right: Blick, Dreamer, Victory, Vergess, and Battery were all there with her—and she knew she would never be alone.

Victory stayed behind with a radio. If his visions revealed anything devastating, he would send word.

Dreamer grazed his fingertips over every Ethereal Squadron sorcerer who passed by, wrapping them in his powerful illusions, masking them as German soldiers so that they could sprint through the enemy lines unimpeded. He held Geist back when he touched her shoulder.

"There will be House Cavell sorcerers here," he said.

She glanced up at him, her eyebrows knit together.

"You take a lot of risks with your life," he murmured. "But

specter sorcery is one of the only ways to counter specter sorcery. We're counting on you."

Geist replied with a curt nod. "I need to go with the others. Stay safe, Dreamer."

Each team met Heinrich at the front of the truck. He handed over the anti-gas grenades and motioned to the pin keeping the precious cargo intact. Geist took her grenade and thanked the man with a look. Heinrich, dead on his feet, answered her in kind. His ghostly complexion reminded her of the high price he'd paid to create the devices—a price paid in blood.

Heavy artillery struck all around the sorcerers, blowing craters as deep as a man is tall in the earth. Men unlucky enough to be caught in these explosions didn't even have time to scream. Their decimated bodies flew in random directions, splattering the warzone in gore. Geist leapt over the bodies, trying her best not to stare at the viscera below her.

Out of the corner of her eye, she spotted the medics—and Cross—rushing in to aid the wounded. The closer she got to the trench, the more Geist felt she needed to keep an eye on her. When bullets whizzed by, Cross ducked down and allowed the French soldiers to return rifle fire.

She doesn't have a gun? Why isn't she armed?

Geist gritted her teeth and made a mental note to speak to Major Reese about this if she survived the battle.

The battlefield, divided by No Man's Land, had two deep lines of trenches. Geist flew over the French soldiers in their trench, never looking down, and sprinted through the barbed wire that separated one side from the other. Vergess, Blick, and Battery followed behind her at a slower pace. With Vergess in front, Blick and Battery had no fear of the bullets, but rotting through the barbed wire took time.

When Geist was halfway across No Man's Land, the deep chill of magic struck her like a wall. A black stallion charged toward her, its rider wielding a gleaming longsword. She slowed and focused on the man riding, her confusion transforming into disbelief as he came into view.

Leopold.

It wasn't unheard of for the man to take to the battlefield. People claimed the crown prince could not be killed, and Geist believed them. Tempest sorcery made Leopold a terrifying presence on the battlefield, and his regenerative abilities protected him from all but the most grievous wounds. She'd already seen the prince take a bullet to the eye and walk away.

And he smiled, she recalled. *He smiled like he lived for this.*

The prince sliced through French soldiers with little effort, each swing amplified tenfold by apex sorcery. His mount, a beast among horses, had all the telltale signs of magi-tech alteration. Opals lined its muscles, and the creature's eyes bulged as if the animal could barely contain the magic coursing through its veins. When bullets pierced its hide, the creature continued forward without a whinny.

One soldier tried to pull the prince from his mount; Leopold laid his hand on the man's face and watched it rot away under his touch. When a group of soldiers fired upon him from across No Man's Land, he waved his hand and blew them away with gale-force winds, sending them wheeling into the barbed wire, which quickly sliced them to ribbons. And, just as Geist had predicted, when he took any slight scratch, he healed almost instantly and pressed forward.

Prince Leopold urged his mount forward, rushing Geist with his sword held out to the side. She froze and met his gaze with a glare. When he was on top of her, he swung, his blade passing through her neck with a whistle but dealing no real damage. In the split-second they were inches from each other, his eyes widened in recognition.

I knew you'd remember me, she thought with a smirk.

And the prince laughed.

The battle—the whole damn war—this really is a game to you, isn't it? When the prince couldn't decapitate her in a single swing, he craned his head back to get a better look, as though intrigued by the challenge she presented.

Geist turned away, unwilling to quarrel with him. She ran for the German lines and found the men had stopped firing when they had gotten a good look at her. Geist hesitated for a moment, but she remembered Dreamer's illusion.

She jumped over the trench, running for the back ranks. Officers shouted, ordering her to return to the front, but she ducked past them and continued, not caring what they said or did as long as they stayed out of her way.

Vergess, Blick, and Battery still lingered behind, but Geist couldn't slow her pace, not while she had the anti-gas grenade in hand. *Just a little farther.*

The shadows of the machine guns cast dark lines over the battle-field as the sun broke over the horizon. Geist squinted through the morning light and she spotted her targets—the Paris Guns—on the far railroads beyond the frontline. Their shadows, equal rivals to the trees behind them, stretched to No Man's Land itself.

Each gun was extraordinarily massive. They rested on a massive all-metal turntable railcar, towering over everything at eighty-two feet, the tips of their barrels seeming to scrape the sky. The gleam of steel blinded her, and Geist took a breath to assess the situation. Magic chilled the area, and she wondered if she was already too late.

But the heavy clang and clink of the gun's titanic turntables erased her concerns. The gunners in charge had to turn massive cranks to physically turn the guns in order to aim, each pop and clank swiveling the huge guns by a foot, maybe a foot and a half. And tilting the barrels up or down took another complex series of mechanisms—it would take a good deal of time before the guns were anywhere close to ready to fire.

The German soldiers, huddled behind makeshift barricades, had their backs to the Paris Guns. An open field lay before her. A straight shot to the railroads.

Geist spotted other members of the Ethereal Squadron rushing toward their assigned guns, but each weapon was sepa-rated from the next by a few hundred feet. Geist could only make out faint spots of people running in the distance. She could see her gun and the next over, but everything else was a mystery. She hoped the other sorcerers would be successful, but she didn't dwell for long.

We need to hurry.

Geist turned her attention back to the last gun on the track and sprinted for it, heedless to anything else going on around her.

Halfway to her destination, Geist was hurled forward by a powerful gust of wind. She hit the dirt and landed on her rifle, the bolt jamming up into her sternum. With a groan, she rolled over and jumped back to her feet, each breath sending sparks of pain through her ribs.

Prince Leopold had followed her. He dismounted, not but thirty feet away, and whistled loud enough to cut through the cracks of rifles in the distance. Two men—no, not men, *abominations*—turned away from the battlements to lumber toward the prince. They wore clothing like Amalgam had worn in the OHL, tight leather straps with hooks, and heavy gasmasks with the glass replaced by mirrors. But unlike Amalgam, they had bulbous humps on their backs, elongated arms, and stout elephant legs, shorter than any normal man's.

Leopold rushed forward. His sword—a king's blade—had a honed edge. It sliced through Geist's neck a second time without touching, but the shiver of death lingered after. The prince wanted her dead, and sooner or later, her reflexes would betray her.

Geist dropped her rifle, pulled out her handgun from her side holster, and then fired. The bullet tore through his gray and green officer uniform, ripping off one of the three general stars, but it didn't harm the man underneath. Apex sorcery. Just like Vergess's, the prince's skin was as solid as steel.

Leopold attacked again, and she dodged out of instinct, but the blade cut through her right sleeve, detaching it from the rest of her uniform. It fell to the ground as she staggered back.

What can I do against him?

The prince must have had a similar thought. He motioned to one of the abominations, ordering it through gestures like a puppet. The monster lunged forward, straight for Geist, its breathing heavy through its gasmask. She leapt from its path, rolling over the dirt. Each swing whistled through the air. Geist knew the monster must have been as strong as Amalgam—strong enough to kill her in a single blow.

"You're *that woman*," Leopold said with a cruel smile. His cold voice sent a shiver down Geist's spine. "What do you think you're doing?"

The abomination slammed a meaty fist into the ground, cracking it with the weight of the mighty blow. Geist staggered backward.

Leopold chuckled. "You think you can fight me? I'll—"

Another round of bombardments drowned out his words. The zeppelins had arrived, dropping shells on the soldiers below. The British biplanes came next, and the dogfights began overhead, adding to the pulse of war around them.

Prince Leopold slashed with his sword, jumping back into the fight the moment Geist let her guard down. Geist ghosted just in time to avoid the deadly blade and leapt away, keeping her eyes on the prince. She couldn't lose track of him. Not once. Not ever.

But Prince Leopold's attention shifted to a man off in the distance. He squinted, confused, as a sorcerer ran for one of the Paris Guns. Geist followed his gaze and held her breath.

Caveat. He hustled to the nearest gun with his anti-gas grenade in hand.

Prince Leopold smirked. "What's this?"

Even with a German uniform, Caveat was distinctly heavyset and shorter than most. He stood out, and Geist knew Leopold couldn't resist such a choice target.

"Run!" she shouted. "Caveat! Back to the frontline!"

Caveat turned to her voice, but Prince Leopold had already started in his direction, taking one of his abominations with him. The prince moved with the speed of a jungle predator, his apex sorcery propelling him forward as swift as any horse. His monster followed behind without tiring. Geist had no way to keep up or stop them. She could only watch in horror as the prince closed the distance in seconds.

But just as the prince swung his sword, Caveat held out his hand, freezing the moment around him, trapping the prince in a web of slowed time. Caveat, sweat-soaked and panting, turned to the monster lumbering forward. He held out his hand again, attempting to stop the beast like he had the prince—but nothing happened. The abomination thrashed about, knocking Caveat to the ground with a bone-shattering swing. Caveat's focus failed him, and the prince was free. Dragging himself to his feet, Caveat held his anti-gas grenade tightly to his chest and stumbled onward.

Geist turned away, searching desperately for the rest of her team, and caught sight of Vergess. He loped across the battlefield, his body tense and his killer focus set.

Finally, allies! We can still win this.

We have to!

THIRTY-FIVE

The Final Argument of Kings

Vergess sprinted over. He grabbed Geist by the shoulder and pushed her toward the Paris Guns, never saying a word. Battery and Blick ran onto the battlefield next, Blick's eyes glowing gold.

"The crown prince is here," he announced as he brought up his rifle, his eyes giving him unparalleled aim. "He's mine if I get a good shot."

"Battery!" Geist called out. "I need you!"

Battery ran over and held out his hand. She grabbed it, taking his power the moment their skin touched.

When she returned her gaze to Caveat, she grimaced. The fight was already over. The monster had no control over its own strength and had already torn Caveat into quarters, leaving entrails splattered across the field. Prince Leopold bent down and snatched up Caveat's anti-gas grenade. Soaked in blood and laughing, he crushed the device in his hand, rotting it away with *ruina* sorcery.

There were six guns. They made six grenades. They didn't have an extra.

"We're in trouble," Blick said, parroting Geist's thoughts. "Geist, what're you still doing here? Take out a gun!"

Battery shook his head. "Oh, God, if the prince is here, he'll kill us all. We need to—"

"You need to get Heinrich," Geist said, pushing Battery back toward the frontline. "Right now, do you understand me? It's top priority!"

"What? Why?"

"We need him if we're going to stop all the guns! Hurry, Battery!"

Battery's face said what his voice could not. *Him? By himself? Would he make it?*

Couldn't he stay with her?

But Geist had no time to answer.

"That's an order," she stated. And then, in a gentler tone, "Trust me."

Battery took in a ragged breath and nodded. Without another word, he turned on his heel and ran back the way he had come. Geist watched him go but stopped once she was sure he wouldn't turn back around.

He'll make it. He's never let me down.

The grunt and growl of the abominations caught Geist's attention. It lumbered forward under the command of the prince. Geist became invisible and lashed out at the first monster that approached. She wanted to reach in and mess with its insides, but the magi-tech suit it wore prevented her hand from passing through. She placed her palm on the chest of the beast to no effect. It swung, feeling her touch, and slammed her to the side. She hit the dirt, reappearing for a brief second before stumbling to her feet. The creature's suit wasn't affected by magic in any way: Caveat's magic was powerless against it, and so was hers.

But bullets still harmed the creature. Blick took aim and fired with supernatural accuracy, striking the abomination in the head, then reloaded and fired again. The beast turned toward him, but it was already too late. Five more bullets and it was stumbling, practically lobotomized.

When the second abomination came, Vergess's brute strength made short work of the monster. He punched the creature in the gut, dazing it, then lifted his opponent into the air and slammed it back to the dirt. A powerful stomp to the throat filled the gasmask with the sounds of wet breaths and gurgling. The abomination flailed on the ground, drowning in its own blood.

Geist straightened herself just in time for Leopold's renewed attack. He galloped in on his steed, aiming for Vergess. Before the prince could reach his target, Geist held out her hand and ghosted it into the horse, raking her fingers along the organs of the gut. She felt no heartbeat, which disturbed her, but when her fingers caught hold of sinew, the horse lost its footing and tumbled to the ground, throwing its rider in the process.

Prince Leopold picked himself off the ground, annoyance flickering across his face, but otherwise he was unharmed. As the prince brushed himself off, Blick hefted his rifle and fired. The bullet removed a small bit of dark hair, but it had no long-lasting impact.

"The eyes," Vergess called out. "Apex sorcery doesn't harden the eyes."

"Is that right?" Blick replied as he reloaded his rifle and fired, striking the prince across an eyebrow, taking another small amount of hair. "Get in there, Vergess. I'll cover you."

Vergess nodded. He and Leopold regarded each other as they circled, each man looking for an opening to strike.

"I ought to have recognized you sooner," Leopold said. "Wilhelm Richter. Traitor to the Kaiser."

Vergess straightened his shoulders and spit in Prince Leopold's direction, his saliva hitting the other man's boots. "You're a dog wearing the skin of a man, and you always will be."

"You'll die for your betrayal."

"Maybe I need a new title. Wilhelm Richter, the Ender of Kings."

Prince Leopold laughed aloud and leveled his sword at Vergess. "I'll enjoy running my blade through your heart."

"You can try."

As much as she wanted to stay and help Vergess fight her former fiancé, she forced herself to turn away. She had a mission to complete, and it didn't involve killing every Magic Hunter, Abomination Soldier, and magi-tech monster that crossed her path. Instead, she ran back to her Paris Gun. No one saw her, not through her sorcery, and she reached the massive supergun without further delay.

A lone gunner occupied the machine's cockpit, and Geist reached her hand inside the man, ripping his throat out with a jerk of her fingers. He slumped and panicked as she ran for the bomb-shell compartment. Two more soldiers rushed to the dying gunner, providing Geist enough time to rip open the hatch and examine the GH Gas shell.

She pulled the pin on her grenade, opened the release on the shell, and tossed the grenade in before the escaping gas could come into contact with her skin.

Geist didn't know if the other teams had made it—Caveat certainly hadn't—but she hoped beyond hope they had. She wouldn't be able to do the entire mission by herself, though she was determined to try to cover Caveat's failure. While everyone else handled one gun, she would have to handle two.

And in the same moment, she realized that Battery's power still lingered with her, far beyond what she could remember his limits were before. *He's stronger than he was*, she realized. *I'll need to tell him that, if we make it out of this alive.*

Geist ran back into the open mud field that separated the Paris Guns from the German army. To her dismay, Vergess and Blick were still locked in conflict with Prince Leopold, and it was apparent who would be the winner.

When Leopold swung with his sword, he cut Vergess's steel flesh, carving piece after piece out of his chest. Their *ruina* sorcery cancelled each other's, preventing Vergess from using his most deadly magic. And when Vergess came in fast, the prince used *tempest* sorcery to unbalance him and leap away.

Blick fired with as much precision as his weapon would allow, but Leopold washed the battlefield in fire, not harming Vergess but burning most of Blick's forearms and catching his rifle ablaze, rendering it useless. When Blick tried to draw his sidearm, Leopold sent a bolt of white-hot lightning arcing toward him, striking him in the shoulder and neck and sending him flying backwards.

Vergess lunged, but Leopold kicked him hard in the side—a sick crunch echoing into the battle, no doubt the result of broken ribs, even after the added fortitude of apex sorcery. It sent him sliding through the mud. Vergess coughed blood and took in breaths as though each mouthful of air was more painful than the last. He struggled to roll sideways, one arm wrapped tight over his shattered ribcage.

Geist ran full tilt toward Prince Leopold, her heart pounding. She sprinted the final distance, right as the prince levied his sword over Vergess, and swiped with her hand, cleaving a chunk of skin and muscle out of the prince's side.

Leopold screamed in agony as he fell to one knee.

Geist dragged Vergess back a few feet, determined to save him. He coughed up another mouthful of blood, his ribs no doubt puncturing his lung. The prince cradled his injury, a wound that would have finished any other sorcerer. But then his flesh knit itself back together, healing the damage almost as fast as Geist had dealt it. His tunic, ripped where Geist had attacked, dripped vital fluid onto his trousers and boots, but the wound itself had already vanished.

"You'll pay for that," Leopold said through gritted teeth. "You stupid *bitch*. You'll regret every decision that ever led to our paths crossing."

Geist let Vergess rest back on the ground and then ran toward Leopold again, her feet splashing in the mud. He watched her footprints as she drew closer and he swung with his sword.

To no effect.

Geist reached a hand into his shoulder and pulled back, damaging him again when no other weapons could. The prince leapt backward, his feet unsteady beneath him. He healed the injury again, but his bravado waned. He glanced around the field, his eyes searching her footfalls in the soft mud.

Then his eyes widened.

"You're Markus Cavell's missing daughter," he said. "That insect he promised to me for a bride."

"The insect ripping you apart," Geist corrected.

Leopold laughed uneasily and wheeled toward the sound of her voice. "You think you can run from me? *Hurt* me? No one can."

Geist rushed forward again. She clawed at his arm, tearing through his uniform and flesh yet again. He healed, faster than the last two times, and held his sword close, his eyes narrowed.

Much to Geist's horror, Battery finally reached his distance limit. She felt his power drain from her body, and her invisibility faded.

"There you are!" the prince hissed.

He raised his sword and slashed downward with incredible force. With the prince's immense strength, Geist was sure he would cleave her skull in two, but not while she ghosted.

"You want to pretend to be a man?" he asked with a laugh. "Then you can die like a man."

Geist stepped back, her legs unsteady. Without Battery, she couldn't attack him.

He swung his hand, and a blast of wind sent Geist tumbling back across the battlefield. Leopold strode toward her, twirling his blade in his hand. "I didn't realize specter sorcery was so powerful. I thought it was all smoke and mirrors. But if it can make a woman into a soldier, our betrothal makes much more sense. The emperors of Austria should have this sorcery. I can't believe it's not in my bloodline.

"Maybe I'll take you for my bride, after all."

Geist honed her thoughts. When Leopold came at her again, she dodged aside and rolled through the mud. As she struggled to get to her feet, he slashed. She stumbled through him, ghosting herself enough to make it past.

In that moment, she realized her own sorcery had improved. She feared using Battery's power would steal from her development, but her clothing shimmered and shifted, becoming just as incorporeal as the flesh beneath. Geist focused harder, and to her immense relief, the invisibility returned, though it took more of her strength to maintain than it had when she'd had Battery's aid. She struggled to move with any speed—her willpower consumed by the strain of maintaining her magic—but the focus made her body feel lighter.

Apex sorcery had become a part of her, something she could rely on, if only a little.

She moved away from Leopold, keeping her feet in patches of grass to avoid detection.

"Show yourself!" Leopold shouted, his voice drowned out by another round of aerial bombardment. When the bombs stopped, he gritted his teeth. "Show yourself, you craven bitch! I'll kill you once I find you! Do you hear me? I'll—"

He stopped himself short.

Then he smiled a cruel smile.

"Drop your sorcery," Prince Leopold demanded. "Or I'll order your family killed."

Geist froze. The tone of his voice, laced with that cruel chuckle —she knew he was serious. He would do it. He'd order them killed. And while she might not have much love for her parents, there was always Dietrich to worry about. Sweet, gentle Dietrich.

He would die because of her.

Geist looked at the prince and then to the Paris Gun. The barrel tilted back and the loading chamber set itself into the firing position. Even one shell would kill thousands, perhaps millions, if it hit the city proper. She had to end the fight—one way or another—before she could handle the gun, lest the prince stop her outright with his overwhelming sorcery.

I have to deal with Leopold before the gun, but Dietrich… She shook her head. *I'm sorry.*

She ran for the prince and she reached out to harm him again. When she drew near, he slashed and jumped back. The blade slashed through her face and cut the shoulder of her uniform before making contact with her corrupted arm—the arm that could not become incorporeal like the rest of her.

In the single swing, it sliced from her elbow down to her knuckles, opening up her forearm like a peapod. Geist stumbled back and grabbed her injury, her invisibility flicking out.

The pain that erupted inside her was blinding.

Keep it together! You can't fail now!

"Geist!"

She turned and spotted Battery entering the field, Heinrich at his side. One part of her felt relief—more confident with Battery nearby—but another piece of her wanted him to run. He would stand no chance against the prince.

Heinrich's appearance sent a ripple through the battlefield that halted movement. He and Leopold made eye contact, staring at each other for a short period of time. Geist took the moment to wrap her dangling arm in bits of her ruined uniform. She bit her lip and tongue to keep from crying out as she dressed the wound as best she could.

Heinrich squinted and moved away from Battery. "Prince Leopold," he called out. "Thank God you're here. I need your help! I was taken hostage by the Ethereal Squadron!"

His declaration surprised Geist. She stared at the researcher, her eyes wide. *What is he doing?* Geist had been depending on his help to stop the last gun. *What're we going to do if he returns to the Germans?*

Prince Leopold smiled.

Geist took note of Vergess's movement. He pulled himself off the ground despite the injuries, his breath still rough and wet.

When Battery turned to help Vergess, Heinrich broke away and sprinted for Leopold. Battery pulled up his Lancaster handgun and took aim. He stopped himself from shooting and cursed under his breath. Heinrich reached Leopold's side with a huff and slight bow of his head.

"Your Highness," he muttered.

"Get behind me," Prince Leopold commanded. "I'll deal with you later." He glanced around the battlefield once more, his cruel smile returning. "This is your last chance, woman. Surrender, or I'll kill your whole family right in front of you, I swear it!"

Heinrich stepped behind the prince. He then reached out and touched Leopold's exposed skin, his fingers lingering on the flesh for less than a second. The one touch—a feather-graze of contact—and the prince screamed. He cringed and doubled over. Geist took in a long breath. The chill in the air that had accompanied Leopold's magic dissipated. Heinrich had stolen it or shut it down, Geist didn't know which. But it didn't matter.

The prince could no longer use his magic.

Geist hurled herself forward, her hand outstretched like a claw, and with all the power she could muster, she raked her fingers through the prince's chest, taking a heavy chunk of flesh with a single, savage swipe. But even this failed to slay him. In the following moment, the prince set his teeth and yanked his sword up, carving into her arm a second time.

Then the prince rounded on Heinrich, but stopped when he saw Vergess heading his way. With an arm over his injured chest—blood pouring from him in almost alarming amounts—Leopold whistled for his horse. The beast had been lying on the ground the entire time, unmoving, but at the sound of the whistle, it dragged itself back to its feet once again. Leopold grabbed the reins and mounted with a pained snarl.

Vergess rushed forward, but in his injured state, even apex sorcery couldn't lend him the speed he needed. Leopold yanked the reins and galloped away, back into the safety of the German back ranks.

The clicking of the turntables stopped.

Time was up—even the German soldiers knew it. Men from the frontlines were backing up and soldiers filtered out in the open field.

"Vergess," Geist called out. "*Vergess, I need your help!*"

He limped over, his breathing laboring.

"Get Blick," she commanded.

"Geist, I—"

She shoved him in the opposite direction. Vergess nodded as he attempted to do what Geist had done—apply pressure and stop the flow of blood from his wound.

Geist, shaking, turned to Battery and Heinrich. "We don't have any time. We need to go. Now."

"What're we doing?" Battery asked.

"Come with me. Vergess and Blick too. To the gun."

She ran toward the gun Caveat had been assigned—the only one locked into position—and tried to ignore the strange cocktail of emotions pounding through her veins. The battle raged, but she couldn't focus on any of it. Her body acted on autopilot as it ran straight up to the enemy's weaponry, her newfound apex sorcery giving her the endurance she needed.

Geist withdrew her sidearm from her side holster and shot the gunner, but she knew that wouldn't matter. Her fight with Leopold had consumed too much time. The gun had been set and the machines were in motion. The next few soldiers who rushed up were killed by Battery's Lancaster.

Heinrich glanced around, shielding his eyes with one hand. "This is going to fire," he said. "Where's the anti-gas grenade?"

"It's gone," Geist replied. "We have to set the shell off now. Right now. Before the gun fires."

"If we do that, the gas will be released. Right here."

"I know, but it's the only way."

I'm sorry, Vergess—I'm sorry, everybody.

"We'll die," Battery murmured, his eyes round.

Geist grabbed him by the hand and then grabbed Heinrich. "Not if we're immune," she whispered. "Do you trust me?"

Before she heard their answer, without even looking them in the eyes, Geist turned around and opened the hatch to the Paris Gun. The shell within, locked into the firing position, sat before her. She didn't think. She didn't want to think.

The instant Vergess made it back with Blick, Geist ripped off the paneling and triggered the shell. They had two seconds to duck and find cover and Geist pushed them behind the solid metal of the gun's turntables. They hit the ground as the explosion went off—an explosion of gas and shrapnel. The field, filling with German soldiers, was suddenly covered in a fog of yellowish-green.

And the gas came for Geist and her team.

But Heinrich's sorcery worked much like her own. His anti-magic, when empowered, encompassed more than just himself. Geist, Battery, Vergess, and Blick all remained intact while the GH Gas swirled around them.

Battery gritted his teeth and scrunched his eyes. Every second got worse and he dug his nails into his scalp as he lay on the ground. Geist furrowed her brow. "What's wrong?" she asked. "Battery?"

"It... hurts."

His back bled. The opals in his spine couldn't handle the anti-magic bubble that was keeping them alive. The jewels trembled under his skin, like they wanted to wrench free of their moorings. Geist could see it even through the canvas of his shirt. If Battery lost focus, his magic would leave Heinrich, and everybody except for the German researcher would die to the gas.

Geist took hold of Battery's hand. Her fingers were slick with blood, but she laced them through his and squeezed. She didn't say anything—there wasn't anything to say. He squeezed her hand back, his fingernails cutting into her good hand. She didn't care. She didn't feel the pain, not from her arm, or injuries. It was all too much to take in. All she knew was that she needed Battery to stay strong for everyone else involved.

Geist closed her eyes. She didn't want to know if Battery failed. If she was going to die, she would rather it strike her unawares, rather than melting away like Cutter, Buttons, or Little Wick. Even a bullet to the chest would be preferred to the terror of the GH Gas.

Please, God, she thought. *Let this work. Let this work.*

The gas whispered.

Geist almost opened her eyes. She could almost hear words as the mist drifted in and out of her ears. They were terrible things— the stuff of the most unspeakable nightmares—but she couldn't make out more than a few syllables. What was the GH Gas made of? What was it trying to tell her? Geist shook her head and counted her heartbeats, trying hard to pray.

Time refused to move. Geist could hear gunshots and shouting and even screams, but they were distant, as if coming through a fog. She waited and waited, never once opening her eyes.

After some time, Battery pulled on her hand. Geist looked up. He stared back at her, his sweat-drenched hair sticking to his face.

"It's over," he said.

Geist looked around. The GH Gas had moved on. The open field, once comprised of mud and grass, resembled the floor of a meat-processing plant. Bodies in various states of decay and lique-faction lay strewn across the battlefield. Clothing had fused into the flesh and become one with the charnel. Clouds of the GH Gas lingered on the farthest corners, swirling around as if waiting for more victims.

Geist turned away and shut her eyes again, finally allowing herself to breathe.

They had done it.

They were the saviors of Paris.

THIRTY-SIX

The Great War

Geist sat on a broken fence post on the road to Fort Belleville. The field just beyond the horizon was still littered with bodies, and the faint odor of viscera was still detectable on the evening wind, but as she stared at the orange rays of the sunset piercing the deep purple clouds overhead, something like peace entered her heart and warmed her from the inside out.

It was these small moments that made life worth living.

Tomorrow, at dawn, they would bury the soldiers who had died in battle among the serene French hillsides, including the enemy soldiers. Some thought burying an enemy soldier among their allies was an insult, but Geist knew the truth. At some level, they were all very much alike.

Staring at her mangled hand made that clear. Cross couldn't fix her, no matter how many times she had tried. Geist pulled a long glove over the hand to cover it. The loss was a small price to pay for victory, and she would happily pay it ten times over if it meant keeping the people of France safe.

All of France cheered for the victory over the Germans. Morale ran high.

The crunch of dirt under boots jolted Geist out of her reverie.

To her relief, it was only Cross, approaching out of the fiery light of the sunset.

"You found me," Geist commented as she turned back to the sun. "Are you done with your work?"

"Yes. Everyone's back on their feet."

"Even Vergess and Blick?"

"Vergess was shaken. I don't think he's as used to pain as the others. But once I healed him, everything was fine. He's resting now. Blick is already flirting with the nurses—take that as you will."

"They sound back to normal."

Cross walked over to the broken fence and smiled. "Battery sings your praises at every turn. He says you gave him the strength to keep the gas at bay."

"I'm glad," Geist replied. "I know he looks up to me, but the truth is I would've been lost without him. This whole operation—I couldn't have done it all without him."

"The opals in his spine need to be replaced. They were cracked by the gas. It's a delicate procedure, but I'll make it happen."

"If anyone can do it, it's you."

"Oh—and Tinker is starting magi-tech production."

Geist's stomach turned. More magi-tech meant more weapons. And more weapons meant more war. Just like Heinrich had predicted.

"He's also crafting more anti-gas," Cross added in a happier tone. "In the future, we won't have to worry about it so much. All thanks to you."

"Thanks to the team, you mean."

"Indeed. They must feel the same way. Both Vergess and Dreamer have requested to stay as part of your unit."

Geist had almost forgotten that Vergess and Dreamer were Verdun sorcerers. "I couldn't imagine going on another mission without them," she said. But her voice shook. She had never thought any soldier would accept her for who she was, and now all of her friends knew—and willingly stood by her side.

"They know what you are now. Don't they?"

Geist nodded.

"And *who* you are?"

Another nod. "It had to happen. It was that or abandon the mission, and I couldn't… I couldn't let what I am stop me again. And I figured they would report me, but the others… they accepted me. All of me."

"You have the soul of a knight, Florence," Cross said. "That's what they admire so much about you. You're a good soldier—in every regard."

Geist didn't know what to say.

"Pardon me."

Geist and Cross glanced back. Victory stood on the road, his uniform hat in hand. He smiled at Cross, a glint in his eye as though amused. She stifled a girlish giggle and gave Geist a quick wave.

"We'll speak again soon," she said.

The pair walked off into the sunset, whispering affectionately to each other. She watched them until they disappeared down the road, no doubt looking for a more private spot to enjoy each other's company.

Geist's thoughts went immediately to Vergess. They still had a war to finish before anything could be final, but having him close made some fights bearable.

The last of the sun faded, leaving a wake of darkness in its passing.

The gold sunsets of France.

The stars that bloomed as the light dimmed.

Love.

Although darkness threatened to tear the world apart—although madmen with weapons beyond their understanding wanted to warp the world into their own twisted image—Geist took comfort in the fact that these beautiful moments had not been tarnished.

And then, as if the world could hear her thoughts and respond in kind, the moon came out from behind a cloud and bathed the world in brilliant silver light. The soft light, the warmth of the night air, resonated within Geist as though she were walking in a dream, somewhere even the worst of the war could never touch her.

She'd remember this moment for all time.

About the Author

S.A. Stovall grew up in California's central valley with a single mother and a little brother. Despite no one in her family before her earning a degree higher than a GED, she put herself through college (earning a BA in History), and then continued on to law school where she obtained her Juris Doctorate.

As a child, Stovall's favorite novel was *Island of the Blue Dolphins* by Scott O'Dell. The adventure on a deserted island opened her mind to ideas and realities to which she had never given thought to before—and it was at that moment Stovall realized story telling (specifically fiction) had become her passion. Anything that told a story, be it a movie, book, video game or comic, she had to experience. Now, as a professor and author, Stovall wants to add her voice to the myriad of stories in the world and she hopes you enjoy.

You can contact her at the following addresses.

https://www.facebook.com/SAStovall/
   https://twitter.com/GameOverStation
   https://sastovallauthor.com/
   https://www.facebook.com/groups/766178373588392/

9 781734 758771